THE
NIGHT
LETTERS

THE
NIGHT
LETTERS

DENISE
LEITH

VENTURA

This book is published by Ventura Press
PO Box 780, Edgecliff NSW 2027, Australia
www.venturapress.com.au

ISBN: 978-1-920727-48-2 (paperback)
ISBN: 978-1-920727-49-9 (ebook)

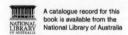 A catalogue record for this
book is available from the
National Library of Australia

Cover design by Emily O'Neill
Typesetting by Working type
Printed and bound in Australia by Griffin Press of Ovato Book Printing

 MIX
Paper from
responsible sources
FSC® C009448

The paper this book is printed on is certified against the
Forest Stewardship Council® Standards. Griffin Press holds
FSC® chain of custody certification SGS-COC-005088. FSC®
promotes environmentally responsible, socially beneficial
and economically viable management of the world's forests

For the women of Afghanistan

Beneath the Sweater and the Skin

How many years of beauty do I have left?
she asks me.
How many more do you want?
Here. Here is 34. Here is 50.

When you are 80 years old
and your beauty rises in ways
your cells cannot even imagine now
and your wild bones grow luminous and
ripe, having carried the weight
of a passionate life.

When your hair is aflame
with winter
and you have decades of
learning and leaving and loving
sewn into
the corners of your eyes
and your children come home
to find their own history
in your face.

When you know what it feels like to fail
ferociously
and have gained the
capacity
to rise and rise and rise again.

When you can make your tea
on a quiet and ridiculously lonely afternoon
and still have a song in your heart
Queen owl wings beating
beneath the cotton of your sweater.

Because your beauty began there
beneath the sweater and the skin,
remember?

This is when I will take you
into my arms and coo
YOU BRAVE AND GLORIOUS THING
you've come so far.
I see you.
Your beauty is breathtaking.

Jeannette Encinias

THE MOUNTAIN PEAKS were silhouetted dark against the disappearing night as the morning call to prayer rang out across the ancient city. In a few minutes the sun would rise above the buildings, sending shards of light to splinter the icy peaks of the Hindu Kush before being reflected back in the windows of Kabul.

Sofia looked down at the men as they emerged from the dark corners of Shaahir Square, drifting toward the mosque in the half-light. She couldn't see their faces but she knew each one by the way he moved and the direction from which he had come. On the mosque's steps they took off their plastic flip-flops and old slippers, placing them in neat rows before disappearing behind the heavy wooden doors and into the arms of their beloved Imam Mustafa and his great and glorious god.

Shivering in the cool dawn, Sofia pulled the shawl more tightly around her shoulders before tucking her feet up under her to wrap warm fingers around icy toes. It was not yet winter in Kabul but already there was a gathering chill in the air. Soon shoppers would desert the square by late afternoon and the shopkeepers would huddle together around open fires in old metal drums. And then one morning the city would wake to find itself blanketed in a mantle of drifting white, and before it had turned into dirty brown slush, and before people had time to curse their city, this drab and smelly place would sparkle like a bright, shiny jewel.

For more than three thousand five hundred years, ancient Kabul had breathed and it had grown. It had been conquered, ruled, abandoned and all but destroyed by any number of dynasties, empires, sects and madmen. It was mentioned in the sacred Rigveda text of Hinduism and the Avesta of Zoroastrianism, and at least two centuries before Jesus was crucified on the cross, Buddhism had settled over the land. Eight hundred years later, Mohammad, from the warring Quraish tribe of Mecca, declared himself the last true prophet of the one true God. Two hundred years later, the great Persian warlord Ya'qub ibn al-Layth al-Saffar brought this new religion to the land. Sofia knew the history well, but for a few precious minutes it felt as if dawn over the Hindu Kush belonged to her.

Had her obsession with the country grown from the stories overheard late at night about the grandfather who had served in the British Army in Afghanistan? Or had this man she had never met planted the seeds of Afghanistan in her genes more than a century ago? None of that seemed to matter anymore because what Sofia did know for sure was the exact point in time when coming to Kabul had become inevitable. All the befores and afters led to and from the moment she had been told about a Dr Jabril Aziz seeking a female doctor to work with him in Kabul. The next moment in time – the one that assured she would remain in Afghanistan – had been in a village high in the Hindu Kush.

Sofia picked up her tea from where she had left it on the windowsill. Taking a sip, she stared up at the mountain range, remembering the village but also the man there who had looked at her with something more than longing, and had made love to her with something more than desire. Over the years, though, his memory had begun to falter and fade until Sofia could no longer put the whole of him together again. At first this had troubled her, but in time it became less troubling until his memory had become little more than a vague, worrying shape, a watery dream that might have belonged to someone else. And yet, if the hour was right, or the day had been of a particular sort, he might return and she would find herself turning each memory over and around, examining its colour and size and shape until she could see again – the way he smiled at her, or a particular way he moved or laughed – and she would feel again the pain of loving someone who had never loved her.

Sofia held the tea in her hands, drawing comfort from its warmth because in two hours he would be standing in front of her. She had no idea how she felt about that. Excitement? Fear? Apprehension? It had been five years. Would he even remember her? Placing the cup back on the windowsill, she leaned down and picked up the newspaper lying at her feet, opening it again to page two.

Dr Daniel Abiteboul from the United Nations arrived in Kabul yesterday. He will be spending the next month assessing the country's most pressing needs on behalf of the organisation...

Without registering the name of the sender, she had flicked the email from the United Nations representative on to her receptionist, Iman, and it was she who had replied on Sofia's behalf. But then she had seen his photo in the paper last night and pulled the email up again, reading it carefully for any hint of recognition, but there had been none.

Staring down now at Daniel's photo, a long-forgotten memory began to form: hands strong enough to pull a broken bone back into place but delicate enough to sew tiny stitches into the face of a baby, and sensitive enough to set her skin on fire. She leaned back in her chair, following the memory. The first night he had come to her he had arrived in silence, placing his finger to her lips, waiting until she understood. Only then, when he was absolutely certain she wanted him as much as he wanted her, did he lean in and kiss her. Every night after that, when the village had settled down for the night, Daniel would leave his bed in the mosque and return to her. And every morning, before the village began to stir, he would go. As they worked together during the day, not a word was spoken of what had passed between them in the dark, but there had been times when she would look up from her work to find him watching her, as if she was a puzzle he could not solve. And then he had disappeared, and his leaving, like his lovemaking, had been a surprise.

It had been such a strange, haunting affair. Without the distraction of life outside the village, time and movement had slowed to a gentler pace until each moment was intensified. When Sofia worked with the village women, or she gazed up at the mountains, or made love with Daniel, there was nothing in the world but that single, complete moment.

Flipping the newspaper shut, she found herself looking at a photo of the aftermath of a suicide bombing outside Kabul's main police headquarters from the day before. She had not heard that particular explosion, but she had heard enough.

The first bomb had been a couple of weeks after she had arrived in Kabul, and so close to the square that the sound of the explosion saw her hitting the floor in terror. Trembling like a terrified animal, she had waited until the gunfire ceased to be replaced by the sound of ambulances. Crawling over to the window, she had pulled herself up and looked out. A thick black plume of smoke was rising in the air about four blocks away. In the square below a few people had been standing in groups talking, but most were going about their business as if nothing had happened.

Over time, Sofia had come to react to explosions just like every other resident of Kabul. The initial, unconscious response was an overwhelming sense of relief that the bomb hadn't gone off under her, after which she tried to work out where it was and whether any friends might be in the vicinity. She would then try to call them, which was always problematic considering everyone else was doing the same thing and the signals were often jammed. Eventually, she would go back to whatever she had been doing beforehand, hoping no bad news would find its way to her door.

It was unsettling just how quickly she had adjusted to living with the constant threat of violence until the next explosion arrived, and her heart somersaulted in her chest and the adrenaline smashed through her veins and she was aware once again of the underlying tension that permanently fizzed through her body.

Like all the residents of Shaahir Square, Sofia had come to see the safety of the square and the danger of Kabul as two completely different, albeit interconnected, worlds. It was, she knew, a particularly dangerous illusion.

2

IN THE COURTYARD below Sofia's window and out in the square beyond the gate, the day was beginning to unfold. Ahmad, the owner of the tiny hole-in-the-wall shop that sold all manner of household goods, was entering the darkness of the square. Ahmad didn't go to mosque in the morning. From the gossip that passed Sofia's way she suspected it was because the blind cleric, Imam Mustafa, was especially fond of the time after morning prayers to let his thoughts wander off to distant and random horizons, keeping the worshippers – according to some – on the cold mats far longer than was strictly necessary. Ahmad, with his serious, frowning eyebrows and his thick black moustache, was a man in a hurry. And yet, thought Sofia, as she watched him heave up the heavy metal shutter on the front of his shop, time was one of the few things her friend had an abundance of.

In the shadow of the shop awning Ahmad lit a cigarette, and as he drew the nicotine deep into his lungs the glow illuminated the craggy corners of his young-old face until he coughed, pulling raw pieces of tobacco out of his mouth with tar-stained fingers. Sofia thought him too young to have such fingers, but Ahmad had been a village boy addicted to nicotine from the age of eight. As he smoked he straightened out his moustache with his thumb and forefinger, contemplating what the day might bring: enough money to put food on his family's table and perhaps a little left over? *Insha'Allah.*

As the sun began to lighten the sky and the darkness of the square turned a cold unwelcoming grey, she could see Ahmad more clearly in his white *perahan tunban* and raggedy old suit coat. Stamping the cigarette out on cobblestones that were older than the square, she watched him stretch the last of the sleep out of his whippet-thin body before rolling out his prayer mat and hurrying through his solitary salutation. Finishing, he rolled up his mat and lit his second cigarette of the day. It was always thus: shutters, cigarette, stretch, prayer, cigarette and wait. Always wait. Wait for the customers who seldom came. Wait for Allah to look favourably upon his miserable soul. Wait for the sake of waiting; wait for the timeless monotony of time slowly passing, just as generations of Ahmad's forebears had done before him.

Afghans were good at waiting, Sofia thought. The English were good at queueing; the Brazilians good at partying; the French good at eating; the Afghans good at waiting. They were also good at accepting, which was probably what made them good at waiting. *Insha'Allah*, thought Sofia. If God wills, it will happen. She wondered what Australians were good at and decided it was fun. Australians were good at having fun.

The doors of the mosque swung open and men began pouring out. Collecting their shoes, they called out greetings before disappearing back around the corners of the square to their homes or places of work to make ready for the day ahead.

Iqbal, the old cobbler, with his dishevelled clothes and misshapen leg, headed back to the warmth of his bed for just one more hour of sleep, while Omar, the local apothecary, in his immaculate *perahan tunban* and jacket to guard against the morning cold, was crossing the square to his shop until he veered off course to disappear behind the high gate that separated the courtyard from the square. When he reappeared a few seconds later he was stuffing something into the pocket of his vest. As Sofia was registering this oddity she was distracted by her landlady, Behnaz, who appeared in the courtyard below her window. After hanging the canary cage she was carrying on one of the low branches of the pomegranate tree, she removed the cover, blew the husks off the seed bowl, checked the water and then headed out the gate with her broom to clean the square of the previous day's dirt and disorder.

On the opposite side of the square, Hadi, who owned the shop next to Ahmad that sold various dried goods in hessian sacks and canned goods that lacked use-by dates, raised a hand to Ahmad.

'*As-salaam alaikum*,' he said, the greeting carrying all the way up to Sofia's window in the stillness of the dawn.

'*Wa alaikum as-salaam*,' Ahmad replied.

As Hadi began the ritual of opening his shop, Ahmad was finishing, carrying his green stool outside to position it in exactly the right place to afford him the best view of the comings and goings of the square. Hadi, when he finished, would also set a stool out front, close enough to Ahmad so the two friends might pass the time of day but far enough away to define which business belonged to which man. On particularly slow summer days the two friends might pull their stools together, lay out an exquisite bone and inlaid mother of pearl backgammon board they had borrowed from Babur many years before and had forgotten to return, and begin a new game.

Babur was folding back the shutters of his *chaikhana*, the tea house that had been in his family for more than three hundred years, before firing up the coals of the grill that in summer radiated a scorching heat onto the square and in the depths of winter became a gathering point for the men. With the tea house also producing meals these days more elaborate than the usual street food, the tantalising aromas of onion, garlic and fragrant, sizzling goat would soon be filling the square, causing those who had just finished breakfast to begin dreaming of lunch.

'Babur makes the best *palau* in all of Afghanistan,' Jabril would often say to Sofia, swearing her to secrecy because his wife, Zahra, who was Sofia's best friend, had put him on what he liked to call 'Allah's Eternal Diet'.

Considering everyone in the square – and probably half of Kabul – knew that on most weekdays between the hours of one and two, or thereabouts, Dr Jabril and Imam Mustafa could be found outside Babur's *chaikhana* tucking into large plates of rice topped with skewers of succulent chargrilled goat and braised eggplant drenched in fresh yoghurt that Babur made especially for them, Sofia suspected this couldn't have been much of a secret from his frighteningly perceptive wife.

After calling morning greetings to Ahmad and Hadi, Babur placed the table – his only concession (other than food) to pretensions of a restaurant – out the front of his café for his two favourite customers. From there Dr Jabril and Imam Mustafa would be able to enjoy their food while greeting old friends, discussing the affairs of the day, and lamenting with Babur on the passage of time and old age that none of them could believe had arrived so promptly. In winter Mustafa and Dr Jabril ate inside with Babur's other customers, perched on a raised wooden platform against the wall, but on fine Kabul days, between the hours of one and two, or thereabouts, the table outside the famous *chaikhana* belonged to them.

Sofia suspected that Jabril would have preferred to sit inside, for the tiny café chairs balanced on the ancient cobblestones were far too precarious for his ample girth, but he believed that his friend preferred the table outside, and so that was where they sat. On the other hand, Mustafa's painfully thin and wiry body, hidden under his black robes, probably felt the cold even when there was none, making the table in the square far too draughty for his tastes. The imam would have much preferred to eat in the warmth inside, but knew that his old friend liked to keep an eye on the comings and goings of the square, and so that was where the two friends sat, each satisfied that he had ceded his own little bit of comfort for the happiness of the other, and no one in the square, including Sofia, was ever going to tell them otherwise.

While Babur's family had been in Kabul since 1504, when his famous relative Zahir-ud-din Muhammad Babur – a warrior from the far north and a direct descendant of Genghis Khan – had conquered the tribes of Kabul and built the first Mughal Empire, the *chaikhana* had only been around since the late 1600s. A famous teahouse and inn along the Silk Road, the *chaikhana* served all manner of thieves, charlatans, wise men and traders, who arrived with dreams packed high on camel trains. Gradually, Shaahir Square had grown around the family's famous inn, and while the other establishments had not survived the demise of the Silk Road, Babur's *chaikhana* and the square that framed it had, along with the pistachio and fig trees that marked its centre and had once been part of a beautiful garden built by Babur's namesake.

Ancient and beautiful Kabul, with the majestic Hindu Kush mountains rising high above, had so captivated Babur's great-great-great-grandfather that he had asked for his body to be buried there and his tomb to be inscribed with the words, 'If there is a paradise on earth, it is this, it is this, it is this.'

The tea house's other great claim to fame was that the Diamond Sutra, the oldest complete book in the world, had spent at least one night under its roof while on its way to the British Museum in London, where it rests to this day in safekeeping for the not-so-grateful Chinese. Babur's relatives were said to have held the Diamond Sutra, a Buddhist text written in Chinese script six hundred years before Gutenberg had even begun to dream of a machine that would print words, although there were some in the square who called this claim false. Whatever the truth, Babur's *chaikhana* had a sign hung outside that read, 'The Diamond Sutra, the oldest book in the world, slept here.' The sign had disappeared during the time of the Taliban when Babur feared any affiliation with a book other than the Qur'an might see the *chaikhana* go the same way as the giant buddhas of Bamiyan, but on that morning, as Sofia sat at her window watching the square come to life, the sign was there for all to see.

In all its rich history, Sofia believed the *chaikhana* had never seen such mismatched friends. Western-educated and urbane Dr Jabril Aziz was short, rotund and debonair, with a thick

thatch of curly black hair receding on top. The village boy
Mustafa, lacking any formal education other than the extraordinary ability of perfect recitation of the verses of the Qur'an,
was tall, thin and wiry, with unseemly strands of scraggly grey
hair that stubbornly resisted all efforts of capture under his tight
black turban. While Mustafa, a much revered and admired qari
of Kabul, looked at the world through the surety of his holy
book, his love for his fellow human and his watery unseeing
eyes, Dr Jabril looked at life through the imperfect and glorious
vision of an idealist.

Tapping his way past the shops each day at the allotted time,
the blind imam would stop exactly one step before the table,
reach out his hand to find the back of the chair Dr Jabril had
positioned just so for his friend, and sit before taking up the
menu Babur had only recently introduced to the *chaikhana*.

'And what might we have today?' the imam would enquire.

'Perhaps what we had yesterday?'

'Good choice.'

The two men would place the unseen menus back on the
table for Babur to take before bringing out the *palau* and goat
that had been their lunchtime repast for as long as anyone in
the square could remember.

There is a beauty to rituals that bind us, Sofia thought, as
she watched Babur disappear back inside the *chaikhana*. This
ritual between the imam, the doctor and the *chaikhana* owner
belonged to all who lived in Shaahir Square, and while it
remained so Sofia was sure the world she knew would retain
its centre.

3

LIKE MOST MORNINGS, Jabril had woken in a good mood, but as he was about to open his front door his heart sank. Would he find another note pinned on the other side? Three notes in three weeks, all with the same message: *If you don't stop, someone will get hurt.* Jabril had no idea what it meant. Stop what? Who will get hurt? Not for the first time he wished whoever penned these notes could be a little less obtuse. When the second had arrived Zahra had told him he had to do something, but what did you do about night letters when you didn't know who sent them or why?

'Maybe I'll tell Chief Wasim,' he had offered when the third note arrived.

'Ha!' Zahra had scoffed, discarding the idea as easily as spoilt milk. 'What can he do? Our friend might be the chief of police, but everyone knows he's a puppet for the men above him and cannot control those below. Don't bother with Chief Wasim. Pay someone to protect us like everyone else in Kabul does.'

Jabril knew that something had to be done about the night letters, he just didn't know what. He considered Zahra's idea again that morning and found it as unappealing as it had been the week before. Surely if someone wanted to kill him they would have done it by now? Why wait three weeks and why send these stupid notes? He and Zahra had received notes like these six years before when she had been supporting a group working to improve the rights of widows and they'd come to nothing. Probably the best idea was to forget about them. Steeling himself, Jabril opened the door. No note. With a sigh of relief, and with his good mood restored, he set off for Babur's *chaikhana* for his morning tea.

As he entered the square, Jabril was surprised to see Sofia still sitting at her window until he remembered this was the day the man from the UN was coming to see her. He wished he knew why; he hoped it wasn't to poach Sofia away. When she smiled and waved to him his happy mood only got better. Jabril loved Sofia like a daughter. Her arrival in the square had been the greatest of blessings.

'First impressions count,' Zahra had said the morning he was to collect the new Australian doctor from the airport. At the time he had been disappointed that his wife was not coming with him to meet her, but in retrospect it had been a blessing. The gabardine pants he had chosen to wear were possibly a little too shiny and the shirt, with the buttons straining and his flesh trying to escape underneath, a little too tight. And, of course, there had been the sign. Five years on and the thought of that sign still made him squirm.

The day before he was due to collect her Jabril had asked their driver, Tawfiq, to make a sign for him to hold so the new doctor would know him in the crowd at the airport. Unfortunately, there had been a little miscommunication and the sign read *Dr Jabril*. By the time Jabril had discovered the problem it had been too late to fix.

'I'm Dr Jabril Aziz,' he had said when the young woman with the striking red hair walked up to him. 'Welcome to my country. How was your trip?'

'It was very good, thank you. It's a pleasure to meet you, Dr Aziz.' He could see she was a little nervous but so was he. He also noticed she had automatically put out her hand to shake before pulling it back. He would have been happy to shake her hand, for he had lived in the West long enough, but it had pleased him to see that she had made an effort to understand and respect his culture.

'Welcome,' he had said again with his hand on his heart before leading her to his car and introducing her to Tawfiq. Again, he was pleased to see her attempt to greet Tawfiq in Dari. It needed some work but at least she was trying.

'You will find it very rewarding working in Shaahir Square,' Jabril had said as they drove out of the carpark and headed for Kabul, 'but you might not get rich.' He knew he should be saying only good things about his country, but it was also important that this new doctor had realistic expectations.

'Oh, I don't want to get rich,' she said happily.

Jabril had been thrown by her comment. Who didn't want to get rich? He didn't think he had met anyone before who didn't want to get rich. But her response, together with her efforts to learn their language and culture *and* her smile, had reassured him that Dr Sofia Raso from Australia could very well be the right person for the job, and absolutely nothing since that morning had given Jabril cause to change his mind. Of course, it would have been preferable to hire an Afghan doctor, and before Sofia had arrived the women of the square

15

had not been backward in telling him so, but no suitable female doctors had been available at the time.

His happiness with her efforts encouraged him to venture further. 'I should also point out that the situation is probably not what you are used to, but what are riches when you're working for the good of others? Being a doctor is a service, is it not?' He had turned around from his seat in the front to watch her response.

'It is,' she had said, offering him another glorious smile.

'You're happy to be here?' he asked, a little baffled by her enthusiasm.

'Oh yes! I've wanted to come to Afghanistan forever.'

Jabril turned back around in his seat, considering her comment. He thought it a little strange that someone had wanted to come to Afghanistan forever. Who wanted to come to Afghanistan? Still, this must also be seen as a positive.

In his growing enthusiasm, and Zahra's absence, he decided his wife should become part of his plan to reassure this Western doctor that the situation for Afghan women was not as it was always portrayed in the Western press.

'My wife, Zahra, sends her apologies for not being here to meet you today, but she is a very busy woman. I'm not always sure what she's very busy doing,' he had said with a smile for Sofia, 'but she's very busy doing it.' After some consideration he added, 'I think maybe she's with one of her women's groups today. No,' he said, after considering other possibilities, 'maybe some unsuspecting public servant, who thought women were unimportant, is meeting his match as we speak.' Jabril laughed, imagining the scene, until he noticed that Tawfiq was unusually quiet. 'Do you know where my wife is today, Tawfiq?'

'She's at the hospital, Dr Jabril.'

'There you are,' Jabril had said, as if the puzzle was solved. 'You will soon learn, Dr Sofia, that my wife is a force of nature, answerable to no man, least of all to myself.' Jabril could almost hear Zahra's voice in his head telling him to stop right there. He had gone too far.

'I look forward to meeting her. She sounds interesting.'

'Oh, she's more than interesting. During the time of the Taliban she secretly schooled five girls in our home. She would have been killed if the Taliban had found her. She also looked after women's health under the Taliban, even though she wasn't trained, but there were very few female doctors left in our country and women weren't allowed to go to male doctors. Of course, some of the women Zahra saw were her friends and she had to examine them intimately. She would see them in one room in our surgery and then come to mine to relay their symptoms. It was difficult for everyone, especially when Zahra started to argue with my diagnosis.' Jabril laughed at the memory before shaking his head. 'My wife ... you would have to be a miracle worker to understand my wife, but she can understand everything. Everything! Without even studying medicine she knows what's wrong with my patients; she knows why someone she's never met has done some inexplicable thing she's read about in the newspaper, and she knows how to fix Afghanistan, and that,' he said, holding up his finger to emphasise the point, 'is probably the singular greatest miracle of all.'

Jabril could hear Zahra's voice in his head. *You need to stop talking right now, Jabril.* He tried very hard to take her advice and was successful for a time, but having lived for twelve years

17

in Boston he was worried about how foreign and chaotic Kabul would appear to someone who had been used to a modern, functioning metropolis. Jabril had discussed these concerns and how they should deal with them with Zahra, but in the end she said, 'If she cannot handle it I think it best we all find out immediately.' Of course, she was right.

On the side of the road, and in the rubble of the sidewalk, local vendors had set up shop, plying their cheap wares from wheelbarrows with faded beach umbrellas, tarpaulins and bits of ripped plastic to shield them from the burning sun. Behind these were small dark shopfronts with metal roller doors opening out onto the footpaths, or directly onto the street. A pharmacy, a silversmith, a rug merchant, a tailor shop, a bookseller, a shop selling household goods and another selling fruit and vegetables sat side by side as crowds of men and women moved in and around them. A lot of the women were wearing long shapeless coats and headscarfs, or long pants and tops, while others were fully covered in the shiny blue burqa that the West now associated with the Taliban but which had been around for over a hundred and fifty years.

A few buggies drawn by horses or donkeys vied for position on the broken roads alongside pedestrians, intrepid men on rusty bicycles, clapped-out yellow and white taxis, overcrowded minibuses, brightly decorated 'jingle' trucks and the ever-present SUVs with their blacked-out windows and missing numberplates.

'Kabul was once very beautiful,' Jabril began, wanting so desperately for her to see the Kabul of his youth. 'We used to have modern universities and beautiful houses, summer villas and gardens, fountains, and shops and movie theatres where men and women could go together. In summer, music would float out onto the streets and there were concerts in the parks.' Jabril had felt his heart expand. It was always like this when he thought back to what had become, in his memory, an idyllic life. 'Yes, it is true in the villages we still had the traditional women, but many women in Kabul were modern and wore miniskirts, shorts and make-up, and their hair was free.' He looked back at Sofia, who had turned in her seat and was watching everything pass by with an enraptured smile. She really wants to be here, he had thought in surprise. He had not expected such enthusiasm.

He turned back around to the front. 'But then the Russians came and they destroyed – the Russians only ever destroy. They cannot see beauty, only ugliness. Of course, there are many beautiful buildings in Russia,' he had added, 'but they're from the time of the tsars, not from the Communists. I tell you, Dr Sofia, while the Communists cannot see beauty, the Taliban cannot bear to see it. Between them they succeeded in destroying our world and, of course, we had the five years of civil war. I tell you, Afghans are tired of war.'

After leaving the main roads they had passed the maze of old streets and back alleyways in the oldest part of Kabul, with its ornate wooden houses in various states of repair. Turning a few streets off the main road, they had stopped in front of a small passageway barely wide enough for a car to pass through. After Tawfiq pulled in their side mirrors they drove slowly down the alley to stop in front of a small mosque with stone steps and a beautiful domed roof, which sat at the entry to a large cobbled square with an ancient pistachio tree and fig tree at its centre. On three sides of the square were small shops and homes, but to the right, and the furthest from where they entered, was a line of beautiful old timber houses with deeply ornate and intricately carved fretwork that had long fallen into disrepair. As if to highlight their abandonment, a hen and her chicks had emerged from a broken window of one of the houses to scamper across the square and disappear around the corner.

'Ah,' said Jabril, slightly embarrassed to see Dr Sofia had noticed them too. 'They'll be someone's dinner tonight,' he laughed.

'They're beautiful houses,' she had said. 'Does anyone live in them?'

'No one but chickens,' he had said, laughing again. 'They were originally used by the artisans who worked for the king, but no one lives in them now. I don't think anyone knows who owns them anymore.'

'Shame.'

Jabril nodded in agreement. 'From time to time a family might move in, but Chief Wasim – who, by the way, will be your landlord – gets rid of them pretty quickly.' Jabril had sighed. 'When we have so many homeless it pains me to see these beautiful houses abandoned, but Chief Wasim is right. They are far too dangerous for people to live in. As you can see, the rest of the buildings are newer, except for Babur's *chaikhana* here,' he had said, pointing to his left and indicating for Tawfiq to drive over.

Inside could be seen Babur's worn wooden serving bench laden with trays of tea glasses, freshly washed and draining. Beside them were stacks of mismatched plates and the chunky old teapots used to cook *chainaki*, the traditional goat or lamb soup loved by all Afghans. Although Babur had made the financial decision to expand the *chaikhana* from serving only tea and simple street food to more elaborate meals, it still looked as it might have done two hundred years before. Two raised wooden platforms covered in old Afghan rugs lined opposing walls, while between the ancient copper tea urns placed strategically along their length men were sitting smoking, drinking tea and eating Babur's superb *bolani*, a flatbread stuffed with potatoes or leeks, until the car pulled up out front and the men all turned to stare, each wanting to be the first to catch a glimpse of the new woman doctor from Australia.

'So,' said Jabril, looking around the square, 'this is Shaahir Square, and as we are near the oldest part of Kabul, and because Babur's *chaikhana* is probably one of the oldest buildings in all of Kabul, it means that we're in the centre of my country's history. I like that idea.'

'Me too,' she had said, a smile in her voice as she looked out over the square.

She has a very promising attitude, thought Jabril, indicating to Tawfiq to move slowly forward. 'You will rarely see cars in the square,' he had added, 'because they don't usually like to come down that little road we just entered, which means we are, in many ways, also hidden from the world. I like that idea too. That's Omar,' he had said, waving to an old man sitting in the middle of the square on a plastic chair. 'He's our apothecary. And see the pistachio and fig trees?' Jabril had pointed to the two trees behind the old man. 'They were once part of a magnificent garden on a fine estate, but the house and most of the garden, apart from a few trees, these cobblestones and the wall and gate of where you will be living, all disappeared a long time ago. And this,' he had said, as they pulled up in front of a high dry-stone wall with a large ornate gate, 'is your new home.'

21

When Sofia didn't move Jabril began to worry that perhaps she was not happy with the home Zahra had chosen for her. He had looked up at the house. Like many homes in Kabul, it was hidden from the world by a high wall behind which was a courtyard, but unlike many of the homes in Afghanistan, this one had a famous history, or at least the wall and gate had a famous history. Part of the old estate, the stone wall once surrounded a smaller garden called Baagh-e-shaahir or Poet's Garden, after which the square was named. It was said that Babur's relative, who built the house and gardens, could often be found in Baagh-e-shaahir reciting Rumi, while writing love poems to his beautiful wife.

The other thing this house had that marked it within the square was a small enclosed balcony on the first floor, which looked very much like it might have been an afterthought, which it was. Jabril well remembered the day he had come into the square to see Chief Wasim balancing on a ladder hammering wood over the balcony's crooked timber frame before lifting windows into the space above. That had been eight years before and since then the timber underpinning the balcony had begun to sag from this unplanned weight. Not for the first time, Jabril wondered if he might come into the square one morning to find the balcony sitting in what used to be the famous poet's garden.

Jabril inspected the house again. By Kabul standards it was a very good house, but perhaps it was too much of a step down from Dr Raso's life in Australia?

He had turned around in the seat to look at her. 'After a great deal of consideration, Zahra chose this lodging for you, Dr Raso, and by her own reckoning it's a very safe house.' Why bother mentioning the balcony when it would not strengthen his argument? 'By the way, I would like you to know that the owner, Chief Wasim, is the chief of police of all of Kabul, but I think I already told you that. You cannot get much safer than that, can you?'

Jabril had thought about this and decided that maybe you could. What chief of police didn't have enemies?

4

AFTER WAVING TO Jabril, Sofia wandered back into the kitchen, tipping the cold tea down the sink before heading off to the bathroom where she stripped naked before turning the shower on. When the water became mildly warm she would jump in because in slightly less than three minutes it would run cold again. On the mornings she washed her hair she would be rinsing off under cold water. Winter was not Sofia's favourite time in her Kabul shower.

Initially she had dropped hints to her landlady, Behnaz, who was also Chief Wasim's wife, that she might need a new water heater for her bathroom, but Behnaz had not been interested. After deciding money might be the problem, Sofia had offered to pay for it, which only provoked a stern lecture on the extravagance of heated water and the possibility that more than a pitcher of warm water to wash every day might be verging on the criminally wasteful. The memory made Sofia smile. She had fallen in love with the dusty cobblestone square with its two gnarled trees marking its centre the first time she had seen it, but life in Kabul, and the chief of police's wife in particular, had proved to be far more acquired tastes.

'This is Behnaz,' Jabril had said on that first day as a short, dour woman, covered from head to toe in black, opened the gate. With a large round face and thick red hands, cracked and dry from a lifetime of scrubbing, there was no smile of welcome to tempt the corners of her downturned mouth.

'I'm happy to meet you,' Sofia said with her hand on her heart, only to see the woman look nervously toward Jabril before looking back at her.

'Welcome,' she said in heavily accented English.

'Behnaz is learning English,' Jabril had offered, picking up Sofia's suitcase and following Behnaz through the courtyard to the house. 'That was also an important consideration in Zahra's choice of lodging for you.'

'Room up, Mrs Doctor,' Behnaz had said, pointing up the stairs. Sofia noted that a little clarification might be in order further down the track, but at that moment she didn't think her schoolbook Dari, or Behnaz's English, would be up to the challenge of correcting this misperception.

With a great deal of effort, Behnaz, who was nearly as wide as she was high, had ascended the stairs using the walls as leverage. Puffing by the time she reached the landing, she searched in a hidden pocket of her coat for a set of keys. After opening the door Behnaz had stood back, motioning for Sofia and Jabril to enter. 'Please, you see.'

They entered a space that Sofia had guessed might have once been a large bedroom but had been divided into small rooms. Off the tiny sitting room was the sagging balcony she had seen from the square. To the right was a bedroom and on the left a small kitchenette and bathroom.

'Behnaz is very modern and proud that her place is furnished like a Western house,' Jabril had said, before translating his words into Dari for Behnaz's benefit as he waved Sofia forward, encouraging her to inspect further. 'I think it would probably be best if you looked around. I believe you are her first tenant and she needs to see that you approve.'

The walls were painted a dull green, the floor wooden, while thick exposed timber beams splattered with white plaster held up the roof. The little sitting room had two cane chairs, a table with a vase of plastic roses as its centrepiece and a standard lamp. On the wall Sofia recognised a photo of Mohammed Zahir Shah, the last king of Afghanistan. The little closed-in balcony reminded her of the verandah at the front of the old red brick house where she had grown up in Leichhardt, only that verandah looked out onto a busy arterial road.

Walking over to the balcony, Sofia had pulled back a pair of fresh lace curtains to look over the courtyard and its pomegranate tree out to the square. From this vantage point she understood that, apart from the tiny access road through which they had arrived, the other three corners of the square were pedestrian access only. When she heard a canary singing she found the cage hidden in the pomegranate tree in the courtyard.

'When you here you open window,' her landlady had said slowly in English. 'Not here, lock window. Bedroom.' With that she had turned and led them back inside.

'Your English is very good,' Sofia offered. Her landlady had looked to Jabril for clarification, but when he'd translated all Sofia got was a 'humph'.

The bedroom had an overly large single bed with a nylon floral bedspread, a bedside table in dark timber, a small desk, a chair and an old wooden wardrobe. A naked light hung from the exposed wiring in the ceiling, while a beautiful, ancient and threadbare Afghan rug lay on the floor by the side of the bed.

'As I said, Behnaz is very proud that she has this modern furniture for you.'

'From police station,' Behnaz had said, pointing to an overly large and decidedly ugly desk.

'*Tashakur*,' Sofia said, practising her new language. She wondered if the police knew the table was no longer in their possession.

'I show you where wash. Not clothes. I wash clothes,' Behnaz had said as she headed off to the bathroom with Sofia and Jabril following close behind.

'There's no need for that. I can wash my own clothes.'

Behnaz had turned to Jabril, looking a little distressed, and spoke so quickly in Dari that Sofia had no idea what she was saying.

'She says it is what was agreed with Zahra.'

'Fine,' said Sofia. 'Thank you.'

Behnaz had pushed open the door to a tiny room with a toilet, rust-marked mirror and miniature handbasin. With a dramatic flourish she pulled back what looked like a new pink floral shower curtain revealing an ancient shower rose halfway up the wall and a small water heater above it. Most of the tiles were off-white, but a few were green. Being the same size as those that had fallen out, the new green tiles looked like they had probably been chosen for their utility rather than their aesthetic appeal.

'We were lucky that the tanks were too big to enter the square,' Jabril had offered, as he too leaned in to inspect the bathroom, 'but as you can see there was some damage during the wars. But it's safe and serviceable, which is what you need.'

27

Leading them out to the archway that led into the kitchen, Behnaz stood back so they might inspect. 'Mrs Doctor, see.' She stood with her hands clasped worriedly in front of her, waiting for Sofia's reaction.

Jabril had cleared his throat. 'Dr Sofia is not married,' he said in Dari. 'So you don't need to call her Mrs Doctor.'

'Why?'

Jabril sighed.

Sofia had been inspecting the kitchen as they spoke. It looked like prefab timber laminate that had been popular in the seventies, but this kitchen was clearly new. It had a little two-ring camping stove fed by a gas bottle that took up precious bench space, while a tiny circular table had been pushed against a wall, together with a pair of mismatched chairs. Another vase of plastic flowers sat on a doily in the centre of the table. Sofia could see that her landlady, who was now twisting her apron between rough, work-stained hands, had gone to a great deal of trouble for her first tenant.

'The kitchen's perfect and the flowers are especially lovely.'

'You like?' asked Behnaz in English.

Jabril had leaned over and whispered in Sofia's ear. 'You must be careful. If you show interest or compliment something an Afghan owns, they may think you want it and might feel they have to give it to you. On the other hand, the reverse is also true. If they compliment you on something you own, they may want it.'

Sofia had heard this from her refugee tutor and was only now beginning to see how it might be a problem. 'Everything is perfect,' she had offered. 'Thank you so much and thank you,

Dr Aziz, for recommending Mrs …' Sofia stopped, unsure what to call her landlady.

'Behnaz. We usually only use first names here in Afghanistan.'

'Oh, I'm sorry, I forgot. Behnaz.'

Sofia had suspected she was not the tenant the dour-looking woman had been expecting. She later learned from Zahra that when Behnaz, who didn't much like foreigners, had understood that her first tenant would be a young Australian doctor she had nearly reneged on the deal. With a great appreciation of Behnaz's interest in money, Zahra had politely reminded her of the promise she had made to help her nieces and nephews back in the village and how Sofia's afghanis would contribute handsomely to that cause.

When Behnaz stopped torturing the apron she had spoken in English again. 'Is good?'

'It's perfect. I love it. Thank you … Behnaz.'

With such high praise her landlady's face had lit up. It would take some time for Sofia to understand that Behnaz viewed life as a singularly unrewarding thick and murky soup one was forced to wade through. Laughing, being happy, making jokes were not part of the recipe. Behnaz's smile was such a rare occurrence that Jabril had looked genuinely shocked.

'I also want to thank you and your wife for organising all this for me, Dr Aziz.'

'Jabril. You should call me Jabril.'

Sofia had been wondering what she should call her boss. She knew from the refugee that you normally referred to people by their title because a title opened doors and showed respect. People would be offended if you didn't use their title.

'Are you sure?'

29

'Yes, please. I lived in Boston long enough to find this normal.'

With the niceties finished they were down to the serious business of money. 'Pay two thousand afghanis on Sunday and I clean. No men.'

'I assure you, Behnaz, that Dr Sofia is not interested in bringing men here, although I believe you will not object to my presence from time to time as the need might arise?'

From the look on Behnaz's face it looked like she might very well object to Dr Jabril's presence.

'I clean and shop on Monday. You cook. This is what Zahra arrange.'

'Thank you, that will be fine, but there's no need for you to clean or shop for me.'

'Yes, clean. Okay, no shop. You still pay two thousand afghanis.'

'Of course.'

'I clean tomorrow.'

'Really, there's no need for you to clean tomorrow.'

'Is Monday. I clean Monday.'

With all the rules and financial arrangements agreed to and her authority firmly established, Behnaz had left.

'She is a very nice woman,' Jabril had offered as they listened to her footsteps descending the stairs. Sofia didn't think Jabril sounded too convinced of that. 'My wife tells me her life has been hard. You'll also find Behnaz's husband, Chief Wasim, very nice, but you may also notice that although my friend might be the chief of police for all of Kabul, he is not always the chief of police in his own home.' Jabril laughed at his joke. 'These things don't matter though. What matters is that you're safe and happy in your new home.

'This afternoon I'll show you the surgery before taking you to meet my wife, who has invited you to dinner.'

* * *

JABRIL AND ZAHRA's home, which was close to the square, was an extravagant two-storey affair with windows painted mauve flanked by bright green shutters, and a high white concrete wall with a large metal door shielding the courtyard from the street. Entering the home, they had ascended a curved staircase that led to a room so large it could have been the foyer of a small hotel.

With handmade silk and woollen Afghan rugs scattered across a white tiled floor, the room had a number of white leather lounges and matching poufs, while the ornate gold and marble coffee tables and brass side tables were heavy with vases of Afghan roses, bowls of sugared almonds, dried fruits and books. The wall directly opposite where they had entered boasted two impressively large arched floor to ceiling windows, regally framed by red velvet curtains tied back with elaborate gold tassels. Through an archway to the side Sofia saw a deeply carved baroque dining table with a set of high-backed velvet chairs matching the curtains. Over the table, which must have sat twenty people, were three enormous crystal chandeliers.

The walls of the lounge room were covered with rich tapestries threaded through with gold, interspersed with coloured family photos showing a young Jabril and Zahra and a boy and girl at various ages. Old black and white and ancient sepia photos of an Afghanistan that no longer existed filled what wall space was left. Sofia had stopped in front of one of the photos.

'Where is this?' she asked.

'Ah,' said Jabril, coming to stand beside her. 'This is the

Kherqa-ye Sharif in Kandahar where the cloak of Prophet Mohammad – peace be upon him – is kept. And this,' he had said, turning to one of the photos of the children, 'is our son, Jaweed, and our daughter, Salmar, who are both living overseas. Of course, they are much older now.'

Jabril had been about to say more when they heard a voice behind them.

'Ah, you're here.'

Sofia had turned to see a tall, slender woman walking toward her. With raven black hair, golden-brown eyes artfully smudged with kohl, and lips painted a brilliant magenta, Zahra was striking in a tight green silk dress. At the end of a pair of long legs were two perfectly manicured feet resting in impossibly high gold sandals. Sofia's heart sank. Against this woman she looked, and felt, like a peasant in her suitcase-crushed trousers, sensible walking boots and khaki jumper. She had just received her first lesson in middle-class etiquette: Afghans are particular about their appearance. Sadly, the refugee hadn't mentioned anything about dress codes in private homes and on social occasions.

'My wife, Zahra,' Jabril had said proudly. Sofia guessed that Zahra was as tall as her, but in her heels she stood at least two inches taller than Sofia and six inches taller than her husband.

'Welcome, Dr Raso,' Zahra had said warmly, taking Sofia's hand as she leaned in to kiss her three times. 'May I call you Sofia and you can call me Zahra?'

'Perfect.'

'I can't tell you how much we've been looking forward to meeting you. I hope you enjoy your time here with us in Shaahir Square.'

5

AFTER HER SHOWER, Sofia was in her bedroom getting ready for work when her phone rang. Looking at the caller ID, she felt a familiar rush of guilt.

'I've done it again, haven't I, Dad? I'm sorry. I should've rung.'

They had an agreement: whenever there was a bombing in Kabul, Sofia would make contact to let him know she was safe.

'Well, you're obviously okay. That's all I need to know.'

Sometimes she wished he wouldn't be so understanding. It only made her feel worse.

'So did you hear the news about Michelle? She's getting married.'

Sofia searched for the right response. Why the hell would Michelle, who went through life blowing up social norms, bother getting married? 'That's wonderful news, Dad,' she said, summoning up an enthusiasm she didn't feel.

When Sofia was twelve years old she had watched her mother's body wasting away and the light in her father's eyes fading. Michelle had been eight at the time, and it seemed to Sofia that when they lost their mother they had lost her too. From a vivacious child, Michelle had grown into a girl without a smile. At ten years old she was truanting from school; at fourteen she had a pierced nose, an eyebrow ring and tattoos and was snorting cocaine; by sixteen she had left school, and at eighteen she was dealing and living on the streets. As Sofia's sister's behaviour tore holes in her father's battered heart, she tried to mend them by becoming a more perfect daughter, which only seemed to infuriate Michelle further until the two sisters found themselves caught in a vicious cycle that neither of them knew how to stop.

'What's he like?'

'I haven't met him yet.'

That didn't surprise her. As far as she knew, her father hadn't seen Michelle for two years, although her sister would ring him if she needed money. 'Well, I hope he's a good influence, Dad.'

'That's what I'm hoping too. I'm also hoping he might be a good father.'

Sofia could barely breathe. How was Michelle going to look after a child when she couldn't even look after herself? She had no idea how to respond to this.

'You might want to ring her,' her father offered, breaking the silence.

'I will.' No point in reminding him that Michelle didn't take her calls. 'But in case I can't get through, can you tell her how happy I am for her? Hard to imagine Michelle pregnant.'

Her dad cleared his throat. 'Apparently, she's already had him, a little boy called Jack.'

'Oh god, Dad.' There was no possibility of pretence now.

'I know.'

'Have you seen him?'

'No, but she's gonna bring him around tomorrow, and the

34

boy's father too – at least, I assume the man she's marrying is the bub's father.'

'Oh god, Dad …' Silence down the phone again. 'Sorry, I'm sounding like a broken record. How about you ring me after you've seen them and we can talk?'

When Sofia hung up she sat on the edge of the bed, feeling a familiar sense of hopelessness. The little baby would be just one more worry her father added to the mountain he already carried around in his heart about both his daughters. My poor father, she thought. He didn't deserve all this heartache.

All he had ever wanted for his daughters was a better life than he had been able to give them: a 'normal life', he used to say, where they found steady jobs, met nice young men to marry, produced one or two beautiful, well-adjusted kids and lived happily ever after. She understood why this was so important to him but he couldn't understand why it wasn't to her. Sofia wanted to experience more of life than 'normal', and now that she had there was no way she could ever step back into the 'normal' of Sydney. And yet, she often thought that if her father could see her days he would be shocked, not because they were extraordinary but because they were so ordinary – normal even – if you ignored the fact that it was Afghanistan.

When Sofia applied for the job in Kabul, Jabril had warned her things didn't happen quickly, and he had been right. It had taken five months to clear her visa with the Afghan authorities, during which time she hired the Afghan refugee to give her conversation lessons. Most of these centred around him asking her in English why she wanted to go to Afghanistan when he had risked his life to get out of the place, followed by her halting replies in Dari about doing something exciting with her life, none of which impressed the refugee or was going to help her converse with her new patients. With the refugee spending much of his time telling her in English she was crazy, she eventually told him that it was okay to say that, but could he please at least say it in Dari. 'It might be a sentence I have some use for in the future.'

The night before Sofia was to leave she had been sitting with her father and Michelle at the kitchen table. No one had eaten much of the celebratory pizza and cheesecake he had brought home after finishing his night shift early. It hadn't much felt like a celebration, Sofia thought as she had looked from her father to her sister; more like a death in the family.

As Michelle concentrated on twisting her can of Coca-Cola around in circles in the little pool of condensation forming on the old formica table, Sofia realised her father had started crying.

'Oh, for Christ's sake,' Michelle had said when she dragged herself away from her Coke to see why they had suddenly gone quiet. Pushing back her chair, she stormed out of the kitchen.

For once her father ignored Michelle's histrionics. 'Why do you have to go to a place where there's a war, Sofia?' he had asked the daughter who, until the Afghan madness, had never given him a moment's worry.

'It's not war, Dad. There's no fighting in Afghanistan anymore. The Americans defeated the Taliban.'

'If you believe that crap you have no right going,' he had said, before apologising for the harshness of his words.

Like all taxi drivers, her father thought he knew everything about everything because he spent his waking life listening to parliament and talkback radio, or poring over the newspapers while waiting for customers, and when he had customers he

36

talked to them about their lives and world events. He also spent a good deal of his time talking to other taxi drivers who, in turn, spent their days listening to talkback, reading newspapers and earbashing anyone who was unfortunate enough to get into their cabs. Sofia believed that while taxi drivers might not know everything, they did know a lot more about life and the world than most people.

'It'll be fine,' she had said, reaching across the table to take his hand. The truth was, now the time had come to leave she was regretting her decision. Scarcely able to admit it to herself, she was not about to admit it to him. 'I'll be back in a year. Twelve months, that's not too long. You'll see.'

The following morning Michelle had left the house before Sofia woke so there could be no sisterly goodbye. After checking in her luggage and collecting her boarding pass, Sofia and her dad had sat sipping coffee and trying to make cheery conversation, none of which concerned Afghanistan. When the parting could no longer be put off they had stood together outside the departures gate. Their conversation had run dry. Pulling his daughter into his arms he had whispered how proud he was of her before abruptly letting go and pushing her away.

'Go on, girl. Get out of here. The sooner you leave the sooner you'll be back.'

Twenty-four hours later Sofia had been flying over Afghanistan in the freezing predawn, the folding black velvet night shadows of the barren central plains and valleys gliding by slowly below her. She knew the land was dotted with villages and crisscrossed by roads and dirt tracks but there was not a light to be seen.

An aid worker would later tell Sofia that the imagination

was always worse than the reality when you were travelling to a new location. He had been right. On that first flight into Afghanistan, Sofia had felt herself riding a terrifying emotional rollercoaster – from fear, to wonder, to elation and back to fear, all in a matter of minutes. But then the dusty city of Kabul had come into view, and as the plane began its descent, dawn broke and Sofia saw the Hindu Kush for the first time and her heart soared. This was it: the place she had dreamed of.

Despite her outward enthusiasm on that first drive into the city with Jabril and Tawfiq, Sofia had found the city confusing, and would soon find it cold and unfriendly. It was impossible to hide her foreignness, and her rudimentary language skills were problematic, making it hard to diagnose her patients' illnesses. In those first few weeks she had felt like she was sinking. She was also painfully, achingly lonely. She had made a mistake. The dream was a nightmare. Most nights she lay awake thinking about how she was going to tell Jabril and Zahra that she wasn't the right person for the job and that they needed to get someone local. And then one morning, Ahmad and Hadi had smiled at her and then Omar had waved to her and Babur offered a free lunch, and as she was crossing the square one of her patients stopped to ask how she was settling in and her world began to change.

Focusing less on her own fears and inadequacies, she had started to understand that, yes, there were cultural differences, but the people in the square were fundamentally the same as Australians. They had jobs to do, bills to pay, shopping, cleaning, cooking, children to look after and friends to meet. Within six weeks she had realised she was having real conversations with people. She was starting to find a rhythm and life began to feel comfortable. Throughout these difficult times her anchors had always been Jabril and Zahra, who propped her up when they could see she was faltering while going out of their way to make her feel welcome.

After being in Kabul for six months, Sofia still hadn't known whether she would be staying past her contract, so Jabril had suggested she take some weeks off to see more of the country. That was when she had travelled to the little village in the Hindu Kush and met Daniel Abiteboul and decided to stay. Two years after making that decision Sofia had found herself lying on her bed, trying to find the courage to ring her father and tell him the thing he probably already knew: she was not coming back.

'I know that every life is precious everywhere, Dad,' she had said, as she tried to explain what he would never accept, 'but somehow it seems like life is more precious here. I don't know, maybe it's because death is so much closer. When I'm away I miss Shaahir Square and everything about it.'

'People are in pain here too, you know,' he had offered.

'Yes, I know, Dad.' How did she tell him it really wasn't the same for her? 'Through all of this is their kindnesses and generosity,' she had added, 'and their ability to laugh despite all their difficulties. I don't see that in Sydney.' Her father didn't respond. She had tried again, wondering whether she could make anything better, or whether they should just hang up and let the dust settle. 'Do you remember when I went to Norway on holidays last year and how happy you were that I was away from Kabul? Well, that wasn't how it felt for me. I've got to tell you that every single kilometre I moved deeper into the perfect orderliness of that beautiful, cold, dark country, the more I longed for the heat and chaos of Kabul.'

'I see.'

No, she had thought, you don't see. He didn't want to see and she couldn't blame him. How she wished it were different. 'Perhaps it's as simple as the fact that I'm part of a community here now, Dad. I never really felt that back in Sydney ... apart from you,' she had added too late. The conversation had been as difficult and painful as she had imagined.

* * *

SOFIA CHECKED THE time on her phone and realised that if she didn't hurry, she'd be late for work and her meeting with Daniel.

After pulling on the long, loose black pants known as *tunban* and a long-sleeved shirt that reached below her butt, she draped a scarf loosely over her hair. Sometimes she replaced the shirt with a dress over pants, but mostly she stuck to a uniform of long black pants or jeans and long shirts, which she layered with the changing seasons. Wearing her long red hair loose wasn't illegal so no one would arrest her, but as a tall Western woman with such fair skin it would have only drawn unwelcome attention. She could have worn high heels like the young women of Kabul, but traversing the worn cobbles of Shaahir Square every day and Kabul's crumbling footpaths made that a treacherous option. She didn't smile at a strange man in the street because it would probably shock him, and she didn't offer her hand unless someone offered theirs first. Outside the square she felt she had to curb her natural propensity for openness and happiness, and not laugh or talk too loudly. She had also learned to be a little vague about herself if strangers asked too many questions. Everything was about not offending or calling attention to herself while being respectful in her attire and behaviour, which conveyed respect for those she met.

Sofia slipped on her flat shoes and looked in the mirror. Make-up or no make-up? The young women of Kabul were dedicated followers of fashion, keeping up with the latest clothes, hairstyles and make-up looks. It had been one of the things that had surprised Sofia the most when she arrived in Kabul, which also reinforced how much she'd accepted the Western stereotype of Afghan women.

Sofia inspected her naked face. Lipstick and mascara would do for Daniel, she decided. She then added a touch of blush as an afterthought.

Grabbing her bag and laptop off the bed, Sofia was about to leave the apartment when she saw the woollen scarf, freshly laundered and neatly folded on the bedside table. Picking it up, she ran her fingers over the familiar wool. She had been intending to give it back to Daniel. Placing it back on the bedside table, she headed out the door.

6

In the courtyard the rug from the entrance was hanging over the lowest branch of the pomegranate tree, ready to be beaten to within an inch of its life. The canary cage had been moved out of harm's way and was sitting on the ground by the gate.

'Good morning, Behnaz,' Sofia said in Dari. As soon as Sofia had learned the language Behnaz had stopped trying to speak *Amreekawee*. Despite Sofia mentioning the word 'English' a number of times, the language had steadfastly remained *Amreekawee* in Behnaz's mind and learning it, she had said, 'hurt her brain'.

Behnaz stopped sweeping the courtyard to lean on her broom beside the little pile of litter she had collected from the square earlier that morning. 'Good morning, Dr Sofia.'

'I hope you slept well last night, Behnaz.'

'Not so well,' she said with an exaggerated sigh. Sofia knew what that meant.

Behnaz happened to be one of Sofia's patients and had told Sofia more than once – a lot more than once – that she had thought of killing her husband, Kabul's chief of police, because his snoring had kept her awake for nearly forty years and she'd had enough. Initially, Behnaz had given Sofia a running tally of the number of hours of sleeplessness this represented in the long torment of her marital bed until one day she had watched a pirated video about Abu Ghraib prison in Iraq and discovered that sleep deprivation was a form of torture. It had been Behnaz's eureka moment and was, as Behnaz liked to tell Sofia, the only useful thing she ever learned from the *Amreekawees* apart from *Amreekawee.*

With this new-found information damning her husband's snoring, Behnaz no longer felt the need to count hours of wakefulness as testimony when torture was far more damning. In the last few months Behnaz had taken to wondering aloud whether torture might be a good line of defence in any possible court case should Chief Wasim be discovered dead in the marital bed. Given that Sofia's bedroom was above Chief Wasim and Behnaz's, she could sympathise with her landlady, and at two o'clock in the morning when she had not yet fallen asleep, she too fantasised about killing the chief of police who lay blissfully unaware in the room below.

Rather than share these thoughts with Behnaz, Sofia had advised that, in her not-so-learned opinion, it probably wasn't a good defence. She had also tactfully suggested things Wasim might like to do to minimise his snoring so Behnaz (and she) could get more sleep, but Behnaz had refused to pass this information on to her husband, claiming that it would have shamed him if he discovered she had spoken to Sofia about such an intimate male problem he didn't have. Understanding Behnaz's twisted logic, Sofia could only smile and console herself that at least she had tried. Despite Behnaz's long-suffering laments and threats, Sofia knew she loved her husband in a coarse and familiar way, and that her words were essentially all habit and bluster.

It hadn't taken Sofia long to discover that being a doctor in a small community – even if it was in the middle of a large city – was a balancing act between intimate secrets and public behaviour. Routinely needing to forget the secrets she was told if she wished to maintain some semblance of normality in day-to-day life with friends and neighbours, Sofia was also required to recall every exacting detail when the next instalment arrived, for her patients would have been deeply offended if she had forgotten some pivotal piece of information and needed to be reminded. Rarely did she make a mistake, which was another thing that endeared her to her patients. They may have felt differently if they had known that, having long ago discovered she was not capable of remembering all the intimate minutiae that found their way into her surgery, Dr Sofia had taken to privately recording notes of their conversations in a secret file on her laptop. She hoped she would not live to regret this.

'It feels like it might be a bit cooler today, Behnaz.'

'I think it's not so hot today.' It was always not so hot that time of year in Kabul.

'You're out early,' Sofia offered, without receiving a reply.

If Behnaz had nothing to say she simply said nothing. It was a skill Sofia had long admired but failed to master for, contrary to popular opinion, silences said a lot, and in this regard, Behnaz's silences were usually commanding.

'You know, I think this canary could use a mate.' Sofia stopped and crouched down in front of the cage, making useless cooing noises that only ever succeeded in silencing the bird.

'No mate,' Behnaz said, still leaning on her broom.

'It might be lonely,' Sofia said, looking up at her.

'No mate.'

'I'll pay for it,' Sofia said hopefully as she got to her feet again.

'No mate.'

'Okay.'

When Behnaz had first returned from the bird market with a canary it had taken her twenty-four hours to decide that her bird was defective because it didn't sing half as loudly or as long as her friend's canary. Marching back to the bird market with the hapless bird swinging wildly in its cage, the furious Behnaz had demanded a bird that wasn't 'broken'. The stall owner distinctly remembered this particular woman, who had haggled him down in price until his profit had all but disappeared. Normally he would have explained to a customer that he charged more for male canaries because they sang better than the females, but all this woman had been interested in was paying as little as possible. Faced with the impenetrable wall of Behnaz's fury, and a growing crowd of curious onlookers, he had swapped the female for a male canary free of charge, sending a little prayer to Allah that he would never have the misfortune of dealing with the woman again.

Opening the gate to reveal the square beyond, Sofia was assailed by familiar sounds and the unwelcome smell of fresh donkey droppings. Looking down she saw the offending item sitting warm and grassy in a patch of sunlight on the dusty old cobblestones just outside the gate. Behnaz, who had been following close behind Sofia, registered the mess and promptly began cursing in her native Pashto.

* * *

OMAR, WHO HAD been sitting patiently in the middle of the square waiting for Behnaz to come through her gate to discover the donkey's calling card, smiled to himself when she began to swear. Not many people got one up on his cantankerous neighbour, but the donkey always did. It was a small pleasure he would accept on this worrisome morning.

In wintertime Omar could be found sitting at the counter in his apothecary shop in front of his dusty old electric bar heater with a warming blanket wrapped around his shoulders. During the height of summer, when the Kabul days were unbearably hot and sticky, he would be sitting in front of the new electric fan he bought from Ahmad for what he considered an acceptable price, but when the power went out – which it did on a regular basis – he would take his sandals off and rest his feet in a bucket of water. As the mornings became cooler, but not yet too cold, Omar carried a plastic chair out into the middle of the square in search of a spot of sunshine to warm his old bones, but as the sun began to move across the square, Omar would pick up his chair and follow it until by mid-morning he could be found sitting back in a patch of sun by the front door of his shop where, more often than not, he would be sleeping.

On this morning, Omar settled back in his chair in the middle of the square, and as he turned his leathery old face to take the full measure of the sun's meagre warmth, he found himself contemplating a nap. Old age had a few small pleasures, but youth, Omar thought as he drifted off, now that was something else.

As a young boy growing up in a desolate village in the hills of northern Afghanistan, and lacking any formal education, Omar believed he could see his future. He would build a square mudbrick house with two rooms next to his parents' home, and like his father, he would become a goat herder. In time he would marry a local girl and, *insha'Allah*, she would be beautiful and he would have many fine sons. With his easygoing manner and the much admired green eyes he had inherited from his Iranian mother, it was often said that Omar would marry well, although even Omar could see that marrying well in such a poor community might not mean very much. When he was fifteen fate had intervened and Omar had been summoned to Kabul by his father's wealthy brother. With no children, the brother had decided to test each of his nephews to see who might be smart enough to inherit his apothecary business in Shaahir Square.

In time Omar won the coveted prize, but what he had experienced during his two years of training with his uncle in Kabul had changed him forever. He had seen more food in the city's markets in one day than he had seen in his entire lifetime. He had smelled smells and his eyes had seen sights that he had found both thrilling and frightening but also hard to understand. The exoticism and sheer size of Kabul had made the young Omar's head spin. There were more people in that great city than he had thought possible in the entire world. He saw women and young girls walking the streets in short skirts with painted faces and their hair hanging free. When one of these beauties smiled at Omar he would often stumble, unable to find the appropriate response, for nothing in his village had taught him how to react to such wanton seduction.

After returning to his village Omar had been restless. The place was too small and the people backward, and yet he had no choice but to wait until his uncle summoned him back to Kabul, or the man died, at which time the apothecary shop would become his. The villagers quietly noted these changes in the once carefree young man and began to speculate about what terrible things must have happened to him in the city until he became a cautionary tale for their children, a warning of the dangers lurking in the streets of Kabul and the modern world. In 1976, five years after he had left Shaahir Square, Omar's uncle had died and he had returned.

As the square's apothecary for more than four decades, Omar took pride in moving with the times by stocking over-the-counter Western drugs, although his heart of hearts belonged to the ancient art of the apothecary. His uncle's beautiful old cabinets, made from the magnificent cedars of Lebanon nearly a century before, and the exquisitely crafted timber drawers lining the shop's walls were still crammed full of all manner of herbs, spices and mysterious tonics and potions, some of which dated from before his uncle's time, and while they were mostly a mystery to him, he could not bring himself to throw them out.

There were those in the square who swore that Omar's concoctions were better than Western drugs and could cure any disease known to man. As was to be expected, the true believers tended to be the older residents of the square and its nearby alleyways, while the younger generation, and those with more formal education, generally dismissed these claims as quackery. Omar was aware that Dr Jabril and Dr Sofia were not always happy when he talked their patients out of the Western painkiller, cough medication or antibiotic they had suggested in favour of one of his potions. It was, in Omar's mind, a bit of a game to see who had the most influence in the square. So far he believed it was split fifty-fifty, which afforded him a certain amount of pride.

With regard to the perceived magic or otherwise of his own wizardry, Omar was a true believer up to a point. Of late he had felt death's hot breath on his burning skin and was wise enough to know there was no miracle potion to be found in his beautiful cabinets for the creeping sickness destroying his body. He also knew that if Dr Jabril or Dr Sofia knew what ailed him they would be greatly concerned and most certainly would prescribe a concoction of Western drugs, which happened to be the main reason he hadn't mentioned his illness to anyone.

It was not so much that Omar wanted to die but that he acknowledged death's inevitability. The thing he found hard to accept, though, was that it had arrived a little too soon for his liking. Sometimes the thought of his imminent demise saddened Omar a great deal, but whenever he felt that sadness in his heart he would take a little more of his special 'draught' and force himself to smile. While it eased the pain, Omar had long ago understood that a smile lit your heart. It was an even stranger thing to discover that the great men of science in the West supported Omar's self-evident truth. *Smiling rewires your brain's circuitry to override its natural tendency to think negatively*, they proclaimed in their learned journals, as if they alone had discovered a new truth. It made Omar chuckle. All those years of learning when all anyone needed to do was sit in the middle of Shaahir Square and watch their friends. For the square had become Omar's university, an ever-changing tableau he watched with equal measures of amusement, confusion and enlightenment, and at times great joy and great sadness, but always with eternal interest. He would miss it when he was gone.

Just as Omar was beginning to think about how he wished he could find a way of bottling some of this truth found in a smile, his eyes flew open. Had he been dreaming? He blinked and blinked again to know he was truly awake before looking around the square, reassuring himself that all was as it should be until he saw Behnaz and Sofia out the front of Behnaz's gate and he remembered the night letter he had taken off that gate that very morning when he had been returning from the mosque. Carrying it back to his bed, he had taken the time to consider its contents in private. Unfortunately, he had been unable to find enlightenment.

Perhaps it was time to investigate, Omar thought. With his rheumatic old bones taking a while to warm up these days, and the pain in his limbs making movement less pleasant, Omar rose slowly and made his way over to the two women.

7

'AND HOW ARE you this morning, my friend?' Sofia asked when Omar joined her, Behnaz and the donkey droppings by the gate.

'I have not long for this world, Dr Sofia,' he said, careful not to step into the mess. His words made Sofia smile, as they always did.

'You know you've been saying that to me for the past five years, don't you? I'm convinced you're going to live forever.'

Omar placed his hand on his heart. 'That, Dr Sofia, would not be my wish. Not forever, but maybe for just a little bit longer.'

'I require you to live to a very old age, Omar. What would Shaahir Square be without you?' Sofia hitched her laptop and tote bags higher over her shoulder ready to head off across the square as Behnaz mumbled something unintelligible under her breath. Sofia turned to her. 'And I'm sure Behnaz agrees with me too, don't you? Shaahir Square wouldn't be the same without Omar, would it?'

Omar knew Dr Sofia was teasing Behnaz, trying to get her to say something nice about him, but Behnaz retreated into one of her silences so Sofia said her goodbyes before setting off across the square to her surgery.

It had become Omar's habit to ignore Behnaz's general displays of disapproval over the latest mysterious offence he had committed. On this morning he did what he had done a thousand times before and turned his back on Behnaz to make his way back to his chair and its beckoning patch of sunlight, only to discover she had followed and was now standing over him, blocking out his sun and its warmth. Omar sighed. What had he done to deserve the abuse that was surely about to rain down on his head? When he remembered the night letter his heart gave a leap, sorely testing the fragile organ.

'She's out of your reach,' Behnaz snapped.

Omar looked up, but with the sun behind her he was finding it hard to see Behnaz's face. It was probably not a bad thing, he thought, squinting. 'Who?'

'Dr Sofia.'

'Ah,' Omar said, nodding as he relaxed back into his chair, relieved that she didn't know about the night letter. 'As always, you're right.'

Omar shifted in his chair so that he might see Behnaz's face more clearly and gain a little more sun. He could see now that she was still glaring down at him but also looking confused. Omar tried to hide his satisfaction. He knew Behnaz well enough to understand that she was not entirely sure how to take his words. It was so satisfying to still have the ability to unsettle her. Teasing Behnaz had always been one of the more pleasurable pastimes of his youth.

Throwing a 'humph' in Omar's direction, which was as near a perfect sign of disapproval as she was able to muster in the circumstances, Behnaz marched back across the square to her famous gate, making a point of slamming it shut behind her.

Chief Wasim would soon need to fix those hinges again, thought Omar with a smile.

Changing position once more in the chair to relieve the ache in his right hip, Omar's amusement began to fade as it was replaced with a familiar sadness. Why did Behnaz have to be like this? They were old now and he was not long for this world. Why could she not find it in her heart to forgive him?

Omar was aware that many in the square said Behnaz was not a friend of happiness, but he remembered the young Behnaz who had come here as Chief Wasim's bride. She had been a young girl bursting with happiness, but over the years someone, or something, had stolen that happiness from her. With all his heart Omar hoped it had not been him, for such a burden was not something he wished to take with him to his grave. He thought again of the self-evident magic of smiles and knew that if he possessed a jar of smiles he would have given them all to this woman he had once loved.

Noticing the old stirring between his legs, Omar could only feel gratitude. It was thinking of the young Behnaz, with her raven black hair and laughing dark eyes, that had given him this gift, just as it had all those years ago. Omar wondered how long it was since he had felt this pleasure and thought back to the last of his three wives, who had died fifteen years before. Or was it sixteen? Omar could not rightly remember, and in truth it no longer mattered. He had loved the last one just as he had loved the two before her, even if they had all so grievously failed him. Each of his three wives had produced only daughters, seven in total, all of whom had married and moved away. He should have kept that last one so she could look after him in his illness, he thought, but at the time the bride price of two goats offered by his old friend back in the village had proved far too tempting.

And where are those goats now?

I don't see them looking after you.

It disturbed Omar that there were now two voices in his head. His first wife, who he believed understood him better than the others, used to say that if he took the voice out of his head and sat it down beside him and listened to its incessant jabbering for just five minutes he would never listen to the voice again. 'That voice is not your friend,' she had warned him. What would she think if she knew there were now two voices? While Omar had never been able to understand how she knew so much about the voice in his head, he had thought it excellent advice and had gone to great lengths to impart his new-found wisdom to his friends and customers until she had suggested he stop.

'You old fool,' she had said not too kindly, her hands planted firmly on her hips. Omar couldn't quite remember when she had first started addressing him as such, but it was the only way he could remember her now. He was sure she had not been like that when he had first taken her as a young bride.

Too late Omar realised that all these bad thoughts about voices and his first wife had chased away his pleasure, his thoughts returning to the problem he had: discovering the secret of the *shabnamah* from the Taliban he had taken off Behnaz's gate. Everyone knew the Taliban's night letters meant only one thing, and if Behnaz or Dr Sofia were in danger then he must take action, for had he not seen the destruction of the great Buddhas of Bamiyan by the ignorant zealots? The Taliban must never be allowed in Shaahir Square.

Yes, yes, he said to his second wife who was in his ear. *I know the women of Afghanistan suffered greatly under the Taliban too. Have we not had this conversation a hundred times already?*

Even from Jannah she would not let him be. Surely she had better things to do in paradise than torment him.

Poor Afghans like the village boy Omar didn't travel for the sake of travelling. Travelling was for necessity only, not something one did for pleasure, but when Omar had left his uncle's shop in Shaahir Square, safe in the knowledge that the apothecary shop would one day be his, he had taken a detour on his way home to visit his cousin in Bamiyan Province. Although Omar had been intoxicated with the capital and all it had to offer, what he saw in Bamiyan he believed was the closest anyone could ever come to knowing Allah in the work of men. Omar had stood in front of the giant Buddhas carved out of the cliff face with tears pooling in his eyes.

Since that day Omar had witnessed, with a degree of equanimity, the assault on his beloved capital by the Russians and the mujahideen during their five years of civil war and the abuses of the ignorant Taliban, but when those fanatics destroyed the great Buddhas of Bamiyan they had gone too far. Retreating to his bedroom for three full days and four nights, Omar had been inconsolable for he understood that not one other human being on this planet would stand before the work of Allah again as he had. The enormity of that realisation had crippled him. In the confines of his room he had raged against the horror of that unspeakable, ungodly act and then, when all his passion and rage had been spent, he emerged with a deep and abiding hatred of the Taliban that he would carry with him until his dying breath.

Omar could not let the Taliban and their threats destroy the square or the people he loved.

***

IT WAS IMPOSSIBLE for Sofia to cross the fifty metres of the square that separated her apartment from her surgery without little diversions, and she would not have had it any other way. The charm of living and working in the incessantly noisy and sometimes smelly square was always the people.

While she had fascinated the men when she first arrived, they had been wary. Over time, and with Afghans' natural disposition for hospitality and respect, the men of the square had come to trust that this tall, exotic Australian doctor with the astonishing hair was not going to shame or shock them, or corrupt their wives and daughters, and they had welcomed her into their world as their 'dear sister'.

Unlike the men, the women had never hidden their fascination with Sofia and would frequently arrive at the surgery with make-believe symptoms of confusing illnesses. With only eleven months of experience in an inner-city Sydney hospital before arriving in Kabul, and fumbling her way through a new language, communication and understanding had been somewhat problematic, making it difficult for Sofia to diagnose the women's problems. In her search for answers her questions had moved haltingly from physical symptoms to life in general, and as the women's natural reserve began slipping away, they moved on to family and home life and marital concerns. As a result, these increasingly convoluted consultations often lasted more than an hour, and when Sofia's patients told her they no longer felt the ache or pain they had arrived with she was often left puzzled as to how she had helped.

It didn't take long for the word to spread among the women of Shaahir Square that the new foreign doctor they had originally told Dr Jabril they did not want was a sympathetic ear who could be trusted with their secrets, and the floodgates of female dissatisfaction descended upon Sofia's surgery. Although the women were soon arriving with legitimate and mostly diagnosable illnesses, a precedent had been set and the women came to expect their consultation time to exceed an hour, covering a wide and varying range of concerns, which might or might not include the marital, familial, social and political. What the new doctor wasn't told about a neighbour's wayward son, a cousin's useless no-good husband or Afghanistan's corrupt politicians was not worth knowing. Unwittingly, Sofia had become a therapist for the women of Shaahir Square.

At first Jabril could not understand why his new partner's consultations were taking so long until Sofia confessed she was not up to the task of diagnosing Afghan women's health issues. After a couple of questions Jabril had guessed what the problem might be, but when the curious husbands began to worry about the time their wives were spending with the new doctor, he smiled and shook his head, as if the ills of women, and the harmless ministrations of a Western doctor, were beyond a simple Afghan man's powers of reasoning. With Sofia continuing to apologise for her deficiencies, Jabril decided the time had come for him to share his insights. Lowering his bulk into one of the seats on the opposite side of her desk, he had told her what he saw as the reality of the situation.

'My dear Sofia, the women of Shaahir Square leave your surgery far happier than when they arrive. Is that not true?'

Sofia considered this. 'Mostly, yes.'

'Precisely. Which means that their husbands are happier and their children are happier.' Sofia had watched the smile light up the face of her quirky boss. 'Which means all the people who live in the square are happier. Everyone is happier! You are doing Afghanistan a glorious service.' Jabril laughed, shaking his head at his powers of reasoning. 'You're a saint. Truly, we should call you Saint Sofia of Shaahir Square. Yes,' he had said, rising from the chair, 'that has a certain pleasing ring to it. Afghanistan will soon have its first Catholic saint. I must inform the Pope immediately!' Sofia could still hear him chuckling as he made his way back through her reception area to his surgery.

Like everybody in the square, Sofia loved Jabril. It also helped that he really didn't seem to care that the duration of her consultations meant she often failed to contribute her fair share of income to the business, an inconvenience that was exacerbated by the fact that some of her patients couldn't afford to pay while others paid a random amount, and still others only paid every other visit. In time Sofia would learn that the viability of both of their surgeries was not reliant on this income but on subsidies from Jabril's seemingly bottomless bank account.

8

STANDING OVER THE first flames of his grill, Babur wiped the beads of sweat from his brow with a greasy rag before waving and calling out to Sofia as she passed: *'As-salaam alaikum.'* Just as she was returning the greeting she was nearly knocked off her feet by her young receptionist, Iman, who had come running up from behind to thread her arm through Sofia's.

Iman's father, who held a high position in the Ministry of Foreign Affairs, and her mother, who taught Pashto and Dari to expatriates at a small privately run school, encouraged Iman to be an independent woman, all the while tempering their enthusiasm for female emancipation with warnings about not drawing too much unwanted attention. Sofia thought both pieces of advice commendable if not somewhat contradictory, which probably went a long way to explaining why Iman adopted the first while generally ignoring the second.

Sofia had not missed Babur's look of disapproval and knew that Iman's habits of talking too loudly on her mobile phone, not covering her hair and always wanting to change everything were generally seen by some of the older generation as an affront to the good order of the square.

'I believe that women must also take responsibility for the subjugation of women in Afghanistan society,' offered Iman, who had a habit of randomly picking up on a past conversation without warning. 'I know this isn't a popular idea, but it's true, don't you think, Dr Sofia?'

Sofia had heard this argument before and wondered where the conversation was going this time. Sofia decided that until she knew it was probably best not to respond.

'Think about it,' continued Iman. 'It's mothers who teach their daughters to serve men and don't insist their daughters are educated. It's also mothers who treat their sons like kings and their daughters-in-law like servants. Even my friends, the way I hear them talking about each other makes me crazy. Why don't women in Afghanistan support each other like they do in the West?'

'Woman don't always support each other in the West, Iman. There's a lot of competition between women there, a lot of bad behaviour.' She still had no idea where the conversation was going.

'But there is also support, right?' she asked, sounding disappointed.

'Of course, but as I've said before, everything isn't perfect in the West for women. What's this all about anyway?'

'I'm organising a protest to highlight the subjugation of women in Afghanistan.'

'Interesting.'

'Don't say that!' Iman let go of Sofia's arm. 'People only say "interesting" when they don't agree with you and want to be polite,' she said, petulantly.

60

Sofia remembered too late that Iman hated the word. 'I promise I shall wipe the offending word from my vocabulary immediately. So how will you protest?'

'We'll ride our bikes in the streets of Kabul.' Iman saw the look on Sofia's face. 'There's nothing in the Qur'an that says girls can't ride bikes. Boys ride bikes everywhere. Why can't we? I want to point out this inequality.'

'I'm just a little worried about the safety issue. The traffic here's so dangerous.'

'I've already thought about that. We'll take over all the lanes and then the cars will have to wait behind us so they can't knock us off our bikes even if they wanted to.'

'I think your protest is admirable.'

'Good. Then you'll join us?'

Sofia was aware that Iman saw her as a role model, but the presence of a Western woman would undermine the validity of Iman's protest by giving its detractors the opportunity to dismiss it as Western-led. There was also another problem. A big part of Sofia's ability to continue living in Kabul was her skill at staying 'under the radar'. She couldn't afford to be part of Iman's demonstration. 'I don't have a bike.'

'Maybe I could find one for you,' Iman said, pulling her hair back behind her shoulders.

Sofia hoped not. 'What did your parents say?'

'I haven't told them.'

Sofia raised an eyebrow. 'They might like to be forewarned. There could be repercussions for them.'

'I know. I will.'

For the first time Sofia noticed that Iman was wearing her best clothes. 'You look especially beautiful today. Something happening?' Sofia had given Iman the morning off because Daniel was coming and there would be no patients.

'Khalif's taking me to breakfast.'

'Somewhere nice, I hope.'

'He says it's a surprise. By the way, I saw the photo in the paper of the man from the UN you're seeing this morning. He's *veeeery* handsome.'

'Do you think so?'

Iman made a point of turning to watch her. 'You think he's handsome too, don't you?'

'I didn't say that.'

'You didn't have to. I can see it in the smile on your face. Okay, I'm going to be late,' she said, as they were nearing Ahmad's shop. 'Don't tell anyone about my protest yet.'

'I won't, but think about telling your parents.'

Iman laughed. 'I might be modern but I'm not so modern that I wouldn't tell them.'

***

BRIGHTLY COLOURED KITCHEN implements, faded bottles of shampoo, wooden rolling pins, brittle plastic storage jars, glasses, hand beaters and strainers of every imaginable size were sitting in their rightful places in front of Ahmad's shop. On top of some crates was a new addition, a stack of girls' woven hats made of pink plastic, while men's sandals were sitting in a basket by the front door, paired together with string. Among Ahmad's tin cans, kerosene lamps and beaten tin plates hanging from the wire strung under the awning at the front of the shop was now a used blue plastic bucket. If Ahmad sold two of the engraved tin plates they would pay for food for a week. Plates did well. Kerosene lamps did even better. Proceeds from a second-hand bucket probably wouldn't spread very far.

As Sofia saw it, the problem for Ahmad, and all the other small shopkeepers of Kabul, was that they were all selling the same things. Liberated Kabul had become another dumping ground for the world's cheap, mass-produced merchandise trucked in from Iran, Pakistan and China, and with everyone selling the same goods, no one was making a profit. It was a problem nobody in the square had been able to solve. Sofia's suggestion that they might diversify had fallen on deaf ears. No one had the resources to find new and exciting items from overseas, and even if they had, who in the hidden backwater that was Shaahir Square would buy them?

'*As-salaam alaikum,*' she called as she walked past Ahmad, who returned her greeting.

'Do you think I should paint my shop a different colour so I might have more customers?' he added.

Sofia stopped and walked back to give serious consideration to the question, which, along with the second-hand blue bucket, probably reflected a new level of desperation. 'Well, I'm not sure.' She looked over to the neighbouring shop. 'What do you think, Hadi?'

Hadi considered his answer. 'Green is probably the best colour because it's the colour of Allah.'

'You're right, my friend,' Ahmad said, lifting the rolled, flat *pakol* off his head and scratching through the thick head of hair underneath. 'If it's His will that I don't have enough customers then *insha'Allah.*'

Not for the first time, Sofia thought *insha'Allah* had a lot to answer for.

'What to do? What to wish for?' Ahmad said to no one in particular as he replaced his hat and drew on his cigarette again.

'Better not to wish for anything,' offered Hadi. 'Better not to draw Allah's attention.' Ahmad nodded.

Ahmad, his wife, Badria, and their four small children lived in two cockroach-infested rooms in the alley behind his shop, and in six months' time another baby would arrive. Sofia had known this before Ahmad because she was his wife's doctor. She also knew Badria was happy with her new pregnancy: proud to be raising children, proud to be a good wife and mother, happy to be living in a world uncomplicated by godless possibilities. For Badria it had always been thus, and always would be. She didn't believe in education for girls; it upset the natural order of things. 'They want to leave home and work in a shop. Stupid girls. They dream all the time of a life they'll never have,' she had told Sofia. 'It's better that they have children and let their husbands work and not waste time on foolish dreams.'

Badria, who was not quite thirty, had her future written for her at the time of her conception back in her village. It was the same future that had waited for generations of women before Badria, and all those who would come after her, until someone in that long line of female history rebelled. As Sofia had delivered each of Badria's daughters she had wondered whether this might be the one, whether this girl child would be history in the making.

Ahmad and Badria were cousins and had married because that was what was expected. From what Badria had told her one emotionally charged day in the sanctity of the surgery, Sofia was not sure Ahmad knew what love was but he would have known what right was, and it had been right to marry

Badria. She also had not questioned her fate, but unlike her cousin, Badria knew what love was. When she was thirteen years old a young boy had come to work in the neighbour's field. Watching him through the crack in the wall of her mudbrick home, Badria had experienced the first breathless quickening of love, but then, as mysteriously as the boy had arrived, he had disappeared, taking her heart along with him. Badria's pain had been so cripplingly raw and all-consuming that she vowed she would never suffer such a thing again. Badria was very sure she knew what love was and it was not for her.

Sofia was aware that Ahmad had not been so happy with this new pregnancy. Another baby would mean another mouth to feed, but if Allah wanted them to have more children then *insha'Allah*. Like so many Afghans, the future for Ahmad was a fear he carried around in the pit of his stomach.

'Old before their time,' her father had once said when Sofia had told him about her friends' woes. Her father's casual dismissal of their struggles had hurt her deeply. It had also taught her a valuable lesson: to keep her own counsel. For completely different reasons she had also learned not to talk with her Afghan friends too much about life in Australia.

'You're talking crazy,' Hadi had said when she once told them about the pension system. 'Our government can barely pay people for the work they do. There's no money for pensions.'

'There used to be,' offered Ahmad, 'before we had the wars.'

'That's true,' nodded Hadi thoughtfully. 'Pensions are a luxury of peace.'

There had been nothing in either man's frame of reference that would allow him to compute life in modern Australia. Why would a family of four need a house with eight rooms and two bathrooms when three rooms were an extravagance and two would do well enough? Who would need more than one perfectly good pair of comfortable shoes, or twenty-eight different brands of shampoo to choose from? Such things made your head spin. Sofia's world in Australia was wanton, extravagant, debauched, and she could see this as clearly as they could. She also knew it was a wanton, extravagant and debauched life most of them would have sold their souls for. And she, the strangest of all creatures, had left all this to live and work among them in Shaahir Square. They loved her all the more for it.

Before Sofia had arrived in Kabul, Western extravagance had come to the city with a glittering new shopping mall that rose phoenix-like out of the rubble and poverty of the city. Nine storeys high, the Kabul City Centre mall was all shiny chrome and glass, with high-fashion shops stocking handbags that cost more than ten years' hard work for the average Afghan. It had moving stairs and glass elevators to effortlessly carry the residents of Kabul from one dazzling floor to the next. The stores inside displayed things that many residents had never seen before and, as was to be expected, the poor residents of Kabul treated it like an amusement park. On weekends families came to gawk at the glass and chrome and all the pretty things they could never have, while the teenagers of Kabul hung out, dreaming of the day when this life of iPhones and designer plenty would be theirs.

With Ahmad and Hadi beginning a familiar discussion about the cost of educating their sons, a potential customer arrived and Hadi retreated inside his shop while Sofia headed off to her surgery. It hadn't escaped her attention that neither man had mentioned educating their daughters. Nor did it escape her attention that she had not questioned this, even though the issue of female education was something she was passionate about.

The subtext of so many of Sofia's conversations with her Afghan friends was that she should not interfere. She understood and accepted this. What right did an outsider have to tell people how they should live and behave in their own country? From the moment she knew she was going to Afghanistan, Sofia had made the decision not to become involved, even though she knew there would be things she would find confronting and hard to accept. Initially she had been able to rationalise the decision by telling herself it would only be for a year. When the option came for a second year she told herself it would only be for one more. After five years of living in Afghanistan she was finding her silences harder to hold, and yet remain silent she did. The stakes were simply too high to do otherwise.

Silent and invisible was what Sofia needed to be.

9

'*As-salaam alaikum*, Dr Sofia,' offered Rashid, the security guard who Jabril had hired three years previously to keep watch at the bottom of the stairs that led up to her surgery. When Sofia had questioned whether the business could afford to carry another salary, Jabril had explained that the ex-soldier was there to protect her and her patients, because without patients, or her, there would be no business. Sofia suspected Rashid's hiring had more to do with Jabril's good heart.

Rashid, who was Hazara and related by marriage to Babur, had lost his two eldest children to a Taliban suicide bomber on a school bus and had been desperate to get his Hazara wife and surviving twins out of the country. When Jabril heard the story, he not only hired Rashid but had given him a small 'appreciation' payment to take care of the expenses for his surviving family to travel to Iran, plus the first six months' rent on an apartment.

It had been Rashid's first security job and Sofia thought he was taking it all too seriously. When she had complained to Jabril he had patiently explained that Rashid was supposed to take his job seriously. Security was a serious business in Afghanistan. It had

taken a while for Sofia to dissuade Rashid from waiting outside
Behnaz's gate each morning to escort her across the square with
his AK-47 pointed at her friends, but once he was convinced that
they were not a threat to her he had become a welcome fixture in
her days and the life of the square. Sitting at the bottom of the
stairs every day, Rashid seemed happy enough listening to the
Kabul security situation on the little transistor radio Dr Jabril
had given him for this purpose, but when Dr Sofia was not in her
surgery he would venture further afield, talking to the *bazarris*
and shopkeepers, who Rashid believed were far more reliable
sources of the city's pulse than whatever came over the radio.

'You're happy this morning,' he said.

'I'm always happy, aren't I?'

'Mostly.'

Sofia laughed. 'There will be no patients this morning
because a man from the UN is coming to see me. Can you
please send him up as soon as he arrives?'

'Of course, Dr Sofia, but I'm sorry, Farahnaz is already
waiting for you.'

Sofia looked at Rashid in confusion. 'Upstairs?'

'Yes.'

'Right.' Sofia considered this. 'If the man from the United
Nations comes while Farahnaz is still here, can you please ask
him to wait?'

'Of course.'

She was about to go up the stairs when she hesitated. 'I've
never asked you before but is that gun of yours loaded?'

Rashid looked at his gun as if the answer might be lurking
there. 'Of course. Do you think I might need to shoot Farahnaz
or this man from the UN for you?'

69

Sofia looked at him in horror until she saw the smile Rashid was trying to hide. In the years she had known him she had never seen him smile, nor had she ever known him to make a joke.

'That was funny, Rashid,' she said, nodding her head in appreciation as she disappeared up the stairs two at a time. 'Really funny.'

The reception area was a long thin room, accommodating Iman's desk at one end and the stairs at the other. Behind Iman's desk were two banks of filing cabinets, while six chairs lined one of the walls in front of the desk. Iman quite liked this formation, which gave her and the waiting patients ample opportunity to gossip. On the opposite wall to the chairs were two photos: the village in the Hindu Kush and the Sydney Opera House. Two doors directly opposite each other led to Sofia's and Jabril's surgeries, but because it would not do to have men and women sitting together the reception area was only for the women, while the men accessed Jabril's surgery by a separate set of stairs on the other side of the building.

With Jabril not having a secretary, or reception, the men generally wandered in whenever they liked. If his surgery door was closed it was a sign they should wait, but if their need was not immediate they might come back later, otherwise they would knock to let Dr Jabril know someone had arrived. The system was ruled by happenstance and a little too chaotic for Sofia's liking, but it seemed to work well for Jabril and the men of the square.

When Sofia saw Farahnaz sitting on the end seat closest to Iman's desk her good humour disappeared. The young woman had aged twenty years since she had last seen her. Pulling off her scarf, Sofia led Farahnaz into her surgery, but instead of taking her seat on the opposite side of the desk she sat down next to Farahnaz and took her hand.

'Please tell me what's wrong.'

Through a veil of tears, Farahnaz poured out the story of Rayi, her ten-year-old brother who lived with her parents in the Kabul slum of Jamal Mina and had been missing for two days. As Sofia listened, her blood ran cold. This was the fourth boy to go missing from the area in the last two months. The first two had disappeared within a few days of each other, and then last week she had been told by her friend Taban, who ran a clinic in the slum, that a third little boy had disappeared. Farahnaz's brother made the fourth.

'I'm sure he'll show up soon,' Sofia had said, forcing a smile as she squeezed Farahnaz's cold hands. 'People don't just disappear. In the meantime, let's see what we can do for you.'

When Farahnaz left, Sofia stood by her window watching the young woman walk back across the square. With her shoulders slumped and her head down, Sofia guessed she was crying and hoped the anti-anxiety tablets she had prescribed would kick in faster than normal. She leaned her forehead up against the window. All she had been able to give Farahnaz was sympathy, medication and lies. People *did* just disappear and Farahnaz knew it. The lie had left a bad taste in her mouth, but what else could she do? Sofia shook her head. It was Jamal Mina. Poverty offered ripe pickings for those who preyed on the weak and vulnerable.

During the civil war, many of the inhabitants of Kabul who had lost their homes in the fighting had begun building makeshift shelters on the barren hills ringing the city. After

71

the Taliban secured Kabul and the fighting intensified in the countryside, they were joined by their country cousins. When the West pushed the Taliban back, Afghan refugees – some of whom had lived their entire lives in the camps of neighbouring Pakistan and Iran – had been forcibly repatriated and they too joined the relentless drive upward in what would eventually become the slum of Jamal Mina. The final ingredient in this potent mix of misery and despair was those who had seen opportunity with the flood of Western aid dollars and had willingly abandoned the uncertain perils of living and working on the land in Afghanistan for the uncertain promise of living in a capital city bulging with opportunity. When their dreams of a better life in the city failed, they too were trapped in the pitiless slums with their magnificent views. Life in Jamal Mina was not for the faint-hearted.

Like everyone else in Afghanistan, Sofia and Jabril knew about *bacha bazi* or 'boy play', but neither had been directly confronted by it until a couple of weeks after the first two boys went missing from Jamal Mina. Walid, a young man who worked with street kids and those at risk, had arrived in Jabril's surgery to tell him about a young boy who had started hanging around with the street kids. Walid soon learned that the boy had been part of a stable of young boys owned by a moderately wealthy merchant from Jalalabad. The boy had eventually escaped the merchant by hitching rides to Kabul, offering to pay the fare with his body along the way. Luckily for him, *bacha bazi* was generally a class phenomenon seen in some quarters as giving wealthy men status. Poor truck drivers, like those who stopped to give the boy a lift, frowned on the practice.

If an owner became 'besotted' by a child, Walid had

explained to Jabril, he might become the man's *ashna*, his beloved, and be lavished with presents and special treats, but as far as Walid could tell this boy had only ever been a commodity. He described how the child continually lived in fear of being found and taken back to the merchant, but was also riddled with shame for what had been done to him and guilt that the merchant would take retribution on his family for his disappearance. The boy was now marked for life as *bacha bereesh* and vulnerable, excluded from society and probably selling himself on the streets to survive. A little confused about why Walid was telling him the story, Jabril had asked Walid what he thought he could do.

'Help these boys,' Walid had said. 'You're a good man, Dr Jabril. I was hoping you could help these boys.'

Later that evening, as he sat on the lounge with Sofia and Zahra enjoying an after-dinner tea, Jabril had told them about the boy before asking what they thought he should do.

'You already spread yourself too thin,' was Zahra's response. 'There are other people dealing with *bacha bazi*. Leave it to them.'

Jabril had turned to Sofia.

It was an inflammatory issue, an open secret that no one wanted to touch because you never knew what powerful person might be involved. She shook her head slowly. 'I've no idea what we can do.'

'No,' Zahra had said, seizing on her words immediately. 'There is no "we" here. You definitely are not getting involved in this issue, even if Jabril does.'

Agreeing that Sofia should not become involved, it had taken Jabril twenty-four hours to devise a plan. Using his influence among his rich and powerful friends in Kabul, he would create a public, high-profile campaign to raise awareness of the evils and prevalence of *bacha bazi*. 'Get people talking,' was how he explained his idea to Sofia. 'Get the subject out in the open. Put pressure on the politicians to force the police to crack down on those who traffic in little boys.' Jabril knew his plan would meet resistance, but in his idealism he had faith.

Without exception, everyone Jabril spoke to had put his hand on his heart, solemnly condemned the practice, agreed unequivocally that it was a terrible business and that it should be stopped and the perpetrators brought to justice, and had done nothing. There was simply no plausible upside for a high-profile person to have his name linked to *bacha bazi*.

'Not to put too fine a point on it,' Jabril would later say to Sofia, 'no one wants anything to do with *bacha bazi*, probably because their powerful friends might be involved.'

Minister Massoud was the only person to show any interest, but because *bacha bazi* was not covered under his portfolio as Minister of Counter Narcotics he would not be able to help. He did, however, ask Jabril to keep him informed of his plans and the two men spoke often, although the general lack of support for his project had left Jabril hurt and frustrated. A month ago, he had made the decision to fund the campaign himself. And now, thought Sofia, there are four little boys missing from Jamal Mina. Were they related to *bacha bazi*?

When the second little boy had gone missing from Jamal Mina about a week before Walid had arrived in Jabril's surgery, Sofia, Jabril and their friend Taban had begun to suspect someone was targeting Hazara children from the slum. In a country still torn apart by violence, the disappearance of a couple of little boys from poor Hazara families was of little interest to anyone. And although the disappearance of the third boy last week had seen Chief Wasim expressing some sympathy for the grieving families, he had told Sofia that he didn't have the resources to launch an investigation when there was no evidence of abduction.

'Three boys have gone missing,' Taban had said when Sofia passed on the chief's message. 'There'll never be evidence of abduction until someone starts looking for it! The loose change of history,' she had said, looking up at Sofia with tears in her eyes. 'No one records these children's births or deaths here because no one cares.'

As Sofia watched Farahnaz disappear down one of the access paths to the alleys behind the square, she remembered her father's parting advice: *Pick your fights*. It had proved wise counsel, but how many times should you turn away, she wondered. How many times was too many and what would the price of that turning away eventually be? Surely there came a point when you could no longer live with yourself? Were these missing boys a fight worth picking? She decided they were. She could not remain silent any longer.

10

OMAR SUSPECTED ALLAH had been playing games with him that morning by tempting him with memories of the young Behnaz. Lost in these pleasant thoughts, Omar had forgotten the fact that Allah had not seen fit to bless him with sons, or that He had done nothing to stop the slow creeping death now stealing through his body, and in this bliss of forgetfulness he thanked Allah the Merciful and the Compassionate for his infinite generosity on that fine sunny morning. As Omar was revisiting all these pleasing thoughts – which were bringing happiness to his heart but not his manhood – he thought again of the Viagra hidden in a drawer under the counter in the shop.

Which, by the way, has not been the seller you anticipated, has it?

Omar would have preferred to ignore the voice, but annoyingly, it captured his attention. When he had seen the ad on the internet for 'Erection Medication – Discreet – Express Delivery', he realised immediately that, although he had no use for it himself, he would be doing his old friends a favour. With some quick financial calculations indicating that the Viagra would also do his profit margin a favour, the deal had been sealed. The thing he hadn't figured into the profit margin was the fact that he didn't have any idea how to advertise something he was embarrassed about keeping. He also hadn't taken into his profit-margin calculations the fact that when he finally found the courage to tell his friends about the Viagra, not one of the old snakes would admit to needing it.

As the wind picked up, carrying the dust and dirt in little eddies around the square, Omar decided it was not so pleasant sitting by the pistachio tree any longer. With the sun about to arrive at the front of his shop, he picked up his plastic chair and slowly made his way back. Once comfortable again, Omar felt inside his pocket to check the night letter was still there before looking around the square to see if anyone was watching.

Babur was busy in his shop preparing lunch, while his cook was outside finishing the last of a cigarette. Rashid and a friend were squatting by the stairs to Dr Sofia's surgery where Iqbal would normally have set up his shop but had not yet reappeared after prayers. This was becoming a habit lately. Omar knew Iqbal's leg was causing him more trouble than normal and decided that when he mixed up another of his uncle's pain draughts for himself he would make a little extra for Iqbal. Like everyone in the square, Omar never dreamed of charging the cobbler. The square looked after its own, Omar thought with a sense of pride.

He could see Hadi lost in thought as he sat smoking on his stool, while Ahmad was busy securing his pile of pink hats which had been toppled by a gust of wind. The first time Omar saw those hats he knew they would be a good seller for Ahmad. As if to prove his point, a couple entered the square with their young daughter who, having spied the hats, was pulling her mother to them. As Omar was smiling at the scene he realised his mind had wandered away from the problem at hand again:

the Taliban's *shabnamah*. With one last look around the square, he pulled the letter out of his pocket.

Tell your friend to stop.

Omar looked up, staring into space, as if the answer might come flying past. That was all. *Tell your friend to stop.* He could not help feeling a little disappointed at the brevity of the message. It was simple enough, but that was what made it all the more complicated. And really, when he thought about it, this didn't look like something the Taliban would write. They wrote long missives, telling you what you had done wrong and how you needed to fix it and what would happen if you didn't.

But if it wasn't the Taliban, who was it?

Omar was searching his mind for possibilities when a terrifying thought parked itself at the station, which happened to be the place in his brain where Omar liked to think all his thoughts arrived and departed from. Maybe this night letter was for him? Maybe he was the friend the Taliban was telling to stop? As soon as the thought arrived, Omar was convinced it was true. He had to get rid of the Viagra. Yes, definitely, he had to get rid of it that very evening.

But how did a Talib, if indeed it was a Talib, know about his Viagra? Omar sat outside his shop pondering this difficult question until the answer arrived at the station, horrifying him. One of those snakes who called himself a friend had told the Taliban! But then a new, more confusing thought arrived at the station to shunt the last one further along the tracks and almost out of view. Why would the Taliban be against Viagra? Didn't they want all men to be virile and impregnate their wives? And if the night letter had been for him then surely it would have been left on his door? He could feel the flood of relief surging through his body. He and his Viagra were safe, but he still had the problem of who this friend of Behnaz's might be and what they had done.

But why does it have to be a friend of Behnaz?

Exactly, thought Omar. Why can't it be a friend of Chief Wasim or Dr Sofia? They live in the house too.

Or maybe it is Dr Sofia who needs to stop?

As Omar contemplated these new possibilities, he was unable to shake the feeling that he was missing some vital piece of information. Surely it could be for a friend of Chief Wasim or a friend of Dr Sofia as much as a friend of Behnaz? He realised that the only way to find the answer was to ask around the square, but just as he was thinking this was a very good idea and was rising from his chair to begin his investigation, he realised it was a very bad idea and sat back down again. How did he ask around the square about who this friend might be without people knowing he'd stolen the night letter? Omar sighed. He sincerely hoped another thought was on its way to the station to tell him how he should proceed.

Omar had been finding thinking very tiring work lately. Not only was he having more than the usual difficulty holding onto a thought for too long but now it seemed he had two voices in his head. The preferred explanation for these failings was that he'd been self-medicating a little too generously. The other option was not something he wished to contemplate too closely. What Omar was sure he was not confused about, though, was the fact that the night letter had become his responsibility and he needed to take action to discover who was being threatened, by whom and why, and then he would be able to warn them.

As Omar sat in his chair, waiting for the correct thought to arrive, he drifted off into a blissful sleep again.

Sofia watched the family disappear under the awning to see them reappear again with the little girl holding one of Ahmad's pink hats. Further out into the square Omar was asleep outside his shop, while Behnaz had just stepped outside her gate to throw a bucket of water over the remains of the donkey droppings as the United Nations SUV slowly manoeuvred its way into the square. Stepping away from the window, Sofia waited until it pulled up in front of Ahmad's shop then leaned forward to catch a glimpse of Daniel getting out of the car before he disappeared under the awning.

As long-lost memories of Daniel in the village came flooding back, she was shocked at the power of feeling that just seeing him again could elicit, and yet, something was wrong. Sofia stood back from the window again. She had no idea what it could be.

***

After leaving Tawfiq in a lowland village, it had taken one and a half days for Sofia and her guide to reach the village in the highlands where the doctor she'd read about from Médecins Sans Frontières was working. At the end of the second day they had climbed a ridge to find themselves standing on a small plateau shrouded in cloud. In front of her were about twenty squat stone huts with flat thatched roofs and tiny windows. The ground around each hut had been swept clean, with a few scrawny bushes clinging to life between large grey boulders dotted around the village where woolly goats were scavenging for invisible scraps. It was a desolate place, dominated on all sides by menacing, razor-sharp mountain peaks.

An old man with a raggedy turban and a thin grey beard who was squatting outside his hut smoking watched as they approached. As word began to spread of the strangers' arrival, other villagers began to appear, including a group of children who gathered around Sofia, giggling as their hands darted out to touch her arm or hand before being pulled back to safety again. When a severe-looking man with a long, hooked nose and a bushy black monobrow had appeared from one of the huts barking something at the kids, they quickly ran off, only to reappear around the other side of the village.

Mafuz, the village headman, informed Sofia's guide that the male doctor from Kabul was in a village further down the mountain and was not expected back until the following day, but Sofia could stay as long as she liked. Making sure she was welcomed and protected by the headman, her guide had left, promising to return in four weeks' time to take her back down to the lowlands where Tawfiq would be waiting.

While Sofia's Dari had been passable for Kabul, the village spoke a dialect of Dari, which caused some confusion and had Sofia believing the small hut they were standing in front of was her lodging. With no one wanting to offend the strange Western woman, who seemed to prefer the grain hut to the women's hut, it had been quickly swept clean and a bed pad laid out for her. The last thing Sofia saw as the door was closed behind her was the faces of the village children, each vying for a closer look at the curiosity that had arrived like magic in their world.

The hut had one tiny window covered by a rough hessian cloth and little light coming in under the door or through its rough-hewn timber planks. Sofia had no idea what to do. Lying down she had discovered the hut was too small to stretch out so she turned on her side, curled her legs up and fell into a deep sleep, only to wake freezing in the middle of the night. Noticing a weight on her legs, Sofia reached down to find a prickly goat hair blanket which she pulled up under her chin, and then fell back to sleep, only to be woken at dawn by the call to prayer.

Turning on her back, Sofia had stretched her cramped legs up the wall until she found a natural stone shelf to rest her feet on and lay listening to the sounds of the new day unfolding outside. In the distance a tiny bird was singing, while further afield a rooster began to crow. When she heard the tinkling of tiny bells around the hut, she was initially unable to place the familiar sound until she remembered the goats from the day before. With the grey light of morning creeping in through the cracks and under the door, Sofia had noticed a small bowl of rice, an earthenware pitcher of water, and a tiny piece of pale waxy soap sitting atop neatly folded clothes. As she picked up each garment and examined it, she decided the women must have thought these clothes were more suitable for her to wear in the village than those she had arrived in.

Wanting to wash but concerned about standing naked behind a door people had obviously been coming in and out of with their deliveries, she had washed under her clothes before changing into a roughly woven undergarment that possibly resembled something her great-great-grandmother wore back in Italy before the First World War. Pulling on a pair of long cotton pants, she had slipped a faded blue skirt over them before tying a rope around her middle to keep it from slipping down. Finally, she put on a thick padded jacket made of rough goat's wool. After rolling the cold rice into balls and eating it with her fingers, Sofia threw a shawl around her shoulders, her scarf around her head, laced up her boots and stepped out into a fresh clear morning.

With the cloud gone she could see now that the tiny village sat precariously atop a rocky plateau that rose like an island in midair. Hardly breathing, Sofia stood perfectly still, and in that moment, as the chill of the air caressed her skin and she felt the weight of the peaks towering above her, she understood what few people ever do: her own insignificance. It no longer mattered whether she lived or died, for in the scheme of things, in the length and breadth of this living, breathing planet, what did it matter that she had ever existed? She was nothing, and in that moment of knowing this – that purest moment of perfect certainty – Sofia touched the divine. And yet, just as she was recognising this one, true thing she could feel it already slipping away. She wanted to call out to it, to grab it, to hold it, to know it just a little bit longer, but in the moment of recognition it was gone.

Sofia knew then that this was the reason she had come to Afghanistan. This was the gift her soul had always known was waiting for her here.

Coming out of that moment, she looked around to see the

everyday: a young boy near her hut was using a switch on the goats' woolly hides, gathering them together to herd them out of the village and down to more fertile feeding pastures below. The welcoming crusty smell of the flat naan bread being cooked inside the huts for breakfast had reached her as the smoke from the fires began to curl up in the chilly mountain air, to hang thin and wispy over the village. Watching her as he walked past with a bundle of sticks balanced high on top of his white turban was the old man she had seen the day before.

'*As-salaam alaikum,*' he had offered with a shy, toothless grin.

'Hello … good morning … yes, how are you?' she had stumbled, laughing at her clumsy inability to remember even one word of Dari.

A woman working nearby, who had been splashing water from a bucket over the bare ground in front of her hut, laughed before exchanging words with the old man, which caused them both to laugh and Sofia to smile. Looking around the village, she had tried to imagine being back in busy, noisy Sydney, plugged into her phone with her head buried in a book as she caught the bus to the hospital where she had worked. She knew then that she never wanted to return to that life.

As the wind began to pick up and wisps of hair tickled her face, Sofia had reached up to thread them back under her scarf when she felt someone watching her. Turning toward the ridge she saw a tall Afghan man walking toward her.

'Daniel Abiteboul,' he had said, offering his hand when he reached her.

Surprised and a little confused by his English, together with the fact that he'd offered his hand, Sofia had hesitated only a second. 'Sofia Raso.'

'From MSF,' he added.

'Oh, right,' she said, finally understanding. 'For some reason I'd expected … but you're not Afghan, are you?'

'No,' he said, looking as confused as she had been until he looked down at his *perahan tunban* and large woollen coat and began to laugh. 'I tend to wear these because they're comfortable and don't draw attention.' He drew his hand down the growth on his face. 'Not shaving and being dark also helps a bit.'

'You might want to rethink that strategy,' Sofia had said, nodding toward the villagers who were standing around watching them.

'I think we can safely say it's probably you they're more interested in. I'm sorry, but why are you here?'

'Oh, I'm sorry,' she said, remembering he had no idea about her. 'I'm a doctor too and I read in the paper that you were coming to work in this village, so I rang your office in Kabul and asked if they thought it would be okay if I joined you. They said you probably wouldn't mind and told me how to get here.'

'So you've come to work here too?'

'If you don't mind.'

She watched his smile broaden. 'Not at all. I could do with the help. So, Raso?' he had said, turning his head to the side as he examined her face. 'You've got an Italian name, but you don't look Italian.'

'Really? What does Italian look like?'

She watched his amusement. 'Until a few minutes ago I would've said nothing like you, but I guess I'd be wrong, wouldn't I?'

'Half wrong. My mother was Scottish and my father's Italian and I'm Australian. Actually, my name is Anna-Maria Sofia

Raso. My parents couldn't agree – my dad wanted Anna-Maria and my mum wanted Sofia. My name's a result of indecisive parents. So where does your surname come from? I can't place it, or your accent.'

'French-Moroccan.'

Sofia had smiled at Daniel. 'So maybe neither of us is who we appear to be.'

'This morning is certainly full of surprises,' he said, laughing. 'I'd like that. It'd be nice to be someone else.'

'I think that depends who you want to be.' Turning away from his scrutiny, she look up at the peaks. 'It's beautiful here, isn't it?'

'It is.'

Taking his backpack off and leaning it up against the wall of her hut, Daniel suggested they take a walk around the village.

She had thought Mafuz's hut marked the end of it, but after passing between his hut and the one next to it they came to a construction made of branches and tied together with vines where washing was hung. Past this the ground fell away sharply to reveal a few more stone huts that had been hidden from view. Falling down the slope, each hut was connected to the one above by a common wall, as if to anchor it to the ground and the village above. Reaching the end of flat ground they had turned to the north, passing by a fallow garden where children were playing, chickens scratching around in the dirt near them. On seeing the strangers the little boys abandoned their game and began following them.

'Yesterday I discovered my first cases of drug addiction in the village below,' Daniel had said. 'At present it looks to be limited

to just two men, but it'll spread.' He turned to look down at Sofia.
'You didn't happen to bring anything for addiction, did you?'

'I'm sorry, no.'

'Me neither. Stupid, really. I guess I just didn't think it would
get its claws into people who were so isolated. I'll talk with
Mafuz and the other headman and explain what this might
mean for them.'

Having arrived at the northern end of the plateau the path
turned right again, leading them to the ridge, which she could
now see was the only possible access route to the village. Other
than this ridge, and where the hidden houses were, the sides of
the plateau disappeared in terrifyingly sheer drops to the valley
floor far below. About two hundred metres down the access
path they could see five women returning to the village with
water containers balanced on their heads.

'I can't tell you how glad I am you're here because I haven't
been able to examine the women, or even ask them questions.
This village lost a fifteen-year-old girl in childbirth last month
and I'm pretty sure that with the proper care, she and her baby
would have survived. Obviously, you need to decide what your
priorities are while you're here, especially if winter sets in early
and our time's limited, but from what I've seen some midwifery
skills wouldn't go astray.'

'If they're receptive,' Sofia had offered, wondering how
the village women would appreciate her telling them how to
birth their babies. When a cloud passed in front of the sun she
shivered.

Daniel had looked up at the peaks. 'Those snow clouds have
been gathering for the last few days and they're telling me now

that the snows might arrive early again this year.' He turned to look at her. 'How long are you planning on staying?'

'A month. I read that was how long you were here for.'

Daniel had nodded. 'If the weather turns ugly, though, we might have to leave early, or risk being trapped in the village for the winter.'

'Then I have a problem because I've got no way of contacting my guide to tell him to come earlier.'

'Well, let's see what happens,' he had said, turning back toward the village. 'You might have to come back down with me.'

12

ON THAT FIRST day they had worked together examining the children, with Sofia concentrating on the girls. The following day they had trekked to the lower village about an hour's walk away, and by the end of that day she knew Daniel was right: midwifery could make a huge difference to the lives of the women and children. She just had to work out how to approach the women about this. Perhaps offering a quid pro quo deal: she'd teach them her skills and they could teach her their skills and natural remedies.

Late that afternoon Sofia had been sitting on the ground outside her hut enjoying the last of the day's sun when two barefoot boys, their clothes and skin covered in thick layers of grime, came to sit in front of her. The youngest had a shaved head and a thick rope of snot streaming from his nose. The older boy was wearing a dirty grey rag that might once have been white tied around his head, and an old ripped suit jacket that fell below his knees. They had come to show Sofia their toys, two large wasps each tied with a length of string that they let free to fly in front of her face. While she had tried to look suitably impressed, she couldn't help ducking each time a wasp flew too close. When she told the boys their toys were great, they looked at her for a few seconds before turning to each other and collapsing on the ground laughing. Sofia had no idea what she had said wrong but she was soon laughing with them.

Daniel, who had been sitting outside the mosque watching her and the boys, got up and made his way to them. 'What's happening?'

'I think I said something stupid. Won't you join me?' Moving over, she had patted the ground next to her as the boys ran off.

After sitting in silence for some time she realised that Daniel had leaned his head back against the wall with his eyes closed. Taking the opportunity, she had examined his face. His skin was smooth and naturally dark, although she had seen the tan line on his arms when he'd rolled his shirtsleeves up as he worked. His black hair was probably due for a cut and the beard was a result of not shaving since he'd arrived in the village. With the angle of the setting sun, dark lashes were casting long shadows over his cheekbones.

'I grew up in Marrakech,' he had said. Although his eyes were still closed, she had the feeling he had known she'd been looking at him. 'I spent a lot of time hanging out with our cook's family in their village and the local kids tied wasps to pieces of string there too. What was it like growing up in Sydney?'

'Well, we didn't tie strings to wasps.'

'What *did* you do?'

'I read books, mostly.'

With his eyes still closed he had smiled. 'That figures.'

She turned to look directly at him. 'What's that supposed to mean?'

'You're the bookish type.'

'I'm not sure how I'm supposed to take that.'

She watched his smile broaden. 'It means you're inquisitive and intelligent, both of which seem to be borne out by the fact that you're here in a village hardly anyone knows or cares about on this crazy plateau in the Hindu Kush. Despite the fact that my mother is a writer, I didn't read many books when I was young, so I'm impressed that's the first thing you say about your childhood. It must have been important to you.'

Sofia leaned back against the hut. 'I guess it was an escape. My mum died when I was twelve.' She bit her bottom lip. She had no idea why she had told him that.

Daniel opened his eyes then and turned to look at her. 'I'm sorry.'

'It's okay.' It wasn't okay really, but she'd been saying it was for so long it was starting to sound like the truth.

'What do you remember about her?'

Sofia slowly began pulling up pictures. 'I remember how she loved me. How our family used to be before she died, and how she read to me and laughed a lot. I also remember how she always said I'd stolen her hair.' She had turned toward him then. 'I hated that.' Leaning back against the wall, she watched the purple and pink of dusk beginning to fade. 'When Mum died, Dad tried to make it better by telling me my hair was a special gift from her. He used to say that someday some man would fall in love with me because of my hair just like he'd fallen in love with my mum. Seriously?' Sofia shook her head, as if talking to herself. 'How could anyone possibly think that would be a good thing? Who wants someone to fall in love with you because of your hair?'

'Better than falling in love with you because of your bank balance.'

'Well, that's never going to happen,' she had said, laughing as she threw her head back, only to crack it against the rock wall of the hut. 'Shit, shit, shit.' Bending forward, Sofia had rubbed the back of her head. 'Damn that hurt.'

'Are you alright?'

'Yeah,' she had said, sitting up straight to look at him as she continued rubbing her head.

'You sure?'

'Yeah.'

'So why are you here, anyway?'

'Are you my therapist, Daniel … Shit, I've forgotten your last name already,' she said, still rubbing the bump.

'Don't worry, it's a hard name to remember. You've obviously never been in therapy.'

'And you have?' she had fired back, regretting the words as soon as they were out of her mouth. 'This ground's a bit hard, isn't it?' she said, moving around to get more comfortable, hoping he'd forget what she had just said.

'Trust me, this isn't therapy. I'm just interested, that's all.'

'So are you asking what I'm doing here in the village specifically or in Afghanistan in general?'

'Either. Both.'

'I registered with an international medical agency doing overseas placements and a friend who worked for the agency told me about a job for a female doctor being advertised in Kabul and I applied.'

'And here in this village specifically?'

'Jabril – that's the guy who hired me – thought it might

be a good idea if I saw some of the country before I returned home, and I saw the article about your trip here in the paper so I contacted your office. You know the rest. How did you end up in this village?' Sofia reached up, rubbing the bump on the back of her head again.

'I'd passed through it years ago trekking in the mountains and always wanted to come back. Do you want me to have a look?' he had asked, reaching out to feel the bump, their hands touching. 'It's a big one.'

'I'll be fine.'

He withdrew his hand. 'How long have you been in Afghanistan?'

'Nearly six months,' she had said, changing position again, 'and I've got no idea if I'm going to stay, if that's your next question.' It was a question Sofia had been asking herself since the day she arrived and she still didn't have an answer. 'This is definitely therapy.'

'Come on,' he had said, standing and holding out his hand to help her to her feet. 'Therapy's over. We're having dinner with Mafuz tonight.'

* * *

ABOUT FIFTY METRES behind Sofia's hut was Mafuz's, which had the same mud and straw floor as Sofia's only his was bigger – as would befit a headman – and lined with beautifully ancient and threadbare rugs. Along the walls woven cushions had been stacked atop neatly folded blankets, which were resting on the thin mats the family used for sleeping at night and sitting on during the day. With the only light entering the hut coming from two small windows high in the wall, Mafuz's home was nearly as dark as Sofia's storeroom.

As they were entering Daniel had touched her hand to pull her back. 'We need to wait to be invited to take a seat. Oh, and I need to warn you that if you eat everything on your plate they'll keep piling more on. They need to see that you can't eat everything to know you're full.'

After being invited to take the seats of honoured guests furthest from the door, Mafuz's wife had lit a kerosene lamp and laid a brightly patterned piece of floral vinyl on the floor before presenting them with mounds of naan bread, a watery soup with rice and vegetables, and cups of salty tea. As they ate and drank, Sofia had answered the headman's questions about her homeland, but it had been a long day and she could feel her eyes growing heavy. After Daniel had made their excuses and was walking her back to her hut, he pulled a battered old English–Dari dictionary out of his pocket. 'Here,' he said.

She looked at the dictionary and pulled a face. 'Am I that bad?'

'No,' he laughed, 'but you're still learning and it might help while you're here, although this dialect has its differences.'

When they stopped outside her hut Sofia realised she didn't want him to leave but had no idea how to say that.

'I think your dad was right,' his voice soft as he reached out to thread her hair back behind her ears.

'About what?'

'Your hair.'

'That a man will fall in love with me because of it?'

'No, that it's beautiful. That you're beautiful.'

They had become lovers that night.

***

Out in the square, Sofia could see Behnaz holding the empty bucket, the donkey droppings now spread further out across the cobblestones. She was trying to see what the foreigner was doing in Ahmad's shop but the UN car was in the way and she soon gave up to disappear behind the gate.

Further out in the square, Babur and his cook were out the front of the *chaikhana* watching the foreigner while Jabril had quickly finished his second cup of tea and was now making his way across the square to Ahmad's shop.

Sofia shook her head. Soon everyone would know the stranger from the UN was there to see her and they'd want to know why. She could almost hear the rumour mill shifting up a gear.

This man from the UN is here to take Dr Sofia away. They don't like that she does good work for us.

This man is here because he loves Dr Sofia and has come to take her away.

Sofia suspected the last might be the most popular with the women because her unattached state had become a serious concern: thirty-two years old and not married, not widowed and no children. The problem needed fixing. Regrettably for Sofia, Zahra had recently joined the ranks of concerned females, although Sofia suspected Zahra's concern was more for her own amusement. The previous week they had been having lunch in one of the Western cafés when Sofia had complained to Zahra about the lack of romance in her life.

'Don't worry,' Zahra had said, reaching across the table to pat Sofia's hand. 'I'll find you a good husband.'

'I don't want a good husband. I want a good lover.' Sofia's last boyfriend had been an American marine. The romance had lasted two months, the relationship six. When his tour was finished they'd made promises to keep in touch, knowing they never would.

'Phhh,' Zahra had said, blowing away Sofia's comment. 'These soldiers and fly-in-fly-out NGO types you keep company with are not good long-term prospects for marriage. I'm watching out for you, don't worry.'

'That's exactly what does worry me.'

'Nonsense,' she said, signalling the waiter for the bill. 'I'll find a good man for you.'

'I wish you wouldn't.'

'Maybe an Afghan politician?' Zahra said, mischief in her eyes. No one wanted an Afghan politician. 'Don't worry.' Zahra had waved the idea away. 'Not an Afghan politician.'

From Iman and Zahra, Sofia had learned that some of her patients thought she was too educated to attract a husband, while others argued it was because she didn't have a family to find her one. There were also those who were sure it was because of the exotic nature of her skin and hair: no man wanted a wife who attracted so much attention. No, it was because she was too tall – a man didn't like to look up at his wife. Definitely it was because of the way she walked (too purposefully), talked (too frankly), laughed (too immodestly). The young, educated women like Iman dismissed all of these claims as ignorant old women's chatter. Dr Sofia didn't have a husband because she didn't want one.

As Sofia waited for Daniel to reappear she realised what had been wrong. She had only ever seen him in the loose-fitting *perahan tunban* and the thick woollen coat and scarf of the people from the village. In all her imaginings he had never been any other way. This Daniel was in Western dress – jeans, a white open-necked shirt, a coat – and he was clean-shaven with short hair.

'He's here!' Jabril said breathlessly, rushing into the surgery to join Sofia by the window.

She looked at him. 'For goodness sake, Jabril. Did you just run up the stairs? You're going to give yourself a heart attack.'

He ignored her. 'He's very tall. A very handsome man, I think.'

Sofia was aware of Jabril's insecurity about his height. 'Men aren't necessarily handsome just because they're tall, Jabril. Besides, I'm not really sure men are the best judges of the handsomeness of other men.' Sofia turned back to the window. 'Although I agree he's not bad looking.'

'You've seen him already?'

Sofia had not told Jabril or Zahra that she had met Daniel before. 'I saw him get out of the car.'

Jabril looked back out of the window to the awning. 'You've ascertained a great deal from the top of his head.'

'I also saw his photo in the newspaper.'

'Ah yes.' Jabril was obviously satisfied with this answer. 'Zahra tells me that black hair and blue eyes are very attractive to women.'

'How does Zahra know his eyes are blue? You can't see that in a black and white photo.'

'My dear Sofia, I came to the conclusion a long time ago that my wife has supernatural powers. Look,' he said, pointing to Babur's cook, who was now making his way over to Ahmad's shop. 'Our friend's customers are multiplying before our eyes.'

'And no doubt my reputation will be ruined before my eyes.'

'No, no, not at all! Your mystique will only grow with this mysterious visitor.'

'Ha, I wish!'

'My dear Sofia,' Jabril said, more earnestly this time, 'it's obvious to me that you underestimate your attraction.'

'And it's obvious to me that we don't have enough excitement here in the square. Look at that,' she said, pointing to the people standing around looking into Ahmad's shop.

'Perhaps we should've asked Mustafa to announce your guest's arrival in the mosque this morning and saved our friends the indignity of eavesdropping.'

Sofia smiled. A few minutes ago Jabril had been one of those eavesdroppers. 'Well, what did he say to Ahmad?'

'I think he said he didn't want a vest.' Jabril laughed. 'I couldn't hear much. He was asking about you but Ahmad was more interested in selling him a vest.'

Sofia groaned just as Daniel stepped out from under the awning and Jabril made a hasty retreat to his surgery.

13

SOFIA HAD BEEN planning to look busy when Daniel arrived, but by the time she had sat back behind her desk and opened her laptop he was already in her doorway. She looked up.

'Daniel?'

His name had come out all wrong, a question; as if she was unsure it was him; as if she was surprised to see him standing in her doorway; as if she hadn't been waiting for him for the last five years.

'It is. And it really is you,' he said, offering the smile she had loved.

'Depends who you think I am.'

'I think you're the woman I met in a village in the Hindu Kush who wasn't sure she was going to stay in Afghanistan. Are you going to invite me in?'

'And if I said no?'

'I'd probably take my chances and come in anyway.'

'Then you'd better come in.' Getting up from her chair she walked around her desk to offer him her hand, but instead he leaned in and kissed her on both cheeks. The smile, the kisses and the remembered scent of him were unnerving. 'Please,'

Sofia said, returning to her desk as she pointed to one of the patient's chairs. 'I'm interested to know if you knew it was me when you asked for the meeting.'

'I thought the Australian doctor called Sofia with the Italian surname might be you, but when I heard you had red hair I knew it was.'

She gave him a smile. 'So my job description included red hair?'

'It might have.'

'You remembered me by my hair?' Was she flirting with him?

'Didn't your father say something about men remembering your hair?'

'Actually, he said they'd fall in love with me because of my hair, but close enough.'

'Maybe he was right.'

She ignored the comment. 'What else do you remember?'

'That your mother died when you were little and you read a lot growing up.'

'You didn't mention anything in your email about having met before.'

'I wasn't sure you'd remember me.'

'Of course I remember you.' She thought it strange that he would think otherwise considering they had been lovers, even if it was only for ten days. Maybe Daniel Abiteboul took random lovers whom he randomly forgot? 'You grew up in Marrakech. You spent a lot of time with your cook's family, and despite the fact that your mother was a writer she didn't encourage you to read. I also remember that you looked very different back then. You had a beard, longer hair and wore Afghan clothes.'

'I did, didn't I?' He looked pleased, as if she had just reminded him of something he'd forgotten.

Sofia looked at her laptop and straightened it up on the desk, wondering if she should say what she was about to say. 'I didn't think I'd ever see you again.'

'And yet, here I am.'

'And yet, here you are,' she repeated. What had it been? Three minutes, and she could already feel herself falling into him again. It had been the same in the village, and like in the village, she had no idea how to protect herself from this man, but protect herself she must. She had no intention of being hurt again.

The note of love is true, her father would say with tears in his eyes whenever he spoke about the first time he had seen her mother. Finding a love like that and then losing it must have been the worst thing. 'Her hair was just like yours,' he would say. 'She was the most magnificent woman I'd ever seen. When this happens to you, Sofia, you'll know. Love can be nothing else.' Sofia didn't believe in love at first sight. Attraction was immediate; love, real love, took time.

'I'm sorry, Daniel, it's a little hard for me to take this all in at the moment. You … me … here,' she said, pointing to him and then herself with a half smile.

When he spoke his voice was softer, less sure of himself, as if his words were a private thought, awkward to share. 'It was strange for me too when I knew I'd be seeing you again.'

The intimacy of his words threw Sofia off balance. Everything about him threw her off balance. She fiddled with her laptop again, pushing it away before lining it up with the edge of her desk. What she really wanted in that moment was for him to leave and come back again when she'd had time to gather herself. She needed to move their conversation to safer neutral ground. 'Tell me how you think I can help you.'

Sitting back in his chair and crossing his legs, he looked more relaxed again. 'The short version is I'm here to assess what the country's health requirements might be in light of the imminent US and Western troop withdrawals. With the suspected deterioration of the security situation and the very real possibility that the Taliban will regain power, a lot of aid agencies will be pulling out, so the UN needs to know how best it can support the indigenous and grassroots organisations still here on the ground. And while it's not officially part of my brief, I'm particularly interested in the women's organisations here and how we can help them. When I began to ask around about who I should talk to, your name kept coming up.'

Maybe that was a little too businesslike, she thought, starting to laugh. 'How long have you been practising that speech?'

It made him laugh too. 'Only the first part, which I already feel like I've said a hundred times. The last part was just for you.'

When Sofia found herself wondering how long it would take for them to become lovers again, she knew she needed to get the conversation back on track. Pulling her laptop toward her, she pushed it away again. She had to stop playing with her laptop. 'I live a quiet life here. I don't know how you think I can help you.'

'You've got your practice here in Kabul that deals with women's health issues, right?'

'This isn't my practice. I work for Dr Jabril.'

'Okay,' he said, a little less sure of himself, 'but you've been working as a women's doctor in Kabul for what – at least five years now? If that was the only thing then you'd already have a perspective I'd like to hear, but I understand you also work in the Kabul slums and in remote villages training midwives.'

Rather than being put off by her lack of enthusiasm, he appeared to become surer of his footing. She was trying to underplay her work; he was refusing to let her, she thought, wondering which of her friends he had been talking to. 'I usually work one day a fortnight in Jamal Mina, which, as I'm sure you know, is one of the biggest slums in Kabul. And yes, I train midwives in various places around the country, which was something I started back in the mountain villages, thanks to you.'

'I remember, and I'm glad you continued with that.'

'All I do is turn up and provide the technical knowhow. It's the women who do all the hard work.' He wasn't reacting to anything she was saying, which made her suspect he probably knew all this already. 'Someone has to set these groups up and find the women to be trained, and that can be really difficult. Each of the women probably needs to get permission from her husband or father or some other male in the family, and they need to make the commitment to turn up one day every month in between all their other responsibilities. If that isn't difficult enough, each woman needs a male relative willing and able to escort her to the meetings and wait to take her home again at the end of each day. When that's all in place then I turn up. My job's the easy part. But how do you know all this about me?'

'Is there a problem?'

You betcha there's a problem, Sofia thought. 'There might be.' Sofia went to move her laptop again before returning her hands to her lap. 'It's important to keep my work with the village women under the radar, especially in a place like Kandahar, where I've been working lately. If the Taliban found out a Western woman was training them it could be really dangerous. So yes, there's a problem.'

'And danger for you.'

She shrugged. 'Danger for everyone. I need to know who told you.'

'A friend who works with MSF. I'm afraid I can't tell you how she knew.'

Sofia sat back, considering this. Only the previous week she'd accepted what she'd known for a while: she had to stop the midwifery training with her Kandahar group. With the upsurge in Taliban control in the region it had become particularly dangerous for her to travel there, and while she could choose to put her own life in danger, she had no right to put Tawfiq and Rashid's lives in danger. She realised now that she should never have taken on the group in the first place but she hated to say no to requests where there was a great need, and Fatima, the woman from Kandahar who coordinated the group, had convinced her of the need. Sofia was planning to return one last time to tell them of her decision, and to deliver boxes of medical supplies she had collected for the group, which was beginning to feel like a Judas kiss: an apology for her betrayal. Jabril and Zahra had been adamant that she didn't need to return in person to tell them but she did. The women had shown such dedication and had sacrificed so much to learn from her that they deserved at least a personal apology and an explanation.

'It probably doesn't matter anymore because my work with the women in Kandahar is about to end. Actually, I'm going there on Friday for the last time to tell them I won't be finishing their training.'

Daniel sat up in his chair looking genuinely concerned. 'Can I ask why?'

'The Taliban.' Sofia shrugged as if the words were self-explanatory. 'It's become too dangerous for us to travel there again, plus the danger is increasing for the women every time they meet with me. I'm still not entirely sure what you want from me.'

'I'd like to hear what the day-to-day concerns are for the women who visit your surgery and if the UN could address any of those issues for Afghan women. With regard to the midwives,' he said, 'I understand it's probably impossible for me to talk with the women, but would it be possible to talk with the woman who coordinated this group? And, of course, anything you can tell me about what you do in the slums would be great. On top of that, I'd be interested in an overview of what you think needs to be done in Afghanistan.'

Sofia bristled. She hated that question and was surprised he'd even asked. He should have known better. She might be living in Afghanistan but she would always remain an outsider, and as much as it wasn't her place to say how the people should live, it also wasn't her place to say how the problems of Afghanistan should be solved, even if she knew, and she didn't.

'What I see here are essentially the same problems that are found in any society that doesn't support its most vulnerable: the lack of a functioning healthcare system, the suppression of over half its population, extraordinary levels of domestic violence and a country that constantly seems to be at war with itself.'

'You paint a grim picture,' he said, while nodding in recognition.

'And what would you want me to paint for you, Daniel?'

He laughed. 'I wouldn't have expected anything else from you, Sofia Raso.'

She had no idea what that meant. 'But you know all this, surely?'

'I haven't worked with women like you have and I don't work on the ground here. You'd really be an invaluable resource.'

It was Sofia's turn to laugh, releasing the tension in her body. 'Well, there's a first. I've never been called that before.'

'Perhaps I could have worded it a little bit better,' he said, a little embarrassed.

'Oh, please don't. I quite fancy being an invaluable resource.'

Sofia glanced at the clock on the wall behind Daniel. 'This is what I can do for you. I'm going to Jamal Mina tomorrow, and if you're free you're welcome to come. I can introduce you to my friend Taban who works there. She trained as a nurse and runs a clinic in the slums and will be able to answer all your questions. I'll also introduce you to my boss, Dr Jabril. Those two can tell you all you need to know about the medical needs of Afghans. With regard to my private patients, I'm happy to talk with you in general terms about women's issues but that's as far as it can go.'

'Your contact with the midwives?'

Sofia considered this. 'I'll talk with Fatima; she's the woman who runs the group. If she's willing to speak with you and you're able to come with me on Friday then we might be able to arrange something. Alternatively, you could simply talk with her on the phone.'

'In person would be better if that's possible.'

'Would you be able to come on Friday and back late Saturday night? It's a quick trip.'

'I could.'

Sofia sat back and smiled at Daniel. 'It's nice to see you again.'

'Ditto.'

She checked the time on the clock again. 'I'm sorry but I've got a patient coming soon.' The lie had slipped out so easily it surprised her. 'Let me walk you out.'

14

Iqbal had finished setting up his little workshop in his usual spot next to the entry to Sofia's surgery. A pile of broken shoes were stacked neatly beside him while the tools of his trade – a bottle of glue, a miniature hammer, an old paintbrush with half its bristles missing, a bundle of rags, and a small tin with the lid cut off to hold his tacks – were spread out at his feet. With his walking stick stowed safely behind him, Iqbal was ready for his first customer.

Having been taught the cobbling trade by his father when he was six years old, Iqbal would reminisce with Sofia about the golden days when rich Afghans had ordered beautiful shoes in soft new leather from the family shop in central Kabul. While those days were long gone and rich Afghans didn't find their way into Shaahir Square seeking the services of an old cobbler with failing eyesight, Iqbal still loved his trade. For the most part he charged a few afghanis to tack on a sole or stitch a loose flap on a neighbour's shoe to help it last through another winter, but if there was no money he would perform the service for free and, in return, he might be given a warm meal or a special sweet.

Although Iqbal's face had grown as dark and brittle as the old leather he worked on, whenever he saw Dr Sofia it crinkled into tiny creases of love. As Sofia and Daniel stepped out into the square, Iqbal looked up at them, lifting his hand to shade his eyes from the sun.

'And who is this beautiful stranger you've brought my way today, Dr Sofia?'

Sofia looked over at Daniel and saw the smile. He had understood every word Iqbal had said. 'This is Dr Daniel, a very important man from the United Nations who has come here to help Afghans.'

Iqbal motioned for Sofia to bring Daniel closer so that he might see better. Over the years Sofia had bought Iqbal cheap reading glasses from Chicken Street, but inevitably he had lost them. When she had offered to replace the last pair he had begged her not to bother wasting her afghani. He could still see well enough to repair a shoe. He didn't need to see more than that.

'*Insha'Allah*. Let us pray that this one, who I think is prettier than most, might do something for us. You must tell this prince of heaven that our lives are very hard here, Dr Sofia.'

'Why don't you tell him yourself, Iqbal? Dr Daniel speaks perfect Dari.'

Iqbal chuckled without a trace of embarrassment before looking at Daniel with renewed interest. 'You are a prince, my friend. I see you and I see that you have been blessed.'

As Daniel and Iqbal began talking, Hadi and Ahmad wandered over to join Sofia in their open examination of the visitor. She was enjoying the scene being played out before her. Iqbal was dear to her heart while Daniel was still the kind and gentle man she remembered from the village, but she could tell already this was not the same man she had taken as a lover. Something had changed for him. Something for the better.

She noticed Iqbal eyeing Daniel's soft leather boots and knew her friend would be itching to touch them. Daniel must have noticed this too because he sat down on the little wooden stool Iqbal kept for the comfort of his customers and took one boot off before offering it to the cobbler. 'It is by the graces of Allah that Dr Sofia has brought me to you this day. Perhaps you would be so kind as to repair my boot for me?' Daniel showed Iqbal where the sole had begun to lift.

Taking the soft boot in his bony old hands, Iqbal began examining it. 'This is a very fine boot. No,' he said, offering the boot back to Daniel. 'I'm not worthy of this beautiful boot.'

Daniel refused to take the boot back. 'I can see that you're the finest of craftsmen and I'm sure Dr Sofia will confirm this, and that there could be no one better in all of Kabul to fix this boot for me.' Daniel looked up at Sofia.

'Indeed, it's true, Dr Daniel. Iqbal is the best in Kabul. Probably in all of Afghanistan.'

Iqbal's thin chest visibly expanded as he began examining the boot again before lifting his old brush, dipping it into his pot of glue and painting it across the offending sole. When he'd finished he weighed it down with rocks to set. Picking up a rag not as dirty as the rest, he insisted Daniel take off his other boot so that it might be polished to a soft caramel lustre while they waited for the glue on the first boot to dry. After the sole had been tested for fastness, Iqbal polished the repaired boot before handing them both back to Daniel. When Daniel offered Iqbal payment the cobbler furiously shook his head.

'No, no, no, I cannot take money from a man who is here to help my country.'

When the hurdle of accepting money had been overcome, Iqbal insisted that Daniel was offering far too much. Sofia knew there was a fine balance to be drawn here. Too much money and Iqbal would feel it was charity; not enough and he would be offended that Daniel didn't think highly enough of his work. Daniel insisted again that Iqbal was a master craftsman and that it would be offensive for him to pay anything less than the notes on offer. With an amount finally agreed on that pleased both men, they said their goodbyes.

'That was kind of you,' Sofia said, as she walked with Daniel to his car.

'I needed the sole repaired.'

'Still, it was kind.'

As they stood outside Ahmad's shop making arrangements for their trip the following day to Jamal Mina, Sofia was aware that Ahmad and Hadi were perched back on their stools, listening. 'And I'll get back to you regarding the midwives,' she said, trying to make their plans sound businesslike.

'Thanks. Oh, and I also need to thank you for returning the dictionary. You didn't have to, you know.'

After returning to Kabul from the village, Sofia had visited the MSF office, ostensibly to return Daniel's scarf and dictionary but in reality wanting to know where he was. It surprised Sofia to learn no one in the office knew because he still hadn't returned from the mountains. If Sofia wanted to leave the dictionary, scarf and a message, the receptionist would be happy to pass them on to him when he returned and before he left for his new posting at MSF headquarters in

Geneva. Sofia left the dictionary and took the scarf. There was no message, she said.

'I've still got your scarf, you know. I've grown fond of it, but you can have it back if you want.'

Daniel laughed. 'That seems like an offer I'm meant to refuse.'

'It is.'

'Then you must keep it.'

'Well, if you ever change your mind you know where it is.'

Daniel hesitated before getting into the car. 'I was wondering if you'd like to have a drink? I'd like to hear what's been happening in your life since the mountains. I'd also be interested to hear what convinced you to stay in Afghanistan.'

She smiled up at him. 'Oh, that's easy. You did.'

Daniel looked confused. 'I changed your mind? Really?' She nodded. 'Then we definitely have to have that drink. I need to hear about this.'

There was no way she was going to turn any of that into a business arrangement for Ahmad and Hadi's benefit. As Sofia walked back to her surgery she was smiling until she remembered Farahnaz and what she had to do.

Taking the stairs two at a time, she crossed reception to knock on Jabril's surgery door.

'We've got a problem,' she said as she entered, taking one of the patient seats on the opposite side of the desk. By the time she'd finished telling him about Farahnaz's brother, Jabril was slumping in his chair.

'This is not good,' he said, shaking his head.

'No, it's not. Do you think the disappearance of the four boys is related?'

Jabril sighed. 'I don't know, possibly. Let's hope someone has taken them as free labour. It certainly wouldn't be the first time kids have been stolen to work in factories or on the poppy farms in this country. If these boys are in a village somewhere someone's sure to notice them, but will they say anything? Probably not. We need the police to make their disappearances public.' Jabril began patting down the strands of hair combed over in an attempt to cover his bald patch, a sure sign he was worried.

'Do you really think they've been taken for free labour?' she asked.

'No,' he said, shaking his head and resting his hands on his desk. 'No, I don't. We can only hope that they're still in Afghanistan and that they've been taken by someone who intends selling them on to a rich man, because that might give us time ... at least for these last two boys. If he's an agent he'll probably want to train them in dance and make-up to raise their value before selling them on. If we're lucky he might also need to leave them virgins. I'm sorry about my bluntness, my dear,' he said, blushing.

'It's okay, Jabril. I'm a big girl.'

'If we're looking at some sort of paedophile ring there just might also be the possibility of buying the boys back – if we find who's taken them, that is.'

'If only the police would take this seriously,' Sofia said, feeling her anger rising.

'Yes, of course, but whatever happens, Sofia dear, you must promise me that you'll keep out of this. If it turns out to be some sort of ring taking these boys then it's far too dangerous for you to be involved. Leave it to Taban and me, and hopefully the police.'

'Speaking of which,' Sofia said, brushing off his warning as she rose from the chair, 'do you want to ring Chief Wasim to tell him about Farahnaz's brother or should I?'

'I'll ring him.'

'And I'll give Taban a call to see if she knows anything about Rayi's disappearance. Okay, I'd better go. I'm supposed to be giving a talk to one of Zahra's women's groups for lunch today about my work with the midwives and I haven't organised any notes.'

Jabril pulled a face. 'Be careful. Those women'll eat you alive.'

'They're okay,' Sofia said with a smile. Opening the surgery door, she turned back to look at Jabril. 'I've never caused you any trouble, have I?'

'No, my dear,' he said, sounding nervous.

'So I understand all the reasons why I shouldn't get involved, but I think you need to know that this one is hard for me to let go of. This one's personal. Farahnaz came to me. I didn't go looking for it and I know Rayi and his family, so I'd like to help.'

Jabril patted down his hair again as he leaned back in his chair. 'I understand. You must follow your conscience, but I have to warn you that in my opinion conscience can be an untrustworthy emotional master sometimes. Conscience may not always be the wisest choice.'

She nodded. 'Message received.'

'I'll make some enquiries and speak with the politicians again,' Jabril said. 'Perhaps now, with these boys going missing, someone might think my campaign against *bacha bazi* has its merits. They might even want to pressure the police into taking their disappearance seriously. Oh, and how was your meeting with the man from the UN, my dear?'

'Good.'

'What did he want?'

Sofia thought about their meeting and shrugged. 'What he said he wanted: to talk with me about the women I work with. Oh, and I'd like to introduce you so you can talk with him about health issues in general in Afghanistan. Would that be okay?'

'Of course.'

Back in her surgery, Sofia rang Taban, who said she'd already heard about Rayi's disappearance but had no further information. 'Bad news has better reception here in Jamal Mina than our phones, it seems,' she added. 'I have no idea how many more little boys need to disappear before anyone takes notice.'

'We've got to get the police involved.'

'Of course, but how?' Sofia didn't have an answer. 'What about your friend, the chief?'

'We asked him when the first boys went missing. We'll ask him again.' Taban's silence on the end of the phone gave Sofia all the answer she needed regarding her thoughts on that.

As Sofia began preparing her notes on midwifery for her talk to Zahra's women's group, she couldn't help thinking what a waste of time it was. It would be a nice talk that they'd probably remember for a week, or maybe less.

Losing her enthusiasm for the subject, Sofia stopped typing and sat back in her chair. It was going to be a waste of her time and theirs. She thought about the events from that morning and deleted the document she'd been working on and started a new one. She was about to pick a fight.

15

AFTER HER LAST patient had left for the day, Sofia was packing up when Iman wandered in to flop down in one of the seats on the opposite side of her desk. She wanted to know how Sofia's talk had gone.

'Not too good.'

'Well, what did you expect?' Iman said, examining the cuffs of her shirt.

Iman generally dismissed Zahra's friends as the trophy wives of powerful warlords, politicians and rich businessmen. 'I told you they wouldn't be interested in the village women. They've all conveniently forgotten that their mothers used to be village women and that they'd all still be village women if they hadn't sold themselves off to the highest bidder. All they do is talk, talk, talk. They never do anything good.'

Sofia sat back in her chair. 'That's just not true, Iman, and you know it. Some of them are politicians themselves and members of powerful NGOs. They don't owe their status to their husbands. They're vocal and they fight for women's rights in this country. I think they should be admired.'

'I suppose,' Iman said, giving Sofia a petulant look.

She decided Iman was in a bad mood. 'I was thinking about our chat this morning. I don't think you should be so hard on the women of Afghanistan. All those gutsy Afghan women of the seventies and eighties haven't just disappeared, you know. They're still around and they've had daughters like you and your friends. What about Zahra and your mother and their friends? They're strong and outspoken women. What about the Afghan Women's Network? They get out on the streets and demonstrate and they're telling the world that Afghan women aren't going to disappear back into their homes ever again. There's much to admire in those women.'

'I guess.' Iman shrugged. 'Until the Taliban come back.'

Sofia decided to ignore the Taliban remark but wondered whether she should go further. It saddened her that Iman wasn't proud of her fellow women and what they'd achieved, but like all young people she was impatient and nothing happened quickly enough. 'Your fight for equality here has been far more difficult than it's been for women in the West, where, by the way, women still haven't got all the equality they want. If we're still finding it hard to emancipate in the West, what makes you think Afghan women should be any further along that path? I meet amazing women here all the time: in the villages and in my surgery and in Jamal Mina every day. They mightn't always be out there on the streets protesting like you want, or walking around without their hair covered, and they mightn't be particularly vocal, but they're doing what they can in their own homes and communities. The strength and tenacity of these women humbles me every single day, Iman. You have a lot to be proud of.'

'That's what my mum says. I just wish they'd speak out more. They don't stand up for themselves enough.'

'It's not always as easy for others as it is for you here in Kabul, and with the parents you have, but things *are* changing. Women can protest on the streets now when they couldn't before, and that's because of these women who came before you. Remember the protest back in 2009 against the new laws governing Shia women that sanctioned rape in marriage and marriage to underage girls? How gutsy and brave were those women to come out in the streets and continue to demonstrate when they were spat on and stoned?'

'My mother was part of that,' Iman said with evident pride.

'See? And so was Zahra, and yes, I agree that there's still a long way to go, but please don't put Afghan women down because they're not so visible as you.'

'I suppose.'

Sofia could see she had got through to her and was glad. Iman took everything so personally, which was understandable, but it did tend to make her look on the negative side of things too often. 'Come on,' she said, trying to brighten Iman's mood. 'You know I'm right.'

Iman shrugged again.

Sofia had an idea that might help lighten Iman's load. 'Have you ever met any of the women from the Afghan Women's Network? I could introduce you, but I'm sure your mother would know them too. Why don't you take your protest idea to them? Join forces and make it bigger?'

Iman ignored her suggestion, sinking deeper into negativity, so different from her mood that morning. 'What's going to happen when the West go and the Taliban get back into power? What's going to happen to our rights then?'

Sofia shook her head. It would be a disaster for the women of Afghanistan: everything they had worked for could be lost again.

'I only have this one life to live, Dr Sofia,' Iman said, sitting forward in her seat. I don't want it to be wasted under the Taliban. I don't want men telling me how I should live and who I should be.'

Sofia could see she was scared. She had every reason to be. 'I know, Iman. I know.'

Iman pouted. 'Khalif was going to take me to his friend's *tabang wallah* near Shahr-e Naw this morning. We had a fight.'

'Ah.' She understood. Modern young Kabul women like Iman didn't want to be taken out to eat street food near Kabul's central park. They wanted the city's hip Western cafés. There was no way of making Khalif's choice attractive so she didn't even try. 'You might be interested to know that I didn't talk about the midwives to Zahra's group today. I talked about what life is like for the children of Jamal Mina and how they're going missing and how no one cares.'

'No! You didn't!' Iman said, sitting up straight, and more animated now. 'Wow. I'm not surprised it didn't go down well. You must've really upset them.'

'Maybe, but I understand their reaction. It's not a pleasant subject to be ambushed with.'

Iman wasn't listening. 'Wow, I'd have given anything to have been there. The looks on their faces must've been priceless.'

Sofia saw the looks on their faces and priceless wasn't how she would have described them. She had also seen the look on

Zahra's face. It wasn't priceless either. It had been wrong to ambush her friend like that. Part of her wanted to apologise, but another part of her said she had nothing to apologise for. Something needed to be done about paedophilia and the first thing that needed to be done was what Jabril had been trying to do even before the boys had gone missing: start an open conversation about the taboo subject. These women needed to be part of that conversation. If just one of those powerful women would be moved enough to do something then it had been worth it. 'I assure you, it didn't feel too priceless.' Sofia stood up, closed her laptop and put it in its bag before walking to the coat stand to pull her scarf off and wrap it around her hair. 'Come on, let's get out of here,' she said, hitching her bag and the laptop over her shoulder.

'Well?' Iman asked as they were walking down the stairs.

'Well what?'

'What was the man from the UN like?'

'Nice.'

'Nice?' Iman stopped, tapping Sofia on the shoulder so she'd turn around and look at her. 'That tells me nothing. Nice,' she said, pulling a face. 'Nice is as bad as interesting. Was he handsome, like in the paper?'

Sofia leaned up against the wall and shrugged. 'I suppose so, if you like that type.'

'What type would that be?' Iman was having fun.

'I don't know.' Sofia was about to continue down the stairs when Iman spoke again.

'And do you like that type?'

'It's irrelevant what I like.'

'Maybe I should have been here to meet him. I wouldn't have found it irrelevant.'

Sofia walked down the stairs. 'Maybe you should have.'

'Oh, by the way,' Iman said when they'd reached the square. 'I saw Farahnaz leaving the surgery when I came back this morning but I didn't see any notes about her visit on file.'

'There won't be any.'

'Okaaaay,' Iman said, drawing the word out and nodding her head.

Sofia knew exactly what Iman's 'okaaaay' meant. She sniffed a secret and was now obliged to uncover it. The young woman got bored too easily and fell into gossip. Maybe the kindest thing for Sofia to do would be to fire her so she would finally go to university.

After locking the door to the stairs and saying goodbye to Iqbal, Iman and Rashid, Sofia headed off across the square only to find Rashid following close behind her. She waited until Rashid came alongside before she began walking again. 'What's going on, Rashid?'

'Nothing.'

'Then why were you following me?'

'It's my job.'

Sofia stopped and turned to him. 'I thought we settled this a long time ago. You don't need to walk across the square with me.'

'But I do.'

Sofia searched Rashid's face. With his warm swarthy skin, golden bright eyes, a long aquiline nose and abundant soft dark curls framing his face and neck beneath his *pakol*, she had always thought Rashid a handsome man. She believed he was her friend and would do just about anything for her, just as she would for him, but it was an odd friendship where there had never been any personal exchanges, unlike with her driver, Tawfiq. She accepted that was just the way most Afghan men were. It didn't mean he cared any less. She often wondered whether the warmest part of him had been lost with the death of his two oldest children in the suicide bomb, or if it remained in safekeeping with his wife in Iran.

'But you don't,' she insisted, adding a smile so he would not mistake her words as criticism.

'But I do.'

She let her smile broaden. 'Okay, this isn't really getting us anywhere, is it? Can you tell me why you're doing this?'

'Dr Jabril said I have to.'

Sofia arched an eyebrow. 'I see. And when did he say this?'

'Every time you leave the surgery and every time you leave Behnaz's house, unless you're with Tawfiq.'

'No,' Sofia said, shaking her head, 'I mean when precisely did he tell you that you needed to follow me?' She saw the confusion. 'Was it this morning? Did Dr Jabril tell you this morning to do this?'

'Oh no,' Rashid said, looking relieved he could finally understand. 'He told me at lunchtime.'

'Okay,' Sofia said as they started walking again. She made a mental note to ask Jabril what this new security was all about.

Once back in her apartment she made a cup of tea and lay down on her bed before calling Taban to see if she had any further news about Farahnaz's brother. When the call dropped out she wasn't surprised; the network in Jamal Mina was notoriously unreliable. Thinking about Taban and remembering her conversation with Iman, she thought it might be a good idea to introduce the two women. Iman would see that Taban was one of the gutsy women of Afghanistan worth admiring.

Rolling over, she sat up on the side of the bed and was about to get up to make dinner when she saw Daniel's scarf. Maybe she shouldn't see him again. Of course, she'd have to take him to Jamal Mina and introduce him to Jabril because she'd promised that, but he didn't have to come to Kandahar with her. She'd just say Fatima didn't want to meet him. It would be easy enough to do.

16

OMAR HAD SPENT most of that day thinking about the night letter he had taken from Behnaz's gate until by a matter of logic he discovered the answer to who the 'friend' had to be: Hadi. Everyone knew he had been stealing from his friends for years, skimming a little off the top of everything he weighed. With the knowledge he felt a great weight being lifted off his shoulders. It also gave him the answer to what he had to do. He felt happy because his thoughts were working well this afternoon: one thought at a time, just like a train running to a timetable. Lately, though, it was true that Omar had noticed a bit of congestion and a number of collisions. No matter, he was old and sick and these things were bound to happen. All in all, he didn't think he was doing too badly, considering he'd solved the mystery of who Behnaz's night letter was for and why, although he hadn't discovered who sent it.

Omar needed to warn his friend but he was aware of the difficulties this presented. He must warn Hadi without giving offence or – and this last point was crucial – without letting him know the night letter didn't rightfully belong to him. Omar began to feel the train of doubt creeping back into the station behind the one that had been parked so satisfactorily there only a few minutes before.

What if you're wrong? What if it isn't Hadi?

Omar's good mood fell away but then he began to smile again. Although there had been a little confusion of thought lately, he realised that the answer to this new dilemma not only made perfect sense but it had arrived in time to clear the station of doubt – no crashes and no congestion – and it also possessed a certain pleasing symmetry. Even if it wasn't Hadi, all Omar had to do was tell Hadi and Ahmad about the night letter – being careful not to mention that it wasn't actually his – and not only would Hadi be warned but, because everyone knew Hadi and Ahmad liked to gossip, by evening half the square would have been warned, and by the following day half of Kabul. Omar really was feeling quite pleased with himself.

To a fool the right answer is silence.

The words of the Prophet had come from that second annoying voice in his head. No disrespect to the Prophet but sometimes the words of Allah the Merciful, the Compassionate and the Generous were a lot like the words of his second wife, who had an irritating knack of having an answer for every-thing. So should he stay silent or should he warn Hadi? He was beginning to wish he'd never taken the night letter off Behnaz's gate. Perhaps the answer to his problems was to put it back on the gate and forget about it? Omar considered this as the congestion at the station began to clear again and he became, once more, sure of the correct path. Leaving the comfort of his chair, Omar made his way across the square.

'Excuse me, my friends,' he said, interrupting a conversation between Ahmad and Hadi as they sat together outside their shops smoking. 'It's a bad day, my friends,' he began. He noticed the look Hadi gave Ahmad but, having practised his excellent opening line as he walked across the square, he ignored it and continued. 'This morning I found a *shabnamah* on the gate.' No need to mention whose gate. He also realised he shouldn't have called it a *shabnamah* because the idea of a Taliban night letter might not be correct. Too late now because he'd already said it. 'At least, it might be a *shabnamah*,' he offered.

Both men looked more interested now in what Omar had to say until a frown creased Hadi's forehead. 'But you don't have a gate, Omar.'

Of course he didn't have a gate. What a fool he'd been. 'Did I say gate? I meant on my door.'

No, no, no, you shouldn't have said my *door.*

Ahmad and Hadi exchanged looks again before Ahmad asked him what the *shabnamah* said.

Omar had seen the look again and was feeling hurt and flustered. Didn't his friends believe him? His eyes darted around, scanning the dark interior of Ahmad's shop and then back to the two men. He needed to find something solid and mundane to focus on so he didn't make any more stupid mistakes. He wished he'd never crossed the square to talk with them. He wished he'd taken less of his draught after lunch. Apart from just walking away, he had no option but to answer. 'It said my friend had to stop.'

'What friend?' they asked in unison.

If only they'd get up off their stools, Omar thought, feeling uncomfortable standing over them, but his days of squatting for a conversation with some old friends were long gone. 'That's the problem,' he said, wiping the sweat off his brow. 'I don't know.'

'Stop what?' asked Hadi.

'I don't know this either.' He could feel his breath shallow in his chest and knew this was not good for him. He took a deep breath. 'I think this person might be cheating his customers.'

Ahmad looked at Hadi, who Omar thought had visibly paled. He and Ahmad were now both looking at Hadi, waiting for him to respond.

'But what if this man needs the money to feed his family?' Hadi asked.

Omar was starting to feel calmer again as he considered these words. It was a valid point. 'I agree that would be a problem, but what does it matter that his family goes a little hungry compared to the possibility of losing his life?' The blood drained from Hadi's face again. Maybe he'd gone too far with the 'losing his life' comment. Omar was beginning to feel sorry for his friend, and also a bit bad about maybe exaggerating a little and causing so much pain, so he offered the possibility that it might be a friend of Behnaz. He thought this a good option to cover all possibilities but saw immediately it had been a mistake.

Hadi was frowning. 'Why would it be a friend of Behnaz if it was on your door?'

Omar could feel the panic rising again. He needed to stick to the script. No more embellishing. 'I don't know, but it might be … or it might be a friend of Chief Wasim or Dr Sofia. It might be a friend of anybody. We have to think of all possibilities so we can warn them.'

'No,' said Ahmad, 'there's only one person in the square it can't be for and that's you, Omar.'

Omar was very glad to hear that Ahmad thought it wasn't about him but he needed to know why.

'Because it said "your friend", didn't it? So if it was on your door then you're the only one it can't be about.'

Omar could feel his heart lighten with this news, wondering why he'd never thought of that himself. In his happiness he also thanked Allah the Merciful that neither Hadi nor Ahmad had thought to ask how he had come to the conclusion that the message was about someone cheating. Trying to describe the trains that came and left the station in his head would have proved a little tricky, as would the truth of the matter. Now he had delivered the message he was also feeling a great deal of sympathy for Hadi.

'Well, my friends, I'll leave it to you, but if you have any ideas, please let me know.' Shuffling back across the square, Omar was feeling satisfied with how things had worked out. It had been a good plan and he had executed it to near perfection, apart for those mistakes about Behnaz and the gate and calling it a *shabnamah*. And, of course, as Ahmad had pointed out, the threat could not be about him.

As he was locking up his shop for the day, he noticed Hadi had already locked up and gone home, but Ahmad was crossing the square to talk with Babur and his cook. Soon they would talk with their customers who would talk to their friends. The message was being spread. All his careful planning had saved his friend from real danger, and if he was wrong and it wasn't about Hadi then whomever it was about would soon be warned.

While making his way up the stairs to his beautifully soft bed, Omar realised he had perhaps been a little too hasty in his decision to throw his Viagra away if it definitely wasn't about him. He also wondered who had sent the night letter, because the more he thought about it the more he realised it wasn't anything like a Taliban *shabnamah*. Tomorrow he would think about correcting that misunderstanding in the square, but right now he needed to sleep.

***

AFTER AHMAD TOLD Babur and his cook about Omar's *shabnamah*, the three men moved inside the *chaikhana* to discuss this worrisome news further. Taking the seats that gave them the greatest privacy from Babur's other customers, they relaxed back on the cushions to enjoy the tea the cook had prepared for them. After engaging in an initial conversation about how the Taliban and all the invaders had ruined their country, Ahmad and the cook began considering who this 'friend' of Omar's might be.

The cook pointed out that if it could be a friend of Behnaz then it could also be a friend of Chief Wasim or Dr Sofia. He also pointed out that everyone in the square was a friend of Omar, Behnaz, Chief Wasim and Dr Sofia, which, as far as Ahmad was concerned, was not a particularly instructive comment. What Ahmad really wanted to know was whether they had guessed the *shabnamah* might actually be about him not going to mosque in the morning. When he noticed that Babur was uncharacteristically quiet, he asked him who he thought the friend might be.

Babur looked at Ahmad a little aggrieved. 'Why do you ask me? What makes you think I'd know?'

Ahmad was taken aback by the tone of his friend's response. 'Well, I don't know, do I? I was just asking.' He waited, expecting Babur to apologise, but there was no apology. Ahmad decided he needed a different approach. 'Who do you think the Talib might be in the square?'

Although this had been Ahmad's initial thought when Omah had told him of the *shabnamah*, it was obvious that neither the cook nor Babur had considered this. The three men looked out into the square as if they expected the culprit to make himself known.

'Not Iqbal,' offered Babur, scratching his head under his turban.

'Not Rashid,' said the cook.

'Couldn't be Chief Wasim because he's the chief of police, and it can't possibly be Dr Jabril because everyone knows he hates the Taliban.'

'Omar hates the Taliban too.'

'Everyone hates the Taliban,' offered Babur miserably.

'Obviously someone doesn't. Isn't that what people normally do, anyway?' asked the cook. The two men looked at him, waiting for an explanation. 'Don't people cover their tracks by pretending to hate something when they really love it?'

'True,' offered Ahmad, nodding.

'It could be someone who only visits the square,' offered the cook who, being the only one not worried that he might be the focus of the *shabnamah*, had grown tired of the conversation and made his excuses to leave. 'And who says it's the Taliban anyway?' he said in parting.

In his absence Ahmad and Babur agreed this was a very good point, but it didn't solve the problem of who was being threatened and why.

***

AFTER AHMAD AND the cook left, Babur waited for his last customers to finish before closing early for the night. Retreating back to his cushion on the platform, he poured himself another tea and sat watching the darkness descending on the square. In the previous hour Babur had moved from shock, to terror, to an explosive anger and finally to emptiness. As he sat alone in the dark he wondered if the *shabnamah* was really meant for him.

Only two nights previously he had told his no-good brother-in-law about his purchase of alcohol that he hoped to secretly sell in the *chaikhana* to increase profits. As Babur thought about his brother-in-law, he felt his anger rising. He'd never much liked his sister's husband, who had always been too pious for his liking. He also suspected that he was jealous because Babur owned the famous *chaikhana*. He had no doubt the brother-in-law would be unhappy about him increasing his profits and realised he'd been a fool to confide in him.

Babur finished the last of his tea and thought about going home, but what was the point? There was no one waiting for him other than the cousin he shared the flat with. The *chaikhana* was where he belonged, he thought, as he looked around at the teapots bought by his father and the walls blackened by centuries of smoke. The rugs he had crawled on as a baby, played on as a toddler, were still there. To this day he knew every perfect and broken thread on those carpets. Over the years he had wondered in what village they had been made and how old they might be, but even his father couldn't say. They had been in the *chaikhana* forever.

For a while now he had been thinking of moving into the *chaikhana*. Turning the two small rooms out the back, which had once been the rooms of the original inn but were now full of old furniture no one used, into living quarters.

Babur took a long drag on his cigarette. He wasn't so sure the threat had been the Taliban. It was probably his brother-in-law, but if it was a *shabnamah*, and if it was about him, then why hadn't it been posted on *his* door? Why post a threat on someone's door telling them to tell their friend? As far as Babur could see, none of that made sense. And if it were his brother-in-law, why would he post a night letter on Omar's door? He had no idea who it was from or intended for, but could he ignore it? The *chaikhana* was worth far more to him than a small potential profit from alcohol. As far as he could see, he had no choice but to get rid of the alcohol. Having made up his mind, Babur walked to the back of the shop and phoned the man he'd been dealing with to ask if he would like to buy the alcohol back. When he declined, Babur offered to return it for free.

No matter what happened, Babur thought as he locked up the *chaikhana* and made his way home alone, he would get rid of the alcohol, even if he had to tip it down the drain and smash the bottles to little pieces. And he would move into the two back rooms of his beloved *chaikhana*.

17

WITH INEFFICIENT VEHICLES and power shortages that had people burning everything from rubber tyres and plastic to trees for fuel, Kabul had become one of the most polluted cities in the world. When Sofia woke early the following morning it was to a cold white fog swirling ghostlike around the square, but by the time she came out of the house the sun had burnt through to reveal a brilliant, cloudless blue sky and unusually fresh air. Outside the gate Tawfiq and Rashid were leaning up against the side of the SUV talking and smoking, while Behnaz was off in the square collecting the previous day's litter.

'*As-salaam alaikum,*' she said, feeling the lightness of the morning. 'Isn't this a beautiful day?'

'*Wa alaikum as-salaam,*' the two men offered in unison, pushing themselves off the car.

'We're going to the Serena Hotel this morning, Rashid, and then on to Jamal Mina, so you're free until after lunch, unless you need to come with us?'

Rashid dropped the cigarette he had been smoking, grinding it out on Behnaz's newly swept cobblestones as he waved the lingering smoke out of his eyes. 'No, I don't need to be with you when you're with Tawfiq, unless you're leaving Kabul.'

'So I'll see you again around lunchtime,' she said, opening the car door and sliding across the back seat. As Tawfiq climbed in and closed his door behind him, the locks clicked into place. The sound had become such a background noise to Sofia's travels that she didn't register it, although she might have if it didn't happen.

When she had first arrived in Kabul, Sofia had made Tawfiq uncomfortable by taking the seat next to him in the front of the car. Not knowing how to broach this delicate subject with the new Australian doctor whose Dari wasn't so good, Tawfiq had asked Zahra to explain to Dr Sofia that an Afghan woman didn't sit in the front with the driver unless he was her husband.

'So what's going on?' Sofia asked Tawfiq as they manoeuvred their way out of the square for the fifteen-minute drive to the hotel.

He looked at her in his rear-vision mirror. 'I don't know what you mean.'

'This new security? Rashid following me across the square again?'

'Ah, that,' Tawfiq said, not sounding too concerned. 'Dr Jabril told us to take more care so we're taking more care.'

'Why?'

'I don't know. You'll have to ask him, but he didn't seem worried. Why are we going to the Serena today?'

'To collect someone.'

Tawfiq was watching her in the rear-vision mirror, which was how a lot of their conversations happened: him in the driver's seat and her in the back and the mirror between them. 'The man who came to see you yesterday?'

Sofia looked out the window so their eyes wouldn't meet. 'That would be the one.'

Out on the main road they found themselves locked in behind a military convoy. With military vehicles being prime targets for attack, together with the fact that being stuck behind one in Kabul traffic could double your travel time, Tawfiq manoeuvred his way out before speeding off.

'He's a friend of yours?' he asked.

'Why would you ask that?' Their eyes met in the mirror.

He looked away. 'Ahmad said you had something that belonged to him and that you didn't want to give it back.'

'My, word travels fast in Shaahir Square. A scarf. It was just a boring old scarf.' She really couldn't do much without the square knowing, and while she had got used to it over the years, she still didn't like it.

***

SOFIA HAD SPENT most of the day in the high mountain village working with the women on their health and, in return, they had taught her where to find the best mountain herb for a toothache, what bark to boil up to relieve indigestion, how to set a fire that wouldn't go out halfway through the cooking, and the secret of their naan bread. In the late afternoon she had been outside her hut packing up her things when she looked up to see Daniel walking toward her with a group of women. The sight of him, tall and elegant in his *perahan tunban* with a group of village women, was one of the visions anchored in a powerful emotion from that time and, thus, not forgotten. It had been the moment she realised she was in love with Daniel Abiteboul.

'You've got a delegation,' he had offered with a cheeky smile.

Sofia had looked at the women. 'So I see.' She looked back at Daniel. 'What's this about?'

'They're curious about you and want to ask some questions. They've asked me to translate so there's no miscommunication. Is that okay?'

'Of course,' she smiled at the women, acknowledging their request.

As they all sat down in the dirt in front of her hut, the questions began. Where was Australia? Was it like Afghanistan? Why didn't she know how to make a fire and cook naan? Why had her father let her come to their village without a chaperone and why wasn't she married? When she said she hadn't found anyone she loved, they looked unhappy with her response.

'Not sure the concept of love has anything to do with life in the village here,' offered Daniel.

'Okay, tell them my father hasn't found anyone for me yet.' When Daniel translated, they nodded. They could understand that, but it opened a discussion about why her father might have found it difficult. One woman suggested it might be because of the colour of her hair. When Daniel had asked the woman what she meant she told him that men wouldn't be comfortable with a wife who drew unwanted attention.

'There you go,' Sofia had said when Daniel translated, although she'd understood most of the conversation. 'It's my hair again.'

Searching her face for a few seconds, he had turned back and spoken again to the women.

'What did you say?' Sofia had asked, not understanding the last word he used.

'I said men in my culture would find your hair intriguing.'

'Oh,' she said, not knowing what else to say.

What is the ocean like, they asked. Sofia had no idea how to describe the ocean.

It was growing dark by the time the women left to prepare dinner, leaving Daniel and Sofia to relax back against the wall of her hut as the afternoon shadows moved across the face of the mountains and the floor of the valley below fell into darkness. 'The women think your hair is beautiful, you know,' he had offered.

She turned to look at him. 'That's not what they said, was it?'

'No, but that's what they say when you aren't around. The men also find it fascinating.'

Sofia had groaned. 'It's my curse. They should write on my gravestone: *She had red hair.*' When the sun had disappeared behind the peaks and the night air descended, Sofia had shivered. Reaching into a pocket of his coat, Daniel pulled out a soft woollen scarf. 'Here, have this.'

'Don't you need it?'

'I've got another.'

Taking his scarf, Sofia had wrapped it around her neck and up over her lips to breathe in the now familiar scent of her lover.

* * *

THE DISCORDANT SOUND of music blasting out of a car full of young Afghan men, together with the pungent smell of an overflowing sewer, brought Sofia out of her reverie just as they were turning into the entry of the five-star Serena Hotel. With its extensive gardens, fountains, swimming pool, members' lounge and dining experience, together with its security and high walls locking out the chaos of Kabul, it tended to be the preferred choice of foreign visitors and dignitaries with little or no interest in getting dirty in the reality of Kabul.

The walls and very visible security may have imbued confidence in its well-heeled guests, but with three terrorist attacks on the Serena Hotel since 2008, security was so beefed up that it sometimes took twenty minutes to get through the various checks before reaching its impressively ornate front doors.

As they pulled into line to wait for the boom gate to open and begin the first security check, Sofia asked Tawfiq how his mother was faring after recently undergoing a cataract operation paid for by Jabril. The groan he gave in response had Sofia regretting her question.

'I tell you, Dr Sofia, my mother doesn't respect Kaamisha, and now that she can see again everything's worse.'

Tawfiq's wife, Kaamisha, and their three young sons remained in the compound of his parents' house in Mazar-i Sharif, the fourth largest town in Afghanistan and about seven hours north of the capital. While traditionally it was the daughter-in-law's job to look after her husband's parents, Tawfiq considered himself a modern man and had been trying to save enough money to buy a small flat in Kabul where his wife and children might join him. For the past six years he had shared a two-bedroom apartment with five other men in one of the worst suburbs of Kabul. With the responsibility of sending money to his parents each month, together with his share of the rent and food for the apartment, there was little to put toward a deposit.

'It was better when my mother couldn't see,' Tawfiq said. 'At least then she couldn't see the dirt that isn't there. Kaamisha, she must clean all the time, but it's never clean enough. I tell you, Dr Sofia, my mother's giving me grief, my wife's giving me grief. I am grief,' he added with a dramatic flourish, laying his head on his hands which were resting on the steering wheel.

'You don't look like grief, Tawfiq,' Sofia said with a smile.

'What?' he asked, lifting his head and turning around in the seat to look at her.

'Never mind. I was being silly.'

They sat in silence watching the car in front being screened until Tawfiq spoke again. 'Is it true that life gets better when you get older?'

Sofia was only six years older than Tawfiq but it was obvious that he considered her much older. She didn't take offence. She was a thirty-two-year-old woman in a country where thirty-five was considered old. Someone of her age in a village might have been married at fourteen and a grandmother by thirty. 'I'm not so sure,' she said.

Tawfiq flopped his head on his hands again, forcing his woollen *pakol* further back on his head. Clearly, it had not been the answer he'd been looking for.

From the moment she had arrived in Afghanistan, Tawfiq had been a stable presence in her life. On their initial excursions around the city alone he had pointed out landmarks, recalled the history of a building, or where the war had a particularly major impact. He showed her where she could find the freshest food, a trustworthy tailor, and the safest Western cafés. In time, Sofia felt she knew the capital as well as Tawfiq. When they travelled outside Kabul her lessons in Afghan history continued, often leaving them both laughing at the absurdity of something an Afghan might do or despairing over the seemingly insurmountable problems facing the country they both loved. During those drives Tawfiq's family had been a constant in their conversations until Sofia felt as if she knew them well.

'I will be your guide,' he had said to her on their first foray into the city. He had become much more. He had become her brother.

When the car in front was released through to the next security check, Sofia leaned over and tapped Tawfiq on the shoulder. 'I think we can move forward now.'

'Perhaps things do improve when we get older,' Sofia offered as the Serena guard began running a mirror under the car. 'Perhaps then you get a better perspective on life and you don't worry about things so much.' Tawfiq's head did not move from where it was back resting on the steering wheel. Sofia watched as one of the gardeners moved around with his broom, sweeping up the litter that had blown in from the street the night before, restoring the Serena to its perfect order, an oasis of calm and cleanliness in a city of dirt and chaos.

While she loved to hear about Tawfiq's kids, Sofia had long ago exhausted her enthusiasm for the running saga of discontent between his mother and wife and was happy to let the subject drop, but Tawfiq lifted his head off the wheel, his soft brown eyes with the long lashes looking at her in the rear-vision mirror. 'Perhaps you're not old enough to know these things,' he offered.

Sofia shrugged. 'Perhaps you're right. Can I take that as a compliment?'

'If you want,' he mumbled, his head on the steering wheel again.

Maybe Tawfiq was right. Maybe you didn't know life was

better until the 'better' had passed. Or maybe people talked about how much better it used to be because they'd forgotten how bad it was.

They passed through the second security point to pull up in front of the impressively tall columns of the Serena's portico. 'Maybe when you're older you're able to rewrite history in a kinder light,' she mused.

'I don't understand.'

'Honestly, neither do I.'

Sofia was beginning to suspect that something more than Tawfiq's woes about his wife and mother was worrying him but there was no way she could ask. Tawfiq might be her brother but he was a proud Afghan man first, and if Tawfiq wanted to confide in her then he would.

Noticing that the two heavily-armed security guards had turned their attention to their stationary vehicle, she asked Tawfiq to wait for her in the little parking area near the entrance. 'I'll be right back.'

As Sofia walked towards the Serena's entrance a handsome man in formal Afghan dress with an old-fashioned curled moustache and pointy clipped beard was opening the door, beckoning her into a haven of softly piped muzak and the gentle hum of purified air.

18

As HE SAT waiting for Sofia, Tawfiq thought about this idea of rewriting history and decided that on his way home that night he would stop in at his local internet café and look it up.

What are you thinking? Do you want to die?

He sank his head back onto the steering wheel. How could he have forgotten so quickly?

The previous evening Ahmad had told Tawfiq about the *shabnamah* pinned to Omar's door. His friend had been sure it was meant for him because he had not been going to mosque and wanted to know who Tawfiq thought the Talib in the square might be. But Tawfiq knew that the Taliban couldn't have cared less if Ahmad was missing morning mosque. It was more likely that they would be interested in what he had been doing on the internet late at night.

Even though he had been very careful to delete his browsing history before leaving the café, he knew nothing was ever truly private and now it was possible that the Taliban had found him. Apart from the crippling embarrassment and shame, Tawfiq had spent the previous night worrying about how he was going to let the Taliban know he had stopped until he realised that he didn't have to. If they knew what he was doing they would know that he had stopped. He would have liked to have told Ahmad that it didn't matter. The Taliban didn't have to be in the square; they could be in America, or England, or even Russia.

Yesterday had not been a good day. Not only did he have the worry of the Talib but now Dr Jabril had instructed him not to let Dr Sofia out of his sight when they left the square, and he'd just let her walk away. Tawfiq turned around in his seat to see if Dr Sofia was coming out again only to discover she had not gone in and was still talking to the doorman. Just as he was considering getting out of the car to join her, she disappeared behind its doors.

He would have to clarify his instructions with Dr Jabril further.

* * *

'CAN MY DRIVER wait over there?' Sofia asked the impressive doorman who was holding the door open for her. He looked to where she was pointing. 'Please,' Sofia said, offering him a smile while trying to scan the lobby behind him for any sign of Daniel. 'I'll only be a second. My friend's waiting for me in the lobby.' Sofia was pretty sure the doorman had seen her scanning and hadn't been fooled by her lie.

'Okay, but only three minutes,' he said, looking displeased with his decision.

She thanked him and hurried into the hotel, thinking that with such lax security there was sure to be another attack on the Serena.

Feeling the fizz of anticipation at seeing Daniel again, she was moving past the luggage trollies on her way to the reception desk when she saw him coming around the corner with a breathtakingly beautiful African woman on his arm and, like a junkie, her emotions came crashing down.

On seeing Sofia, Daniel quickly extricated his arm and waved while the woman turned to look at her, until her phone rang and she waved him on with a wrist heavy with silver bracelets.

'I'm so sorry,' he said on reaching Sofia, bringing with him a whiff of some exotic perfume. 'Am I late?'

'No, not at all. She's very beautiful,' Sofia said, nodding toward the woman who was talking on her phone, watching them.

He looked over as if he'd never seen her before. 'Clementine's an old friend. We were having breakfast and I'm afraid we lost track of time.'

Sofia looked back at Clementine and decided, on reflection, that she wasn't so much beautiful as striking. Standing over six feet tall and dressed in traditional African clothes, she was making heads turn.

'Clem's a doctor with MSF,' he offered. 'She's the one who told me about your work with the midwives. She's also been here for the last six months, so coming to Kabul had an added attraction.'

'I can definitely appreciate the added attraction.'

Clementine finished the call and was gliding across the floor to envelop them in a cloud of the perfume Daniel had brought with him.

'Clementine Ntuyahaga,' he said, making introductions, 'I'd like you to meet Sofia Raso.'

'Dr Raso,' Clementine said, taking Sofia's hand. 'I know it's a cliché but I've heard only good things about you, and not just from Daniel, who now seems to have joined your long queue of admirers.'

'Is that right?' Sofia said, looking up at Daniel.

'It is,' smiled Clementine, 'and we have another mutual friend. Taban.'

That's interesting, Sofia thought, making a mental note to ask Taban about Clementine.

'She told me about your work with her in the slums, plus my MSF colleagues in Kandahar had mentioned your work with the midwives there. So your name came at me from two sources I trust, and now I find Daniel, whose opinion I respect above all others, is also singing your praises.'

Sofia ignored the comment about Daniel singing her praises. She was more interested in the MSF colleagues in Kandahar. 'How did your colleagues know about my work with the midwives there?' Sofia was aware she wasn't being particularly friendly toward the woman.

Clementine looked surprised by the question. 'I don't know,' she said, shrugging as if it shouldn't matter.

Sofia was about to ask her to find out but decided it really didn't matter now the group was about to be disbanded.

'As you can imagine,' Clementine continued, 'after hearing about you from Taban and my colleagues in Kandahar, I was interested in meeting you, and now I've discovered Daniel has known you for years. How extraordinary.'

'How extraordinary,' Sofia repeated, suspecting Clementine was fishing for information, which meant Daniel hadn't told her much. While she was trying to fathom Daniel and Clementine's relationship, Clementine was probably trying to work out theirs. Was Clementine feeling the same little twists of jealousy she was trying to ignore?

'Perhaps we could all get together? Friday maybe?'

Clementine looked from Sofia to Daniel. 'You could both come to my place for dinner perhaps?'

'Sofia's going to Kandahar on Friday, Clem.'

She turned back to Sofia. 'To see your midwives?'

'They're not my midwives,' Sofia said. Again, she knew she'd been rude. 'To tell them I won't be coming back.'

'Can I ask why?'

'It's too dangerous, and my presence could be putting the women in danger.'

'Yes, I see,' said Clementine, looking as if she had retreated into her thoughts.

'Okay, we need to go now,' said Daniel.

'Just a minute, please,' Clementine said, grabbing Daniel's arm to stop him moving, although she was looking at Sofia. 'I don't know if you're aware, Dr Raso, but MSF has recently opened a maternity unit in Kandahar and we're desperately short of trained staff. I was hoping … Well, I've been wondering since I heard about your … the midwives if it might be possible to discuss our maternity staff teaming up with them, and now, with you not being able to continue their training … I'm thinking out loud here,' she said. 'I assume their training isn't finished?'

'That's right.' Sofia was wondering where Clementine was going.

'Well then, perhaps MSF could help finish their training? It would definitely take the load off our maternity ward if there were competent midwives in the villages.'

The offer had come out of left field. Sofia's first reaction was to not let herself get too excited. She had no idea whether it was genuine or not. So many foreigners made so many promises that came to nothing. This might be the same, but if it was genuine then this was an offer Sofia couldn't afford to ignore. 'You do understand I can't speak for the women?' she said.

'Of course, I know what village women are like.'

Sofia bristled. What *are* village women like, she wanted to say, but decided against it. She wondered whether her dislike of Clementine was obvious to Daniel.

'Look, I was intending going down sometime next week,' Clementine was saying, 'but I could change plans and go with you this Friday to meet the women.' She looked over at Daniel. 'I know Daniel's interested in hearing about what you're doing there so he might like to come too. Daniel?'

'We've already discussed this, Clem. It's not Sofia's choice. She needs to hear back from her contact with the midwives.'

'Of course,' Clementine said, as if his point was irrelevant, 'but really, it makes perfect sense. If we travel down in the MSF cars with their security guards then Dr Raso will be better protected, and she could introduce me to the midwives so I could discuss the possibility of MSF finishing their training with them directly.'

'Clem, you need to back off,' Daniel said. He didn't sound too happy, and while Sofia could clearly see Daniel's annoyance, Clementine didn't seem to notice or didn't care.

Sofia was not liking how Clementine was trying to hijack her last trip to Kandahar, but if there was a possibility that MSF would continue the women's training then she wasn't about to jeopardise that. 'It's possible,' she said carefully, 'but I'd have to run things by Fatima and she might want to discuss it with the women first.'

Clementine flashed Sofia a perfect smile before turning

back to Daniel with the same megawatt smile. 'It seems like a good idea, don't you think?'

'The idea has its merits, but it's Sofia and her contact's decision.'

Rummaging around in her handbag, Clementine retrieved a business card and handed it to Sofia before finding her phone and checking the time. 'Okay, I really do have to go.' She turned to Daniel. 'Will I see you tonight?'

'Probably not.'

It was only a second, but Sofia registered the woman's disappointment. She had clearly expected to see him. 'Okay, call me.' Leaning in, she kissed Daniel on the cheek and said goodbye to Sofia before hurrying out.

'Clem's a bit of a whirlwind,' Daniel said as they followed her out the door, 'but if she says she'll train your midwives she will.'

They were lovers, Sofia decided, but he was not in love.

19

BECAUSE PEOPLE OF Daniel's importance rarely found their way into the middle of the slums, Taban had promised Sofia that, barring any unforeseen emergencies, she would wait for them in her clinic.

After driving as far as they could into the mountain suburb before they had to get out and walk, Tawfiq pulled up beside a pile of plastic bags bursting with rotting garbage. Locking the car, he lit a cigarette before wandering off to look for some boys he could pay to watch over the car until they returned. With the morning heating up, the stench from the garbage would soon become unbearable.

'What's your poison?' Sofia asked Daniel. 'Do we wait here for Tawfiq to return and risk passing out from the smell or do we head up to Taban's?'

'Let's head up.'

The sturdier homes they passed along the dirt path were built from rocks or cinder blocks, but they sat alongside more flimsy dwellings. Carrying the whiff of impermanence, these places were constructed with varying degrees of desperation: offcuts of plywood, the rotting hardwood of old crates, sticks, cardboard, rusting tin, ripped plastic sheeting and anything else people could scavenge from an unguarded worksite, on the streets of Kabul or from the putrid garbage dumps. Halfway up the hill the track narrowed and they had to stop, leaning in against the wall of a house to let a man leading a donkey loaded with empty plastic bottles pass.

'They're for water,' Sofia explained, wiping the sweat off her forehead under the scarf. 'The only taps are down there.' Sofia pointed back down to the bottom of the slum. As the man and his donkey disappeared around the corner they saw Tawfiq labouring up the hill. 'Are you okay?' she called to him, pulling the top she was wearing in and out to let air circulate over her wet skin.

'Tell Taban that I'll be requiring oxygen and a stretcher when I arrive,' he called back.

'Me first,' she said under her breath as they continued up the hill. Within fifteen minutes they had reached an outcrop of boulders with a rough path carved through them. Above the boulders sat Taban's clinic, painted a dirty shade of pale blue that had been created by Taban after combining a large can of tan paint some American soldiers had given her with a small can of deep blue she already owned. It definitely made the clinic stand out from the raw stone and whitewashed buildings surrounding it. It didn't make it attractive. Taban was standing in the doorway of clinic, her hand shading her eyes as she watched their approach.

Taban had a beautiful round face, high cheekbones, a flat nose and the almond-shaped eyes of the Hazara, but the scar of a harelip 'fixed' badly by a Russian military doctor marred her natural beauty. Wearing a long grey skirt, a large shapeless shirt and a thick woollen vest over her thin body, Taban's only concession to femininity was the soft unruly curls escaping from her chador. As a modern woman living in a conservative society, Taban bowed to most of the rules with the exception of her hair, which she regularly cut short, something that was almost unheard of among Afghan women.

It had been four years since Taban had left her job with an international NGO to set up a clinic for the poor in her parents' home near Jamal Mina. When they had become unhappy with the constant stream of strangers knocking on their door, Taban had secured a little bit of money from her former employers and moved her clinic to the only suitable building she could afford in the slum, which happened to be near the top.

Jabril and Sofia had followed Taban's efforts with the clinic from the outset, watching as it quickly expanded from addressing the purely medical needs of the community to meeting all manner of social and economic emergencies, until they could see she was drowning under the increasing demands on her time and meagre funds. With Jabril and Sofia donating medical supplies and each spending a day a month in the slum, some of the burden on Taban had been eased, but it was only when her brothers began to help financially, and Jabril found Parsa, that Taban was truly able to breathe again.

Jabril had met Parsa when the young man had come into the square begging. Jabril, who Zahra said with some affection would talk to a wall if it would listen, had bought Parsa lunch at Babur's *chaikhana* in exchange for his life story. This was a new experience for Parsa; no one wanted to know about beggars. When it became obvious to Jabril that Taban needed help beyond what he and Sofia could give he had immediately thought of Parsa, who he judged to be an honest and intelligent young man who would thrive with work. Parsa had quickly learned nursing skills from Taban, proved to be exceptionally good with the people who came to the clinic, and was soon flourishing in the job. Only recently he had proudly informed Sofia that the wage Jabril was paying him allowed him to support his family so that his brother and sisters could go to school rather than beg on the streets. It had made Sofia smile. Exactly how much was Jabril paying Parsa?

It was obvious to Sofia that Parsa was in love with Taban, but the shy young man was too much in awe of his boss to say anything. When Sofia had suggested to Jabril that she might mention her suspicions to Taban he had cautioned against it.

'Love has a way of seeping through the cracks. It's not up to you and me to point this thing out to Taban. It's there for everyone to see, and if she can't see it then either she's not ready or she doesn't want to.'

Sofia had looked at him with a smirk. 'When did you turn into such a love guru?'

The idea of a love guru had tickled Jabril. 'I've always been a love guru, didn't you know?'

'Oh no,' said Sofia, the smile leaving her face as she waved him away, 'too much information, way too much information. I don't need to hear that!'

With five brothers, all married and living prosperous lives as entrepreneurs in Kabul and Pakistan, Taban's parents had been content to have their only daughter return home at the end of each day to tend to their needs, as long as she didn't bring half the slum with her.

'It's Allah's will that my daughter is so deformed and no

man wants to marry her,' Taban's mother had once confided to Sofia, who had to control an overwhelming urge to hit the woman. 'She can look after us in our old age, but she must stop this nonsense clinic.'

Adopting their mother's mantra that no one would want to marry their sister, her entrepreneurial brothers were horrified to learn that Taban had left the security of the NGO job to work for no money in the slums. Once reconciled to the fact that she would continue on this path no matter what they said, their entrepreneur genes kicked in and the brothers began pressuring Taban to charge more for her services. Steadfastly refusing to do so – for most of her clients had no jobs and hence no money – she came halfway to satisfying her brothers' demands by accepting 'gifts', which she promptly redistributed to the more needy of the slum.

When Jabril had learned of the brothers' demands he had paid the three, who then still lived in Kabul, a social visit. The brothers soon discovered that the rotund little doctor wanted to talk only about the five pillars of Islam, professing a special interest in the third pillar, *zakat*, or almsgiving. The brothers, who unlike Jabril really were devout Muslims, could find no offence with such a subject, and after his visit had begun supporting their sister's work financially, soothing their natural predispositions to hoard and exploit with the promise of a greater reward in Jannah. Describing her brothers' new-found generosity toward the clinic, Taban had told Dr Jabril with a smile that it was nothing short of another one of Allah's great miracles.

'Praise be to Allah,' Jabril had agreed, eager to escape before Taban started thanking him. Despite all his good work, Jabril still had no idea how to take a compliment.

Considering the success of Taban and her brothers, Sofia thought there must have been an intelligence gene somewhere in the family but it had obviously bypassed Taban's mother, while the compassion gene had clearly bypassed everyone except Taban.

'Welcome, my friend,' Taban said as she and Daniel reached the clinic.

'Why do you have a clinic so far up the slope?' Sofia asked between laboured breaths, wiping her face with the end of her scarf.

'Why do you ask this same question every time? The need does not always happen at the bottom of the mountain. Dr Daniel,' Taban said, turning to him, 'welcome to Jamal Mina and thank you for making the effort to trek up to my little clinic.' Stepping back, Taban pulled aside the cloth from the doorway for them to enter.

The interior's mud walls had been thinly – and somewhat haphazardly – painted white by Taban, with the roller strokes still visible. The mud floor was a sickly brown-green, while through an open door Sofia could see the two cots Taban had scavenged from the US military, covered in white sheets for their next patients.

'I'm sorry, I don't have anything to offer you to drink until Parsa arrives with the water.' She held out her hands in apology. 'Unfortunately, the government has supplied us with pipes to carry water but not the water to go through them. Now you must tell me, Dr Daniel,' she said, sitting cross-legged on the floor opposite them, 'what is it you want to know?'

'I want to know what you will need here in Jamal Mina when the foreign troops pull out.'

154

Taban laughed. 'Nothing will change when the foreign troops pull out. Yes,' she said, waving toward the beds in the next room, 'from time to time they have given me a bed or some medical supplies, and I'm grateful for that, but we don't see them here. So to answer your question, there are many things we need: jobs, health care, sanitation, running water, equality, protection, education for girls and the end of gender violence. But this is not what you came here to learn, is it?'

'You've already told me something important: that you don't get enough help and that won't change with the withdrawal of the foreign troops.'

'I would like to know what your conclusions are from what you have seen so far in my country,' Taban said as she innocently flattened out the folds of her skirt with short, bony fingers before pulling down the sleeves of her shirt to cover her wrists. Sofia knew the question was a test. Taban had seen too many Westerners arrive in her country and after ten minutes make decisions about what should happen. Taban would not waste time on Daniel if he were one of them. She was also not above telling him to leave.

'You're the one who knows Jamal Mina. I need you to tell me.'

Satisfied with his response, Taban stood. 'Come with me.' If someone was serious, Taban believed it was better to let them see Jamal Mina for themselves. That way they were left with powerful, visual and emotional images that would stay with them far longer than any fine words she might offer. As they were standing, Tawfiq arrived with Parsa, who was carrying a large jerry can of water balanced high on his shoulder.

'Ah, the tea has arrived,' declared Taban. On seeing Parsa's confusion she told him not to worry. Before she introduced

Parsa to Daniel she spoke with him in Dari, explaining that Dr Daniel was a very important man and that they needed to impress him because he might be able to help them. Sofia cringed. She should have warned Taban that Daniel spoke perfect Dari.

'Ah,' Parsa said, looking over at Daniel again and nodding.

'We'll wait outside,' Sofia said, hurrying Daniel and Tawfiq out while Taban gave Parsa his instructions for the morning.

Outside the clinic they looked down on the flat roofs of the houses of Jamal Mina. In summer these were used for drying fruits and for the men to sleep on the hottest nights, but in winter they were often deserted. Halfway down the hill that day they could just make out an old woman sitting cross-legged on her roof weaving on a loom, while to the left of her two little boys were trying unsuccessfully to launch a kite. In the sky above a hawk was circling, gliding ever higher in the updrafts.

'Have you been back to the village?' Sofia asked him.

Daniel turned to look at her. 'No. You?'

She shook her head. 'I've often thought about it.'

'It was a strange time for me ...' Daniel began, but before he could finish Taban came out with a package tucked under her arm.

'Let's go,' she said.

As they set off at a brisk pace back down the hill, Sofia wondered what Daniel had meant.

20

MIRWAIS HAD BEEN sitting cross-legged on the ground outside his house playing with his youngest son, who was snuggled in his lap, as they waited for the important visitors Taban had told him about. When he saw them coming his smile disappeared and the child, sensing the change in his father, huddled further down. Five kids constantly sick and a wife who had just come through a difficult pregnancy meant that Sofia knew the family well. Unlike his brothers and sisters, though, she had never been able to draw this child out. He clearly had developmental problems, but without tests she had no idea what could be done for the boy. Realising Mirwais was nervous, Sofia tried to reassure him with a smile, but he had eyes only for the tall man walking beside her.

Lifting the child off his lap, Mirwais stood to greet his visitors, but with the boy clinging tightly to his trouser leg he was forced to bend down and pick him up again. After the introductions, Taban nodded for Mirwais to invite them inside.

The house, built by Mirwais when he'd had permanent employment, was one of the sturdier constructions in Jamal Mina. Made with mudbricks, it had a well-fitted front door and two matching windows facing out to the magnificent view and the open sewer that ran close by. On the hard-packed dirt floor inside was a mattress, a pile of old blankets and two cardboard boxes storing cooking utensils and the family's clothes. While Daniel, Sofia and Tawfiq found places on the floor to sit, Taban spoke quietly with Mirwais before she joined them. Putting the child down, Mirwais took the package she had handed him and began walking toward the box of utensils, but the child scooted across the floor on his backside until he had caught up with his father and grabbed hold of his leg again. Mirwais bent down and picked his son up.

Sofia took the opportunity to study the boy. He was five years old, quite small for his age, and still not walking or talking. About eighteen months previously Sofia had asked if she might run some tests, but Mirwais and his wife had refused, which had been confusing for her considering Afghans would normally jump at any opportunity of free health care. Perhaps they didn't trust the hospital, or were frightened of what the results might say? In time she hoped they might change their minds.

With one hand free, Mirwais opened Taban's package. Pulling out a small cellophane packet of pistachios and emptying them into a bowl, he returned to sit cross-legged with his son in his lap again before placing the nuts on the floor between them.

'Mirwais,' Taban began, 'can you please tell Dr Daniel what life's like for you and your family in Jamal Mina?'

As Mirwais began speaking, Taban translated until Daniel interrupted her in Dari to say he understood the language. Sofia could see that Daniel's value had just gone up another notch in Taban's eyes.

Like many of the men who lived here, Mirwais had become a day labourer on construction sites in Kabul until the Western dollars, and the work, started drying up. For over a year now he'd had no work.

'Every morning I look for work but no one's hiring because the Americans are leaving, and now we have no money to buy food. Sometimes my wife and children beg,' he said, the shame thickening his voice. Sofia's heart ached for the father. He was a good man. 'It's better that my children and my wife beg because they get more money. I don't get so much.'

As tears began to well in his eyes Mirwais looked down, pretending to examine the back of his son's shaven head. Sensing his father's distress, the boy curled up into a tighter ball in his lap, burying his face in the rough cotton of the man's *perahan tunban*.

Daniel turned to Taban. 'How many children from Jamal Mina do you think beg on the streets?' Sofia was aware Daniel probably knew the answer to that question but he'd asked it to give Mirwais privacy and time to collect himself.

'There are many. Mothers and children also wash windscreens during traffic jams and unfortunately now some are stealing.'

Mirwais started talking again. 'In our village people helped us, but there's nothing left in our village to go back to.' Mirwais looked down and began picking at the plastic strap of his torn sandal. 'If there's money I buy food. If we have food at night there'll be no food for the morning. In winter I might buy firewood if I have money, but if I do there'll be no food that day. My children are always sick and hungry.' Mirwais looked away from Daniel to Sofia. 'Dr Sofia and Dr Jabril give me medicines for my children. I cannot pay them. It shames me.' Again he looked down at his son's head.

'Mirwais,' Sofia said softly, 'we've spoken of this many times.' She turned to Daniel to explain. 'Dr Jabril and I get the medicines free so there's no need for Mirwais to pay.'

This was not strictly true. Jabril and Sofia had become good at getting money out of Jabril's rich friends to support their work in the slum, using the drug samples they got from their suppliers and reaching into their own pockets. Like Mirwais, Sofia knew she would have been embarrassed to ask for handouts for herself, but she would have got down on her hands and knees – and sometimes nearly did – to get the drugs needed for families like Mirwais's. Sofia had no idea where Taban got her supply from and never asked, but she had noticed that a lot of the medicines were either out of date or close to it. She suspected her source was the black market in Pakistan.

Mirwais looked directly at Daniel. 'This is how it is for us.'

'I see.'

Mirwais looked over at Taban, apologising with his eyes for what he was about to say. Hitching the little boy higher on his lap as he sat up straighter, Mirwais turned back to Daniel. 'I want to work. I don't want people to give me things. I don't want my family to beg. I'm a man. I can work hard. It's not a problem for me because I'm still strong. I need a job. If you could give me a job ...'

Sofia guessed Mirwais had been thinking about what he might say to this man from the UN from the moment Taban had told him he was coming, and for a short time he had probably allowed himself to hope. The words would have cost Mirwais dearly. Sometimes their stories broke her heart and she would be disturbed for days, but whenever that happened she reminded herself that she had a home and a bed and enough food on the table. She wasn't the one suffering. An Afghan friend had pointed out to her once that if she did not appreciate and enjoy what she had then these things were wasted on her. So every night she would give thanks for the roof over her head and the life she had and every month she would return to Jamal Mina and do the best she could. As she waited for Daniel's response, she knew what it had to be. They all knew except Mirwais.

'I can see that you're a man who works hard for his family. If I was here to employ people you would be just the sort of man I would be looking for, but I'm here to see how my organisation might be able to help make life easier for all the people of Jamal Mina.' Daniel waited for the father to respond but his words had dried up along with his hope.

'Your input has been invaluable, Mirwais. Thank you,' Daniel offered lamely.

Sofia could see how it had affected Daniel also, remembering how gentle he had been and how hard he had worked with the villagers in the mountains. She understood what both Mirwais and Daniel were going through – the one who had to beg and the one who had to disappoint – but Daniel had done the right thing. Too many Westerners gave false hope. As hard as it might be, in Sofia's experience, it was usually better to give no hope than false hope.

'It never gets any easier,' Sofia said to Daniel as they left Mirwais's home.

'And nor should it,' he replied.

***

THEY VISITED TWO more homes, each sheltering a family whose story was similar: no work, no money, hungry bellies and constant illness. Underlying each story was a visceral sense of despair.

'In winter your UN has given us plastic sheeting, clothes, blankets and fuel,' Taban said as they left the last home, heading back to the point where she would leave them to walk up to her clinic, 'but there's more needy people than there are blankets to go around. Did you know twenty-eight children died in this neighbourhood from the cold last winter?'

'I did.'

Taban stopped walking and turned to look up at Daniel. 'Either you're lying or you're exceptionally well informed. Somehow, I think it's the latter.' Taban started walking again. 'I know it's not a high percentage of attrition for your organisation but it's twenty-eight tiny souls who should have lived, twenty-eight shattered families.'

'Do you think this man will do anything?' Tawfiq whispered to Sofia as they walked behind Taban and Daniel along the rocky path.

'I hope so.'

'He should see the villages so he can see what it's like in the country, not just here in the city.'

'Somehow I think he already knows what it's like in the country.' Sofia stopped in a little cleared area between a few houses to let Daniel and Taban move ahead. Beside them a plastic pipe was coming out of the wall of a house, emptying into a running drain channelling waste downhill. 'Do you remember when I first came here and you drove me to the village in the foothills of the Hindu Kush so I could go up to the highlands to work?'

'Yes.'

'Well, Dr Daniel was the man I worked with up there. That's where I first met him.'

'Ah,' Tawfiq said. 'He's a good man, I think.'

'I've always thought so.'

'Why can't Afghans have good things like everyone else?' Tawfiq asked as they began walking fast to catch up with Daniel and Taban again.

'I don't know, my friend.'

She had that feeling again that things were not right with Tawfiq and decided that she may as well ask him. 'Is something wrong?'

'No.'

'Are you sure? Because if there's anything I can do, you know you've only got to ask.'

'Thank you, but there's nothing you can do.'

Hearing someone running up behind them, they all turned to see Aisha, the eldest daughter from the family they had just left.

She was a beautiful child with a tangled mass of rich chestnut curls. On her feet she wore an old pair of scuffed sandals Sofia had not seen before. No doubt hand-me-downs from a family who could no longer find any use for them. Over the dirty pair of pink tracksuit pants she always wore she had a brown and pink dress.

'I want to go to school and learn how to read,' she said, as she tried to catch her breath.

Daniel crouched down to Aisha's level. 'Don't you go to school?'

'No,' she said, shaking her head.

'As you saw, Aisha's family don't have the money,' offered Taban in English so Aisha couldn't understand.

'I see.' Daniel looked back at Aisha.

'Please,' she said, putting her hands together in supplication. 'Please.'

'Aisha, I understand your need and I know what I'm about to say won't be enough for you,' Daniel said in Dari, 'but I promise you I will talk with your government about building a school here in Jamal Mina and I *will* make sure they see how important it is.'

'But that will be too late,' she cried. 'I need to learn to read before the Taliban come back.'

Taban spoke in English again. 'She won't be able to go to school even if you succeeded in getting a school built next door to her home because, like all the children born here, the government won't give her an identification card, and without that she can't go to school. In any event, her family can't afford to send her. They need her to beg.'

'What can be done?' Daniel said in English, standing again and looking from Taban to Sofia.

'Your UN could make the government give the children identity cards so they might at least have the opportunity to go to school if they could find the money. Could you do that?'

Aisha had been watching the adults talking, looking from Taban to Daniel with no idea of what they were saying. She looked up at Daniel, her hands together in supplication again. 'Can I go to school?'

'I hate it when they do that. I hate it when they beg. She's learned that on the street,' said Taban in English.

Aisha turned to Taban. 'Taban *jan*, if my government builds the school, will you tell me so I can go?'

Taban looked at Daniel. 'What am I supposed to tell her?'

Daniel and Taban stood looking at each other. He had no answer.

Taban turned to the little girl and spoke in Dari. 'I will tell you, Aisha. I promise.'

As Aisha ran off, Taban turned back to Daniel. 'We need medical assistance, access to good food and clean water, identity cards for these children, health awareness, better midwifery, infant care, sewerage, streets and streetlights and police – there's a lot of crime here at night. You name it, Dr Abiteboul, we need it, and the kids need to be able to afford to go to school.'

'I understand.'

'Do you?' Taban stopped. They had reached the point where she was to leave them. Taban was looking up at him again. 'Do you really? I'm not meaning to be rude, because I think you're sincere, but isn't this just another desperate place competing for the UN's resources? Can you see us as any different, or any more needy, or worthy? Did Mirwais's plight move you? Did any of them move you? Do we matter to you? Because that's what I'm trying to do here – I'm trying to make these people matter to you more than the next terrible place you go to and the next terrible stories you hear.'

'I'm looking to help people or organisations like yours that are already on the ground, who know what the priorities are and how to move through the regulations, and who can absorb and respond to what we can give them quickly and efficiently.'

'My clinic's too small for your important organisation to fund.'

'Not necessarily.'

Taban laughed. 'That's what they all say, but we continue to wait.' She held out her hand for Daniel to shake. 'You've been a witness to our suffering in a small way, Dr Daniel. Please don't let that be all you do. Just pick one thing – one thing you think you might be able to help us with and that would be enough.'

As they were about to part, Sofia asked Tawfiq and Daniel to head back down to the car and she'd catch up with them. 'Any news about Rayi and if there are any other boys?' Sofia asked as Daniel and Tawfiq walked away.

'No, but I'm thinking we can't wait for the police anymore. We have to try to find them ourselves before more boys are taken.'

'Where do we start?'

'God knows,' Taban said, looking around her as if to say you could start anywhere.

'I believe Jabril's spoken to Chief Wasim, or was going to, but I'll talk to him also. To change the subject, do you happen to know an African woman called Clementine who works for MSF?'

'Sure.'

'What can you tell me about her?'

'In what sense?' asked Taban.

'She says she's interested in organising the MSF facility in Kandahar to take over the training of the midwives.'

'If that's what she says, believe her. She's a dragon lady, but she gets things done.'

***

'I KNOW IT's short notice,' Daniel said as they neared the UN compound where they were to drop him off, 'but I was wondering if you're free tonight for dinner?'

'Oh,' Sofia said, pulling a face as she turned in her seat to look at him. 'I really would have loved that but I've got a fundraiser tonight for a new orphanage.'

'Well, maybe another time.'

'It happens to be at your hotel,' she offered, thinking of suggesting they have a drink together before or after the function.

'Do you think if I throw my weight around they might let me in?'

Sofia shook her head as if disappointed by his suggestion. 'I don't think so, Daniel, but maybe if I throw *my* weight around you might have a chance.' She couldn't help laughing at the surprise on his face. 'My boss happens to be on the committee for the orphanage,' she added.

'Please, by all means, use your influence on my behalf, and maybe we can have a drink afterward?'

After dropping Daniel off, Sofia was sitting in the back of the car smiling to herself when she remembered Tawfiq and looked up to see him watching her in the rear-vision mirror. 'We're just friends.'

'I didn't say anything.'

Sofia could see the smile in Tawfiq's eyes.

21

'I'LL NEVER GET used to it,' Tawfiq said as they drove into the square.

Sofia knew what he was talking about. 'I quite like it,' she offered, looking at Behnaz's turquoise gate.

Three months previously Sofia had returned from her annual holiday in Sydney to find Behnaz's old brown gate painted vivid turquoise. When she complimented Behnaz on the gate's makeover the only response she got was a 'humph'. When she queried Behnaz about the colour choice she got the silent treatment. It was left to Iman to fill Sofia in on the scandal of Behnaz's turquoise gate.

Behnaz's nephew, who had been staying with his aunt while Sofia was away, had been put to work painting the gate. Being an enterprising fellow, and careful with his afghani, the nephew secured a half-used can of turquoise paint from a friend for half a packet of cigarettes. While most people, including Ahmad, Hadi and Tawfiq, didn't like the turquoise gate, Iman said the reaction of Ahmad's wife, Badria, had been particularly harsh, although she suspected that the 'miserable' Badria had not only been offended by the vibrancy and beauty of that particular shade of turquoise but had felt betrayed by Behnaz, who she consider to be a kindred dour spirit. Iqbal found the whole thing an amusing diversion in the square, Rashid had no opinion, and Jabril and Zahra, whose home had mauve trimmings, quite liked it, but Iman positively loved it.

For once someone was 'thinking outside the box', she claimed, ignoring the fact that the paint was turquoise because Behnaz and her nephew were stingy with their afghani. So inspired was Iman by the gate that she told everyone about a village in Indonesia where they had painted their homes rainbow colours to attract the tourist dollar. Wouldn't it be a good idea if everyone in Shaahir Square did the same thing? When Iman pulled up photos on her phone she had to concede that the Indonesian village might have gone a little overboard with their cans of paint. Shaahir Square didn't need to be so radical – at least until everyone got used to the idea, Iman had argued. She suggested everyone painted only their door or gate a rainbow colour to begin with. 'Imagine,' she said, 'if Shaahir Square became famous and tourists flocked here from all over the world?'

There were those who weren't so sure this argument furthered Iman's plan for her 'Rainbow Shaahir Square', although it did have its devotees. Omar had shown some enthusiasm by offering to paint his shop door purple if someone else would paint theirs orange first. Unsurprising, Ahmad, who initially hadn't liked the turquoise gate, quite liked the idea of hordes of tourists flocking to the square and began toying with the idea of painting his shutter red, until he made the mistake of telling Badria. According to Hadi, who had eavesdropped on the entire conversation, Ahmad had quickly folded and his idea of a red shutter was brought to its inevitable end. After some consideration, Babur became a convert. Surely if tourists flocked to the square his famous *chaikhana* would become even more famous? Within a couple of weeks, however, Iman's 'Rainbow Shaahir Square' campaign had gone the way of Ahmad's red shutter and Omar's purple door, although Behnaz's turquoise gate remained turquoise.

During all this Behnaz had remained silent, although secretly pleased with the drama she had caused. Not only did she love the colour (which in her mind had become her idea) but she loved the controversy *and* the fact that she had got all of that for nothing.

As Tawfiq pulled up in the car in front of the turquoise gate, Rashid was squatting, talking with Behnaz who, with full shopping bags in both hands, appeared to have just arrived home.

'Is this a meeting we're not invited to?' Sofia asked with a cheeky smile.

'No,' they answered in unison, finding the question strange. With her Aussie humour being lost on its intended victims, Sofia was about to head to her surgery when she saw Chief Wasim enter the square, heading home for lunch. Seeing her husband, Behnaz quickly disappeared into the house to prepare the lunch that should have already been waiting. With Chief Wasim sailing past as he acknowledged Sofia, Rashid and Tawfiq, Sofia quickly followed him through the gate before closing it behind her so Rashid and Tawfiq might not hear what she had to say.

'Chief Wasim, can I have a word, please?'

Unaware that she had followed him, Wasim stopped mid-stride and turned to look at Sofia. 'Of course. What is it I can do for you?'

'Do you know about Farahnaz's little brother?'

He raised his thick black eyebrows questioningly. 'No. What about Farahnaz's little brother?'

'Rayi's gone missing.'

'I'm sorry to hear this,' he said, as if he said these words a thousand times a day.

'It's possible he's been kidnapped.'

Wasim frowned. 'Who's saying this?'

'No one, but we think he might have been.'

'Who's we?'

'Dr Jabril and Taban … and me.'

'What evidence do you have for this claim?' he said rather stiffly.

Sofia was confused by the chief's antagonism. 'It's not a claim, more a fear, and we have no evidence yet. What are the police doing? I mean, what do you do in these situations?'

Wasim offered Sofia an empty smile before walking over to the canary cage hanging off the lowest branch of the pomegranate tree. Sticking his little finger through the bars, he made cooing noises to the surprised canary. As the canary began backing away from the intruding finger, the chief lost all interest.

'I never liked that bird much,' he said, turning back to Sofia. 'Now, what were you saying? Ah, yes. To be truthful, Dr Sofia, there's not much we can do. Sadly, little boys go missing in Afghanistan every day and we rarely find them.'

'But this is the fourth boy to go missing from Jamal Mina. Two went a couple of months ago and now another two have gone in the last week. For all we know there might be more. Someone has to be taking them.'

171

'Are you sure about this?'

'Well, not about someone taking them, but four boys have disappeared in a short space of time. Don't you remember Dr Jabril told you about the first two?'

'Ah, yes,' he said, as if he had forgotten. 'And now another two are missing, you say?'

'Yes, maybe more.' Sofia had the feeling the chief was more interested in getting to his lunch than getting to the bottom of the missing boys. She felt the desperation rising. She couldn't let him disappear into the house before she got some sort of commitment. 'What do you think is happening to them?'

'Was each incident reported to the police?'

'I don't know, but I'm sure Taban would have, or their parents. Perhaps you can make enquiries and see what's happening?'

'I'll look into it,' he said, turning away.

'Taban knows everything about the boys,' she said. She was losing him. 'You could start by talking with her.'

The chief turned back to Sofia and gave her a smile that came nowhere near his eyes. 'Leave it to me, Dr Sofia. As I said, I'll look into it.' He turned away again and she grabbed his arm, immediately letting it go in horror at what she had done.

'You'll let me know what you discover?' she pleaded, knowing she had tried his patience for far too long.

'I will, but you must remember,' the chief said, pointing his finger at her, 'if these little boys want to run away, there'll not be much chance of finding them.'

'Four? Four boys from the same neighbourhood in two months? Four boys with desperate parents? Don't you think there's something wrong?'

The chief sighed. 'As I said, I'll see what I can do, but if you will excuse me now, Dr Sofia, I must have my lunch and return to work.'

Sofia watched him disappear into the house before returning to Rashid and Tawfiq squatting outside the gate, talking. 'It's lunchtime,' she said. 'Aren't you two interested in eating?'

'We're waiting for you,' Tawfiq said. 'Do you need me this afternoon?'

'No, and it looks like I mightn't need you tomorrow because I'll probably be going to Kandahar with MSF, so both of you can have the weekend off.' The bonus of going with MSF was that the organisation seemed to be off limits for attacks from insurgency groups.

Tawfiq slid up the wall until he was standing. 'We will take you like we always do.'

'Wouldn't you rather take the car and visit your family?'

'Of course, but I have a job. Rashid and I will do this.'

Sofia put her hands on her hips, looking from one man to the other as Rashid flicked the butt of his cigarette into the square before standing also. 'What's really going on here?'

'I think Dr Jabril will want us to do our job.'

Sofia shook her head. 'This is the new security thing, isn't it?' Neither man spoke. 'Okay, I'll speak with Dr Jabril, but right now I'm going to the surgery. Rashid, do you need to walk me across the square?'

'I do, Dr Sofia.' As they walked off, Tawfiq headed over to Babur's for lunch.

'How are you today?' she asked Iqbal when they reached the stairs.

'Better than most days.'

She stopped. 'And why is that?'

173

'I think we have a little intrigue here in the square.'

'Ah,' Sofia said, crouching down in front of him. 'And what intrigue would that be, my friend?'

'I can't tell you, can I, if you might have a part in it?'

She raised her eyebrows. 'Have I got a part in it?'

'I don't know yet, do I?'

Deciding it had to be about Daniel, Sofia stood up again. 'I'm pretty sure I'm not involved in any intrigue, Iqbal. I'm thinking there are too many vivid imaginations in the square.'

'What else do we have to do?' she heard him say as she disappeared up the stairs.

22

SOFIA ENTERED HER surgery to see that Iman had moved the two patients' chairs to the window where she was waiting to have lunch with her boss. Smelling the food Babur had prepared for them, Sofia realised she was famished.

'You know what I imagine when I walk down the street?' Iman said, after taking a mouthful of her tangy braised *sabzi* with Afghan *challaw* rice.

'I cannot even begin to think.' Sofia knew from past experience that when Iman had that dreamy look on her face, whatever she was about to say would be highly entertaining and probably outrageous by Afghan standards.

'I imagine I'm wearing a pair of sparkly gold sandals and a beautiful, short rainbow-coloured dress that fits tight around my body.'

'Good for you. I see the rainbow theme's still alive and well then?' Babur's kebabs drenched in yoghurt were delicious, as always.

'Ah! We're too dreary here. I need colour in my life.' Iman ate some more food before continuing. 'I can see this dress swinging from my hips as I walk.' She considered this image to find it wanting. 'No, I don't walk, I flaunt.' Iman tilted her chin up in imaginary defiance. 'I flaunt that I'm a woman and that I'm powerful and proud of it, and those pious young men with their stupid scratchy beards and ignorant old men who are frightened of women will all blow a fuse when they see me walking down the street in my rainbow dress and gold sandals with attitude.'

Sofia laughed as she speared a piece of okra. 'I can see it now, Iman. They're definitely blowing their fuses.'

Iman became serious. 'I'm a good Muslim and I know what's in the Qur'an. I don't need those ignorant mullahs to tell me what I can and can't do, and if I want to wear a short rainbow dress I can. I'm not ashamed of being a woman.'

'And neither should you be. Do you happen to own a short rainbow dress, by any chance?'

Iman laughed. 'Where would I buy something like that in Kabul? When I go to America I'll buy my short rainbow dress.'

'Ah, you're going to America?'

'One day.'

'And will you wear your short rainbow dress with your gold shoes in the street when you come home?'

'Probably not.' Iman gave Sofia a rueful smile. 'I'm not that crazy, but in America I will and maybe one day I can here too. Did you know that before the civil war women used to wear dresses and shorts like women everywhere?'

'I did. Dr Jabril's told me many times about Kabul back then and I've seen photos of Zahra outside the Darul Aman Palace wearing a short skirt.'

'I wish it was like that now. Oh, why was I born too late? Zahra's still beautiful, isn't she? My mother says Behnaz was beautiful once too when she was young.'

'She was,' Sofia said, remembering the photo she'd seen of her and Chief Wasim on their wedding day.'

Iman grimaced. 'Really? I'm sorry but I'm finding that too hard to imagine. I've heard my mother's friends talking about Behnaz. They say there was some sort of scandal.' Iman pouted. 'She won't tell me what it was. Do you know?'

'No, I've never heard that before.'

The two women ate in silence for a while. 'Are you frightened of growing old and being ugly, Dr Sofia?'

Sofia stopped eating and looked at Iman. She wondered how best to respond until she thought of the poem she loved.

'How many years of beauty do I have left? she asks me.

'How many more do you want?

'Here. Here is thirty-four.

'Here is fifty.'

'Why do you quote me a poem?'

'Because it says things better than I can.'

'Mmmm,' Iman said, twisting her mouth into a moue as she considered this. 'So are you?'

Sofia began packing up the leftovers of the lunch, taking Iman's empty food container and packing it into hers. How did she answer this?

'My mother never got the chance to grow old, but I'm sure she would've given anything in the world to. I don't think she would have given a damn about losing her beauty. In fact, I suspect she would have traded it in a millisecond just to have the opportunity to watch her children grow up and to grow old with the man she loved.'

'That's sad.'

'It is. It's always sad when someone dies young, but I think

people should stop worrying about growing old and realise
how privileged they are just to be able to do that. Besides, I
don't think you necessarily lose your beauty when you grow
old. All the lines on our faces are a testament of our life with
all its inherent joys and heartache. I like the idea that in the last
years of my life, if I'm lucky enough to grow old, my face will
bear testament to my life, hopefully a life well lived. I'm going
to celebrate getting old. It's a privilege.'

'I never thought about it like that,' Iman said, sitting back in
her chair as she considered the idea. 'On another note, have you
seen Uzma around lately?'

It was only when Iman asked the question that she realised
she hadn't. Uzma had been married to a man who beat her.
In the sanctuary of Sofia's surgery, Uzma would cry about the
horror of her marriage and the shame that forced her to stay.

'Why is the shame on the woman?' Sofia had asked Zahra
the first time she had seen abuse in her surgery.

'The reputation of the family rests on the woman. If
the abuse remains hidden then she doesn't bring shame to the
family, but if she leaves her husband then there is shame.'

Every time Uzma arrived in her surgery Sofia would steel
herself against what she might find beneath the burqa. Believing
that one day the man would kill Uzma she had encouraged her
to go to one of the women's shelters in Kabul, but she had
refused. Not only was there the shame but also three of her
children were over seven years old, and under Afghan law she
would lose custody to the father.

On one occasion Uzma's injuries had been so horrifying that
Sofia had taken her to hospital where an organisation helping
abused women had convinced Uzma to lay charges. While the

husband was serving his short jail sentence his parents had taken over the abuse of their daughter-in-law, whose 'lies' had sent their 'innocent' son to jail and brought shame on the family. When Uzma's husband died a short time later of a stroke, Sofia had felt both relief and increased anxiety. The future for an uneducated, unskilled widow with no support other than in-laws who abused her, no prospect of work and no government handouts was bleak.

'No, now that you mention it. I haven't seen her. What's happened?'

'I heard the old woman kicked her out.'

'And her children?'

'The old woman kept them. See? That's what I mean about women not supporting women.'

Sofia was more interested in what had happened to Uzma. 'Do you have any idea where she is?'

'Begging on the streets?' Iman raised her arms in the air and stretched. 'What else could she do?'

'Oh, Iman, you sound so cold.'

'I'm not cold. I'm angry,' she said, jabbing her finger on the arm of the chair. 'Things should not be like this.'

'I know.'

'How do I change this?'

'Slowly.'

Iman stood up and held out her hand for the empty lunch boxes. 'Do you want to give me those?' With Iman taking the containers, Sofia began returning the patients' chairs to their place in front of her desk until she realised Iman was standing in the doorway. 'Something weird happened yesterday. When Hadi weighed the chickpeas for my mother he gave her an extra scoop. Have you ever heard of Hadi giving anyone extra?'

179

Sofia didn't need to think about that. 'It's a bit strange, I agree.'

'Do you think something's wrong with him, like he's dying maybe?'

Sofia frowned. 'Why would you say that?'

'Well, people do things like that when they're dying, don't they? They want to set things straight in this life before Jannah.'

Sofia walked around to her chair. 'Maybe it's as simple as he doesn't want to cheat his friends anymore.'

'Are you kidding me?' Imam said, one hand on her hip while the other held the empty lunch containers. 'Are we even talking about the same man?'

'Maybe he was just being kind to your mother.'

'No, he did the same thing for miserable old Badria.'

Sofia thought about this. 'I'm going there this afternoon. I'll be interested to see if he's still feeling so generous with me.'

'Anyway, I've decided to take your advice and my mother is going to introduce me someone from the Afghan Women's Network.'

This is progress, Sofia thought.

After leaving the surgery that afternoon, she and Rashid made their way past Ahmad's shop to Hadi's. He'd recently added a second-hand glass serving counter, but because the shop was too small for the counter it had been pushed up against the back wall so its stock of Coffee Mate, plastic bottles of bleach and various washing detergents could only be reached by moving it away from the wall, after moving the boxes of water and fizzy sweet drinks stacked in front of it. On top of the glass counter sat layers of corrugated cardboard separating dozens of eggs alongside stale cakes wrapped in clear cellophane. The shelves lining the three walls of the shop were bulging with bottles of shampoo, bars of soap, tins of biscuits, light bulbs, brightly coloured boxes of tea from Pakistan, sweet breakfast cereal and cheap vegetable oils, alongside cans of tomatoes and jars of olives. The legumes and pulses, plus various spices, were stacked out the front of the shop in tins or large hessian sacks. More plastic-wrapped bottles of water and fizzy drinks sat in front of the dried goods.

'I'm giving you a little extra,' Hadi said to Sofia as he weighed her lentils.

'That's very generous of you.'

'I would never steal from my friends. You know that, don't you, Dr Sofia?' It was a tough question considering he did steal from his friends.

'You have no idea what Hadi just did,' she said with some amusement to Rashid as they headed off across the square with her bag of lentils.

'He gave you extra?'

Sofia stopped and looked at him. 'How did you know?'

'He's giving everyone extra today.'

'I wonder why.'

'He's frightened.'

'Of what?'

Rashid, the man of few words and no gossip, shrugged.

Back in her apartment, Sofia sat with her cup of tea by the window, watching Hadi and Ahmad packing up for the day. Hadi is frightened and overly generous, she thought, Jabril has upped my security, Tawfiq is worried about something and Iqbal thinks I'm in some sort of mystery that's going on in the square, although it might only be about Daniel. She tried to figure out how all these things might be connected and decided they weren't. There was always some sort of intrigue in the square. Sooner or later she would find out what all the fuss was about.

After finishing her tea Sofia phoned Fatima to tell her about the female doctor from MSF who was interested in meeting the midwives, without saying specifically why, and the male doctor with the UN who was interest in speaking with her about women's needs in Kandahar. With Fatima approving both meetings Sofia phoned Jabril about the fundraiser before texting Daniel to say his name had been added to the invitee list, and if he was still free she'd love to have that drink afterward. She added that she'd be happy to go with him and Clementine to Kandahar on Friday, and while he wouldn't be able to speak with the midwives, Fatima would be happy to answer all his questions. She got a text back almost immediately thanking her for all her efforts and confirming he'd love to catch up for that drink.

After showering, Sofia opened her wardrobe door and stood staring in at the meagre pickings. What to wear to impress? So much for the idea of not seeing him again, she thought, as she pulled out a blue and silver salwar kameez.

23

A PHONE CALL from Clem that afternoon had Daniel agreeing to meet her forty-five minutes before the fundraiser began. With the Serena not having a bar, or serving alcohol, they had agreed to meet in the patisserie on the ground floor of the hotel. The only available table was a small round one by the entry with only one chair. After scavenging a spare from a nearby table, Daniel ordered coffees for both of them and sat down to wait.

He cared deeply about Clem and always would, but for a hundred different reasons it was a difficult relationship built on a shared history and a tragedy, complicated by the fact that they were friends who had become lovers and were trying to be friends again. When Clem had lectured Daniel that morning at breakfast about how much time he spent working, he hadn't reacted. The topic of his work-life balance had been a constant theme of Clem's since Amahoro's death, after which he'd found work a distraction and a salvation and found no good reason to change that. It was a conversation he would not have accepted from anyone else.

From the beginning of each new relationship, including the disastrous one with Clem, Daniel had taken pains to explain he was not long-term relationship material. While some women had been relieved – for neither were they – there were others who thought love would change him, it never occurring to them that he might not want to change, or that he might never love them. Friendship, affection, tenderness, sex, loyalty – he had willingly given all these things, but for some it wasn't enough. He understood that and when relationships ended he accepted the acrimony, although he was never completely sure it was all rightfully his. He had never lied to anyone, including Clem, and he had never promised forever – that also included Clem. After Amahoro and Alice it didn't feel like he had any more he wanted to give.

He had fallen for Amahoro the first time he had seen her in the refugee camp in Uganda. She had been wearing the traditional African dress with a vibrant piece of material tied high around her head as she sat on an upturned crate reading to a group of little children. What first struck him about Amahoro was the way she held herself – her head high and her back straight – and how she spoke, her words soft and lyrical as the wind through the trees. Leaving early for work the following day he had hoped to see her again but she wasn't there. She hadn't been there the next day or the one after that or the one after that. When Daniel asked he discovered the Rwandan woman only read to the children on Tuesdays.

'I saw you watching me last week and now you're here again,' she had said when he approached her as she was packing up her books on that second Tuesday. 'What are you doing?'

'I was wondering if you'd like to have a coffee with me?'

She stopped and looked up at him, the books now piled high in her arms. 'No,' she said, before walking away.

'Why not?' he had asked, following her, desperate that these would not be the last words between them.

'Because you've been asking people about me.'

'Aren't I allowed to ask about you?' He had no idea how to salvage his approach.

'No.'

With the books tucked safely under her arm, he watched her walk off. On his way to work the following Monday, he had found her waiting for him near the place where she read.

'I will meet you at the kiosk this afternoon, Daniel Abiteboul,' she offered, without a smile.

As she walked off, he had called after her. 'How do you know my name?'

'I asked around about you. You'd better be as nice as they say,' she called back, without turning around.

A childcare worker with a local Ugandan agency, Amahoro had left her native Rwanda three years before to work in the camp, the same camp she had been born in. When the genocide ended, her parents, like many Rwandan Tutsi, made the trek back across the border to their villages, only to find they were expected to live alongside those who had forced them out of their homes after killing their friends and family. While her ageing parents and the rest of her siblings accepted the situation, Amahoro found she could not. She had no time for the Rwandan version of 'reconciliation' forced on the population by the government simply because the jails were too full and so she had returned to the only place she knew: the camp.

'What does it mean to love?' Amahoro had asked him as they lay together in his bed many months later, the casual manner of the question belying its seriousness. 'It means to hurt,' she said before he had time to answer. 'You'll hurt me in the end, Daniel Abiteboul.'

'Never,' he had said, pulling her close as he looked into a future he could not even begin to imagine.

And then there had been Alice. The first time he had seen her she had been standing in an MSF clinic in northern Afghanistan, arms akimbo, confronting a man who had just brought his battered and bruised wife in because she had 'fallen over'.

'And you'll sell me a block of flats in Tasmania, right?' she had said in English to the confused husband.

Stepping in, Daniel had assured the man that his wife would be well cared for before politely asking if he would mind taking a seat while the nurse had a look at her. At the end of a long working day Alice had approached Daniel to apologise for her behaviour. Over a drink that evening she explained that she had been working in Iraq for the previous three years and was new to Afghanistan.

'I probably shouldn't have come here,' she had said. 'I probably should have called it quits and gone back to nursing geriatrics in Coonabarabran after Iraq.'

While Amahoro had been tall, elegant, seductive and quietly spoken with a will of steel, Alice was her antithesis, although she too had a will of steel. Short and wiry with curly blond hair, Alice was loud and irreverent, partied until dawn and was a fitness freak. The latter addiction was a means of negating the former, she would often tell him with a smile.

From an Australian country town, Alice knew how to ride a horse, drive a tractor and 'change a wheel with my eyes closed'. 'I

can also probably drink you under the table, Daniel Abiteboul,'
she had said the second time they had a drink together.

'Is that a challenge?' he asked.

'You betcha!'

In every way she was larger than life, but most of all, she was
fun. She had made him laugh at a time when it was what he
needed the most.

'I didn't join MSF to save the frigging the world, you know,'
she said to him late one night. It didn't take Daniel long to
understand that most of her bluster was a façade that had been
developed to protect a sensitive young country girl from the
teasing banter of four older brothers and the offhand cruelty of
adolescent boys in a small town. If anything, Alice was probably
too kind and too sensitive for the work she did.

There had never been mention of marriage or family, but
they had begun to talk in the long term until the day she was
gone. As head of the MSF mission in Afghanistan, Daniel
oversaw the repatriation of five of his colleagues' bodies home
to their loved ones, and one of those had been Alice's. He had
returned Alice to Coonabarabran in a box.

It was shortly after her death that he had travelled to the
village high in the Hindu Kush. At the time Clem had accused
him of running away from his pain. She had no idea what
she was talking about. You never ran away from that sort of
pain, it was seared into your DNA. Clem urged him to accept
the counselling offered by MSF. He refused. He didn't need
counselling. He needed time and he needed distance.

And then there had been Sofia.

The first time he saw Sofia he had returned from a day in the
village further down the mountain. As he climbed up over the

ridge he had stopped to catch his breath and saw her standing outside the storage hut staring up at the mountains, entranced. At first he thought she was one of the young village women until he saw the long strands of red hair escaping from under the scarf. The attraction had been as immediate as it had been unwelcome. There was never any doubt in his mind that going to Sofia's hut so soon after Alice's death had been a betrayal of Alice and he had not been proud of it. Yet the vivid memories of his lover in the village in the Hindu Kush had never left him. In the years that passed he had wondered whether he would ever see her again, but if he did he wanted to explain and apologise for his behaviour. When the job with the UN had come up he began making enquiries among his contacts in Afghanistan about whom he should speak with. It had been Clem who had mentioned the Australian doctor training midwives in the villages. Emailing Clem, he asked if she knew this doctor's name. When she said she didn't he had hesitated, not wanting to pique Clementine's interest, but a week later he emailed her again, asking if she could find out the doctor's name or whether she had red hair.

Clem had replied a couple of days later: *Sofia Raso. No idea about hair!?! What gives?*

The only thing he remembered about her surname was that it was Italian and short. He began to suspect he'd found her again. A few days later he had received another email from Clem.

Your friend is turning out to be quite an interesting character. Not only does she train midwives but she also works as a general practitioner in Shaahir Square in Kabul near the old city and volunteers in the slums with a woman I know. She also has red hair. You owe me a story, Abiteboul.

188

That afternoon Daniel had sent an official email to the practice of Dr Sofia Raso of Shaahir Square, outlining his mandate and requesting an interview. He didn't mention that they had met, not because she might not remember him, as he'd told her, but because she *would* remember him and refuse to see him before he had a chance to apologise and explain why he'd left without a word. A few days later he had received a short email from Dr Raso agreeing to a half-hour meeting in her office. It was all he needed. He would explain, apologise and put his guilt to rest once and for all, but then he had seen her again and the attraction had been as strong and as immediate as it had been the first time and he'd said nothing, but tonight he would. He would also give her the letter, the one he'd been carrying around for the past five years.

'Penny for your thoughts,' Clem said, kissing him on the cheek before flopping down in the chair opposite. Dressed in dungarees and an overly large shirt and jacket, she pulled the scarf off her hair, setting the tight curls free before stuffing the scarf in her handbag.

'Hello, Clem, how are you?' he said formally at her lack of greeting.

'Very well, Daniel,' she said formally back. 'You looked very pensive when I walked in. Where were you?'

He held up his coffee cup. 'I was thinking how I wished this place wasn't dry.'

A couple with two small children wandered in. When one of the kids bumped Clem's chair, she turned to give him a filthy look, but by then he was too busy putting sticky fingers all over the glass cabinet holding the sweets selection.

'God, who'd want them,' she said. Although her face had

189

been side-on to Daniel, he saw her wince. He wished she could get over what had happened and move on. There was nothing either of them could do to change the past.

'Well,' she said, turning back to him with a smile, 'you chose a coffee shop in the Serena to meet. What did you imagine? However,' she said, holding up a finger, the silver bracelets falling down her wrists with a familiar clatter, 'all is not lost. I've got a somewhat depleted supply of hooch back at my place.' Clem shared a flat with two other aid workers close to the MSF office in Kabul. Their place regularly became a party house. He watched her screw up her face in pain. 'Actually, I probably enjoyed a little too much of it last night so there mightn't be much left. Anyway, you know where to come if you're really in need,' she offered when Daniel didn't take her up on it.

Putting a couple of teaspoons of sugar in the coffee he'd ordered for her, she took a sip before pulling a face and putting it back down on the table. 'It's cold.'

'Perhaps if you broke the lifetime habit of arriving late it might still be hot.'

Ignoring him, she turned to catch the eye of the man behind the counter, pointing at her coffee. 'So,' she said, turning back to Daniel and pushing the cup further away, 'I can appreciate your interest in Dr Raso.'

'Who said I was interested?'

'Now you've found her again, what're you going to do about it?'

'Come on, Clem, it wasn't as if I'd lost her and spent the last five years looking for her in some lover's haze. I met her once. We spent a short time together working in a village. That's all. I thought it would be nice to see her again.'

'Nice,' Clem said, raising her eyebrows as if he had used a very strange word.

'We can go to Kandahar to see the midwives if you still want,' he said, changing the subject.

* * *

FIFTEEN MINUTES AFTER the fundraiser had begun Daniel was standing in front of the Serena with Clem, waiting for her car to arrive. With a stream of people still arriving for the function, they moved off to the side of the entrance. As Daniel stood talking with Clem he saw Sofia stepping out of an SUV with a tall, elegant woman dressed in black and a short, older man, who he guessed was her boss. Until that moment he had only ever seen Sofia in shapeless dark clothes, but tonight she was wearing a peacock blue and silver salwar kameez with a matching scarf draped lightly over the back of her head, the long earrings under the sheer material of the scarf catching the fire of the setting sun. She was breathtaking.

'You're seeing her tonight, aren't you?' said Clem, who had her back to the arriving guests.

'Why would you say that?'

'Because you've only just arrived in Kabul and you can't get rid of me fast enough and it doesn't take a genius to guess why. And besides,' she said, turning to look behind her, 'you're not quite with me. Ah,' she said when she saw Sofia, 'I rest my case. Yes,' she said, nodding, 'I can certainly see the attraction.'

They didn't speak again until Clem's car arrived. 'I think she might be good for you,' she said as he opened the door for her.

Daniel shook his head. 'All in your imagination. There's nothing there.'

191

24

SOFIA HAD BEEN more than happy with her choice of outfit
and her long crystal earrings, but as soon as she saw Zahra's
understated elegance she knew it had been a mistake. No one
would say Zahra was a classic beauty, but she was striking
and always immaculately dressed, carrying off her height and
style with aplomb. That evening she was wearing a long black
silk dress that trailed along the ground behind her. The only
adornments on her body were the crystals embroidered on the
hem of the dress and along its sleeves. With a sheer black scarf
barely covering her hair, lashings of kohl to darken her eyes and
ruby red lips, she was turning heads as soon as she stepped out
of the car at the Serena. While Zahra acted as if she was blind
to all this attention, Sofia knew she was always acutely aware of
the impression she made.

'I've been meaning to ask you what all this new security is
about,' Sofia said to Jabril as he directed her and Zahra through
the Serena's front doors toward the Chaman-e-Serena, the
walled garden where the function was being held.

A beautiful formal outdoor space surrounded by a high
concrete wall separating it from the dust and the rubble of

the city, the Chaman-e-Serena was often used for outdoor dining, but on that evening the tables had been cleared away and replaced by rows of seats facing a newly erected stage. The fundraiser was to be a cocktail party – without the alcohol – and would end with speeches encouraging the wealthy and influential of Kabul to put their hands into their deep pockets for the children in the orphanage.

'Why is Rashid walking me across the square again?'

'Oh, that. We're paying him so I think we should use him, don't you?' he said, making light of her concerns.

As they were swallowed up in the crowd waiting outside the doors to the garden, Sofia's phone pinged with an incoming message. After reading it she leaned in and spoke softly to Jabril. 'Taban says there's a possibility there might be more children missing. A few of the older kids said there's been a strange man hanging around the pump house at the bottom of the hill giving the little kids sweets. What do you think we should do?'

'*We* should do nothing, but I'm definitely going to be speaking with Minister Massoud again tonight.'

'Ha,' Zahra said in disgust, 'you think our good warlord turned respectable Minister of Narcotics is going help you find the missing boys? Excuse me if I'm somewhat sceptical. He can't even help you with your campaign against *bacha bazi*.'

'He's no longer Minister of *Counter* Narcotics, my dear.'

'Good, someone realised their error.'

'Zahra,' Jabril whispered, 'please be careful what you say in public.'

She took no notice of him. 'So what ministry does he control now?'

'Justice.'

'Justice. Ha!' she said, throwing back her head. 'That's a laugh. From narcotics to justice. Sounds like they've let the fox into the henhouse.'

Jabril leaned in again, 'Zahra, please keep your voice down.' As they inched forward toward the security screening and invitation check, Jabril greeted acquaintances in the line before leaning towards Zahra again. 'Have you ever met him, my dear?'

'A number of times. His wife's in my Women's Initiative Group.'

As Zahra and Jabril discussed Massoud, Sofia strained to see Daniel in the crowd.

'Well, I think we're a country that must forgive past mistakes or we would have to make enemies of everyone. If you must know, I've already had a number of conversations with Minister Massoud about the missing boys and he's taken my concerns very seriously. I also think he's becoming more sympathetic to my plans to raise awareness of *bacha bazi* and now he's on the committee for the orphanage with me, I think our chances of having something done are improving. I'm sure he'll help.'

'Help?' Zahra said as they reached the security screening. Opening her handbag for inspection and then having the security wand run over her by a female attendant, they inched forward again. 'Help himself to what, I'm wondering. You should work out what the warlord thinks he'll get out of supporting your campaign and being on the committee of an orphanage with vulnerable young children.' With Jabril showing their invitations and having their names marked off the list, they moved into the gardens.

'What are you insinuating?'

'Nothing. I'm insinuating absolutely nothing.'

Massoud was a controversial figure whose appointment to the cabinet some years earlier had been strongly opposed. Like Zahra, Sofia didn't have a particularly good impression of the man, but unlike Zahra, she'd never met him.

'I haven't been able to talk with Chief Wasim yet,' Jabril said to Sofia.

Sofia, who had been looking for Daniel again, turned back to him. 'I did actually. He said little boys go missing in Afghanistan all the time and that there wasn't much chance of finding them, but he's going to look into it. I've got the feeling he's not much interested.'

'I think perhaps you should not bother Chief Wasim. Let me talk with him, my dear.'

'It's no problem.'

'No, I'll do it. Now, Zahra,' he said, sounding brighter as they descended the steps onto the paved central courtyard of the garden where the crowds were milling in their finery, 'can we please debate the merits, or otherwise, of Minister Massoud another time?'

Zahra shrugged as if it the subject was of no interest to her. 'I'm not debating anything.' She smiled sweetly as she waved to another friend. 'Nothing to debate.'

As Sofia took her scarf off to drape around her shoulders and heard Jabril's sigh, she began looking for Daniel again. Like Jabril, she knew there was no use arguing with Zahra once she'd made up her mind about someone or something.

As people continued to enter the garden from behind them, they were pushed forward along the central tiled courtyard lined by blooming Afghan roses and ending in a fountain. With dusk beginning to fall, the lights along the path and the fountain had come on, bathing the garden and its well-jewelled patrons in a warm glow.

Finding himself momentarily free of the demands of greeting friends and acquaintances, Jabril wandered off in search of Minister Massoud. Standing on tiptoe, Sofia used her height to look out over the crowd that was now spilling out from the central courtyard onto the grass and paved areas beyond the rows of pines. She began to think he wasn't coming.

'Seen him yet?' Zahra asked, also taking her scarf off to drape across one shoulder.

'No.' Sofia relaxed down, deciding she should abandon her search. He was not coming. 'Do you know something about Massoud that we should?' she asked Zahra.

'I only know his wife's frightened of him.'

Sofia raised her eyebrow in interest, encouraging Zahra to continue, but she simply shrugged. 'You can intuit things by the way someone talks about their spouse – or the way they don't talk about them.'

Sofia knew that was all she was going to get from Zahra. In a city that loved gossip, her friend was an exception.

'Did you know about this new security?'

Zahra shrugged again. 'We're paying Rashid and Tawfiq to keep you safe. Makes sense to get them to do their job.'

'I thought we were paying Rashid to keep my patients safe.'

'That too.'

Taking Sofia's elbow, Zahra drew her off to one side, away from the crowd to under one of the trees along the perimeter of the walled garden. 'This thing about Farahnaz's brother and these other missing boys ... I think it's best if you don't get involved any further.'

'I didn't go looking for this, Zahra. Farahnaz came to see me. What else could I do?'

'I know, I know, it's a terrible business and, of course, you did the right thing by telling Jabril, but if I may speak plainly on another matter ...' Sofia didn't think Zahra spoke anything but plainly on any matter. 'I wish you had not given that talk to the women yesterday. It didn't go down well.'

Sofia didn't need to be told that. It had been painfully clear, but she still believed it had been the right thing to do. 'You don't think they liked being reminded of the pitiful lives of these children and the dangers they face every day?'

Zahra didn't look impressed. 'No, Sofia, they didn't like a young *Western* woman reminding them of their country's inadequacies, or telling them what they should do about it. Don't you think they know these things? These are intelligent women: politicians, aid workers. They're not stupid. They know what's going on.'

'Then why don't they do something about it?' As soon as the words were out Sofia knew how ridiculous and offensive they were. She was not surprised by the rebuke that followed.

'Have you wiped out the practice in Australia? Have they wiped it out anywhere else in the Western world? We are no different to anywhere else, I think.'

Sofia felt the fire leave her belly. 'Point taken. I'm sorry I put you in that position.'

'It's got nothing to do with whatever position you think you put me in. I can deal with that, and I know you only meant well, I really do. And, of course, I understand your outrage.'

Zahra reached over to squeeze Sofia's arm. 'We're all outraged, Sofia. Appalled. Disgusted. I also understand, and appreciate, that you don't usually interfere, but I have to say to you, as my dear friend, that in this matter you went too far and what you did could put your life in danger.'

'I thought you knew and trusted these women?' Sofia said, looking surprised.

'I do, but I don't know who they talk to and neither do you. The wrong word in the wrong ear … Well, you don't know where it could lead. This place is a small town and it loves to gossip.'

'I didn't know what else to do,' Sofia said, feeling deflated. It had been a long day and she'd been so looking forward to seeing Daniel again, but he obviously wasn't coming.

With the expanding crowd spreading out toward them, Zahra pulled Sofia further away until they were under the shadow of the wall. 'Do you remember I told you that when Jabril and I decided to return to Afghanistan after living in the US we agreed that we wouldn't try to fix the whole country?' A waiter in traditional Afghan dress arrived with a smile and a tray of juices and mocktails. Choosing a drink, Zahra waited for him to move away before continuing. 'We took chances under the Taliban that I'm not willing to take anymore. Jabril was to help the men in the square in his practice and I would work with women. That was what was agreed. That was all we were going to do.' She took Sofia's arm again. 'Don't you see, this is why I'm so upset with Jabril about this paedophilia campaign thing. We promised not to put ourselves in danger again, and I don't want you putting yourself in danger either. This is why I don't want you to pursue this.'

'I understand.'

Sofia could feel Zahra softening. 'What you do with the women in the square is enough. It's more than enough and we're so grateful that you are doing this. We can't change Afghanistan, Sofia. None of us can individually and certainly outsiders can't.' She must have seen the look of hurt on Sofia's face. 'You know what I mean, don't you?'

'Of course.'

'So please, don't get involved in what isn't your business and above all, don't call attention to yourself. Just be our beautiful, generous, kind friend who helps the women in the square and the villages. That's all I'm asking.'

'Ah, there you are,' said Jabril, beaming as he arrived with Minister Massoud. 'I thought I'd lost you.'

In his sixties, Abdul Ali Massoud was a striking, even handsome man, with deep-set dark eyes, black hair, a neatly trimmed beard peppered with grey and a strong beak of a nose. Dressed in an expensive suit cut perfectly to his trim figure, he wore a crisp white shirt and pale blue silk tie. Sofia thought him even more impressive in person than he appeared on TV.

'Minister Massoud, I believe you already know my wife, Zahra?'

The minister nodded, bowing slightly. 'Always a pleasure to see you, *Bibi* Zahra. My wife speaks so highly of you. Unfortunately, she's not well and couldn't join us tonight. I know she'll be upset to have missed you.'

'Please give Tahminah my warmest wishes for a speedy recovery, minister.' Zahra delivered the words without any warmth. Sofia wondered if the minister saw this. If he did, he hid it well.

'And this is Dr Sofia,' Jabril said, turning to her. 'My partner in crime, so to speak.'

'Ah, Dr Sofia,' Massoud said, placing his hand on his heart as he bowed his head. 'It's a great pleasure to finally meet you. Dr Jabril has such good things to say about you that I'm beginning to believe you are one of your Christian saints.'

'No saint, I assure you.'

'My wife told me you gave a rather interesting talk yesterday,' he said, pulling down on the snow-white cuffs of his shirt.

Sofia felt as if she'd been ambushed. 'It's something I feel very strongly about.' She was not about to apologise to him too.

'You're a very courageous young woman, I think. Perhaps, though, this is something we Afghans must address ourselves and not something our guests need worry about.' He gave Sofia a practised smile.

'As I was saying,' Jabril said, eager to get the conversation away from Sofia's talk and back to the news about the boys, 'Taban, who I've already told you about, now thinks there may be even more boys missing.'

Massoud turned his attention back to Jabril. 'Ah yes, the woman who runs the clinic in Jamal Mina. Another courageous woman.'

'Yes, that's her,' Jabril said, sounding flustered. 'She also said that a man has been seen hanging around the boys of late near the pump house. I think it's imperative that we act quickly and find these missing boys and this man.'

'I agree. Have you informed our friend Chief Wasim of this new information?'

'Not yet. We only heard about the possibility of more boys ourselves a few minutes ago but I'll tell him as soon as I can.'

'Good. After Dr Jabril's phone call I spoke with Chief Wasim about the one who's your patient's brother, I believe, Dr Sofia,' he said, turning back to her. 'What's his name again?'

A waiter arrived at that moment with a tray of hors d'oeuvres. As Jabril, Zahra and Sofia examined the tray and made their choices, Massoud stepped slightly back, ignoring the waiter when he offered the tray to him. As the man moved off through the crowd to another group, Massoud leaned back in. Sofia had been watching him. It was as if someone had flicked a switch and turned the man off before flicking him back on again with the waiter's arrival and departure. The handsome, immaculately dressed man oozed power in every considered movement and facial expression he gave to the world. Like a finely tuned robot, Sofia thought, who wasn't used to, and didn't much like, being interrupted.

'Rayi,' she said. 'His name is Rayi.'

'Rayi.' Massoud offered her the politician's smile again. 'That's right. I remember now. I'll ring our chief of police tomorrow to make sure he prioritises this investigation. Now, unfortunately, I have duties tonight I must attend to. Sometimes,' he said, bathing them all in the glory of his smile, 'I think it was easier being an ordinary citizen.'

And when would that have been, Sofia was thinking as the minister turned to her again. 'I do admire your courage, Dr Sofia. Perhaps you have an admirable disregard for danger.'

Sofia could feel her shackles rising, but before she could respond, Jabril spoke. 'We've already told Dr Sofia she must be careful.'

'Wise counsel I suggest you take, Dr Sofia. Now, if you'll excuse me.'

Massoud bowed before turning and walking away, the two men who had been standing slightly apart from their group also turning and following him.

'There,' said Jabril happily, 'the minister's on our side.'

'He just threatened Sofia!' Zahra sounded outraged.

'Nonsense.'

'None so blind ...' his wife hissed under her breath as she shook her head. 'A leopard doesn't change its spots, Jabril. I'm suspicious of what he thinks he can get out of this.'

Sofia felt a light touch on her elbow and turned to see Daniel. 'I hope I'm not interrupting,' he said. After making introductions, they talked about his visit that day to Jamal Mina until the guests were requested to find their seats. The speeches and auction were about to begin. With Jabril slipping away to his seat on the stage and Daniel and Sofia about to separate to their allotted seats, he asked if she would like to join him for a drink after the function, agreeing to meet in the Char Chata Lounge rather than try to find each other in the crowd when the auction finished.

'So that was your mysterious man from the UN. I can certainly understand your interest,' Zahra offered as they took their places in the front row.

'Who said I was interested?'

'Drinks?'

'A coffee at the Serena doesn't mean anything,' Sofia said, giving her attention to the dignitaries, including Jabril, who seemed unable to decide what the appropriate seating arrangement on stage should be.

Leaning in, Zahra whispered, 'Or it could mean something. Besides,' she said, settling back in her seat, 'a little bird might have whispered something in my ear.'

Sofia shook her head. 'Tawfiq has a vivid imagination.'

'Really? You think so? I always thought Tawfiq to be a very perceptive man.'

25

DANIEL WAS HAPPY Sofia had chosen the Char Chata Lounge. With its crimson painted arches, Moroccan brass light fittings hanging low from the pink arched ceilings and intricately carved wooden privacy screens on the windows, it reminded him of Marrakech. The arched walls also provided relatively intimate spaces for its patrons: a perfect space for making an apology and handing over a letter he'd been carrying around for far too long.

Choosing two large seats in an alcove away from everyone else, Daniel was thinking how easy it had been to find Sofia in the garden in her silver and blue salwar kameez among all the heavy blacks, and how he liked that she was confident enough to be different, when she arrived along with the waiter. Making small talk about the fundraiser, Daniel waited until their drinks arrived before lifting his glass.

'A toast,' he said, 'to the village and all its gifts.'

'The village and all its gifts, especially you, Daniel Abiteboul.'

'Me?' he said, after they'd drunk. He couldn't think of one single reason Sofia would consider him a gift.

'You showed me other possibilities.'

He was still confused.

'It was you who suggested I train midwives, and that was an important moment in my life. I think Jabril and I had both realised I needed more than the surgery to stay. Once he heard about my midwifery in the village he used his connections to help me find my next group of village women, and the midwifery grew organically from there. He also introduced me to Taban, which got me into volunteer work in Jamal Mina. So you, Daniel Abiteboul,' she said, pointing at him with a finger from the hand holding the glass, 'showed me what my life in Afghanistan might look like and, thus, you're the reason I'm still here.'

She could have no idea how much he hated the suggestion that he was responsible for her remaining in Afghanistan. He could not, and would not, be responsible ever again. She must have sensed something was wrong because she asked him if he was okay.

'Yeah, yeah, fine,' he said, forcing a smile. 'After that confession, perhaps I should tell you how meeting you changed my life also.' What was it about Sofia that made him want to confess things? It was an interesting experience for a man who was obsessively private.

'By all means.'

As she happily rearranged the cushions in the overly large chair to make herself more comfortable he couldn't help noticing how the glow from the overhead brass light fittings was reflected in the lights in her hair.

'Meeting you made me realise how much I'd been missing normal interaction with people at the time.' Daniel laughed, a little embarrassed by what he was about to say. 'Actually, with a woman, if you want to know the absolute truth.' He was pleased to see his words had gone down well, although he hadn't missed the blush. He wondered if it meant she was thinking about the same thing he was thinking about, which he could feel arousing him. It had not been what he had intended. 'You also made me realise that I'd stopped being curious about the world, and if you're not curious about the world then you're not really living, are you?'

'Seriously, I did that?'

Her confusion surprised him, although it shouldn't have. He knew enough about human nature to know that how we saw ourselves rarely gelled with how the world saw us. As a negotiator for MSF it had been Daniel's job to see past the public projections to the person beneath. Sofia may not have been aware that the sheer joy and wonder of life was what she had been projecting back in the village. It was a compelling trait. 'You were happy and curious and full of wonder about the villagers and the joy of just being there. Everything excited you. Until you came it felt like I was just moving through the days, doing what needed to be done.'

This was the perfect time to make the apology, but he found himself hesitating. He didn't want to spoil the moment.

'Why do you say you were just moving through your days?' Sofia asked. 'Tell me more about you. We never really talked that much about ourselves back then, did we?'

Daniel's attention was momentarily caught by two of Massoud's henchmen in suits taking the seats in the alcove opposite them. He wouldn't have even known who they were if he hadn't been watching Sofia, waiting for her to finish her conversation with the warlord before approaching her at the fundraiser. It could be a coincidence that they had sat so close or it might not.

Turning back to Sofia, he lowered his voice to answer her question. 'No, we didn't.' He knew that had been his fault. He had wanted only to enjoy what they had together rather than muddy it with their pasts. 'After the village I went to live in Geneva, using it as a base to travel to different parts of the world negotiating for MSF. I was in and out of Afghanistan a few times and now there's this UN report. Not much in my life but work.'

'Come on, Daniel,' she said, slipping her sandals off and tucking her feet up under her on the chair. It made him smile. The only other woman he had known who did that was Alice. He wondered whether it was an Australian thing. 'Tell me about you, not what you do.'

'Only child of an Irish mother and French-Moroccan father who was a former soldier turned mercenary. By the time my mother realised he was heartbreak material I was fourteen and she took us both back to her native Dublin, which was a bit cold, wet, dark and dreary for a boy from Morocco, although I did become rather partial to the pubs and the Irish women, especially the red-haired ones.'

He watched her roll her eyes and laughed.

'Well, it's true. Anyway, my mother's still living in Dublin writing reasonably successful romance novels, while my father's reinvented himself as a member of the French parliament.' He laughed. 'He's had two wives since my mother and is recently divorced again. I hear he's going to marry for the fourth time. She'll be the second wife younger than me, which is inevitable, really, when you think about it. He likes them young and I keep getting older. I don't see much of my father, in case you hadn't gathered. A long time ago we discovered we didn't have much in common.'

'I knew your story would be interesting.'

'If it's the only thing you know then it seems ordinary.' Daniel reassessed what he'd just said and frowned. 'It was ordinary, really: a dysfunctional family, only dysfunctional in an exotic place. Aren't most families dysfunctional?' He was aware that he still wasn't really talking about himself. Protective habits of a lifetime were hard to break.

When the waiter arrived to take drink orders from the men he noticed Sofia had nearly finished hers and asked if she wanted another. She declined. He hoped she wasn't about to leave.

'Morocco sounds better than Leichhardt,' she offered.

'Tell me about Leichhardt?'

Sofia pulled her legs further under her. 'Inner-city working-class suburb, gentrifying.'

'Family?' He thought he might have asked this question back in the village but couldn't remember her answer.

She began rattling information off as if ticking a shopping list.

'Mother died when I was twelve, single working father and younger sister. Your normal totally dysfunctional family only in a not-so-exotic place.' Finishing off her drink, she smiled as she put the glass back down on the table between them. 'I escaped by going to Afghanistan.'

'Why Afghanistan?' Was he asking too many questions? It was a bad habit, he knew, remembering that in the village she'd accused him of being her therapist. While he could have written the habit off as the result of a career asking questions, it really had been his natural state since a young boy. Probably it was what made him good at his job, but he was genuinely interested in most people, and especially Sofia.

'No one here frets about how long it's going to take for the plumber to come to fix a leak,' she was saying, 'or how they couldn't possibly manage without three bathrooms and a huge TV. People look out for each other here. I like that. My dad doesn't know the people who live three doors away but I know everyone in Shaahir Square. Everyone.' She opened her arms wide as if to include the whole world. As he listened to this relaxed and animated Sofia, he could see the young woman from the village and wondered what his parents might make of her. He decided his mother would probably love her and his father would try to seduce her.

'I know their kids,' she was saying, 'and their parents and their grandparents. I know their history and what they care about. I suppose some people would find that a little claustrophobic but not me. Maybe it's my Italian roots longing for the great big family I never had.'

There could be no doubt she loved Afghanistan. It was in the way her face and eyes lit up when she talked about it and how animated she became. He could in some ways understand, but the place was far from perfect. 'How do you cope with the danger?'

She didn't seem happy with the question. 'Everyone wants to know that and the only way I can explain it to my friends back home is that they know sharks exist in the ocean but they still go in. It's the same here. You live with it however you can or you get out.' She pulled a face as she smoothed out the filmy blue and silver material covering her feet resting on the chair. 'You've lived here. You know what I mean?'

'Humour me.'

'Well, firstly, Chief Wasim, the Kabul chief of police, is my landlord and lives in the apartment below me.' She laughed at the look on his face. 'He's obviously a powerful man in Kabul, and as long as he remains powerful and doesn't make too many enemies, he's a big part of my insurance policy. I also have Tawfiq and Rashid, my driver and the guy who guards my surgery. Both of them carry guns and are supposed to protect me. For all I know Chief Wasim's wife, Behnaz, carries a gun too. Actually, now that I think about it, Behnaz is probably my best line of defence. No one crosses Behnaz.'

Folding his arms, he leaned back in the lounge and gave her a smile, all the while acutely aware that Massoud's men had stopped talking when Sofia mentioned the chief of police. A large part of Daniel's job with MSF was reading people and their body language, which was sometimes more instructive than what they said and didn't say. He also had to be good at risk assessment. He wouldn't have worried about the proximity of Massoud's henchmen in a public lounge in normal circumstances, and that they had stopped to listen when she mentioned her landlord might be normal curiosity, but his gut was saying it was something else.

'It's such a lovely night,' he said. 'Why don't we go back out to the gardens?'

26

When Sofia and Daniel reached the gardens they discovered it was full of staff clearing away the stage and the chairs.

'Damn,' he said. 'Sorry.' The garden was beautiful in the evenings. He would have liked to sit there with Sofia. With neither of them interested in going to one of the restaurants for a late dinner, he racked his brains for another option. There was always his room, which would give him the privacy he wanted, but it was probably too suggestive. It was also probably not an appropriate place to apologise for being a bastard lover.

'What about the Residents Lounge?' she suggested, but when they got there a group of Arab men, laughing and talking loudly, had claimed the space.

Daniel was starting to suspect the security guards stationed inside the hotel, including along every corridor, were probably already fingering them as suspicious. He looked up at the security cameras. They were also probably tracking their movements by now. When he realised Sofia was also looking at the cameras and probably thinking the same thing, they both started laughing.

'I think we need to sit down somewhere soon and act as

normal as possible before they shut the place down and carry us away,' she said.

Daniel considered his room again and again dismissed it. 'One of the lounges in reception?' he offered. It was probably the only option left.

He watched Sofia check the time on her phone. 'That's probably a good idea because Tawfiq will be returning soon to take me home so I should be watching the door.'

While reception was reasonably busy with people still leaving the two functions in the hotel, it was a large area and there were free lounges. They were also well spaced for privacy. Nothing romantic, or even remotely Moroccan, he thought as he led Sofia to a lounge with a clear view of the cars lining up to collect their passengers outside the front doors. As he sat down beside her he thought about broaching the subject of Massoud. He also still had the apology and the letter.

'You were talking about how you cope with the danger,' he said, taking up the conversation from where they'd left off. 'What about kidnapping?'

She looked at him in surprise. 'You can still remember what we were last talking about? I'd completely forgotten. Okay, Plan A is I leave through a balcony door out the back of the apartment, which means jumping down on the roof of the house next door. As long as I don't break a leg I'm over the wall and away. Then there's Plan B, which is a little trickier. In the event I can't get out of the apartment in time, I break the glass in the kitchen window to make the kidnappers think I've escaped over the roof of the house next door, and then I hide in the broom cupboard, but I'd have to get rid of all Behnaz's cleaning paraphernalia first, and believe me, there's a lot of paraphernalia. I'm also thinking that all the brooms and buckets and bleach lying around on the floor outside the cupboard might be a dead giveaway. Actually,' she said, growing serious, 'there's no plan for kidnapping. That's the whole point of kidnapping, isn't it? It has to be when you least expect it, so I try to keep a low profile and slip under the radar. It also helps that there's no other Westerners living in the square so it doesn't get the unwelcome focus a Western enclave might, which is a bonus for me.'

He realised that not only did she tuck her feet up under her like Alice but she had the same dry sense of humour. 'But not necessarily for your friends?' he offered.

'Exactly. If someone doesn't like me being in the square they could also be unhappy with those who befriend me. Besides, if someone wanted to kidnap or kill me, it wouldn't be too hard because twice a day I walk across the square between my apartment and the surgery. I've also got into the habit of spending a lot of time at my window watching the square. No matter which way you look at it, I'm an easy target.'

If Sofia had been one of his staff and had just told him what she did, he would have flipped. *She kept a low profile and so far she had slipped under the radar?* It was not nearly good enough, but it also wasn't any of his business. 'What about the Taliban, Sofia? What if they get back in power after the Western troops leave? What will you do then?'

'I'll have to leave, won't I?' she said, looking as if she was challenging him to deny it until her shoulders slumped and she sat shaking her head. 'You know, they've already said women can't be judges or president and everyone seems to have accepted that. No one's standing up for the women. Nothing in the US's negotiation with the Taliban has specified protecting women or their rights. I fear it, Daniel, I really do.'

'You think the West should stay?'

'God no. They've been here twenty years and the Taliban are gaining ground again. No, I think the Afghans have to do this themselves, but like I said …' She shook her head again, clearly not wanting to continue the conversation.

Daniel had the feeling he'd asked her far too many questions already, but he needed to know about Massoud.

About six years previously, he had spent three torturous months negotiating with the warlord on behalf of MSF about setting up a new clinic in his area. Massoud had been a mercurial and difficult negotiating partner, hard to pin down, constantly shifting the goalposts, and unreliable with both his word and the truth. It was difficult to strike a bargain with someone like that, but a bargain had to be negotiated and Daniel had stayed at the table until the process was finished and MSF got its clinic.

During that time he'd learned a few things about Massoud, none of which endeared him to Daniel. When the West had arrived with its easy money, the warlord had successfully reinvented himself as a democracy-loving businessman and was elected to the parliament with an outstanding majority in the fraudulent 2010 elections. As famous for his astonishing beauty in his youth as he was for his love of cruelty, the man moved through the world with the slow surety of menace honed through years of brutality. Before his twentieth year it was said that Massoud had slaughtered the inhabitants of an entire village because they had defied him, while more recently it was rumoured he had organised the disappearance of a young man his daughter had professed to love. Over the years

Massoud's name had been linked to kidnapping, torture and extortion, although it was common knowledge that most of the man's wealth now came from the more commonplace practice of poppy cultivation. Understanding the power of mythology, the minister had never commented on any of these matters, or more significantly, no one had ever found the courage to ask him. Daniel's time with Massoud had not been one of his most pleasant memories. It worried him that Sofia might be his friend, although from her body language when they had been talking it didn't look like she cared much for the man.

'I saw you talking with Minister Massoud. Is he a friend of yours?'

'Not at all. I met him for the first time tonight.'

'A friend of Jabril?'

'Not really. He's helping him with something – or at least, Jabril wants the minister to help him with something.'

Daniel could see Sofia was uncomfortable with the subject, although he was relieved to learn they were not friends and was willing to let the subject drop.

'In the last couple of months four little boys have gone missing from Jamal Mina,' she began, 'maybe more. I know one of the boys.'

Daniel turned on the lounge, placing his arm across its back as he faced Sofia while being careful not to touch her. 'Any idea who's taking them?'

'No.'

'What are the police doing?'

'Not much yet.' He heard the frustration in her voice.

No one cared about little boys living in the slums. He remembered something similar happening about five years previously in Jalalabad. The word then had been that powerful and untouchable men had taken the boys. As far as Daniel was aware they'd never been found.

'I spoke to Chief Wasim about them. He said he'd look into it. Anyway, for the last few months Jabril's been trying to get politicians interested in a campaign to raise public awareness about paedophilia, but no one other than Minister Massoud has shown any interest. I know this "boy play" is big in the provinces, but with the media and all the public service programming on television you'd think they'd come up with something addressing the issue to show how damaging it is and how it's against Islam, but no one'll touch it. Jabril wants the politicians to publicly say let's talk about this and stop it. Even if Massoud can't do anything about the whole paedophile thing, we're hoping he can get the authorities moving on the missing boys.'

Daniel knew that if there were nothing in it for Massoud he wouldn't be interested, and if he was interested then he would have questioned why.

Daniel's introduction to *bacha bazi* had come nearly ten years previously when he'd been called to the camp of a warlord to attend a seriously ill boy. He could see that the warlord, who had to be in his seventies, was really fretting over the child and had assumed he was his father or grandfather, but over the next couple of days he watched the way the man and boy interacted and had finally understood. On that occasion he'd been able to save the child's life but not the child. The memory remained a painful one.

A couple of years later a young man had tried to solicit Daniel on the streets of Kabul. He had told Gharib he wasn't interested in sex, but he was interested in hearing all about *bacha bazi.* Buying Gharib his first solid meal for two days, Daniel had sat with the young man as he talked. The two had remained friends over the years, although Daniel suspected Gharib was still part of the world of sex. He decided to ring Gharib in the morning to ask if he knew anything about the missing boys.

Talking about Massoud and missing boys was not how Daniel wanted to end the evening with Sofia. The crowd in the foyer and outside the front doors had begun to thin and her driver would arrive soon. He was running out of time.

'You know, I was here last year and I thought I saw you at a party.'

Sofia turned further in her seat to face him directly. Aware it was too intimate for a public space, he moved slightly back.

'Why didn't you say hello?'

'It was only for a second and I had to leave.' He hesitated. 'After all these years I wasn't sure it was you, or that you'd want to see me again.'

She looked genuinely surprised. 'Why would you think I wouldn't want to see you again?'

'Because I didn't behave particularly honourably last time?'

Sofia leaned back in the lounge and smiled. 'What makes you think I'm not the one who didn't behave honourably?'

Whatever reaction Daniel had imagined over the years it had not been that. Searching back through their time together, he couldn't find a single thing she would need to apologise for. 'I have no idea what you're talking about.'

Sofia sighed deeply, leaning further into the lounge, watching him. She waited. When he still looked confused, she sighed again. 'I don't believe it. You're going to make me do this, aren't you?'

'I truly have no idea what you're talking about.'

'Okay, so maybe I knew something was troubling you and suspected you were vulnerable, and maybe I took advantage of that.' The only way he could describe the look on her face was seductive. 'Some people might say,' she continued, lowering her voice, 'that using your body the way I did wasn't a particularly honourable thing to do. Some people might think I needed to apologise for that.'

Daniel sat looking at her for a few seconds, speechless before he laughed so hard that people were turning around to look. 'My god, Sofia!' he said. 'Do you have any idea how long I've been carrying around this guilt when obviously I was the one who should be feeling aggrieved?'

A sudden memory of a warm night under a rough blanket in a cold hut; of kisses deep and warm; of a hand tangled up in long silky red hair; of breathing in the scent of her; of being lost in her; of her body leading his. The memory was so vivid and visceral that its intensity shocked him. It also aroused him. As they sat looking at each other she smiled. She knew exactly what she was doing.

'Tawfiq's here,' she said, smiling and standing as she motioned to the line of cars outside edging toward the front door. 'I guess it's time for me to go.'

Back in his room, Daniel threw his jacket onto the bed before retrieving the letter out of the pocket. He still hadn't given it to her.

27

RETURNING FROM MOSQUE early the following morning, Omar was not happy to see a second night letter pinned to Behnaz's gate, and although he was itching to see whether it explained the problem better, he left it. The problem was not his. The problem belonged to Chief Wasim and Behnaz. Maybe one of them would know what it was all about.

Carrying his chair out to the centre of the square earlier than usual, Omar sat watching Behnaz's gate until she emerged. Ripping the night letter off the gate, she looked around the square. Omar made himself busy examining the scab on his hand that had been there for the last two months. Things didn't mend so easily these days. Taking his time, he looked up again to see Behnaz pushing the letter deep into the pocket of her coat before heading out into the square to pick up the rubbish.

He had decided that Chief Wasim and Behnaz needed to know about the first night letter also. Getting up off his chair, Omar began shuffling across the square until he realised that he had no idea how to tell her or her husband about the first letter without admitting he had stolen it. He returned to the safety of his chair. Perhaps a better plan would arrive very soon. In the meantime, a little nap could do no harm.

* * *

COMING OUT THROUGH the gate, Sofia saw Omar asleep in his chair in the middle of the square and Rashid walking toward her with Behnaz, who was holding a bag of rubbish. After greeting them she told Behnaz that she'd been trying to ring Chief Wasim but he wasn't answering.

'Sometimes he doesn't,' she said, retrieving her broom from where she'd left it leaning against the wall.

'I know that. I've left messages, but he hasn't got back to me. Do you know how I might reach him? It's important.'

'What messages?'

'Just about something he was looking into.'

'Are you in danger?'

'No,' she said, laughing. 'Will he be coming home for lunch?'

'Yes.'

When it was clear Behnaz wasn't going to elaborate she asked, 'What time do you think he'll finish lunch?'

'When his plate's empty.'

Sofia could see the hint of a smile on Rashid's face as he made himself busy lighting a fresh cigarette. Sofia tried not to smile too. 'Okay. What time do you think he'll start lunch?'

'When he gets here.'

'Perfect,' Sofia said, as if the response was exactly what she wanted to hear. 'Those times suit me.'

'Humph.' Behnaz looked like she was about to disappear behind the gate again.

'Maybe you could give him a message for me.'

'He's not answering his phone.'

220

Sofia wanted to say she knew that. That was how this whole conversation had started. Instead she turned to Rashid. 'Are you ready?' As Behnaz disappeared behind her gate and she and Rashid crossed the square to the surgery, Sofia wondered how the chief of police got anything done if he didn't answer his phone or return calls. Greeting Iman in reception, she ran her eye down the hard copy of her appointments sitting on the corner of Iman's desk and saw she had a full day.

'Everybody in the square is sick and everybody is strange,' offered Iman as she concentrated on filing her nails.

Sofia looked up. 'What do you mean?'

Iman put the nail file down. 'Well,' she said, warming to the subject she had obviously been preparing to ambush Sofia with, 'people are starting to say that something's wrong in the square.'

'I still don't know what you mean.'

'Well, neither do I, that's why I'm asking you.'

'I didn't realise you were asking me a question.'

Iman gave Sofia one of her 'don't be smart with me' looks. 'Are you in danger, Dr Sofia?'

Sofia frowned. 'That's the second time someone's asked me that in the last five minutes. Why would I be in danger?'

'Well, Rashid's walking you across the square again. Why would he start doing that?'

'Because it's his job and Dr Jabril said he should?' Sofia saw that look again. 'What other evidence do you have that everybody is strange and I'm in danger? By the way, are those two things linked?'

'I don't know, but Ahmad's telling everyone he's going to go to mosque every morning now, and Hadi's giving everyone more than they pay for, and Mustafa told my mother that Babur's acting strange, and Omar … Well, he's always acting strange these days, but Iqbal says Omar's up to no good, and Behnaz just told my mother she was too busy to have her usual cup of tea with her, and when my mother asked why she told her to mind her own business.'

Sofia was glad when Iman finally drew breath. 'That was a bit harsh.'

'Exactly,' Iman said, picking up the nail file and pointing it at Sofia before pulling a face. 'Well, she might not have said those precise words but that was what she meant.'

'All seems pretty normal then.'

'This is serious,' Iman said, crossing her arms.

'Sorry,' Sofia said. 'So what's Omar up to that's no good?'

'I wouldn't be asking you if I knew, would I?'

Sofia wanted to say she hadn't realised there had been a question again but it was feeling like they were going around in circles.

'I think Omar's spreading rumours.'

'Really,' Sofia said, pushing the list out of the way so she could sit on the side of Iman's desk. 'What sort of rumours?'

'About someone's friend being in danger.'

'Whose friend?'

'No one knows,' she said, throwing her hands in the air. 'That's the point. That's why I asked you if you were in danger. Why won't anyone tell me anything?'

Sofia was sure this was just the usual rumour mill in a square that really was a little too insular, causing gossip to abound. 'Do we have any more evidence that everyone is sick and strange other than Ahmad going to mosque, and Hadi being generous, and Omar up to no good and spreading rumours, and Mustafa worrying about Babur because he's acting strange, and Behnaz being rude, and my schedule being reasonably full and me being in some unspecified danger?'

'Isn't that enough?' Iman said, pointing to Sofia's list of appointments, as if this was all the confirmation Sofia might need.

Sofia picked up the list to examine it but was unable to identify whatever evidence Iman could see lurking there. 'Sorry, you've lost me.'

Iman began sawing away at her nails again.

If she didn't stop soon, Sofia thought with amusement, she'd have no nails left. She decided Khalif must have done something to put Iman in a bad mood again, thankful that she was not Iman's age. The way things were going between Iman and Khalif lately, she didn't give the relationship much of a chance.

Iman looked up from her nails, pointing the file at her again. 'Don't look at me like that.'

'Like what?' Sofia said, trying very hard not to let Iman see her amusement as she got up off the desk.

'Like you're about to ask me if Khalif and I had a fight.'

'Did you and Khalif have a fight?'

'*Nooooo.*' Iman stared Sofia down.

'Fine.' Sofia decided for her own sanity it was time to make a tactical retreat and headed for Jabril's surgery. She needed to know if he'd heard anything new.

'Dr Jabril's not in yet,' said Iman, not looking up from filing her nails.

'Right.' Sofia did a U-turn, retreating into her own surgery only to realise that Iman had got up from her desk and followed her in.

'Have you ever thought about dreams, Dr Sofia?' she asked, leaning against the doorframe.

'Can't say I've spent a lot of time thinking about dreams.' Sitting down, Sofia unpacked her laptop, plugged it in and turned it on.

'The ones you remember, they're weird, right?'

Sofia stopped to consider this. 'I suppose so.' She typed in her password.

'Have you ever thought about all the hours we spend in those weird invented universes?'

'Not really,' she said, watching Iman now.

'Well, think about it. What do you think that says about human beings?'

'I've no idea. What do you think it says?'

'Well, it explains why people are weird. If we spend most of our lives in these crazy, weird dream places then anything that's crazy in our normal life mightn't seem so crazy after all, right?'

'I suppose so.'

'I'm right, you know.'

'I didn't say you weren't.'

As Iman walked back to her desk Sofia called out. 'Do you think that's why the square is so weird at the moment? Do you think everyone's dreaming too much?'

Iman poked her head back around the door. 'Now you're just being silly.'

As she got ready for her first patient, Sofia was smiling. Maybe Iman should add herself to the list of people in the square acting strange.

***

SOFIA'S FIRST PATIENT of the day was Fawzia. At seventeen years old she was newly married to a man she met the week before her wedding. She was curious to know how this arranged marriage was faring. After the initial greeting Fawzia seemed reluctant to talk, taking an inordinate amount of time taking off her chador before laying it neatly across her lap. She then put her handbag down on the floor, only to pick it up again and rest it on her lap over the chador. When her hands were no longer busy she folded them chastely over the handbag and looked up at Sofia before turning her head to look out the window.

'How have you been, Fawzia?'

She looked back to Sofia. 'Very well, thank you, Dr Sofia.'

'Good.' Whatever Fawzia wanted to talk about was obviously difficult for her. This was going to take some time. Their conversation began with Fawzia's recent wedding before moving on to her new life with her in-laws until Fawzia looked down at the floor and grew silent.

'I have impure thoughts about my husband, Dr Sofia.'

This was a first for Sofia. Was she talking of impure thoughts about sex, or impure thoughts like the ones Behnaz had about killing Chief Wasim?

'Does it give you pleasure to think about him?'

'Yes.' Fawzia looked up, blushing a bright crimson before looking back down again.

Sofia thought she understood. Too many women were married in ignorance of the sex act, other than the fact that they must submit to their husband. They had no idea that they too might find it pleasurable.

'Is your husband kind to you, Fawzia?' The young woman

nodded. 'And you think about the times he is with you … in private … with pleasure?' Fawzia turned crimson and nodded again. Good for you, Sofia thought. 'What you're feeling is normal.'

Fawzia looked eager to hear more. 'You know these thoughts, Dr Sofia?'

'I've had these feelings too. They're normal.'

'But you're not married.'

Here we go again, she thought. Being an untrained, inadequate sex therapist in a devout Muslim country was as dangerous as moving blindfold through a minefield. Never quite sure how explicit she should be, Sofia had asked Zahra, who was her sounding-board on all things cultural. Her advice was to be as honest and gentle as she could. 'I'm a woman and I've felt these things when I've loved a man,' she said, hoping she hadn't gone too far.

Fawzia stared at the floor again as she considered this new piece of information. When she looked up she was smiling. 'I think I understand. You're Australian.'

Sofia wanted to laugh. Did Australians have a particularly lascivious reputation in Afghanistan?

* * *

AFTER HER LAST patient before lunch, Sofia was eager to catch Chief Wasim at home. She knew Jabril had got through to him that morning but she was eager to hear if there was any more news. She also needed to tell Jabril that people were thinking she was in danger because of the new security and that perhaps they should go back to normal so people could stop worrying. As she was about to leave, Iman came rushing into the surgery waving a piece of paper.

'I can't believe it,' she said, looking distraught.

'What can't you believe?'

'This!' she said, waving the paper at Sofia.

'Iman, please calm down and tell me what "this" is.'

'They've cancelled your working visa!'

'What!' Sofia stood, reaching out for the letter.

'The Ministry of Labour has cancelled your visa.'

Sofia took the letter from Iman and read it. Not only had her visa been cancelled but she had only three weeks to leave the country. 'There must be some mistake.'

'Oh,' cried Iman, 'you can't leave. We don't want you to leave. Who would do this to you?'

'I don't know.' Sofia read the letter again. 'This definitely has to be some sort of mistake.' When her phone rang she gave it only a cursory look until she saw the caller ID.

'I've got a name and a location of someone who might know where some of your missing boys are.'

It took Sofia a few seconds to move from the visa cancellation to compute what Daniel was saying. 'Iman, can you give me a minute?' she said. Iman looked even more upset but Sofia followed her to the door and closed it behind her.

'Are you there?' Daniel asked.

'Yes, I'm here.' Sofia walked over to the window and stood looking out.

'Apparently, this man prepares boys before they're sold. Maybe he still has them, or can at least tell you where they might have been taken.'

Sofia turned to sit on the windowsill. 'How do you know this?'

'A friend.'

The way Daniel said 'a friend' meant she couldn't ask more. 'Okay. Who's this man and where can I find him?'

'His name's Afzal. All I know is that he lives near you in the bird market above a tailor shop with a green sign. That's the best my friend could do.'

'Hopefully that's enough.' She needed to catch Chief Wasim before he went back to work and was about to end the call when Daniel spoke again.

'I hope you're going to pass this information on to your Chief Wasim and let him deal with it.'

'That's exactly what I'm about to do.'

'Good. I just needed to make sure you weren't going there by yourself to confront this guy.'

'No, I'm about to cross the square right now and tell Chief Wasim, who's hopefully still at home eating lunch.'

She could sense a change in Daniel on the other end of the phone before he spoke. 'I really enjoyed last night.'

'So did I,' she said, as she walked across the room to pull her scarf off the hook and try unsuccessfully to wrap it over her hair with one hand. She gave up. She would have liked to linger over the conversation but she didn't have time. 'I'll see you and Clementine tomorrow morning around six, okay?'

'Sure. Let me know what happens.'

28

SECURING HER SCARF, Sofia rushed out the door and down the stairs only to discover Iman following her.

'What was that all about? What are you doing?' she asked, hurrying down the stairs behind Sofia.

'I'm going to see Chief Wasim.'

'Is Chief Wasim going to help with your visa?' she called as Sofia set off across the square with Rashid following.

'I doubt it.' With Sofia disappearing through the gate, Rashid took up watch outside it.

Her husband had already gone back to work, Behnaz told her. 'He said to tell you that you're not to worry about anything.'

'I'd better ring him.'

Behnaz shook her head. 'No point. He won't answer.'

'I'll try anyway.'

'Are you in trouble?'

'No. This has nothing to do with me and I'm not in trouble and please tell everyone in the square that I'm not in trouble or danger or anything.'

'That's what he said.'

'Good, then you should believe him.'

As Behnaz stood in her doorway watching, Sofia rang Chief Wasim's number only for it to go through to his voice mail. She hung up.

'I told you,' Behnaz said, folding her arms and looking righteous.

Sofia turned and headed up the stairs to her apartment where she rang Jabril. When he didn't answer she left a message about a man called Afzal who lived over a tailor shop in the bird bazaar. Sitting on her bed, she wondered what to do. Going to the bird market looking for this Afzal was not particularly sensible, especially if he was a criminal and possibly dangerous, but she could feel the panic rising. Time was of the essence and it was running out. This might be the last chance they ever had to find the boys.

Opening her cupboard, she searched for her long coat only to find the thing at the bottom of the wardrobe, crushed under some shoes. Buttoning the coat all the way up to her neck, she wrapped her scarf more tightly around her head this time, taking care to cover all her hair, before getting on her hands and knees to retrieve the shoebox she kept under her bed. Counting out the equivalent of two hundred US dollars, she put the money in the secret pocket in the inner lining of her coat and pushed the box back under the bed before heading off to Babur's *chaikhana*.

'Have you finished?' she asked as she stood over Tawfiq, who was having lunch.

He looked at the shapeless coat through the smoke haze in the *chaikhana* before looking to Rashid, who had followed Sofia in.

'Yes,' he said hesitantly, aware that Sofia only ever wore the coat when they were travelling in the more remote or dangerous parts of Afghanistan.

'I'd like you come with me.'

Tawfiq looked over to Rashid again and then back to Sofia. 'Do we need the car?' he asked, stubbing out his cigarette as he rose from the cushion on the timber platform.

'No.'

Babur, who had seen Sofia walk in wearing the long coat and her hair tucked away under her scarf, knew something was wrong and came over to them, the glass and tea towel he had been using still in his hand. 'Is something wrong, Dr Sofia?'

'No, nothing. Come on, Tawfiq,' she said, walking out.

'Should Rashid come too?' Tawfiq asked cautiously, as he followed her.

They stood in front of the *chaikhana*, Babur inside watching them. 'Maybe ... I don't know.' She wondered whether they should take Rashid for security before deciding it was better not to arouse any more suspicion in the square, or scare this Afzal off with her gun-toting former soldier turned security guard. She looked at Rashid. 'We'll be fine, my friend. No need to come with us.'

'I have to.'

Sofia looked into Rashid's eyes and spoke very calmly and clearly so there could be no mistaking her meaning. 'We're only going to the bird market, Rashid, not too far away. This one time I need you to stay here. Do you understand what I'm saying?'

She watched him and Tawfiq exchange glances again. She had no idea what messages were being exchanged between them. She could also see the conflict in Rashid. This was a horrible thing to do to him. She repeated, 'I need you to stay here this one time. We'll be fine. I promise.' Rashid nodded. If he had insisted she would have taken him, but she believed it would be better for everyone if it was just her and Tawfiq.

'Why are we going to the bird market?' Tawfiq asked as they headed off.

'To find a man called Afzal who lives above a tailor shop.'

Tawfiq frowned. 'There aren't any tailors in the bird market.'

'Apparently there are.'

'I don't understand. Why do we have to find this man?'

Sofia stopped and looked at him, just as she had looked at Rashid. She needed him to understand the importance of what they were about to do and she didn't need any more questions. 'He might know where we can find some missing boys.' She gave Tawfiq time to consider this. 'You've heard about these missing boys from Jamal Mina?'

'I might have.'

Stood to reason, she thought. Nothing was secret in the square for long.

'Wait!' Sofia turned to see Iman hurrying toward them. Pointing down the passageway that led out of the square, she asked Tawfiq to wait for her at the end of it.

'Where are you going?' Iman cried, catching her breath.

'Please don't tell anyone about the visa,' Sofia said. When Iman didn't respond she put her hands on the young woman's shoulders, feeling the blood pumping through her fine young skin. 'I need to sort it out and I don't need people in the square to know or to worry about me for nothing. Please?'

'Okay, I'll try,' Iman said, not happy with this.

'No, Iman,' she squeezed her shoulders. 'You have to do

232

better than try. You need to promise me you won't tell anyone. Do you understand?'

'Okay, but where are you going and why are you wearing *that*?' she said, looking down at Sofia's coat with distaste.

'I'm going to the bird market.'

Iman was confused. 'To fix your visa?'

'No, it's a long story,' Sofia said. 'If I'm not back in time for my next patient, please tell her I was called out on an emergency and ask if she could wait or reschedule.'

'I don't understand anything,' Iman said, her shoulders slumping under Sofia's hands. 'What's going on?'

'There is nothing to worry about. So nothing about the visa to anyone, okay?'

When Iman nodded, Sofia gave her shoulders another squeeze before hurrying off to where Tawfiq was waiting for her.

As they made their way through the crowded maze of backstreets and alleyways of the old city, a man pedalled furiously past them on a bicycle with two passengers clinging on precariously. A small three-wheeled yellow car was overtaking him while threatening to wipe out a man pushing a barrow laden with oranges. After passing the blue-domed Pul-e Khishti Mosque Sofia saw every day from her surgery window, they entered the crowded bird market to be assailed by its distinctively musty smell. They stopped.

Colourful metal birdcages and the more traditional domed cages made of cane were hanging from hooks overhead on the walls of the tiny mud and timber buildings and stacked high on top of each other in front of the shops. Bright plastic feeder trays and water bottles were displayed on walls and dusty old timber benches alongside small sacks full of every type of bird feed imaginable. The tiny street and the even smaller alleyways running off it were so crowded that Sofia couldn't see more than a few metres in front of her. Despite the dip in the economy, it looked to her that at least the bird trade was still thriving.

With one of the world's largest migratory paths passing over Afghanistan, birds were caught in the wild, bred in captivity or shipped in from places like Pakistan and Iran. Some of the more exotic species had their own cage, but many more were crowded into larger wire cages. Canaries, finches, larks, pigeons, tiny parrots, the local chukar partridge and, of course, chickens and quails for the table could all be found in the bird market. There were also the prized fighting cocks. Afghans loved their birds.

Sofia looked down at her feet where a blanket was spread out on the dusty ground. On top of the filthy blanket were second-hand books, DVDs and old music cassettes displayed in neat rows. Her eye was caught by a well-thumbed English copy of the once banned 1969 novel *Portnoy's Complaint*, probably brought to Afghanistan in some hippie's backpack in the seventies. In forty more years it would probably still be on a blanket in some other marketplace in Kabul waiting for the right buyer.

Looking up, she scanned the crowd again only to realise she was beginning to draw attention. Tawfiq had noticed the attention too. 'This is not good,' he said, clearing a way for her to follow him as he moved deeper into the alley.

'You'd think a tailor in a street full of bird sellers shouldn't be too hard to find,' Sofia said, almost to herself. As they passed one of the side alleyways she looked down to see an excited crowd milling around a cockfight, but with word quickly spreading that a Western woman was in the street, men were already beginning to stop and stare.

'I have a bad feeling about this,' whispered Tawfiq. 'I think we should leave. It's not right that you go to this man's home alone.'

'I'm not going alone. I'm going with you and we can't leave. This is about saving some little boys.'

'What does Dr Jabril say?' Tawfiq lamented.

'He doesn't know.' Tawfiq stopped and turned around, looking at her with alarm. 'I tried to call him but I couldn't, and I tried Chief Wasim but I couldn't get onto him either. We had no choice but to do this now. There's no one else and there's no time. This is for the little boys, Tawfiq. Remember that. This is for the little boys.'

She saw the slump in his shoulders and knew what that meant. 'Okay, you can try calling him.'

Leading Sofia over to the entrance of a nearby shop, Tawfiq pulled out his phone and dialled Jabril's number only for it to go to messages. 'Dr Jabril's not going to be happy,' he said, shaking his head as he put his phone away again.

'He'll be very happy if we find where the boys are, though.' Sofia was watching his face. 'I know you're unhappy about this, Tawfiq. I'm unhappy too, but what else can we do? We'll do this as quickly as we can. We'll just go in, ask this man, and then leave.' He looked as uncertain and worried as she felt. 'Come on, let's keep going.'

Tawfiq didn't move. 'It's there,' he said, pointing to a green sign. She realised he'd seen the sign before he'd tried to ring Jabril.

As they entered the shop a bell tinkled. Thousands of bolts of fabric, in some places five and six deep, were stacked against the walls, on shelves and gathering dust on the top of old cupboards. Spools of brightly coloured thread hung from the ceiling, while below them an old man was furiously feeding material into an ancient Singer treadle sewing machine. He hadn't heard them enter over the noise of the machine, but when their shadows fell across his work the machine slowed and he looked up.

'I think it best if I talk,' whispered Tawfiq. Sofia agreed completely. A man would respond much better to Tawfiq than to her.

'Where is Afzal?' Tawfiq asked. Without a word the man stood and led them back out into the street, pointing up a narrow staircase beside the door to his shop that neither of them had noticed.

29

AFZAL LIVED IN the tiny apartment with his wife, four children and mother. After Tawfiq knocked they stood listening to the shuffling going on behind the door as someone made themselves presentable to strangers. A young woman finally opened the door, still making adjustments to her black burqa so that only her eyes could be seen. While Tawfiq was explaining that they were there to speak with Afzal, the woman looked more interested in examining Sofia. When Tawfiq had finished she motioned for them to come in and sit on the floor while she fetched her sleeping husband, who came out of another room with a cigarette hanging out of the side of his mouth while scratching his crotch. Three little children, who had been peeking out from behind their mother when she answered the door, were now gathered around their father as he sat opposite Tawfiq and Sofia on the floor. Sofia smiled at the children. The little girl stuck her thumb in her mouth and buried her head in her father's side. The boys continued to stare.

Two filthy glass doors opened onto a timber deck with rotting boards and a dilapidated timber balustrade. An old flyspecked air conditioner, which looked as if it had given up the ghost decades earlier, was hanging threateningly off the wall above the doors. Training *bacha bareesh*, if that was what this man did, didn't look like it paid that well.

Afzal's two boys, who would have been about five and six years old, had shaved heads. Their younger sister, who had emerged from her father's side, had a head of luxurious dark waves, two little gold studs in her tiny earlobes and gold bracelets jangling on her wrists. Afzal's wife was leaning up against a bench in front of a two-hob gas burner that served as the kitchen. An older woman was holding a sleeping baby. Both women were watching Sofia and Tawfiq. When the wife picked up an old plastic flyswat that might once have been a cheerful red but had faded to a dirty brown, and hit the wall, it seemed to be good enough reason for the two women to start arguing. As Sofia watched, the wife picked up the dead fly with two fingers and threw it out the open window. With that settled, the women turned their attention back to Sofia and Tawfiq.

Afzal seemed immune to what was happening behind him. With a thick smoke haze settling around his head and the cigarette still hanging from the side of his mouth, Afzal looked at them with disinterest.

'Perhaps it would be best if I spoke,' Tawfiq whispered to Sofia again.

'What do you want?' Afzal asked, irritated by the whispering.

'Some boys recently went missing from Jamal Mina and we're trying to find out what happened to them.'

Clearing his throat, Afzal took the cigarette out of his mouth and watched as the ash dropped onto the rug they were sitting on. He shook his head. 'Why have you come to me? I don't know what you're talking about.'

Despite the fact that they were clearly not welcome, the offering of tea to guests was so entrenched in the culture that the two women came into the room carrying glasses of tea, each taking the opportunity to get a closer look at Sofia before they retreated back to the kitchen to stand watch again.

Two slow trails of smoke were leaking out of Afzal's nostrils and circling up in the air, adding to the thickening cloud in the room. He pushed the tea toward Sofia. 'Please, drink,' he instructed. No more was said as they all drank their tea. Sofia was focused on not saying anything while wondering where the conversation could go now. Afzal, who probably didn't want the conversation to go anywhere, was the first to break the silence. 'I don't know why you're asking me these things. What makes you think I know anything about these boys?'

Tawfiq looked at Sofia. He probably wanted that question answered also.

'Someone who knows about these things told a friend that you might know where they've been taken.' She was not happy to be speaking.

'Who told you this?'

'A friend,' Tawfiq said, trying to take the conversation back to him. When Afzal looked like he wasn't impressed with this information, Tawfiq added, 'It's complicated.'

Afzal gave an ironic laugh, shaking his head. 'Everything is complicated these days. You're wasting my time,' he added, waving them away as if they were less than irritants. 'You should go.'

Tawfiq began to rise until Sofia said, 'No,' and he sat back down again. She was not going to give up so easily. This man was their only possible lead to the boys. 'Anything,' she pleaded.

'Can you give us anything? Anything at all to help us find these little boys? We'd be very grateful.'

Afzal stared at Sofia before turning his attention to Tawfiq. 'How important is this to you?'

'Very important.'

'That does not show me *how* important it is.'

Sofia was looking at Tawfiq, willing him to know how important it was, willing him to do whatever he could to show Afzal how important it was. After hesitating for a few seconds, she watched Tawfiq put his hand in under his *perahan* and pull out a large roll of afghani notes from deep within the pocket of his *tunban*. When she looked back up at Afzal she could see the hunger in his eyes as he weighed up his options. With money on display his wife and mother had moved into the room. Money was everything, and in the end greed won.

'There is a house near Ghazi Stadium. You'll know this house because it has a blue star painted on the wall. Maybe the boys are there, maybe not.' He shrugged, his dark eyebrows drawing into a frown as he stared at the money.

Tawfiq was not parting with the money so easily. 'Take us there.'

Afzal's attention turned back to Tawfiq. 'No.' As simple as that. 'I've told you where the house is. That is all I will give you. I will not go there with you.'

Tawfiq stared at the man, looking like he was not willing to part with the cash on such flimsy information. Inside Sofia was screaming at Tawfiq to give him the bloody money so they could get the information back to Chief Wasim and get out of there, but she was not part of this negotiation between two Afghan men and knew she must remain silent. The two men had come to an impasse but then Tawfiq relented and placed the money on the rug between them. As it disappeared into Afzal's pocket, he said, 'If you want to find the boys you need to leave now.' Sofia was already on her feet. She couldn't get out of there fast enough.

'This is very bad,' Tawfiq said, shaking his head as they hurriedly threaded their way back through the old city. 'How do we know he's telling the truth?'

'We don't.'

'He'll probably warn them someone's looking for the boys.'

She shared his concern and picked up her pace. 'Which is why we have to let Chief Wasim know as soon as possible.' When they were a couple of streets away from the bird market Sofia stopped outside a shop and rang Chief Wasim, but he still didn't answer. She swore. 'What fucking police chief doesn't answer his phone? Sorry,' she apologised to Tawfiq. They continued on. 'You had a lot of money there.'

'Dr Jabril makes sure I always have money for an emergency.'

'An emergency like what just happened?'

'Maybe not quite like what just happened,' he said, his shoulders slumping as he walked with her. Sofia reached into the pocket of her coat for her phone again. Tawfiq wanted to know whom she was calling. 'Dr Jabril,' she said, stopping by a bicycle shop as she waited, hoping for Jabril to answer. 'Maybe he can get onto Chief Wasim and tell him.'

Sofia studied her friend as she listened to the ringtone. This whole episode had upset him greatly. She knew it had been wrong to involve him but what else could she have done? She couldn't wait and there was no way she could have gone to Afzal's home without Tawfiq, and even if she had been able to find him she probably would never have got the information out of him. Tawfiq's face was drawn and his eyes dull. Life was hard for him at the moment for some reason and she'd just made it harder. She felt so bad. She had to let him know how invaluable he had just been and how much she appreciated him.

'Jabril!' she said, shocked when he answered. She started walking again, motioning for Tawfiq to join her. After she'd told Jabril about the house with the star, he said he would try to contact Chief Wasim, asking her to inform Taban and Daniel. As they were entering the square she hung up, put the phone back in her pocket and stopped walking. She didn't want what she was about to say to be overheard in the square.

'You did well, Tawfiq. I couldn't have done this without you, and if they find the boys then it will all be because of you. You are my good friend and a good man. I just want you to know that, and I know this wasn't easy for you. I put you in a bad position but I couldn't see what else to do. I hope you can forgive me.'

'I understand,' he said, his face still drawn. 'Is Dr Jabril angry?'

'He's pleased we may have found where the boys are.' He was also furious that Tawfiq had let her go to the bird market to see this criminal. She would have to talk to Jabril and explain how Tawfiq really didn't have an option, because she would have gone with or without him. Nothing was Tawfiq's fault.

'We're good?' she asked Tawfiq when they got to the bottom of the stairs to her surgery where Rashid was sitting, waiting with Iqbal. He nodded and she ran up the staircase and through reception, ignoring Iman who had jumped to her feet as she knocked on Jabril's door.

242

'Chief Wasim's organising to raid the house as we speak,' Jabril said, looking happier than he had sounded on the phone ten minutes before.

'Thank god for that.' Sofia collapsed into the chair on the opposite side of his desk. After filling Jabril in on the visit to the bird market, she made a point of letting him know that Tawfiq really had no choice but to go with her because she would have gone anyway, and she had been much safer with Tawfiq.

'What about Rashid?'

'He was having lunch somewhere. I couldn't find him,' she lied, hoping the matter was settled and he wouldn't talk with either man about it.

Jabril seemed to accept this. 'I happened to inform Minister Massoud of this breakthrough,' he added as she was leaving. 'He was particularly interested to hear about it and that the information had come from Dr Abiteboul. I got the feeling they knew each other. Do they?'

Sofia shrugged and shook her head. 'No idea.'

Jabril smoothed down the hair on top of his head. 'He seemed very interested in Dr Abiteboul. Perhaps I shouldn't have mentioned his involvement.'

* * *

WHEN SOFIA ARRIVED back in her apartment that evening she was surprised to see her passport sitting on her bedside table. She couldn't remember taking it out of the bedside drawer and putting it there. In fact, she was sure she hadn't. On her way out to dinner with Zahra and Jabril that night she knocked on Behnaz's door.

'Did you happen to put my passport on my bedside table?'

Sofia asked when Behnaz opened the door, white flour covering her hands and peppered down the front of her black dress.

'No.'

'Was anyone in the house today?'

'No.'

'Are you sure?'

'Of course.' Behnaz didn't appreciate her word being questioned.

'I think someone must have been in the house.'

'No one has been in the house. I'd know.'

The two women stood looking at each other. 'I didn't touch your passport,' Behnaz said. 'You must have forgotten.'

'No, I don't think so.'

As Sofia walked out, heading for Jabril and Zahra's home, she wondered why Behnaz would take her passport out of the drawer and then deny it. She knew Behnaz sometimes went into her apartment when she had no reason to be there, because she would find things not quite how she'd left them. But why would Behnaz touch her passport, and especially now when her visa had been cancelled? Something was not right.

* * *

LATER THAT EVENING, as Sofia, Jabril and Zahra were having an after-dinner coffee in the lounge room while they waited for news from Chief Wasim about the raid, Jabril brought up the subject of Sofia's visa. As her employer and sponsor, he explained, he had been officially informed of its termination. He agreed with Sofia that it had to be a mistake and had taken the liberty of telling Minister Massoud of its cancellation when he'd spoken to him about the raid.

'We're lucky to have friends in high places,' he said, after explaining that the minister had promised to look into the cancellation. 'I'm sure this will be sorted out soon and we'll all be able to go back to normal.'

'Normal,' repeated Zahra.

Sofia had noticed that in the last few days Zahra had been uncharacteristically snappy. She was worried that it was because of the talk she had given to the women's group.

'These things take time,' Jabril said, answering the question none of them was asking.

'With Chief Wasim, everything takes time,' offered Zahra.

By eleven o'clock they still had not heard from Chief Wasim, nor could they reach him. Jabril suggested they all go to bed, and hopefully when they woke in the morning it would be to the news of the boys' release.

'I wish I wasn't going to Kandahar tomorrow,' Sofia said, pulling the collar of her coat up around her neck as Jabril walked her back through the deserted square which was lit softly by the glow from the apartments above the shops, 'but I don't see how I can get out of it now.'

'There's nothing more you can do here,' he said. 'We all have to wait and trust that Chief Wasim has found the boys.'

'Why doesn't that exactly fill me with confidence?'

30

WHEN JABRIL RETURNED to the house he found Zahra in the bedroom turning the sheets down, but when she saw him she sat down on the end of the bed. 'We need to talk.'

Jabril groaned inwardly. He was in for a lecture.

'You have to tell her.' Zahra didn't need to say more. He knew who, and he knew what. Sofia and the notes posted on their door had been constants in their conversations from the day the first one had arrived.

'Why should we give Sofia more things to worry about when these things have nothing to do with her?' he asked, resting his tired body in Zahra's velvet-covered 'boudoir' chair that he usually avoided, thinking it far too fragile to be of any use to anyone, especially him. 'It's me these ridiculous things are for.'

'You don't know this.'

'They're left on my door. They don't say anything about Sofia. They've got nothing to do with her.'

Jabril didn't need this conversation. He was more worried about why Chief Wasim hadn't rung to tell them the raid had taken place and the boys were safe. He feared something was wrong, but right then – in those very minutes – all he really wanted to do was go to bed.

'What about the visa? Why would her visa be cancelled?'

Jabril's body sank further into the flimsy arms of the chair. 'Clerical error, my dear. Clerical error.'

'Perhaps you should tell your precious Minister Massoud about the letters too and he can fix them for us while he's fixing Sofia's visa,' she said innocently, running her hand over the bedspread to flatten out its invisible creases. 'I have no idea why you put so much faith in that man.'

After more than thirty years of marriage Jabril knew what that tone meant. He also knew it was a waste of time to continue the conversation so late in the evening. Anything he said would be ignored or would lead to further argument. Excusing himself, he escaped to the bathroom. As he sat on the side of the bath waiting for Zahra to get into bed and fall asleep – his wife had the enviable knack of falling asleep the minute her head touched the pillow – he thought back to his conversation with Minister Massoud. He had not said anything wrong, but … Jabril pushed the thought away. Surely not.

* * *

WHEN SOFIA WOKE early the following morning to cold air seeping in through the partially open bedroom window and the vision of a cloudless blue sky, she was about to pull the blanket up around her ears and snuggle down for another half an hour when she realised she'd probably already overslept. Rolling over, she grabbed her phone off the bedside table to check the time and any messages. No messages but she was late. Daniel and Clementine would be in the square in thirty minutes. After having a quicker than normal shower, Sofia raced downstairs to knock on Chief Wasim's door. When no one answered she walked out into the courtyard to see the canary cage already hanging off the lowest branch of the pomegranate tree, which meant Behnaz was out and about. Hearing voices on the other side of the gate, she walked out to find Behnaz and Tawfiq talking. After greeting them, she asked Behnaz where her husband was.

'Work,' she said, narrowing her eyes.

'Do you know if anything happened last night?'

Behnaz put her hand on her hip while holding the broom in the other. 'What might have happened last night?'

'You haven't heard anything?'

'No. What might have happened last night?' Behnaz asked again.

'Did Chief Wasim get home late?'

'Maybe.'

'I'll be back in a minute,' Sofia said. Running up to her apartment, she rang the chief, stunned when he answered. 'What happened?'

'*As-salaam alaikum*, Dr Sofia,' he said politely.

'*Wa alaikum as-salaam.* What happened?'

'Nothing happened.'

Sofia sat down on the edge of her bed, a sick feeling in the pit of her stomach. They were going to lose the boys. 'What do you mean? I thought you were raiding the house yesterday?'

She heard him sigh. 'Dr Sofia, these things take time. It will be soon, I promise you. Today, I think. Now please don't worry yourself about this. I'll ring you when it's done.'

'Chief Wasim, the boys ...'

'Yes, I know about the boys.' She could hear the irritation on the other end of the phone. 'That's who I'm thinking about.

You don't want them to be harmed in a raid that hasn't been properly prepared, do you? Relax, I've got men watching the house. No one can escape.'

Sofia hung up and rang Jabril. 'It hasn't happened.' She realised she was hoping he might have different news or be able to make it happen.

'I know.'

'These men are going to get away, Jabril.' She started pacing around her bedroom. 'We're going to lose the boys forever.'

'Now, now, we don't know that yet.' Despite his words she could hear his worry.

'If only I wasn't going to Kandahar.' She lay down on the bed with her arm resting across her forehead. 'Jesus, I need to sort out my visa too. I shouldn't be going.'

'You need to talk to the women, remember? Listen, I want you to forget about the visa. I'm dealing with it. Go to Kandahar, deliver the medical supplies, say goodbye to the midwives as planned, and by the time you get back the boys will probably be safe at home and your visa sorted.'

Carrying her hastily packed overnight bag and a large box of medical supplies, Sofia headed back out to the courtyard. Omar, who had joined Tawfiq, Behnaz and now Rashid outside the gate, insisted on taking the box from her only to place it on the ground near her feet. Thanking Omar, she turned back toward the house, asking Rashid and Tawfiq if they could help her bring out the rest of the boxes for the midwives.

'You told me no more Kandahar,' Behnaz snapped when Sofia returned with another box.

'Yes, but I have to tell the women that, don't I?' Sofia disappeared back into the house for some more boxes.

249

'What's wrong with your phone?' Behnaz asked as Sofia was about to head back into the house one last time.

'Nothing's wrong with my phone. I want to tell them in person, Behnaz. Besides, I need to deliver these last supplies to the women.'

As Tawfiq came out with the last box he stood examining the two piles, considering his options before placing it on the ground next to them.

'Why haven't you left for the weekend with your family?' Sofia asked Tawfiq after counting the boxes to make sure they were all there.

He flicked his cigarette on Behnaz's newly swept cobble-stones, causing her to run the broom over the still smoking cigarette and his foot. 'Rashid and I will take you to Kandahar like we always do.'

As two MSF vehicles drove slowly into the square, Sofia turned back to Tawfiq. 'MSF have a security car,' she said. 'You don't need to come. I'll be fine.'

'It's our job,' repeated Tawfiq.

Sofia let out a sigh before turning to Rashid. 'Do you have to come with us too?'

Rashid examined the second car and the two security guards inside. 'No.'

Jumping out of the first car, Daniel came around to the gate, ready to offer a greeting until he saw their faces. 'Is something wrong?'

'Maybe.' Sofia was aware that if she rejected Tawfiq's protection he would be deeply hurt.

'Who are you?' Behnaz asked, looking Daniel up and down.

'Daniel Abiteboul.'

Sofia noticed that Daniel had found Behnaz's scrutiny amusing. *At your own risk.* 'Dr Daniel, let me introduce you to my landlady, Behnaz.'

'Ah,' he said in English to Sofia when recognition dawned. 'The gun-toting –'

'Who understands English,' Sofia added.

'It's a pleasure to meet you, Behnaz,' Daniel said in English.

'He's with the UN,' Sofia added in Dari.

Behnaz pointedly looked at the MSF logo on the side of the car and then back at Daniel.

'I'm with both,' he offered, also in Dari.

Behnaz seemed unimpressed. 'Dr Sofia must travel outside Kabul with Tawfiq and Rashid.'

Giving Behnaz his most charming smile, Daniel assured her that MSF would look after Dr Sofia very well. For the first time in twenty-four hours, Sofia felt like she might actually laugh. The man had no idea what an immovable force he had just pushed up against, but he was about to find out.

'No.'

Clementine had remained in the first car talking on her phone, but Sofia could see she was watching, looking unhappy about the delay. They were already late and it was a long drive to Kandahar.

'I think we have to go in my car with Tawfiq,' she said to Daniel. 'But maybe we can take the MSF security car so Rashid doesn't need to come.'

'It's better,' Behnaz offered, as if she was a legitimate part of the conversation.

Sofia watched Daniel assessing the situation. MSF would not be pleased their staff weren't travelling in one of their cars and with one of their drivers. Signalling for Clementine to wind her window down, he walked over to inform her of the new arrangements. Sofia watched her mouth, 'What the fuck?' Without interrupting her phone call, Clementine gathered her things, got out of the MSF car, opened the back door of Tawfiq's car, flung her things in and then climbed in after them.

With everything settled, Omar insisted on helping load the boxes, which made the whole process twice as long as it should have been, but once they were all stowed safely away and Daniel had retrieved his and Clementine's overnight bags, they headed off. As they pulled out of the square he turned in his seat to ask Sofia if there was any news.

'Nothing yet.'

'Are you serious?' he said, looking unimpressed.

She rolled her eyes. 'Chief Wasim's waiting for the right moment.'

***

As Tawfiq and Dr Sofia drove off with the man and woman from MSF, Behnaz gave Omar a withering look before disappearing back behind her gate, but for once Omar barely noticed. He was more intrigued by Tawfiq's insistence that only he should drive Dr Sofia to Kandahar. Omar began considering a new idea. Perhaps Dr Sofia was the friend who needed to stop, and if she was then this changed everything. But what would Dr Sofia be doing that so grievously offended anyone?

'Is Dr Sofia in danger?' he asked Rashid, who had remained outside the gate watching the cars drive away. 'You must know something.'

Rashid shrugged. 'All I know is that Dr Jabril says I have to

252

walk Dr Sofia across the square every day.' With that Rashid, the man of few words, wandered out of the square.

Standing alone by Behnaz's gate, Omar was still wondering what Dr Sofia might have done wrong when he noticed Iqbal setting up shop outside the surgery steps, which got him thinking. Iqbal sat outside Dr Sofia's surgery every day, talking with Rashid. If Dr Sofia had done something wrong and was in some kind of danger then surely Iqbal would know.

'Blessings on you this morning, my friend,' Omar said, after shuffling over to Iqbal who, having finished setting up, was resting with his back against the wall.

'And upon you.'

Omar watched as Iqbal adjusted his position, trying to ease the pain in his bad leg, which had been mangled when he was run over by a car at nine years old. It looked to Omar as if things were getting worse for Iqbal. 'I might have a potion that could help your pain,' he offered.

'My pain has been my companion for so long now, Omar, that I would miss him if he left me, but thank you anyway.'

Omar understood this. Although he had never thought of his pain as a friend until that moment, he saw now that it was. If his pain no longer existed then neither would he.

Omar would have liked to squat down and have a chat with Iqbal but his body would not. 'I have a question for you,' he said, remaining standing. 'Is Dr Sofia in danger?'

Iqbal looked up, squinting with the morning sun in his eyes. 'You want to know if Dr Sofia is in danger?'

'Yes.'

'All foreigners are in danger nowadays. Bombs explode here, there, everywhere. In cafés and hotels. You never know who'll be killed next, although I have noticed the police have been the main target now for a long time, so maybe it will be Chief Wasim.'

Omar stroked his beard as he considered this, only to find spiky hairs stuck to the ends of his fingers. The loss of hair under his *pakol* had been expected but this unwelcome reminder of his illness on his face was not. He brushed them off on his *tunban*.

'Anyway, if she was, why do you think I'd know?' Iqbal asked, shading his eyes with his bony old hand.

Omar shrugged. 'I thought you might have heard something, or Rashid might have told you something.'

Iqbal changed his position again. 'The last time Rashid told me something it was that a black man had become president of the United States. How long ago was that?'

Omar considered the question. 'Quite a long time ago, I think.' As he considered what Iqbal had just said he realised that Rashid had only been in the square for three years and Obama became president a very long time ago. His heart felt heavy in his thin body. Why was Iqbal teasing him?

'Tell me why you're asking this thing, Omar.'

'Well, I noticed that Tawfiq didn't want Dr Sofia to go to Kandahar with the man from the UN, and Rashid's been following her across the square, and Behnaz didn't want Dr Sofia to go to Kandahar. It seems to me that something's not right in the square.'

'Why do you say the man was from the UN when he has an MSF car? I think you're confused.'

Omar scratched the skin under his beard again. He couldn't rightly remember why he thought the man was from the UN. 'Yes, but Behnaz was being very strange also. Maybe the chief has told her something about Dr Sofia. He must know what everyone is doing.'

'It's been my opinion that Behnaz has been very strange for a very long time,' Iqbal offered with a chuckle.

Omar shook his head. 'That's not the point.' Why was Iqbal trying to confuse him?

'Don't you think, Omar, that if Dr Jabril was really worried about Dr Sofia, he would have hired someone better than Rashid?'

It is true, Omar thought.

'Perhaps there is another possibility you've not considered yet.'

'Yes?' Omar asked, hoping this new possibility would clear everything up.

'Tawfiq and Rashid are simply doing their jobs and Behnaz is always worried about Dr Sofia and Kandahar is not a safe place to be for someone like Dr Sofia anytime these days.

'Well, yes, but there are these *shabnamah* …'

'These *shabnamah*? Last time I heard you had only one *shabnamah*.'

'Yes, you're right, it was only one.' Omar felt flustered. 'But there might be more. There might be two.'

'Two?'

'Maybe … maybe not.'

'Careful, Omar, the wound of the sword will heal, but not that of the tongue.' Iqbal was watching him, waiting for his words to sink in. 'I think you need to keep your story straight or people in the square might think you're out to cause trouble.'

Omar felt deeply wounded. 'No, I would never want to cause trouble.'

'I know this, my friend, but you've been talking to people, and now half the square is afraid, so I'm thinking that it might be wise for you to go back to your chair in the middle of the square and catch all the gossip you've created as it comes flying past so everything in the square can go back to normal. Don't dig wells for others because you might fall into one yourself, Omar.' With that, Iqbal leaned his head back against the wall and closed his eyes. 'Now I need to rest.'

Omar wandered back to his chair. He knew Iqbal's words had been harsh because of his pain and he must forgive him. As he sat, his heart made heavy by his friend's words, Omar could feel himself beginning to drift off. When he woke that morning he had used the last of his pain draught. Perhaps he had taken a little too much, he thought, but sleep was a beautiful thing.

As he drifted off, he wondered whether falling asleep forever would not be such a bad thing after all.

31

ONCE THEY HIT the paved, and mostly monitored, ring road from Kabul to Ghazni and then on to Kandahar, Tawfiq reverted to Afghan rally car mode, which assigned the right of way to the fastest driver in the largest SUV. Such driving had more to do with security than machismo. A fast-moving target was harder for Taliban snipers to hit.

Within an hour they were moving through barren hills and flying past sparse villages of dull mudbrick partially hidden behind crumbling rock walls. Occasionally a child could be seen playing in the dirt next to a house, a goat herder grazing his flock among the rocks, black-clad women laying washing over dry stone walls and old men with heavy loads balanced on their heads navigating a path along the disappearing verge of the road. Forlorn little roadside *chaikhanas* and stalls were dotted along the highway selling the street food of *chainaki*, kebabs, *bolani* and chickpeas in a vinegar sauce, together with misshapen fruit, vegetables and dusty bottles of warm water.

When the large SUVs sped past, the owners no longer bothered looking up from the shade of their makeshift shelters, although it had not always been so. When Sofia had first arrived in Afghanistan the stallholders used to wave enthusi-astically whenever they saw a large car approaching, but with the re-emergence of the Taliban, who liked to use their stalls' patrons for target practice, the foreigners in their big cars no longer stopped and the stallholders no longer waved.

They passed a barren stretch of land where the remnants of what must have once been a family compound lay abandoned. Having long lost its battle with the elements, the stone walls of the house lay broken and scattered around the dusty, dry courtyard. What sort of tenacity or desperation, she often wondered, forced people to build in such a place? Life was hard enough in the cities; in the country it could be soul-destroying. People aged quickly and died early in Afghanistan, but it was not always disease, childbirth, bad diet or even war that killed them. Sometimes it was just life.

In her first six months in Afghanistan the poverty and desperation had worn her down, causing her to question whether she should stay. It had been her trip to the village that had changed everything, but not just because of the reasons she had told Daniel. That trip had truly shown her the people of Afghanistan: the highlanders who had embraced her; the guide who had risked his life to bring her back down from the mountain; Tawfiq, the driver she had barely known who cried when he saw her walking back into the village; and the people of the square who had welcomed her home with open arms, as if she was one of their own. Despite everything she had told Daniel, and for all her rationalising, her decision to stay had been because of the people.

Each year, as the seasons changed, Sofia had watched the snows melting on the mountains from her window overlooking

Shaahir Square, and each year she had thought about returning to the village. She told herself she had never made the trek because she would probably never find it again but she knew it was because he would not have been there. Sofia thought again of the man now sitting in the seat in front of her, the lover who had left without a hint or word of goodbye. The memory of that betrayal still had the power to hurt.

* * *

THE DAY DANIEL left the wind had whipped through the village, chasing away the last breath of autumn and bringing with it the bitter winter cold. Winding Daniel's woollen scarf more tightly around her neck, she had breathed in the scent of him and waited. He had not come back that night, or the night or day after that, or the one after that. When her guide from the lowlands arrived unexpectedly to take her back down the mountain, she asked if they might wait one more day. When Daniel had not returned that day she pleaded for another, but the guide would not be moved. The snows would cover the mountains any day now and they would be trapped for months. He would be leaving the following morning, he told her. She could come or she could stay.

The trek back down to the lowlands should have taken a little more than two days at the most. It took four. On the journey down Sofia was so cold she wore most of the clothes she owned, including a blanket the village women had given her, which she had wrapped tightly around her shoulders until it too became heavy with damp. While it snowed every night, by lunchtime the snow had turned into a filthy brown mud that clung to the bottom of her boots, sucking at her every step until the leather had become sodden and the skin on her feet had begun to peel. The wind and horizontal rain that whipped up the mountain passes and between the boulders caused her lips to crack and bleed, while her thick cotton trousers, frozen with damp, rubbed rough against the soft flesh of her inner thighs until the skin became so chafed and raw that it too bled. She dreaded walking, she hated stopping, and whenever she slept she woke frozen from dreams of Daniel.

'How far now?' she began asking the guide on the second day, when they still had not reached the village they'd slept in on their way up.

'*Nazdik*,' he would answer, until 'near' became meaningless and he stopped answering and she stopped asking.

By the third day the land had grown eerily quiet. A heavy fog rolled in, blocking out the thin grey light of the wintry sun, but by late that afternoon the wind had picked up again and blown the fog away, bringing with it sheets of horizontal rain and snow that cut their faces like icy blades. Sofia and the guide had wrapped their wet blankets up over their heads until only their eyes were visible, but she had seen the fear in his eyes. It was mirrored in her own. They had left it too late. On the third day they finally made it to the village for their only respite from sleeping out, covered in layers of wet blankets.

With every kilometre they moved away from the highland village her sense of loss grew. She told herself that whatever she felt for Daniel had been illusory. She told herself that, despite her memories of that last night, nothing had passed between them. She told herself she was a fool to think otherwise. And yet, that was not how her heart felt. She had told herself to forget him. Her heart would not.

***

SOFIA LOOKED UP at Daniel sitting in the seat in front of her. His elbow was resting on the car window frame and his shirt-sleeve had slipped down to expose the tan mark under the fine dark hairs of his arm. She knew what touching that skin felt like. She knew what the curl of his hair felt like as it slipped through her fingers. She knew the scent of him. Sofia turned to look out the window. He was here with her again. He had returned. She had no idea what that meant or whether it meant anything at all.

There had been times, late at night in her bed or if she found herself alone for another weekend, when she would question the trade-off she was making living in Afghanistan against the possibility of a long-term relationship and a family back in Sydney where nearly all her friends were married and having children. Recently she had begun to feel her biological clock ticking away, which wasn't helped by the fact that her little sister now had a baby and every Afghan she met asked her about her husband. She was running out of time. She told herself that was an irrational thought, but a thought wasn't the same as a feeling, and the feeling she was trying to hold down was that of a slow-ticking biological clock. How long until she must abandon the idea of ever having a family? Eight years? Was eight a reasonable number? Too generous? Not generous enough?

Sofia had slept in that morning because, unusually, her father had rung her in the middle of the night, waking her from only a few hours' sleep to talk about Michelle's little boy – his smile, his dimples, his little pudgy fingers and his wide brown eyes. 'I think you've fallen in love,' she had said.

He had laughed. 'I think I have. Well, he's my grandson, you know, I should.'

'Of course he is. How stupid am I? I hadn't even registered that. You're a grandfather! Congratulations, Dad. So what's he going to call you?'

'Hey, he's not even talking. He's only six months old.'

'Nonno,' she had said, offering the Italian for grandfather. 'He'll call you Nonno.'

Sofia's heart sank. It had taken Michelle six months to introduce her father to his first grandchild. The fact would not have escaped him either. 'And how's Michelle?'

When he didn't answer immediately, a sure sign that she was in for a long night, she had turned on her back to stare into the dark, resting her arm across her forehead. Sleep was not about to return anytime soon and whatever her father said was not going to be good.

'She's okay.' Sofia could hear the lie. 'She's much better, actually.'

Much better, he had said, confirming her suspicions that her father knew more about Michelle than he ever let on to her. 'And the guy she's going to marry?'

'Seems like a nice bloke.'

'Uhuh, and what does that mean?'

'Doesn't look like a drug addict.'

'What does he do for a job, Dad?'

She had heard him hesitate again and immediately regretted asking the question. Something about the guy didn't sit well with her father. *He doesn't need my questions.* What had he done to deserve losing his young wife and then having two daughters who caused him such pain? Life was not always right, or good, or fair.

'Well, he doesn't have a job at the moment, but he's been looking. I gather he's in finance or something. I didn't quite understand. Guess I'm getting too old.' Her father's brain was as sharp as ever. If he didn't understand they weren't being transparent with him. 'They're going to move in with me for a while, until he gets on his feet.'

Sofia could feel her skin crawl. They were going to sponge off him. They were going to rip him off. Usual Michelle. 'That'll be nice for you, having Jack and Michelle around.'

'Having family again will be good.'

Sofia had ended the call on a happy note, congratulating him again on being a nonno and having his daughter back and a new son-in-law, but when she had hung up she felt only sadness. She was sure little Jack would lighten his life, but she feared they had only contacted him for a roof over their heads. It wouldn't have escaped her father's notice either. It had taken her hours to get back to sleep.

* * *

AFTER STOPPING FOR twenty minutes at a small mud-walled village so Tawfiq could have a rest and they could stretch their legs and get something to eat, they carried on, passing dry riverbeds marked by dead trees in a parched landscape.

The phone resting in Sofia's lap began to ring.

'You know how my father works in the Ministry of Foreign Affairs?' Iman said as soon as she answered.

'Yes?' Sofia said hesitantly. She didn't like the sound of this.

'I asked him to look into your visa –'

'Iman, what was the last thing I said to you?'

'I know, I know, but he works at the ministry –'

'You promised.'

'I know, but you'll want to hear this.' Sofia waited. 'He said the instructions to cancel your visa came from a very high level.'

263

'What does that mean?'

'It means it was so high my father wasn't allowed to see.'

Sofia had no idea what powerful person she had upset. 'Could it have been a clerical error?'

'I asked him that and he said no.'

'Okay, let's talk about this when I get back. In the meantime, can you please not discuss this with anyone else?'

'Why did you go to the bird market?'

'I can't explain now.'

When Sofia hung up, Daniel turned around to ask if everything was okay. Before answering she mentally threaded her way back through her side of the conversation to see if she had said anything that might alert the others to what she'd been talking about. 'A problem with a patient.'

Ten minutes later her phone rang again. This time it was Jabril to tell her that he still hadn't heard from Chief Wasim.

'What about Massoud? Anything from him?'

'No, I'm leaving him out of this for the moment.'

'I think you should talk with Iman,' Sofia said.

Jabril waited for her to continue. 'Are you able to tell me why?'

'No.'

'Okay, I'll give her a call. By the way, has Taban rung you?'

'No.'

Jabril informed her that Taban's clinic had been broken into the night before. Not much damage had been done, and no one was there so nobody was hurt, but a message had been scrawled on the wall. It said Taban should to go back to her family.

'Do you think it had something to do with –'

'Don't know. It might, but it could also be someone who

doesn't like the work she's doing there. Taban does tend to stir things up.'

'Should I call her?'

'No, I think she's got enough to deal with at the moment.'

'Okay. Call me if there's any news on any front.'

As Daniel and Clementine began a conversation about problems in MSF's Kandahar clinic, Sofia leaned her head against the window. She couldn't understand why Chief Wasim was waiting. It didn't make sense. And now Taban's clinic had been broken into and her visa was cancelled. Were those things linked? It was hard to see how but it all seemed too much of a coincidence.

With the warm afternoon sun pouring in and the rhythm of the road, Sofia felt herself drifting off, only to be pulled out of a dream by the sound of conversation. Fighting to wake up, she sat up straight and blinked a couple of times before looking out the window to see they were coming into Kandahar.

'Ah, you're awake,' Daniel said, turning around to look at her.

Sofia put a hand over her mouth to stifle a yawn. 'How long did I sleep?'

'A couple of hours. You must've been tired.'

'I was.' She looked down at her phone to see if she'd missed any messages. There were none.

'We've made pretty good time so we've decided to stop at a café that belongs to a friend of mine for something to eat then we'll drop Clem off at the hospital and we can go to Fatima's together, if that's okay with you?'

'Sure,' she said as her phone began to ring.

'Chief Wasim's raid was a failure. No one was there,' Jabril said.

'No!' She felt her emotions collapsing in. She had pinned everything on the success of the raid. How would they ever find the boys now? 'Damn it, Jabril, how could they escape if the place was being watched? Damn it. Fuck.'

'He's saying they must have left before his men began watching the place. The good news is they found fresh food and girls' clothing and make-up, so it was probably the right place, especially when the neighbours said there were only little boys there and men.'

'No! Fuck.' Sofia wasn't so sure that was good news at all, other than the fact that they had been given good information.

'We're close,' Jabril said.

'We *were* close. Bloody Wasim. You know what this means, don't you? Either Chief Wasim is completely incompetent or someone warned them.'

'Chief Wasim is thinking the latter.'

'He would! Why the hell didn't he raid the house when you first told him?' Daniel had turned around in his seat again and was watching her, as was Clementine. 'I don't understand who would have warned them.' She shook her head at Daniel to let him know the raid was unsuccessful.

'There's always the possibility it was one of Chief Wasim's men, or even the man who told you and Tawfiq about the house. He could have been happy to take your money and then take some more from these men by warning them? I'm hoping that's the explanation.'

Sofia considered this. 'I suppose that's possible. He was pretty sleazy. What now?'

'We'll think of something.'

Sofia couldn't see how they'd think of anything. 'Shit!' she said, her anger at Chief Wasim boiling up again.

'About your visa … I spoke with Iman and I still don't think we need to worry yet. It has to be a mistake but, in any case, we should give the minister a couple of days to see what he can do, and if he can't do anything then we'll think of something else.'

With Jabril in the habit of shouting a little down a phone line, Sofia was aware that Clementine, who was sitting next to her on the back seat, might have been able to hear everything he said. Hanging up, she dropped the phone back into her lap.

'They didn't find them. Sounds like they were warned,' she said to Daniel. 'In any event, your information was good.'

'Who do you think could have warned them?'

Sofia put her hands in the air and shrugged. 'Who knows?'

'I'm sorry. I'll ask my friend again. Maybe he's heard something new.'

'I'd really appreciate that.'

Sofia worried that the leak had come from someone in their circle, although she had no idea who it could have been or why. It just didn't make sense. Perhaps it was innocent and one of them had spoken to someone they shouldn't have. She thought it was more probable that the leak was at Chief Wasim's end than that Afzal had sold them out, but whatever the reason, she was going to be more circumspect about who she spoke to next time, if there was a next time.

32

It was a hot, windless afternoon with a dense soup of exhaust fumes and smoke settling over Kandahar as they slowly made their way into the centre of town behind a long line of almost stationary vehicles. A man with a high black turban and a bushy grey beard sitting atop an overladen donkey took the opportunity to cross the slow-moving traffic in front of them. Kicking the donkey's sides with his sandalled feet and giving its neck a flick with a stick, he tried to make the scrawny animal move faster, but the donkey only had one pace. A fluffy white dog that looked to be a Maltese but was clipped like a poodle wandered out in front of them, closely followed by a second donkey, who was riderless and possibly ownerless. As the traffic began to move and Tawfiq waited for this donkey to pass, a brightly painted three-wheeled car and three men on bicycles pushed in front of him.

'*Amaq*,' Tawfiq said, annoyed. 'Am I supposed to let all of Kandahar cross the road in front of me?' As he held his hand down on the horn, the last donkey was the only one who bothered to look back to see what all the commotion was about.

Eventually they parked in front of a small café behind yet

another donkey attached to a tray loaded with empty plastic water bottles. Slowly turning its head to look at them, the scrawny animal swished the flies away with his ears before lifting his tail and dropping a pile of grassy turds on the road. Having finished his business, the donkey turned back again to stare desolately at the ground in front of him.

'Donkey droppings are good luck,' offered Tawfiq as they got out of the car.

'Yeah, I can see that. Afghanistan's a real paradise,' offered Clementine.

'Come on, my friend,' Daniel said, wrapping his arm around Tawfiq's shoulders as he led him into the café. 'We're all hungry and some of us can be grumpy when we haven't eaten.'

The entry to Forood's café was beside an alley in which rickety stalls had been set up to display growers' produce. Women in burqas were wandering down the alleyway between the stalls, inspecting pieces of raw meat, running their hands through hessian bags of grain, and picking up vegetables to feel their worthiness. On the opposite side of the alley was a tiny ice cream parlour conspicuously empty of patrons, its throbbing generator dripping water into a puddle that had created a little river of mud running between the stalls.

Inside the café the air was thick with the greasy smell of meat and cigarette smoke. Behind a counter dividing the cooking and the seating areas a charcoal brazier was splattering, flames leaping into the air as skewers of mutton dripped fat onto the burning coals. Along one wall was the kitchen while on the opposite wall was a raised timber bench where half a dozen men were sitting cross-legged, chatting as they spooned food into their mouths with their fingers. Their sandals had been placed just inside the door; their rifles leaned up against the wall behind them.

When the foreigners entered conversation ceased, causing the cook to look up from his work until his face split into a grin. 'Forood! Forood!' he shouted toward the back door of the café before wiping greasy hands on his apron and leaning dangerously over the grill to kiss Daniel on both cheeks. 'My friend, my friend,' he said, before calling out to Forood again. Daniel pointed toward the door and raised his eyebrows questioningly. The cook nodded just as Forood came through the door laden with dishes and saw Daniel standing in front of him.

'Ah!' Forood cried, putting the plates down on the counter before enveloping his friend in a hug and kisses. 'Where have you been?' He stood back to examine Daniel. 'I've missed you, my friend. It has been too long.'

'It has, it has,' Daniel said, slapping him on the back. 'And how is the family, Forood? Humaira and the kids?'

'Ah,' Forood laughed, 'I have five little ones now and another on the way. *Insha'Allah* this will be the last! Move along, move along,' he said, turning his attention to his curious patrons. 'Make room for my special guest and his friends.'

After Daniel made introductions they all settled into the tiny space the men had made for them before being presented with little plates of food dictated by what was available in the alleyway beside the café that day and the whims and impulses of Forood's uncle, the cook. Within a short time the floral *dastarkhan* had disappeared under the weight of food: hard-boiled eggs, rounds of naan, a limp green lettuce drenched in oil, steaming hot bean soup and a bowl of stringy goat floating in an oily liquid. Glasses were filled with tea that had been brewing for so long it was undrinkable to all but Tawfiq, who heaped in the sugar. After they'd finished eating, Forood cleared the dishes away, brought a plate of freshly baked pistachio biscuits to the table and sat down next to Daniel.

'Where have you been, my friend?' he asked, wrapping his arm around Daniel's shoulders and giving him a squeeze.

'Here and there. Too much time in Geneva, I'm afraid.'

'And what brings you to Kandahar again?'

As Daniel explained his work for the UN, Sofia, Clementine and Tawfiq talked among themselves about the dangers of Kandahar, Taban's work in the slum and what might happen when all the Western troops pulled out until Daniel reminded them that it was time to go.

'But when will I see you again?' Forood asked, looking morose before his face lit up. 'I know, come with me tonight. You will be my special guest.'

Daniel turned to Sofia to ask how long she thought he would be with Fatima that afternoon.

'Seven … seven-thirty?' she said, pulling a face as if to say, 'Your guess is as good as mine'.

It was decided that Daniel would meet Forood in downtown Kandahar outside a defunct video store at eight.

Once out in the street again they found themselves surrounded by a bunch of raggedy street urchins, their hands held out for *baksheesh*. Sofia's attention was caught by a little boy of no more than five or six who was standing back from the others. When he turned his head she saw that part of his cheek had been eaten away, lost to leishmaniasis, a potentially fatal but largely treatable disease spread by sandflies. Having also noticed the child, Clementine was crouching down in front of him, but when the other boys realised something was happening they began crowding around.

'If you go to the MSF clinic the people there can do something for your face. Do you think you could do that?' she said in Pashto.

An older boy with a dark fringe flopping in his eyes and dressed in an old *perahan tunban* stepped forward. 'Will it cost money? He doesn't have money.'

Clementine looked up at the boy. 'No, he'll be treated for free.' She stood again, dusting her hands off before pointing to the MSF sign on the side of the security car. 'This is the clinic you should go to. Do you know this place?'

'I know it, but there are others who have this disease,' the boy said.

'Then they should go also.'

'We will get money if we go?'

'No. Your friends will get help.'

The boy considered this. 'Okay, we'll go.'

Sofia had been surprised to hear Clementine speak perfect Pashto, the predominant language of the south. Perhaps she needed to reassess her opinion of the woman, which she was painfully aware had been coloured by an unworthy emotion.

***

AFTER DROPPING CLEMENTINE off at the MSF facility where she and Daniel would spend the night, the two cars headed off to Fatima's single-storey house on the outskirts of Kandahar. Having once belonged to her parents, its mudbrick walls were still washed the original dull ochre with tiny windows all but hidden within deep sills. Thick, rough-hewn timber beams supported the low white ceilings with the hard concrete floors covered in rugs that had belonged to Fatima's family for generations. In summer the cavernous rooms were blessedly cool, but in winter they were bitterly cold.

'Do you think your friend will be able to answer my questions freely with another man in the room?' Daniel had asked as they were pulling up outside the house.

Sofia smiled and shook her head. 'Somehow I don't think that's going to a problem.'

'What do you mean?'

Sofia's smile broadened. 'Fatima's not like an ordinary woman. There won't be any man there to look after her honour.'

After Fatima's elderly guard opened the huge metal gates, they followed him through the courtyard to the cool dark interior where Fatima was waiting for them. After greeting her friend Sofia made the introductions and left, wandering back out into the courtyard. With Tawfiq deep in conversation with the guard, Sofia walked a little further off to sit by herself on a small stone wall that had once been part of the family's enclosed vegetable garden but was now full of weeds. As Sofia watched, the afternoon sun began to fade behind the vast undulating plain, washing the empty sky a soft pink.

From her initial meeting with Fatima, Sofia had been taken by the strength and determination of the female entrepreneur from Kandahar until she eventually came to see her as part of the rich heritage of fierce Afghan women that went back centuries. Aware that one of these women, Commander Kaftar, was her friend's idol, Sofia had once told Fatima that she reminded her of Afghan's famous female warlord. While Fatima had been pleased, Sofia, who had actually met the warlord, knew that would not have been everyone's response.

There were many crazy stories about Commander Kaftar, but the one that had cemented her legend had been an exchange between her and a Taliban leader. Like everything else about Kaftar, though, whether it was true or not was anyone's guess.

New to the area, the Taliban leader, Mullah Baqi, had tuned into Kaftar's radio frequency to warn the local warlord that he intended taking over his land. 'And I will fuck your wife!' he had added for good measure.

Grabbing the microphone from her radio operator, Kaftar had shot back, 'And my husband will fuck yours.'

Until that moment the Talib had been unaware his adversary was a woman, although that was probably understandable in Kaftar's case. She might have had the necessary anatomy to bear seven children but that was where the similarities between her and the fairer sex ended.

'If you come into my valley and kill me then people will laugh at you for killing a woman,' Kaftar had warned Mullah Baqi. 'And if you come into my valley and I kill you then people will laugh because you were killed by a woman.'

The Taliban commander knew a lose-lose situation when he heard one and had made a tactical retreat.

Two years previously Sofia had been working with a group of midwives in Baghlan Province, which was part of Kaftar's personal fiefdom in the north of Afghanistan, when she had received a message through the village imam that the warlord wanted to see her. While she had been intrigued by the request, Tawfiq had been horrified.

'You cannot go,' he had told her as they sat together on the stone steps leading up to a room Sofia was using to train the women. Two girls had come to sit in the dirt in front of Sofia and stare at her. She'd tried talking with them but all they did was giggle. Tawfiq's response had surprised her. It was the first time he had told Sofia what she could or could not do.

'But I want to meet her,' she had said, turning to look at him. 'She's an Afghan legend.'

'Are you crazy? This is an unwise decision.'

'Making what people thought were unwise decisions was what got me to Afghanistan in the first place, Tawfiq. It's also what got me to the village in the Hindu Kush and my work with midwives, which is what got me here today.'

Tawfiq had considered this. 'Yes, those were good unwise decisions. Sometimes this can happen, but making an unwise decision about Commander Kaftar is not a good unwise decision. This one will get you killed.'

'She has no reason to kill me.'

Tawfiq had hit himself on the forehead with the palm of his hand. 'She doesn't need a reason to kill you! This is Kaftar. How can you know she won't kill you anyway?'

'Think about it. Why would she summon me just to kill me? She doesn't even know me.'

Tawfiq had rolled his eyes toward the heavens. 'She doesn't need to know you! She doesn't need a reason to kill you! This is Kaftar! I think this rests my case: if she doesn't know you, why would she summon you unless she wants to kill you?'

Sofia had been resting her head on her knees, staring back at the children in what had become a staring contest she was going to let them win. 'Because I'm a doctor, or because of what I'm doing with the midwives? There could be a hundred different reasons.'

Tawfiq ran his hands down his face in frustration before

placing his hand on his heart. 'Dr Sofia, you know all you have to do is ask. You are the owner of my choice, you are the sand under my feet, but I don't know how you will get there if I cannot take you.'

Sofia looked at Tawfiq, who seemed quite pleased with his logic. She conceded it was a good point. With Tawfiq happy that the catastrophe had been expertly averted, they had both assumed the subject was closed until Kaftar turned up in the village to see Sofia.

Legend had it that Commander Kaftar came by the *nom de guerre* of Kaftar, meaning dove, either by killing with the grace of a bird or from climbing mountains as lightly as a bird. As far as Sofia could see, the birdlike days of the overweight woman sitting in front of her in a floral dress, headscarf and rifle slung over her shoulder were long gone. Large folds of skin covered half the commander's eyelids while puffy bags hung heavy beneath them. Her hands were fleshy fat fists and her nose bulbous. The deep ridges chiselled into the wasteland of her face drew her mouth down into a permanent scowl. She had no front teeth, and was suffering from acute arthritic pain, failing eyesight and, Sofia suspected, depression. Before Sofia was allowed to examine Kaftar, the warlord insisted that she convert to Islam. 'Say the *Shahada. La ilaha illa Allah, Muhammad rasoolu Allah* – there is no true god but God, and Mohammad is the Messenger of God. It's easy.'

Sofia thought the ease of conversion was not the point. 'Aren't you supposed to mean it?'

Kaftar looked confused. 'Don't you want Jannah?'

When Sofia professed that, in all good faith, she could not convert to Islam, they spent the next twenty minutes with

Kaftar refusing to speak or even look at her. As Sofia was trying to work out the best way to leave, Kaftar began describing her aches and pains, all the while lamenting her miserable life. The best Sofia could do was offer the name of an arthritis medication the warlord could find in Kabul and suggest that while there she might like to see an eye specialist about her cataracts.

Not interested in anything Sofia could offer, Kaftar raised the possibility of Sofia helping her, and maybe thirty or forty of her closest relatives, to immigrate to America where she might live out her last years in peace, maybe even have an operation to mend her aching knees and an apartment with a TV.

'You need to talk to the American authorities about that.'

'You're American.'

'No, I'm Australian.'

Kaftar was not interested in living in Australia. Sofia was dismissed.

33

As THE SUN set behind the mountains and Fatima's courtyard was thrown into long cool shadows, Tawfiq and the guard retreated into the shelter of the guard house. Sofia could hear them talking and knew that Tawfiq would be relishing the opportunity to listen to the old guard's stories about Kandahar in the time before the Russians and the Taliban.

Feeling the early evening chill, Sofia wrapped her arms around her body. She knew Tawfiq would be tired from the long drive but he still had to drop Daniel off for his rendezvous with Forood, and she and Fatima needed to shop for their dinner. As she was wondering whether she should go inside to ask how much longer they might be, Daniel appeared.

'So how did it go?' she asked, jumping off the wall to join him.

'You were right. She's not like ordinary Afghan women, is she?'

'No, she's not like other Afghan women, but did you learn anything?'

'I learned a great deal.'

Hearing Daniel's voice, Tawfiq came out of the guard's hut and climbed into the car to take him to Forood.

* * *

In her late forties, Fatima was the sixth of twelve children. As her successful father's favourite child, she had taken over his building company, expanding it into earthmoving and a taxi service. She had never married, nor had she ever wanted children. She also had zero interest in becoming a midwife, but after one of her sisters and a niece died in quick succession in childbirth, Fatima had seen a need and had set about meeting it. After hearing about the foreign doctor in Kabul who trained midwives in outlying villages, she had travelled to the capital to find her, refusing to leave until Dr Sofia agreed to come to Kandahar. On gaining Sofia's consent Fatima had returned to the city to find the women who would make up this group.

She needed women who were both intelligent and curious, but also willing and able to leave their homes one day a month to travel to the outskirts of the city for training. Each woman needed the permission of her husband or father, and in some cases the consent of the village imam or other family members. She also needed a male relative willing to accompany her to the training and to wait around to take her home. The initial formation, together with the continuation of the group, was testament to Fatima's perseverance and the determination and the dedication of each of the women and their families.

When Dr Sofia had arrived at Fatima's home late that afternoon and introduced her to Dr Daniel, a cold claw had gripped Fatima's heart. She was not stupid, nor was she blind.

Over the years Fatima had only had one furtive encounter with a woman. Under their clothes, in a dark cupboard, she had been

279

electrified by the gloriousness of it and the utter fear of being discovered. The woman had been married, but even if she hadn't been there was nothing more they could do. With their lust sated, the two women had stepped out of the cupboard, ashamed by their wantonness. When they met again, which was often enough, for she was Fatima's sister-in-law, they pretended it had never happened. When Fatima met Sofia in Kabul she had carried back to Kandahar dreams of a foreign woman almost too beautiful to imagine, along with hopes almost too painful to hold.

Dr Daniel seemed both intelligent and knowledgeable about her country, and eager to learn from her. She wished it had been otherwise; it would have been easier to dislike the man. After she and Dr Sofia had visited the local market to shop for their dinner, they prepared and ate their usual meal together before beginning to unpack Sofia's boxes.

'The doctor is an interesting man,' Fatima had offered.

'He is,' Sofia said, taking out blood pressure monitors, thermometers, forceps, lancets and surgical scissors.

Fatima picked up a bandage and pretended to examine it. 'Do you know him well?'

'Not really. I met him a long time ago.'

'And you've never forgotten him?'

Sofia stopped what she was doing and looked at Fatima, considering her words. 'Maybe, though perhaps it's not so much that I've never forgotten him as that I've never forgotten the experience.'

'I don't understand.'

Sofia sat back on her haunches, hands resting on her knees in front of the box she had been unpacking. 'I was in a strange place at a strange time and he was part of that. Does that make sense?'

'I think so. I also think perhaps you love him,' Fatima offered, returning to her box. She could see her question had disturbed Dr Sofia. They had never strayed into such territory. She watched as the woman she had fallen in love with searched deep inside her for an answer.

'He's part of a memory of a time I loved, and perhaps, in that way, it felt like I loved him, but perhaps I don't know him well enough to say that now. I think you have to know someone much better to know if it's love rather than attraction, don't you?'

Fatima sat back on the floor, crossing her legs, looking at Sofia. 'No, I think you can love someone instantly.'

'That's what my father believes.' Sofia abandoned the boxes to sit cross-legged on the floor opposite Fatima, their knees almost touching. 'I have something I need to tell you and I don't know how to say it.'

'Then perhaps it's not meant to be said,' offered Fatima, afraid of what she was about to hear.

'I can't come back here anymore. It's become too dangerous for all of us: me, you, Tawfiq and Rashid and the women. It means I won't be able to finish their training. I'm sorry.'

In those few seconds Fatima understood that she would have preferred it if Dr Sofia had confessed her love for the man rather than this. But she could see how hard this decision had been for her and she was not about to cause her more pain. Leaning forward, Fatima took both of Sofia's hands in hers, feeling how delicate and strong they were. It was, she thought, the first time they had touched like this. She let Sofia's hands go to place her palm on Sofia's cheek, her heart aching as Sofia leaned into it, covering Fatima's hand with her own. This was what lovers do, she thought, but they would never be lovers.

'This is a wise decision, I think,' Fatima said, forcing a smile. 'Of course, the women will be disappointed, but they'll understand.'

'But listen, there's a possibility that the woman from MSF who's coming tomorrow might have someone here in Kandahar who can continue their training.' As Sofia told her about Clementine and her interest in the group, Fatima withdrew her hand. Seeing Sofia with the doctor had been difficult, but the idea she would never see her again was worse – much, much worse.

In her bed that night, Fatima carefully began unwrapping her grief. Never again would she shop with Sofia in the markets, never again would they return to her kitchen to share their evening meal like lovers, never again would she be able to watch Sofia work with the women, and never again would she be able to make her memory pictures of the woman she loved above all others. Whatever she had now, and whatever she could make in the morning, would be all she would ever have of Sofia.

This is life, Fatima told herself. What more should she expect?

***

THE FULL CONTINGENT of midwives numbered twelve, but because the commitment to the group was an extra burden on their already overburdened lives, there was rarely full attendance. On the mornings they were to meet, each woman needed to rise early to finish her work for the day in the home or gardens.

That morning, eight women, their chadors and burqas discarded in a tangled heap by the door, were sitting on the floor drinking tea and eating sweet biscuits, babies resting in laps and small children playing at their feet. Nearly all the women were young mothers, and in this regard the group was no different to any other Sofia had worked with before. The traditional village *dai*, who had probably practised village midwifery since she was little more than a child herself, was not interested in a young Western woman telling her how she should do her job.

The exception had been Atiqa, who had turned up to one of Sofia's midwife groups in the north of Afghanistan declaring she was there to learn. In a country where the average life expectancy is sixty years or less, at around fifty years old, Atiqa was considered extremely old. Her withered body had been racked and broken through sixteen full-term pregnancies; six had not survived birth and three had not passed their second birthdays. Atiqa's eyes were deep holes sunk in a face as chiselled as the mountain passes, her back bent double through years of toil, and her skin as ancient as the land she came from, and yet Sofia could only see beauty. Her crinkly face was a map of a life lived full, her hands as elegant and expressive as a bird in flight, and her heart as deep and full as the great Amu Darya. When Sofia's work with that particular group ended she had been grieved by the thought of never seeing Atiqa again.

'You do not need to know the end of every story, little one,' Atiqa had said gently, pinching Sofia's cheek. 'Our lives once crossed. That is enough in this life.'

Had Atiqa been right and would the fact that their lives once crossed be enough for these women? As she sat on the floor next to Fatima, drinking tea and eating sweet biscuits, she looked around the group and thought of all the extraordinary women she had trained over the years. Without any doubt, the women of Afghanistan were marshalling their strength and gathering their resources and would one day be a force to be reckoned with.

'We have something sad to tell you,' Fatima said, the various discussions between the women falling into silence. 'Unfortunately, Dr Sofia will not be returning to us after today. It has become far too dangerous for her to travel here from Kabul.' A ripple of disquiet ran through the room.

Sofia had not discussed with Fatima how they were to tell the women but she couldn't help thinking it might have been better if it had come from her.

She saw the disappointment in their eyes as the reality of what this would mean for each of them settled in. These women were stoic and resilient because they were used to disappointments, Sofia thought. It was part of their strength, but sometimes Sofia agreed with Iman and wished they would rise up and smash the walls down.

34

Just as Sofia was about to talk about her decision and what it would mean for the women, Clementine was ushered into the room by one of Fatima's staff and the women's attention was lost to the exotic beauty in dungarees and boots. Rising from her position on the floor, Sofia introduced Clementine to Fatima before turning to the women. 'Dr Clementine is interested in hearing about your training,' she said, 'but it's probably best if she explains why she's here.' As she sat back down on the floor again, Sofia made room for Clementine between her and Fatima.

Crossing her legs and lowering herself to the ground in one fluid movement, Clementine greeted the women before resting her hand on her heart and beginning a little speech in Pashto. She talked about how privileged she felt to be there and to be able to meet the extraordinary woman trained by Dr Sofia, and how she hoped the MSF staff at the clinic in Kandahar might be able to continue their training.

'The clinic,' she explained, being careful to look around the room to include all the women in her comments, 'is about to expand its services for pregnant women and newborn babies and it will be needing help.'

While the women turned to each other to discuss this news, Clementine waited until the room fell silent and she had their attention again. 'I know you must be disappointed that Dr Sofia won't be able to finish your training, but with Fatima's help, and your permission, our MSF staff would like to finish that process. We would also be able to supply you with all the necessary medicines and support you need during that process.'

Again the women talked among themselves and Clementine waited for their attention to return. 'If each of you could tell me what village you come from, the names of the villages closest to you and what you see as your village's most pressing neonatal needs, I'd be grateful.' As she waited for the women to speak, Clementine rummaged around in her tote bag to pull out a well-worn notepad and pen before turning her phone on to record and setting it down in front of her. The women, who had watched her with interest, remained silent. Sofia was wondering how she could simplify the question when Clementine spoke again. 'Do any of your villages have a doctor?' she asked.

'There are no doctors in our villages,' Afsana said, a baby in her lap and a toddler asleep at her feet. At eighteen years old, Afsana was the youngest and, like most of the rural population, was illiterate. Sofia considered her the most forthright of the women. As Afsana spoke she waved her hand in the air dismissively. 'There's no money for them. We have private clinics in Afghanistan, but they're run by doctors who don't care.'

When Afsana saw Clementine beginning to take notes she stopped. 'It's okay,' Clementine said, looking up to see why Afsana had grown silent. 'I'm just doing this so I can remember things.'

'You are a writer of books?' she asked.

'No, I'm a doctor who's a little bit slow,' Clementine said, giving Afsana her most winning smile, 'and if I don't write down all the important things you tell me then I'll forget them. These notes are just a reminder for me. No one else will ever see them.'

Afsana looked at Sofia and Fatima. They both nodded.

'Okay,' she said, still sounding a little worried that if she said bad things, which she was intending to do, this magic of recording her words might bring trouble to her door. 'These clinics are not always open, and the doctors want too much money, and we can never afford the medicines they want to give us, but at your clinic I'm thinking the drugs are free and the doctors are free. And,' she said, wanting to make a point, 'the doctors care about us, I think. The doctors in these other clinics do not care about us, they only care about our money.' Afsana pointed at Clementine's notebook. 'You can write this down, please.'

'I would like to know what you do at your clinic,' asked Sadaf. At thirty-two years old, she was the senior member of the group and probably the most curious. Married at fifteen to her young cousin, Mohammed, Sadaf had been unable to bear him a child. Three years ago he had taken a second wife, who had also proven to be barren. From initially feeling inadequate, Sadaf had guessed where the problem lay and had moved from hating her younger rival to feeling compassion for the girl who was also about to be replaced. Sadaf considered her husband a fool. A third barren wife would see his whispered failures become a roar in the village. She had told Sofia that when she understood that her home would never be blessed with the sound of children, she had joined the midwives to work with the babies she would never have.

'The staff ensure that mothers and their babies have the best possible care,' Clementine said. 'If, when you finish your training, you can work with them in an outreach capacity then the mothers and babies will be safer and you will lower the incidence of mortality.' A deep murmur of approval ran through the room.

Sofia was becoming increasingly worried that the women might lose their enthusiasm if their imaginings of what was being offered exceeded the reality. Fatima must have been thinking the same thing because she interrupted Clementine to explain the advantages, but also the limits, of the work the midwives might be offered.

'The clinics cost too much money and they don't always have the medicines we need,' added Kamelah, whose husband had died two years previously. She and her children were now living under her brother-in-law's roof, and unless he was able to find her a husband she would be forced to continue relying on the goodwill and handouts of the brother-in-law and his resentful wife. Failing an offer of a second marriage, the only alternatives for Kamelah and her three children were to live on the streets, or for the brother-in-law to take her as his second wife. Sofia hoped for the latter, which reminded her again just how far her values had shifted since arriving in Afghanistan. Not so long ago she would have been appalled at a woman becoming anyone's second wife. Now she could see it as a benefit.

It reminded her, yet again, how few absolutes there were and how naïve she had been when she'd first arrived. Boundaries shifted. Judgements were suspended. Her friends back in Australia would have said she had abandoned the feminist cause, but this had nothing to do with feminism. This was reality, and reality trumped ideals every single day of the week when you needed to feed your children.

As Sofia listened to the conversation she took a moment to look around the room. She decided she would speak to Clementine about widening the brief for the ones she saw as more competent. With extra training and the right support, they would also become extraordinary educational assets back in their villages but perhaps also in the MSF clinic.

For the next two hours Sofia gave the women their last lesson, a little nervous with Clementine watching on, but when she had invited her to participate Clementine had thrown her hands in the air, explaining that Dr Sofia was the expert while she was more of an administrator these days. As the time to leave drew ever closer, Sofia could feel her heart constricting. Would she ever see any of these women she had grown so fond of again, or know what happened to them? She thought not. When the time came to say her goodbyes the words got stuck in her throat, until Clementine reached across and took hold of her hand. It was all she needed.

'You all mean so much to me,' she said, looking at their faces as the sob rose in her throat again. 'I can't even begin to tell you how sorry I am not to be able to finish your training and see you all become midwives, but I do believe Dr Clementine and MSF will be able to step in and finish it for you. If this is somehow not possible I know deep in my heart that each of you will use the knowledge you have gained in the workshops to help back in your communities. I wish every one of you the very best and, *insha'Allah,* we will meet again very soon.'

As they all stood the women began crowding around Sofia, thanking her for her support and telling her how much they would miss her too until Fatima said she would like a group photo. This caused a little concern at first for some of the women who were unveiled, but Fatima assured them that the photo was only for her own memories and would never be shown to anyone.

'Dr Sofia, you must stand in the middle,' Fatima said, directing the women with her hands until Sofia was standing where she wanted her to be.

'Why don't I do it?' Clementine asked, holding her hand out for Fatima's phone. 'You should be in the photo too.'

Looking flustered, Fatima handed the phone over to Clementine before positioning herself on the outside of the group. Directing them all to move in a little closer, and Fatima to stand in the middle beside Sofia, Clementine took three photos. When she asked Fatima if she'd like to check any of the photos she declined to look, although the rest of the women crowded in.

'She loves you,' Clementine said to Sofia as they stood to the side watching the women pass the phone around.

'I love her too.'

'Maybe not in the same way.'

Sofia didn't reply. She knew the way Fatima felt about her and it was none of Clementine's business. Sofia had been thinking about Clementine's reassuring touch and how she might need to reassess her opinion of the woman, then her words had spoilt it.

Turning away, Sofia collected her overnight bag before

making her way out into the courtyard where she found Tawfiq and Daniel sitting on the sandstone wall with Fatima's guard.

* * *

'How DID IT go?' Daniel asked.

'Good. You should ask Clementine,' Sofia said, dropping the bag on the ground and sitting down beside him.

He looked at her for a couple of seconds before turning to Clementine, who had followed Sofia out. 'Clem?"

'It was good. I think we can work together if the women agree. Anyway,' she said, shading her eyes as she looked for the two security guards who she found smoking outside the gate, 'I better get back to the clinic. There's a lot to do before I leave tomorrow. I'll see you guys back in Kabul.'

It had been agreed that one of the security guards and the MSF car would stay behind in Kandahar with Clementine to bring her back to Kabul the following day, while the other guard would travel back with Tawfiq in their car. It wasn't an ideal situation, but with the only alternative being Clementine heading back before her work was completed, or Sofia and Daniel staying on another day, it was accepted as the best option.

'Dr Clementine is an excellent coordinator,' Daniel said to Fatima, who had come to stand with them. 'I hope she told you and the women that our staff are all Afghan. I really think they'll be able to help each other.'

'I'll have to see what the women think first,' Fatima said, before turning to Sofia and placing her hand over her heart. 'I'll always stand in your shadow and keep you close in my heart. You are my sister. You have given me so much.'

Sofia pushed herself off the wall to take Fatima's hand. 'And you, my friend, and all the women have given me so much. I'm really going to miss you.' When she moved in to hug Fatima she felt her friend flinch and let her go. 'Perhaps one day, when things are not so dangerous, I might come back and visit you?'

'I'd like that,' Fatima said, 'but right now I need to go back to the women.' Turning to Daniel, she said her goodbyes before hurrying back into the house.

'Oh god, that was weird,' Sofia said, as Daniel picked up her overnight bag and she followed him out the gate and through the group of men who were sitting around outside the gate, waiting to take their sisters and wives home. 'I feel like a real shit. She must hate me.'

'She doesn't hate you,' he said, putting her bag in the back before climbing in beside her. 'She loves you and she's just a little emotional.'

'And I love her too.'

But not the way she loves you, he thought, remembering the way Fatima had talked about Sofia the previous afternoon. In the last few days he'd seen how Sofia elicited strong emotions in her friends, although he thought some were a little overly protective of her. It was probably because she was so open and gentle, he thought, which people could misinterpret as fragile and vulnerable.

But a fragile, vulnerable woman didn't leave the safety of a comfortable home in Australia to travel to a place like Kabul to work for a man she'd never met. Neither did a vulnerable woman travel to an unknown village in the wilds of the Hindu Kush on a whim after reading an article, or travel around Afghanistan working with village women in isolated locations, or volunteer in the slums of Kabul. Sofia Raso might appear fragile and vulnerable but he knew she was bloody tough. It was there to see if you bothered to look.

'I've let the women down,' she said, breaking into his thoughts as they drove out of Kandahar.

Daniel turned to look at her. She was sensitive, which probably also led to the misperception of fragility. 'I don't think any of those women judge you for your decision.'

'Ha!' she scoffed. 'And therein lies the problem, doesn't it?' She turned to look at him, becoming animated. 'They never do,' she said, waving her hand in the air. 'They expect so little in their lives and now I've just been one more disappointment.'

'They're strong women, Sofia.'

'I know they are. My god, what they have to deal with every day in their lives. The other day my young receptionist was lamenting the weakness of Afghan women, but these women and what they do every day and have to overcome in their lives would leave most Western women for dead. They're strong and resilient and brave and I love them so much.'

'That's probably how they feel about you. Any more news about the boys, by the way?' he asked.

'No.' Sofia clenched her eyes shut and rubbed them with her thumb and forefinger as if to relieve a headache.

'You alright?'

'Sure.' She stopped rubbing to look at him. 'Do you think you could ask your friend again about the boys? His information was good last time and maybe this time Minister Massoud might step in and give Chief Wasim a hurry on.'

The mention of Massoud reminded Daniel of what had happened the night before. 'I can, but do you think you could arrange a meeting with Jabril for me first?'

'Sure. When?'

'Tomorrow.'

'You're not going to tell me what it's about?' she asked.

'I think it's best you hear it together.' He turned to look out the window. Daniel had a threat to deliver. It was not going to be easy.

35

WHEN SOFIA CAME down the following morning she found
Behnaz in the courtyard under the pomegranate tree. Having
gathered the fallen leaves from the two trees in the centre of
the square and from the pomegranate tree in her courtyard, she
had swept them into a little pyramid. The canary cage had been
moved out of harm's way to the front door and now she was
trying to ignite the brittle mound of leaves. Long ago Sofia had
suggested that Behnaz might like to let the leaves decompose
below the trees to fertilise the soil and keep the moisture in
during the blistering summer heat, but Behnaz had politely
thanked Sofia for her 'Australian' advice and continued to make
the bonfires she had been building for the last forty years.

When she saw Dr Sofia, Behnaz gave up on the bonfire and
tried to rise, but with one twisted hand clutching the trunk
of the tree and the other supporting her aching back, it was
proving difficult. Behnaz had arthritis in her hands when Sofia
had first arrived in Kabul, but over the years it had found its
way into her knees, and more lately into her spine. A couple
of years previously Sofia had returned from Australia with
the latest arthritis medicine, which Behnaz promptly gave to

Babur. His need, she said, was greater than her own. Behnaz didn't like medicines, especially foreign medicines. They were part of a Western conspiracy, she said. When Sofia had tried to ascertain exactly what this Western conspiracy might be, Behnaz had told her that conspiracies were secret, so how was she, a stupid Afghan woman, supposed to know?

Sofia hated seeing Behnaz in such pain but knew from experience that if she tried to help her hand would be swatted away. Despite the inevitable rebuke, Sofia couldn't help reaching out, and to her utter amazement her hand was accepted.

'You know, I can give you something to ease the pain, Behnaz,' she said.

Safely on her feet, Behnaz waved off Sofia's hand. 'Give your medicines to Babur,' she said as she dusted down the front of her black dress where she'd been kneeling in the dirt.

'It's not like there isn't enough to go around. There's enough for you and Babur and everyone in Kabul. There's enough for the whole world,' Sofia said. 'That's what pharmaceutical companies do: they make enough medicine for everyone.'

'Humph!' Behnaz threw her hand in the air. 'Enough poison for everyone, you mean! I don't want their poison.' She looked Sofia up and down. 'Are you going out today?'

'Just to work and Dr Jabril's house for a meeting at lunchtime. Is that okay?'

'I think it's good that you're staying in the square. Dr Jabril's is okay, but I wasn't happy with you going to Kandahar with that rude woman and that man.'

Sofia raised her eyebrows at Behnaz's comment about Clementine. She was still trying to come to terms with her conflicting feelings about her. 'Why didn't you like the woman?'

'She didn't greet you. She just sat in the car and talked on the phone. It's rude.'

Sofia considered this, nodding, before she asked, 'And the man? What's the problem with him?'

'You went to Kandahar with someone you don't know.'

'Actually, I do know him.' Sofia felt a little buzz of satisfaction at Behnaz's reaction.

'No, you don't,' she said, planting her hands on her hips in defiance.

'Yes, I do. I met him five years ago.'

Behnaz thought about this for a while before deciding it changed nothing. 'Your mother wouldn't like him.'

Sofia wondered whether her mother would like Daniel and was saddened by the fact that she'd never know. She was also a little taken aback by the idea that Behnaz had a direct line to her dead mother.

'She wouldn't like it if I didn't watch out for you.' Finished with the conversation, Behnaz headed back to the front door, picked up the canary cage and carried it out to hang it on the lowest branch of the pomegranate tree.

'Okay, I'm off,' Sofia said, opening the gate to find Rashid outside waiting for her. After greeting him she called back to Behnaz. 'You'll be happy to know there's no Dr Daniel in sight, or that rude woman, and Rashid's here to escort me across the square.' She turned back to Rashid. 'And I'm pretty sure he'll escort me to Dr Jabril's for lunch.' Rashid nodded. 'So you don't need to worry about me today.'

'I worry about you every day,' Behnaz muttered loud enough for Sofia and Rashid to hear as she closed the gate behind Sofia.

As she crossed the square, Sofia wondered whether Daniel's

friend would be able to find where the boys had been taken again. She also wished Daniel had told her what he wanted to talk to her and Jabril about.

* * *

OMAR, WHO HAD been waiting for an opportunity to speak with Behnaz, watched Dr Sofia crossing the square before making his way over to Behnaz's gate.

'Behnaz,' he called through the gate, not game to cross over the threshold into a courtyard he was no longer invited to enter. 'There's something of a delicate nature I wish to discuss with you.'

The gate flew open. Behnaz gave him her death stare. 'What do you want?'

Omar backed away a little. 'I don't want anything. I need to tell you something.'

'Since when have you had anything interesting to say to me?'

As usual, Behnaz was making Omar nervous. It had not always been like that, especially when they had been young, but it was what he had come to expect now. 'It's about the *shabnamah* you received.'

Behnaz stiffened. 'What are you talking about? I've never received *shabnamah*.'

Things were not going very well, but probably as well as Omar had expected. 'A letter then. I … I think I saw you take a letter off your gate yesterday morning.'

'I didn't see any *shabnamah* on my gate yesterday morning. You're talking nonsense, you old fool.' Behnaz slammed the gate shut. Stepping up to the gate, Omar listened. He could tell she was still standing on the other side of the gate.

'I saw you take it,' he said.

The gate flew open and Omar stepped back again. 'You saw nothing. I took nothing off my gate. Do you understand? There was no *shabnamah*.'

'Is Dr Sofia in danger?'

Behnaz stiffened, drawing herself up. 'What do you know about Dr Sofia?'

Omar could feel the sweat breaking out on his back and under his arms. For a few seconds he thought Behnaz might strike him. 'Why is Rashid walking Dr Sofia across the square again, and why didn't you want her to go to Kandahar with the man from the UN?'

'What do you know?'

Omar took another step back. 'I don't know anything.' It had been a mistake to think he could speak civilly with Behnaz. 'I don't know anything,' he repeated, turning and shuffling away. There was no way he could ever tell her about the night letter he had stolen.

'You're a troublemaker, Omar,' she called out after him. 'Stop spreading rumours and causing trouble.'

He turned back. 'I'm not causing trouble. I only want to –'
Behnaz slammed the gate shut.

Back in his chair, Omar sat unaware of the people passing, or of Babur calling out a greeting, or of the sun that had moved on, leaving him in shade. As he contemplated the terrible mess he had got himself into, a new thought arrived at the station and it seemed like a good thought, and within a few minutes it had grown into a wondrous, shiny-new, proper-right thought. The relief that flooded through Omar's body was pure joy. He knew what he had to do.

***

'HELLO, MY FRIEND,' Babur said, wiping his hands on his dirty apron as he came to stand in front of Omar. 'I saw you talking with Behnaz. She looked pretty angry with you.' He needed to know whether it had something to do with the *shabnamah*.

'She's always angry at me.'

'That's true.' Babur couldn't help feeling sorry for his old friend. Behnaz was a prickly character at the best of times, but these days she seemed to keep the worst for poor old Omar, although Babur could remember a time when Omar and Behnaz had been good friends. He wondered again what had happened, but knowing the young Omar he'd probably done something inappropriate.

'So,' Babur said, making an effort to sound casual as he inspected the stains on his apron, 'any more news about your *shabnamah*?'

'It probably wasn't a *shabnamah*,' Omar said. 'I think you should wait until tomorrow.'

'Why?' Fear prickled under Babur's skin. 'What's going to happen tomorrow?'

'All I can tell you is that you shouldn't worry.' Omar reached out and patted Babur's hand. 'It's not meant for you, my friend.'

'How do you know? I mean, how can you be so sure?'

'Trust me.'

Babur would like to be able to trust Omar, but he had been getting things confused a lot lately. 'Is the *shabnamah* about Dr Sofia?'

Omar stopped patting Babur's hand. 'Why would you say that?'

'Because she came into my shop in a big hurry and needed to go somewhere with Tawfiq and she was wearing her coat.'

As Babur was saying this he noticed his grill was blazing out of control and the cook was nowhere to be seen. He needed to go. 'And how many times have you ever seen Dr Sofia wearing that coat? She was hiding something,' he said, excusing himself as he hurried off.

With no customers in the shop, Babur dampened the flame before reaching for the samovar to pour boiling water into the rose-painted teapot. Soon the aromas of green tea, cardamom pods, cinnamon bark, saffron strands and a hint of rosewater would be filling his nostrils. Pouring a glass for himself, he carried it and the teapot out to the table normally reserved for Mustafa and Dr Jabril.

Maybe the *shabnamah* was about him or maybe it wasn't, he thought as he took Dr Jabril's customary seat. Maybe it was about Dr Sofia, or maybe Omar had got everything confused. For some time Babur had been suspicious that Omar was self-medicating too liberally. He also wondered whether anyone else had actually seen this *shabnamah*. Taking his first calming sips of the brew, he thought about his options again. The safest thing to do was surely to get rid of the alcohol, but the man he had bought it from still had not come to collect it, even though he said he could have it back for free. If it was a *shabnamah*, and it was about him, how did he let the Taliban know when the alcohol was gone – whoever the Talib in the square might be? At least when the Russians were in Kabul, or the Taliban was in control, you knew who the enemy was, but now he had no idea. Babur looked around the square again.

Off to the right he could see Ahmad talking with an early customer. From the body language Babur knew things were not going so well. Ahmad had taken possession of the pair of sandals the man had been inspecting and was now leaning in too closely and talking too fast, causing the man to lean away. Babur could tell the customer was already lost. Ahmad was the only one who couldn't see it. As far as Babur was concerned there wasn't anything inherently wrong with Ahmad's goods, other than the fact that you could buy them all over Kabul. Ahmad's real problem was the way he pressured his customers.

In the shop next to Ahmad, Hadi was perched on his stool reading a newspaper, oblivious to the drama taking place in front of him. Hadi, like everyone else in the square, had seen it all before. Further over in front of Dr Sofia's surgery, Rashid and Iqbal were sitting together in silence. Babur wondered again why the two men seemed such close companions when Rashid seldom said anything and Iqbal preferred his own company. Perhaps it was the silences that bound them?

To the left and directly opposite Ahmad and Hadi's shops and Dr Sofia's surgery, Omar had returned to sit in front of his shop and was now fast asleep. Babur had a soft spot for Omar but that Viagra thing had been a mistake, just as his alcohol had been. Babur looked around the square again. None of his friends were Talib, he decided. Nor would they write threatening notes. It had to be that brother-in-law of his, or else it wasn't for him at all. He wished he knew which one it was.

Iman caught Babur's attention as she came dancing around the corner of the square by the mosque, earplugs firmly fixed to the phone. That 'Rainbow Shaahir Square' campaign of hers had been a madness that would have destroyed his precious square, he thought as he watched her, conveniently forgetting his enthusiasm for it and its tempting promise of international fame for the *chaikhana*.

'*As-salaam alaikum,*' he called and waved as she passed.

'*Wa alaikum as-salaam,*' she called back with a smile.

It was a shame the girl went too far, flaunting things that were better left hidden. Even as he censored Iman he could feel his old heart softening around her. She reminded him of the young women of Kabul he used to know, especially the young Behnaz when she had first arrived in the square. Thinking of how she had been a wild beauty in her day brought back the old sadness. They had all lost so much with stupid wars filling up their years. Sometimes his country broke Babur's heart. He let out a deep sigh, swirling the last of his chai in his cup before throwing his head back and tossing it down his throat. There was no time for reminiscing now. He had a problem that needed to be fixed.

As Iman disappeared up the stairs to Dr Sofia's surgery, Babur scanned the square again with a proprietorial air which, as a direct descendant of Zahir-ud-din Muhammad Babur, who was himself a direct descendant of the great warrior Genghis Khan, he believed was afforded him. Soon Babur had forgotten his problem with the *shabnamah* and was thinking about the long and proud history of the *chaikhana* where the Diamond Sutra had once slept. How he wished he had held the book in his own hands at least once. For years he had told everyone in the square that he would one day travel to England to see the famous book, but he knew now that the time had passed and he never would.

The fact that he didn't have a son to leave the *chaikhana* to had been weighing heavily on his mind of late. His brother expected him to leave it to his eldest son, but Babur had never much liked the boy. Until recently he would have preferred to leave it to his third sister's second son, but she was married to that devil who had caused him all this trouble over the alcohol. Babur sighed again as his thoughts had come back full circle to arrive at the alcohol problem he still had no idea how to fix.

36

AFTER LUNCH AT Jabril's they retired to the white leather lounges with cardamom tea, where Daniel and Sofia told Jabril and Zahra about their trip to Kandahar. Finally, Daniel asked Jabril how well he knew Minister Massoud.

'I suppose you're talking about his past?' asked Jabril, setting his cup down on the small side table beside his favourite chair.

'In part.'

'I know a little about his past, but generally I make it a rule not to judge people on rumour. I also like to believe, or at least hope –' Jabril, who had been watching Daniel, stopped. 'Perhaps you need to tell me what you know?'

'I'm afraid you're not going to like this.'

Jabril nodded. 'I suspect not.'

* * *

AFTER DANIEL HAD finished his interview with Fatima, Tawfiq had dropped him off in downtown Kandahar between a bank and a video shop whose windows had recently been covered with newspaper. It had been a long day, and with Forood more than ten minutes late, Daniel was considering leaving when an old silver Toyota Corolla pulled up in front of him. Apologising for his tardiness, Forood threw his arm around Daniel's shoulders, introduced his three companions, and ushered them all up the stairs.

Under the bright glare of a long fluorescent tube that hissed and crackled, men were sitting three deep on cushions around a cleared space in the centre of the room. Behind them more men were crouching, standing or leaning up against the walls talking, while over by the window three musicians were tuning their instruments. The air was thick with cigarette smoke, the heat of the unwashed bodies and the buzz of anticipation.

After taking their places in a space reserved for them in the front row, Forood claimed Daniel's attention. When Daniel finally had the opportunity to look around he noticed a curtain placed over a doorway being pulled back a little and three young boys wearing jewellery and make-up peeping out. Although Daniel had never been to one of these 'performances' before, there was no mistaking what it was.

'I'm going,' he said to Forood.

'No!' Forood said, grabbing Daniel's arm. The men closest to them had turned to see what was happening. 'You'll make trouble for me if you leave now.' Daniel looked to where Forood was indicating. A group of men was standing against a wall. One of them was Abdul Ali Massoud. When he caught Daniel's eye the warlord smiled and bowed his head in recognition. Daniel did not return the courtesy.

As the musicians began playing a scratchy, plaintive melody, the men in the room began a slow, insistent clap and the curtain was pulled back. One of the boys, barefoot and wearing a pale blue dress with a shimmering orange shawl, came twirling out into the space in the middle of the room. Shaking the bells and bracelets on his ankles and wrists, he began to move, tossing his long hair and flashing his heavily kohled eyes at the men around him.

The excitement and lust in the room increased as the boy danced ever more provocatively. Holding out his arms and shimmying his chest, he dipped and flicked his skirt and hair. Pursing his lips and lowering his mascaraed eyelashes, he circled the shawl around his face before letting it fall to his shoulders. The boy, Daniel thought, was well versed in the art of seduction.

It was the boy's job to make these men desire him because the measure of his success would define his owner's power. At the end of the evening the man might keep the boy for his own pleasure, or sell the child's services on to one of the men in the room. Alternatively, the boy might be given as a reward to a friend, or to a man from whom his owner might one day need a favour.

'This boy belongs to Abdul Ali Massoud,' Forood had said. 'He's a very powerful man and has many friends with the foreign troops. Do you know him?'

Daniel nodded. 'I do.'

'The boy's very beautiful, is he not?' asked Forood.

'How long has he had this boy?'

'A long time, I think. He's his favourite.'

'Does he have any new boys?' Daniel asked, noticing the change in Forood. You didn't ask questions like this.

'Do you not like pleasure with boys, Dr Daniel?'

'Are there any new boys here tonight?'

Forood's body tensed and his smile had disappeared. 'I don't know. Maybe we hear if a new boy is going to dance but I've not heard anything tonight.'

'How would I know if anyone had a new boy?'

'I do not know. Why are you asking these questions?' Forood said, forcing a smile. Sensing something was wrong, the men sitting next to them were trying to eavesdrop. No one wanted trouble.

'How would I find out?'

Forood was sweating now. Realising he would not get anything more out of him, Daniel had risen but Forood grabbed his arm again

'Please,' he said. 'Please sit. This will be very bad for me if you offend Minister Massoud. Please.'

Daniel had pulled his wrist free. As he threaded his way back through the men on the floor, the boy's twirling became more frantic. He was about to end his performance with a swoon, but by the time Daniel had reached the door all eyes had turned to him and the boy was all but ignored. A rustle of disquiet spread through the crowd. No one wanted trouble.

After the fetid heat of the room Daniel had welcomed the fresh night air, but just as he was about to head back to the MSF clinic he heard footsteps on the stairs behind him and turned to see Massoud.

'Dr Abiteboul, wait, please.' Daniel stopped. Massoud came to stand beside him. Taking his time to light a cigarette and drawing deeply on it he had turned to look at Daniel and smiled. 'You are offended by the boy?'

'No, not at all, I'm offended by you and the men like you.'

'Ah, such a pity. In Afghanistan we appreciate beauty in all its forms.'

'Young boys shouldn't be seen as beautiful.'

Massoud's smile had deepened. 'Such foolish notions, Dr

Abiteboul. There can be nothing more beautiful than taking pleasure with a young boy. Are they not like little girls, and little girls are enjoying sex with their husbands every night all over Afghanistan? What can be the harm in this pleasure?'

'You have two sons, I believe, minister? How would you like your sons to be used for this "pleasure"?' Two men walked past, eyeing Massoud and Daniel standing in the light of the stairway.

Massoud bristled. 'My sons have no need for this. I can provide amply for them.' Massoud had contemplated the tip of his cigarette before flicking the ash off with a long fingernail on his little finger. 'I'm sure none of us can pretend to be so naïve or righteous these days, can we, Dr Abiteboul? You're a man of the world. You've travelled widely.' Massoud frowned. 'Aren't there tours for Western men to Asia for such activities? What about your Catholic priests I read about?' He shook his head and smiled. 'You may not like what you see, Dr Abiteboul, but I assure you it is normal.'

Daniel could feel his hatred of the man rising. He had smiled at Massoud. 'I've heard that the Taliban is gaining traction here in your part of the world again. That must be concerning, given that these zealots have a particular distaste for men like you.'

'Men like me,' repeated Massoud, looking amused as he examined his nails. 'I have friends everywhere, Dr Abiteboul, even among these men you call zealots. What is it you say in the West, you and I must agree to disagree? You are an honoured guest in my country. I regret that our harmless little distraction has offended you.' He had turned to look out into the night. 'It's a beautiful evening in Kandahar, is it not?' He flicked the butt into the gutter. 'I believe you are here with Dr Jabril's friend, what is her name? Ah yes, Dr Sofia. She's an impressive young woman, wouldn't you say, although perhaps a little impulsive. I have always contended that our guests should not concern themselves with things that are not their business, don't you think?' He smiled and bowed to Daniel. 'Please give my regards to Dr Jabril. He does such invaluable work in Shaahir Square. It would be a shame if for some reason it all had to end.'

37

When Daniel finished his story about Massoud, Zahra was the first to speak. 'Why am I not surprised? Men like Massoud think their wives are for giving them sons and young boys are for giving them pleasure.'

'I'm sorry, Jabril,' offered Daniel.

'No, no, you have nothing to be sorry for. On the contrary, I should be thanking you.' Jabril shook his head. 'To think I spoke with him only this morning to see if he might be able to push harder to find the boys. In truth, I was beginning to wonder about our good minister when he seemed more interested in where the information came from than where the boys were, and then when we discovered the men had been warned about the raid, well … What a fool I've been.'

'Men like Massoud are chameleons. They've mastered the art of appearing to be whatever you want them to be. You're not the first person to be fooled by him,' Daniel offered.

'He's fooled just about everyone, my husband,' Zahra said, reaching out to touch his knee.

Jabril's hand covered his wife's. 'But not you, my dear. You've never liked him, have you?'

'Well,' Zahra said, as if it was nothing. She sat back on the lounge again. 'Only because I know his wife and I've seen how frightened she is of him.'

Jabril turned his attention to Daniel. 'I'm afraid I told him it was your friend who told us about the house. I probably shouldn't have.'

'It's okay, Jabril. He doesn't know who my friend is. He's safe.' Daniel felt sorry for Jabril. He was a good man who was no match for someone like Massoud.

'By the way, has your friend got any idea where the boys are now?' Jabril asked.

'I'm afraid he hasn't got back to me yet, but as soon as he does I'll let you know.'

'He mentioned you when I spoke with him this morning, Daniel. Minister Massoud wanted me to give you his regards.' Jabril gave Daniel a wan smile of apology.

'And as you've just heard, he wanted me to give you his. He wants us to know that he's not afraid of us knowing about the boy.'

'So it would seem,' Jabril said. 'He's telling us he's untouchable.'

'With good reason,' offered Zahra, rising from her chair and turning to Daniel. 'I'm sorry, Daniel, I have an appointment, but I want to thank you for telling us this. As Sofia and my husband know, I believe they shouldn't have got involved in the first place. Someone's going to get hurt.'

'People are already getting hurt,' Jabril said after his wife left the room.

'I've been thinking,' Sofia said, speaking for the first time. 'What if MSF and the UN took up the cause?'

Daniel turned in his chair to look directly at Sofia. 'You want me to ask MSF and the UN if they'll campaign against *bacha bazi*?'

'Is it possible?'

'It isn't part of MSF's remit. It's not how they operate in a host country. They won't touch it.' Daniel considered what the options might be. 'There are areas within the UN that might be interested, though.'

'Would you also be willing to testify against Massoud if we could bring a case against him in Kabul?' Sofia asked.

Jesus, thought Daniel, I didn't see that coming.

'No,' Jabril interjected immediately before Daniel had time to answer. 'Do you understand what you're asking Daniel to do?' he said to Sofia. 'You're asking him to put his life in danger for this thing that's not his responsibility. I'm sorry but I can't agree with this.'

Sofia turned back to Jabril, her excitement growing as she became more animated. 'I'm not asking on my own behalf. I'm asking on behalf of all the little boys who are being molested. Think about it. I'm not sure such a good, high-profile opportunity will ever come again, and there can be no more credible witness than Daniel against Massoud. And yes, there might be some degree of danger, but I don't think Daniel's a stranger to such things.' She looked over at him. 'Whatever you say will be heard, Daniel, and because you're not an Afghan, you can leave if things get too dangerous.'

And never come back again, he thought.

'No,' Jabril repeated. 'No.'

'Surely you see that this is an opportunity we might never have again?' Sofia turned back to Daniel. 'It might sound otherwise but I don't want you to feel pressured, and I won't think any less of you if you say no, but this is an extraordinary opportunity.'

Daniel wondered whether what she said was true. She probably would think less of him. There was no way she was comprehending the full ramifications of what she was suggesting. He could take risks with his own life, but a court case and testimony against Massoud would put his colleagues at MSF in danger and maybe even his UN colleagues. It would also jeopardise the whole MSF operation in Afghanistan. He didn't have the right to do that. In any event, neither MSF nor the UN would allow one of their employees to initiate a highly public court case against a cabinet minister in a foreign country. He would have to resign first and probably never return to Afghanistan. There was also the possibility that such an action would endanger Sofia and Jabril now that Massoud was linking them to him. Even if someone brought a court case, he doubted they'd be able to find a judge brave enough to convict Massoud.

'Sofia, I ask you to think again,' pleaded Jabril.

'I don't think they'll dare touch Daniel, and people will listen to him.'

She was putting way too high a value on his position while completely underestimating Massoud. Men like him weren't frightened of MSF or the UN. They were untouchable in their own countries. And yet, Daniel understood where she was coming from and her desperation. When he thought of the boy dancing and how his night would have ended, he knew he had to do something, but it couldn't be what Sofia suggested. There had to be another way.

314

'Did Minister Massoud ever admit he owned the boy?' Jabril asked.

As soon as Jabril asked the question Daniel knew where he was going. He thought back to their conversation. 'No, I don't think so, but the inference was always there and Forood said the boy belonged to Massoud, although you'd never be able to get him to say that in court. He and his family would be dead before he left the house.'

Jabril turned back to Sofia. 'I don't see how we can take this to court. We have no evidence. If Daniel were to accuse Massoud his claim would be hearsay, and unless he could prove the boy belonged to Massoud, which I'm sure he can't, the case would be thrown out of court. Besides, I can't think of a single judge in Afghanistan who'd be brave enough to convict Massoud. No,' Jabril said, sounding surer of his argument every minute, 'there can be no legal case brought against Massoud on what we've got so far.'

Daniel watched Sofia's body slump as Jabril's words sank in. When she spoke again she sounded defeated. 'You're right. I'm sorry. I got ahead of myself. I wasn't thinking.'

'Perhaps it would be enough if Massoud knew we had the information on him?' offered Jabril.

'He already knows that,' offered Daniel. 'In fact, he wanted you to know he knows. I'm not sure threatening Massoud is the way to go. In my experience you have to be cleverer with men like him.'

'How?'

'I don't know yet. Let me think on it.'

'What about name and shame?' offered Jabril, sounding excited. 'These men should know that if we find out about their

315

nefarious activities we'll name and shame them no matter who they are and how powerful they might be. We can begin with our good Minister Massoud. If we can name and shame him then others will be warned.'

'Isn't that the same thing?' Sofia said. 'Aren't you asking Daniel to publicly accuse Massoud when we have no proof?'

'Not at all, my dear. I have something much better in mind. Something that will also sort out your visa problems.' Daniel could see Jabril was very pleased with himself. He was hatching something, but he had no idea what it was.

'Oh god,' she said, deflated again. 'It was Massoud who cancelled it, wasn't it?'

'It looks that way to me.'

Daniel looked from one to the other. 'I think someone needs to bring me up to speed here. Have you had your visa cancelled, Sofia?'

After she explained the situation Jabril spoke, only this time they were not the words of a man defeated or frightened by Massoud. 'I believe, Daniel, that good men will always win out in the end. Yes, good men will win. Now,' he said, hoisting himself out of his chair and making his way over to an old, elaborately carved wooden cabinet adorned with family photos. Taking out a half-empty bottle of twenty-year-old malt whisky and two glasses, he held them up for Daniel's inspection. 'We are a good Muslim family here, but when I lived in Boston I did acquire a taste for scotch. I know it is a little early, and I know Sofia doesn't like the stuff, but would you like to join me in a celebratory drink?'

'Are we celebrating something?' asked Sofia.

'We are indeed.'

'What?'

'You'll see soon enough, my dear,' Jabril said with a broad smile.

'Perhaps you could tell us what you're thinking?' Daniel asked.

'I'm afraid not quite yet, but soon you'll see,' Jabril said as he carried the bottle and glasses back to where they were sitting.

Daniel suspected he wasn't going to like whatever Jabril was planning. As far as he could see, Sofia's boss was an innocent. Either he had no idea what depths of depravity people like Massoud could go to or he no longer cared. Either way, Daniel's gut was telling him it was not going to end well.

Placing the two crystal glasses on the coffee table between them, Jabril poured a finger of scotch into each before passing one over to Daniel. 'To brave men,' he said, before remembering Sofia and turning to her. 'And women.'

Her smile didn't last long. She looked as worried as Daniel was. Excusing himself shortly after, Daniel waited until he was in the car before he started making phone calls.

38

UNABLE TO SLEEP, Sofia lay in bed listening to the late-night sounds of people returning home until the square grew silent.

After Daniel had left that afternoon, she and Jabril had called Chief Wasim on speakerphone to learn that there was still no news of the boys. They then told the chief about Massoud. It troubled her that he didn't sounded particularly surprised, just as his comment about little boys going missing all over Afghanistan every day had troubled her. She tried to rationalise that Chief Wasim must have seen the absolute worst that humankind had to offer and nothing much would surprise him anymore.

They all agreed that Massoud was the one who had warned the men in the house about the raid and decided that the one thing they still had going for them was that Massoud probably expected them to stop looking for the boys now. Jabril warned Chief Wasim to be particularly careful with any new information they might discover. Not only was Massoud technically his boss but the minister probably also had informants in Chief Wasim's office. Chief Wasim reminded them that they should *all* be careful with whom they shared new information.

Before she left, Sofia had asked Jabril what he was planning but he had refused to tell her, claiming again that she would learn soon enough.

Grabbing her pillow, Sofia tried to plump its feathery softness up into some sort of shape, but when she lay her head back down again it was as unappealing as it had been two minutes before. Climbing out of bed, she drew back her bedroom curtains to stand looking out into the square, ghostly white under the full moon.

How on earth are we going to find you?

Below her window a man walked into the square, disturbing a dog that had been sleeping outside Babur's *chaikhana*. The dog stood and barked half-heartedly after the man, who walked over to the row of derelict buildings and climbed in a broken window. Sofia guessed it wasn't the first time he'd done that. With the man disappearing, the dog turned in circles before settling back down again, while somewhere behind the square a motorbike fired up. Sofia watched its lights dance between the buildings until it too disappeared into the night.

Far away, the snow-covered peaks of the Hindu Kush were shimmering silvery white under the full moon, just as they had on the last night she had spent with Daniel.

Arriving in her hut he had brought with him the icy cold of the mountain air and, for a few brief seconds, the light from the same full moon. As he closed the door she asked if he would take the cloth off the window. 'I want to see you,' she had said from where she lay waiting for him on the floor.

Their lovemaking had been different that night, more intense but also gentler, as if the feverish rush of lust had given way to the deeper, slower intimacy of love.

319

'You're beautiful,' he had said. Sofia had been watching his eyes as he moved inside her and in that moment she saw his truth: she was beautiful to him.

'I love you,' she had whispered, frightened of her words, not sure if he'd heard her.

Later, as he slept, she had watched her lover in the fading light from the tiny window: the barely noticeable rise and fall of his bare chest, the delicate blue veins threaded through the pale inside of his wrist, the dark hairs on his arm and the tiny scar on his left earlobe. When he turned in his sleep she noticed the tattoos on his shoulder, but he had opened his eyes and was smiling up at her. 'What are you doing? Come here,' he said sleepily, reaching up with his hand to draw her back down to him again.

In the morning, as he was covering the window before leaving, she had asked him about the tattoos.

'They're nothing,' he said.

She had only known Daniel for ten short days but she understood that if he'd had something tattooed into his skin then it meant something. 'What does the Arabic script say?'

'Without pain you can never know joy.' Crouching down, he took her bare feet from under the blanket and kissed the delicate skin of the arches. 'Go back to sleep, my love,' he had said.

'And the numbers?'

He let her feet go, tucking them back into the warmth of the blanket before rising. 'Just numbers.'

'Stay,' she said.

He smiled. 'You know I can't.'

After he left, Sofia lay in the warm hollow where his body had been, smiling with the memory of the night that had passed, gently packing away these new things she had learned about him into the special place now reserved for Daniel. It made what happened afterward more painful.

As she came out of the hut that morning Sofia saw him disappear over the ridge with a man she'd not seen before. In time she had come to accept he had known he would be leaving her that day and the night before had been his goodbye. No longer could she trust the memory of what she thought she had seen in his eyes, or that he had said she was beautiful, or even that she had told him that she loved him.

* * *

WHEN SOFIA GOT out of the shower the following morning she found a message on her phone from Jabril telling her not to worry about anything. He had an idea that would fix the visa situation and Minister Massoud. The message had not given her any comfort. She wasn't so sure Jabril would be able to 'fix' her visa situation, or Massoud, and the fact that he thought he could, and that the solutions to both were linked, worried her even more. Between getting dressed, having breakfast, and heading out the door she had tried to ring him five times, but he'd not answered. In the first break in her appointments that morning Sofia crossed the reception to Jabril's surgery.

'He hasn't come in yet,' Iman said as she was about to knock on his door.

She turned to Iman. 'Did you hear from him?'

'Only to say he'd be late, or maybe not in at all.'

'Did he say why?'

'No.'

Sofia returned to her surgery to ring Jabril's number again. Once more it went to his voice mail. She rang Zahra.

'The last I saw of him was early this morning when he was

leaving for the surgery.' When Sofia informed her that Jabril hadn't arrived at the surgery and had told Iman that he wasn't coming in, Zahra told Sofia to hang up so she could ring him. In less than a minute Zahra was back on the line. 'He's not answering me either.'

'Do you know what he's planning to do about Massoud?'

'I have no idea what you're talking about. What about Massoud?' They both heard the ping of an incoming message on Zahra's phone. It was from Jabril. 'My husband apologises for not taking my call,' she said, reading the message, 'and he's very busy and will see me tonight. At least I know he's still alive. What's going on, Sofia?'

'I don't know. He said he had an idea what to do about Massoud and fix my visa issue at the same time, so maybe it's that.'

'I don't like this one little bit.'

When they hung up, Sofia rang Chief Wasim. He didn't answer either.

Her last patient of the day was Afrooz, whose main concern seemed to be her fifteen-year-old daughter working at a beauty salon when she should have been at home waiting for the family to find a suitable husband for her.

'Perhaps she'd like a career?' Sofia offered.

'She needs to be married before she's too old and no one wants her. We can't be stuck with her all our lives.' Afrooz's hernia was also giving her trouble again, 'but not as much as my daughter. She's my heart of pains.'

Sofia was finding it hard to work up any sympathy for Afrooz. She could help with the hernia, she said, but had little to offer with regard to her daughter and the beauty salon.

By the end of the day she had still not heard from Chief

Wasim, or Jabril, and was beginning to become seriously concerned. With her last patient cancelling, Sofia rang Taban.

'What happened? Are you alright?'

'I'm fine. A few things were broken, nothing much.'

'Jabril told me about a message.'

'It's nothing. Some crank.'

Sofia sat back in her chair. 'Do you think it has anything to do with the boys?'

'No idea, but it doesn't seem any more boys are missing.'

As usual, Taban was playing down her problems. Deciding there was really nothing she could do, Sofia ended the call, promising to talk the following day if there was any news of the boys. As she was packing up for the day, Iman wandered in and sat down in one of the patients' chairs.

'I'm going home now.'

Sofia looked up from making some last-minute notes. 'So I can see.' She saved the document and closed the laptop to give Iman her full attention. 'Something on your mind?'

'Have you heard anything more about your visa?' Iman asked, straightening out the cuffs of the long blue shirt she wore over her skinny jeans.

'I rang the Australian embassy this morning but they're not too optimistic about being able to reverse the decision, especially when I told them the order might have come from someone high up in the government. They wanted to know who I'd offended.'

'Who have you offended?'

Sofia shrugged.

'So what's going to happen now?' Iman asked, grabbing her ponytail and pulling it over one shoulder.

'I've got an appointment next week. Dr Jabril says he's working on something, and if both of those fail I might need to take an unscheduled holiday back to Australia and sort it out from there.'

'Aren't you worried?'

'Yes.'

'You were right the other day,' she said, changing the subject as she changed her position on the chair. 'I did have a fight with Khalif. His mother wants him to break up with me.'

Sofia grimaced. 'That's not good. What does Khalif say?'

'He says he takes no notice of her, but you know what Afghan mothers and their sons are like.'

'All mothers care about their children.'

'Care about their children! Are you kidding me? They're like leeches. While Afrooz was waiting for you she was complaining to me about her daughter working in the beauty salon. Complaining to *me!*' Iman gave a look of disgust. 'Sometimes I hate how polite I have to be in this job. Smiling and telling Afrooz that I understand how upsetting it must be for her when all I really want to do is tell her to get a life. She's not good to her daughter.'

'I guess she's looking after her interests in the only way she knows how.'

Iman frowned. 'Why do you always stick up for these women? Why don't you tell them they're wrong?'

Sofia sighed. 'We've been through this a dozen times. It's not my place to tell them they're wrong. You don't tell them they're wrong when they tell you their problems.'

'Of course not! I'm just a receptionist. I'd get fired. Anyway, they won't listen to me, but they'll listen to you. You're in a position of power. They come to you for advice and you can say these things and they'll take notice of you. If I were in your position I'd tell them. I think you're wasting your power.'

Iman's words hit a nerve. It was always a struggle for Sofia, weighing up how much she should and could say and what right she had to say it. Sometimes she did say things, but then she would worry she had gone too far and some irate father or husband would be on her doorstep. Other times she didn't say anything at all and she disappointed herself. Often it depended on what sort of mood she was in and how receptive she thought the woman might be. In Afrooz's case she knew her words, whatever they might be, would fall on deaf ears. Besides, the change Afghan women sought wouldn't come through a foreigner. Its roots had to be homegrown. It had to come from people like Iman. As far as Sofia was concerned, Iman had far more power than she did, she just wouldn't recognise it. Ninety per cent of being powerless was believing you were.

'Or maybe you think I have more power than I do,' Sofia said. 'You've got power, Iman.'

'Don't be silly.'

'No, I mean it, you do. As an Afghan woman you've got the greatest power to change things for Afghan women.' Iman shrugged. The topic was closed. 'Did Dr Jabril come in this afternoon?'

'For a little bit. He came to see you but you were with Afrooz. Oh yeah,' she said, 'I forgot. He told me to tell you that he would speak with you but he had some important business to do. Sounds suspicious to me. What's going on?'

It was Sofia's turn to shrug.

'Okay,' Iman said, standing. 'Something's going on but I

don't care anymore. I'm going home and I still think you've got more power than me and you're wasting it.'

***

As HE WAS closing up, Omar was aware of Behnaz hanging around her gate watching him. This was not good. He had put the night letter back on her gate that morning, and while he had been feeling relieved, he was also more worried than ever because he had come to the conclusion that the person in danger was indeed Dr Sofia. Why had she been wearing a coat and where had she gone in such a hurry with Tawfiq? When he'd questioned Tawfiq about this he had been suspiciously quiet. Something was wrong, but he had no idea what it was or how was he going to save her. When he saw Behnaz walking over to his shop he locked the door and stood behind it.

'Open this door,' Behnaz said, banging on the glass. 'I want to talk to you. It's important.'

Even Omar could see it really was a bit absurd, standing either side of a locked glass door looking at each other. Perhaps Behnaz knew how to fix this. Opening the door slightly, Omar looked out. 'You didn't want to talk to me yesterday.'

'That was not yesterday.'

'Then what day was it?'

'The day before yesterday.'

Omar was confused. What had happened to the day in between? 'Is Dr Sofia safe?' he asked, watching the frown on Behnaz's forehead deepen.

'What do you know, Omar?'

'I think we have been through this question before, Behnaz. I know nothing.'

'That's what you said before.'

'Exactly.'

Behnaz glared at him. 'Hadi told me you got *shabnamah*.'

'No, I don't think that's right.'

'Ahmad told me you got *shabnamah*.'

'No, I –' Omar was trying to remember what he'd said.

'Babur, Rashid and Tawfiq told me you got *shabnamah*.'

'Maybe I got *shabnamah*. I don't know. Maybe I just got a letter.'

Behnaz planted her hands on her ample hips. 'And what did your letter say?'

'It didn't say anything.'

Behnaz's eyes narrowed. 'It must have said something.'

'No, it really didn't say anything. In fact, I forget what it said.' He wished she'd go away.

'Then it did say something.'

Omar felt his body slumping. He had to concede defeat. Behnaz was far too clever, just like his second wife.

'I was told it said one of your friends had to be careful and stop what they were doing,' Behnaz offered.

'It might have said something like that.' He couldn't even remember what it said. Things were so confusing.

She sighed deeply. 'You're a troublemaker, Omar.'

'Yes, you've said that before too.' Maybe he was a trouble-maker. No, he wasn't a troublemaker. He'd only been trying to help.

'Did it say anything about Dr Sofia?'

'Did yours say anything about Dr Sofia?'

'No.'

'Then neither did mine. Do you think it's about Dr Sofia?' he asked.

He watched as Behnaz drew in a deep breath. 'Stop causing trouble, Omar.'

'What does Chief Wasim say?' he called after her as she strode back to her gate to disappear behind it.

It was not him who was causing trouble, Omar thought, locking the shop door again. It was the night letters that Behnaz wasn't getting and all the secrets their friends were keeping and something mysterious that Dr Sofia was doing that was causing trouble.

As he made his way upstairs to his bedroom, it worried him that he couldn't remember the missing day.

39

No MATTER HOW much Zahra threatened, cajoled or pleaded with Jabril he would not tell her what he was planning to do about Massoud and the visa, which meant they had gone to bed on bad terms. The following morning his wife remained icy, which had him hurrying out the door early to buy his morning copy of the *Afghanistan Times*. Flicking through the pages he was relieved to see there was nothing about Massoud. He rang his friend Ishmael, who was the senior editor of the newspaper, who informed Jabril that the story they had been working on might not appear in the newspaper for a few more days. Jabril's heart sank. Every time he thought about the chain of events he had set in motion he felt ill. The story needed to be published before he lost his nerve and changed his mind. When he asked Ishmael why the delay he was told the newspaper needed to check facts, including whether Massoud was in Kandahar on the night in question.

'You don't believe a special representative of the United Nations?' he asked, affronted on both his and Daniel's behalf.

'I would if I could interview or quote him, but you told me I can't talk with him. You don't want to withdraw the story, do you, Jabril?'

'No, no, no, of course not! What sort of man would I be if I reneged?' The sort of man he despised is what he would be. 'What happens now?'

'As far as I can see, either one of two things will happen when the story breaks about Massoud and his boy. Nobody will touch it because they'll all be too frightened, or it'll be picked up by everyone, maybe even the international press if it's a slow news day.'

Jabril wished he'd told Zahra what he was planning to do, but the right opportunity had not presented itself. Jabril checked the thought right there. There was never going to be a right opportunity, and even if there was, he probably wouldn't have recognised it if it had smacked him in the face. The truth was, he hadn't told Zahra because he was frightened of what she would say.

'There is another possibility, not mutually exclusive of the first two,' Ishmael was saying.

'What's that?' Jabril asked, patting down the hair he swept across the top of his baldness.

'We're both going to get killed.'

Jabril's hand froze and his heart jumped. 'Don't say that!'

'I was joking.'

'It's not funny. You're not the one getting the threats from Massoud.' He was now sure that Massoud was the author of the three supposed night letters left on his door.

By mid-morning Jabril had become so agitated that he did the unthinkable and cancelled lunch with Mustafa so he could join Zahra and Sofia, who were having lunch together at his home. He would tell them together. With any luck, Sofia's presence would curb some of Zahra's fury.

* * *

'Try this new yoghurt from the French Bakery,' Zahra said as the last dish was placed on the table. 'They make it themselves.'

Jabril could stand it no longer. 'Well, I've done it,' he said. It hadn't been quite how he had planned to begin but at least he had begun. There was no going back now.

'Finally, the great mystery is about to be revealed. Well?' asked Zahra, turning to her husband.

Jabril patted down his hair and cleared his throat. 'I've given the story about Massoud and his boy to Ishmael at the *Afghanistan Times* and very soon it'll be front-page news all over Afghanistan.' Just saying it out loud made Jabril feel ill.

He saw Sofia's face. It had gone white, while Zahra's hands froze in midair, causing salad to drop from the servers she was holding. At that moment he would have given a great deal to be having lunch with Mustafa in Babur's *chaikhana* like any other day of the week.

'No,' she said, shaking her head. 'No, no, no, no, no, *no!* Tell me you're joking. Tell me you didn't really expose a man like Massoud.'

'I did, but we're not using his name. We're saying "a former warlord turned politician".'

'Oh, that's alright then.' Zahra threw the salad servers into the bowl, causing more lettuce to jump out onto the table. 'Have you gone completely mad? Have you lost your mind? You've just signed your death warrant!'

'Nonsense, my love.' Jabril could feel the sweat breaking out on his forehead, prickling under his arms. It was not going as well as he had hoped but probably as he had expected. He looked to Sofia for help but she was looking just as upset as Zahra.

'Massoud is going to kill you!'

'I think not, Zahra, but I've made arrangements that if something does happen to me his name will be made known and then everyone will know who did it.' This was the only comforting thought Jabril could muster out of the entire affair, other than the fact that a paedophile would be exposed and the government would be forced to do something about the abominable practice.

'Oh, so that's your logic, is it? I'll no longer have a husband, but I can be comforted by the fact that everyone will know who did it. Is that it? Is that your reasoning?'

In thirty years of marriage he couldn't remember seeing Zahra so angry.

'Perhaps your friend won't publish the story,' Sofia offered quietly.

'Jabril,' Zahra, said, ignoring Sofia as she leaned over to take her husband's hand, 'what have you done? Can you not see the danger you've put yourself in? Weren't the letters enough for you?'

Sofia looked from Zahra to Jabril. 'What letters?'

Zahra turned to Sofia. 'About a month ago we got a night letter posted on our door. Since then we've got another two.'

Jabril's heart sank. Zahra had promised she would not tell Sofia.

'My god, Zahra,' Sofia said, her eyes wide with fear. 'What about?'

'That's precisely the point,' Jabril said, cutting Zahra off before she could answer. 'They're vague, my dear, but along the lines of "if you don't stop, someone will get hurt".'

'Who's going to get hurt, and stop what?'

'Yes! Exactly! I've considered posting a letter back asking if they could offer a little more clarification.'

'This is not funny, Jabril,' his wife said.

'No, Zahra, you're right. It's not. In any event, we've had these types of letters before and they've come to nothing. I'm sure it'll be the same this time.'

'So you upped my security because of the letters,' said Sofia.

'Notes. They're more like notes, but yes, and only when we got the last note and only as a precaution.'

'Why haven't *you* got security?' Sofia asked. 'Considering you're the one getting the notes, it seems to me you're the one who needs security, Jabril.'

'We're Afghans, my dear.'

Sofia shook her head. 'I don't know what that means. How does that keep you safe? Are all those people being killed in bombings not Afghans?'

Jabril had no answer. 'At least now we think we know who sent them.'

'Oh no,' Sofia said, her hand flying to her mouth. 'And I've made everything worse by speaking out at Zahra's women's meeting the other day, haven't I? His wife was there. She told him. No wonder Massoud said what he did to me.'

'And now,' said Zahra, turning back to her husband, 'you've commissioned an article outing Massoud as a paedophile.'

'Not Massoud. A former warlord turned –'

'Oh please!' snapped Zahra. 'Don't you think everyone will know who you mean? I believe you want martyrdom, Jabril. Why have you bought enemies with all your saved currency?' she cried. 'You've done so much good and yet you throw your hard-earned coin away on this?'

It pained him to see her fear and to know that he was the cause of it, but it had to be done. There was no going back now. 'What would you have me throw it away on?' he asked, turning around in his chair to face his distressed wife. 'Is not paedophilia worth throwing away my saved coin on? If Dr Abiteboul – a stranger to our country – was willing to testify, shouldn't I also be willing to do as much? Am I any less a man?'

'No, Jabril, you are the most wonderful, kindest, most principled man in the whole world, but there are so many other issues in this country you could fight for. Why pick this one? You didn't think.'

'A man can only think for so long before he must act. Everything I've done to stop this abomination has been for naught. No one in power listens. No one cares or wants to be involved in my campaign but then Dr Abiteboul gave us his information. Even Sofia knew we had to do something with it.'

Zahra turned to her friend in disbelief.

'I'm sorry, Zahra. I didn't mean for this to happen.'

'I knew it was the weapon I needed,' Jabril said, pulling Zahra's attention back to him. 'Can you not see, Zahra, that I had to do something bold with this? I can't sit by with this information about Minister Massoud and not do something with it. He's a paedophile. He keeps young boys. What more do we need to know?' He could see the tears gathering in Zahra's eyes.

'And why is it your responsibility to do something?' she asked.

'It's not just my responsibility,' he said, leaning forward. 'It's everyone's responsibility.'

'I don't see everyone out there throwing their lives away naming powerful politicians.'

'Because they don't have the information we have. Shh, my love.' Jabril took his wife's hand. 'Everything will be alright. I promise.'

'No, Jabril,' she said, pulling away. 'Everything will not be alright. You must stop this nonsense right now.'

'It's too late. I can't.'

* * *

Sofia left Jabril and Zahra arguing, and even though she had a full schedule that afternoon she found it hard to concentrate. Jabril's threatening night letters, or notes, or whatever they were, had to be from Massoud, warning Jabril to stop, and now she had made it worse by speaking out, and he had made it a thousand times worse by commissioning the article. Sofia had no doubts it was also Massoud who had cancelled her visa, and for the first time she had to consider the very real possibility that she might have to leave Afghanistan for good. Sofia sank her head onto her hands on the desk. How had everything spun so out of control in just one week? Hearing the ping of a message on her phone, she looked up to see who it was just as the phone began to ring.

'I've just texted you an address,' Daniel said. 'It's where two boys were taken this afternoon. I've also been told that the men who have them are pretty spooked after the first raid, so whoever goes into the house will have to be very careful.'

'Oh god, thank you!' she said, sitting up. 'I'll ring Chief Wasim right now.' After hanging up she rang the chief but it immediately went to his voice mail. She could feel the panic. They'd lost the boys before. They couldn't lose them twice. Every minute was crucial. She rang the chief again and again it went to his voice mail. This time she left a message before walking to her surgery door. 'How long until my next patient?' she asked Iman.

'Soraya in five minutes.'

'Can you try to ring her and tell her that I have an emergency? She can either wait or reschedule.'

'What's wrong?' Iman asked, rising from her chair.

Sofia waved her concern away. 'Nothing,' she said, before closing the surgery door. She began pacing the room as she rang Jabril. No answer. 'Will someone please answer their fucking phone! Shit, shit, shit,' she said under her breath, turning in circles. She rang Daniel back. 'I can't get through to Chief Wasim or Jabril! We can't let them get away again. What are we going to do?'

'Hang up. I'll ring you back.'

Sofia flopped back down into her chair to discover she couldn't sit still. She rose again, pacing with the phone in her hand. Time was passing. Too much time. She rang Jabril again and left an angry, confusing message. Walking to her desk she looked at the address she'd written down on her notepad. There was no way she could go there to rescue the boys. Her phone rang again.

'Okay,' Daniel said. 'I've just spoken with a friend who's head of the UN in Afghanistan and told her what's been going on. Apparently, she has an open line to your chief. She's just rung him and he's taking some men to the house now.'

'Oh my god,' Sofia said, the relief flooding through her body. 'So now we wait?'

'So now we wait. Oh, and Chief Wasim said to tell you that he got your message but he didn't ring back because he didn't think you'd want him to waste time ringing you instead of saving the boys. He'll contact you as soon as they're safe. We're nearly there, Sofia, just another hour and it should all be over.'

Sofia choked back a sob. 'I just want to hear the boys are okay.'

'I know, but there's nothing more you can do except wait. Did I ever tell you about the guy who's been giving me the information?' As he began recounting the story of Gharib she was drawn into the details until she realised it was simply a way of distracting her while she waited for news.

'You're a good man, Daniel Abiteboul.'

'Not so good.'

'No, I think you are.'

'Let's see what you think when you know me better.'

Sofia thought about the implication in his words. 'I want to apologise. I should never have asked you to testify against Massoud.'

'You've already apologised. Forget it. On another note, do you know what happened with Jabril's plan?'

'Oh god, I do and it's terrible. Sorry, I should have told you. The *Afghanistan Times* is going to publish the story of Massoud and the boy in Kandahar, leaving you out of it, of course.'

Daniel was silent for a few moments before he spoke slowly. 'Does Jabril understand the ramifications of what he's doing? Does he understand that he's putting both himself and whoever's publishing the story in grave danger? Massoud's not going to let this go. He can't.'

'We've tried to talk him out of it but he keeps saying it's too late.'

'It can't be too late. Tell him that I've been working on something that might not only help but will keep everyone safe.

I've got a friend who works for the Afghanistan Independent Human Rights Commission –'

'Jabril's already spoken with them. They said they've got too many issues and not enough resources, or something like that.'

'What if they got a request from the head of the UN to investigate *bacha bazi* and a grant to go with it? I've already spoken with my friend at the UN and she thinks they'd jump at the chance, and with the proper encouragement they might put some focus on Massoud in that report.'

'Is this really going to happen?'

'The preliminary talks are encouraging. In any event, Jabril's got to stop the article and the rest can be sorted out afterward. I can't stress that enough.'

After she hung up from Daniel, Sofia got through to Jabril to tell him about the raid and also about Daniel's plan, but he still wouldn't change his mind. An hour later Chief Wasim rang Sofia to say two boys had been rescued. One of them was Rayi.

'Now, Sofia,' he said, before she could hang up. 'This situation has ended well, but this is not always going to be the case with these things. I would like you to promise me to keep out of this *bacha bazi* business and not talk about it anymore or have anything to do with this campaign Jabril has been trying to organise.'

'How do you know about Jabril's campaign?'

'Everybody knows about it. Now, are you going to promise me to leave all this alone?'

'Absolutely. I promise.'

40

JABRIL WOULD HAVE liked to celebrate the boys' return that evening with Zahra, but she still wasn't speaking to him and had gone to bed early with a book. Sitting alone in the dark in the lounge room, nursing a scotch as he contemplated the events he had set in motion, Jabril was startled to hear a knock on the front door. Going downstairs he opened it to see Chief Wasim. 'Is there something wrong with the boys?'

'No, they're fine,' he said, placing a reassuring hand on Jabril's shoulder before the two men headed upstairs to the comfort of the lounges. 'A little shaken, but that is to be expected. As far as we can tell they've not been interfered with.'

Turning on the lights, Jabril picked up his glass of scotch and carried it to the cabinet before asking Wasim if he might get him anything to drink. Pouring them both pomegranate juices, he sat back down again in his favourite chair. 'The men who took them told you they weren't interfered with?' Jabril asked.

'The men who took them told me nothing. They're dead.'

'I see. Will the raid be in the papers tomorrow?' Jabril asked, taking a sip of his juice.

'No.'

'I see,' he said again, nodding. 'Like it never happened?'

'It's for the best.' After taking a sip the chief removed his glasses and began cleaning them on the hem of his *perahan*.

Only if you're a paedophile, Jabril thought. It was clear to Jabril that Wasim was not comfortable and the visit was not a social call. He also sensed that whatever Wasim had come to tell him was probably not going to be good. Jabril felt his exhaustion and the heavy weight of his own body in the chair. He wasn't sure he could deal with more worries, but he had to ask. 'What about the other two boys?'

'We will not find them, Jabril. You need to accept this. You should also stop your campaign and not publish the article,' Wasim said, not looking up from cleaning his glasses.

Jabril was shocked. 'Who told you about the article?'

'It doesn't matter who told me. What matters is that you don't publish.' Wasim held his glasses up to the light, checking for fingerprints before putting them back on his nose. 'No one wants to know about this business, and if you publish you'll be a social pariah. Do you understand, Jabril? A social pariah.' Wasim waited for Jabril to respond, but he was still trying to come to terms with the fact that Wasim knew about the article. 'You won't stop the men who do these things and you will have wasted all your money. Of course, you might save a few little boys, but it will all have been for nothing.'

'A few little boys are not nothing, Chief Wasim.'

The chief sighed deeply. 'Yes, you are right, they are not nothing. They are definitely not nothing but do you care so little for your own life, my friend?'

Jabril sat forward. 'Why do you think my life's in danger?'

'Because I know these men.'

340

'If you know these men, why don't you arrest them?'

The chief ignored Jabril's question. 'On another matter, Dr Sofia must stop talking about these things or she will be in danger also.'

'What do you know that you're not telling me, Wasim?' Jabril wondered whether after all these years he really knew his friend at all. Of course, as chief of police Wasim had a life none of them were part of. Jabril was just surprised he had never thought about this before.

'That's the thing, I *am* telling you what I know. That is the whole point. Let us just say that these are powerful men and as chief of police I hear things, and what I hear is that certain people are not happy with you and now with Dr Sofia. That's all I can say. Cancel this article and forget about this business, Jabril, please.'

'I can't cancel the article even if I wanted to. I have no choice anymore.'

'You always have choices, my friend. Everyone has choices.' Almost as an afterthought he added, 'Some just have more choices than others.'

'Not this time and not in this matter.'

Wasim sat forward. 'Has someone threatened you, Dr Jabril?'

'Only you.'

Wasim's shoulders sagged. 'I understand that you might feel this way but believe me, I'm not threatening you; I am trying to save you. I understand you want to publish. It's a terrible business.' The chief was becoming more animated. 'No one will deny that, but can't you see that nothing good will ever come from what you're doing? You have to stop.' Wasim gathered himself, sitting even further forward. 'Tell me, what is it that I can say to convince you to stop?'

'There's nothing.'

For the first time Jabril saw the years in his friend's face and the grey in his hair. 'I'm sorry, Wasim.'

Wasim sat back, shaking his head. 'I wish you would change your mind.'

Jabril finally realised why Chief Wasim was there and why Zahra had gone to bed early. 'It's Zahra, isn't it? She asked you to come here tonight to talk me out of the campaign and publishing, didn't she?'

'It doesn't matter who it was anymore,' Chief Wasim said, all emotion drained from his words.

The two men sat talking for another ten minutes about the boys and their rescue before Chief Wasim's phone rang. 'This thing never stops,' he said to Jabril, taking the phone out of his pocket and looking at the caller before standing up. 'I have to go.'

As Jabril stood at his gate watching Wasim walk away, he noticed for the first time how bent his friend's back had become and how slow his gait. When had Wasim turned into this old man? Going back upstairs with a heavy heart, Jabril returned to his scotch. Time was passing. They were all getting old.

In the last few years Jabril had started imagining grand-children around him in his old age, but only two weeks previously his daughter, Salmar, had rung to say she was going to marry an American man they had never met. Her home, she said, would be in Athens where the prospective husband's family lived.

'Athens!' Jabril had said to Zahra in disgust. 'Athens, Greece I can understand, but Athens, Alabama? Why not New York or Boston, at least? A man needs his daughter.'

When he saw Zahra's raised eyebrow he realised his mistake.

How did he explain to his wife that a father does not love one child more than the other, but Salmar was his baby girl and Jaweed ... well, his son had always been an enigma to him. After Salmar's news they had rung Jaweed to tell him only to discover he already knew and had even met the fiancé. It had been another knife in Jabril's heart.

During the conversation with Jaweed he had finally asked the question he had wanted to ask ever since his son had finished his engineering degree the previous year. When might he be returning home? Never, Jaweed had said. He saw no reason to build something beautiful in Afghanistan only to have it destroyed. Jabril's heart felt as if it had been shattered into tiny pieces.

'He wants us to come to Paris to live,' Zahra had informed him when she got off the phone with Jaweed.

'What would we do in Paris?'

'Shop, visit the Eiffel Tower, the Louvre, spend time with our son.'

Jabril looked at his wife in horror. 'Tell me you don't mean that.'

'What? That I would like to spend time with my son?'

'No, no, no, I'm sure you'd like to spend time with Jaweed just as much as I would, but then what?'

'You're right. We can't live in Paris. How could I live without Chicken Street?'

'This is not a laughing matter. There is no sense of family or obligation anymore with children,' Jabril lamented. 'We should never have taken them to America in the first place.'

'And what should we have done? Brought them up in the middle of a war? How would you have got your degree in our country, Jabril, when it was chaos? No, we did what we had to do

343

and now we'll live with the consequences. We have no choice.'
Zahra moved from the lounge to kneel in front of her husband.

'I know this hurts you,' she said, taking his hands. 'It hurts
me too, but our children are living the lives they want to live.
Didn't we teach them to be independent? Didn't we encourage
them to have wings and fly? They've left us, Jabril, and that is as
it should be. We need to let go of our dreams for our children:
they were never their dreams.'

***

WHEN JABRIL'S PHONE rang he answered it immediately. 'I'm
sorry,' he said, before Daniel had time to speak. 'It was remiss
of me not to have rung and thanked you for helping find the
boys. We couldn't have done it without you.'

'All I did was pass on information from my friend, but that's
not why I'm calling. Sofia told me about the article you're
planning to publish.'

'Not you too?' Jabril said, exhausted.

'Pardon?' When Jabril didn't respond Daniel continued. 'Are
you sure you want to publish? It'll be dangerous.'

'I'm not worried about Massoud if that's what you're
thinking, because once the article comes out he wouldn't dare
touch me.' Jabril downed the last of the scotch in his glass and
walked to the cabinet to pour himself another.

There was a long silence before Daniel spoke. 'I think you're
wrong. You'll have publicly crossed him and he can't let that
happen without exacting a high price. A price so high no one
will ever consider doing the same thing to him again. That's how
the man operates. He has his reputation to protect, Jabril, above
and beyond anything. His power comes from his reputation.
You can only come off worse with this man.'

'No, he's a minister and this will ruin him.' Jabril had returned to his chair and made himself comfortable by pulling up a pouf with his feet. 'He won't do anything to me because it would be linked directly back to him after the article came out.'

'Do you honestly believe that? I'm not sure there's much anyone can say about Massoud that hasn't already been said, and I've never seen him held accountable for anything he's ever done. Think about it. In the end he'll just deny the paedophilia and none of us can prove it. *I* can't even prove it. It'll just be your word against his.'

The logic of what Daniel was saying sank in. In truth, Jabril had always known he'd be paying a high price, but what else could he do? No one understood that this was about more than Massoud and paedophilia now. Far more was at stake.

After he hung up, Jabril considered his options again. Was there another way? Definitely it would have been preferable to leave everything up to Daniel and the Human Rights Commission if they could do an investigation. He could also see that his own plan to bring down Massoud was probably naïve, but how else could he get Sofia's visa reinstated before she had to leave unless he brought down the man who had cancelled it? Minister Massoud had to lose his power or Sofia had to go. It was as simple as that. There was no other way. Taking his empty glass out to the kitchen, Jabril got ready for bed.

In those lonely night hours, when fears are at their darkest, Jabril could feel himself sinking. The life he knew was slipping away. Was he going too far with the article? Was his life really in danger? Was Sofia's life in danger?

As Jabril was going over his options he grew increasingly despondent until he discovered a new option, and while it was

345

also dangerous it was definitely preferable to publishing. He was about to ring Ishmael and tell him to hold off on publishing until he realised it was already two o'clock. He would ring him in the morning.

* * *

Relieved to see that the article hadn't been published yet, Jabril was in such a good mood that when he came into the kitchen he was humming.

'You sound cheery,' Zahra said as she dried the last of her breakfast dishes.

'Did you ask Chief Wasim to talk me out of publishing the article?' Jabril asked, pouring himself a coffee.

Zahra was looking at him in as if he'd gone mad. 'And why would I do that?'

'Because he paid me a visit last night.'

'Really?' she said, turning around from the kitchen sink. 'Chief Wasim would not be the first person I'd call to try to talk you out of publishing. So have you changed your mind because I see the article isn't in the paper yet.' She placed his breakfast dishes on the table in front of him.

'Maybe.'

'What does maybe mean?'

'I've got a better plan.'

Zahra shook her head as she leaned back against the kitchen bench. 'I'm glad to hear that, but does this better plan happen to involve Massoud?'

'It does.'

'Then I don't want to hear about it.' With that she walked out of the kitchen.

Jabril had decided that Daniel had been right about Massoud.

He wouldn't normally be affected by accusations, but paedo-philia was no ordinary accusation, and if the minister was given the opportunity to avoid such a thing there was a very good chance he might take it. That was what Jabril was going to offer Massoud. He would tell him about the article before offering him an option: reinstate Sofia's visa and he would promise not to publish, and neither he nor Sofia would talk about this issue in public again. How could the man refuse? Then, once the deal was made, the Human Rights Commission could write its report, which would have nothing to do with Jabril or Sofia. It was a good plan.

Jabril was humming again as he got ready to leave for the surgery. As far as he could see, nothing would be lost with this deal: no lives would be put at risk, and in the end Massoud would still get his just desserts. As he left the house he decided lunchtime would be a good time to visit Massoud, and after the deal was struck he'd call Ishmael to cancel the article. When lunchtime came, though, Jabril found himself particularly hungry. Nothing would be lost by having the conversation with Massoud after he had eaten.

As he and Mustafa were finishing their teas, Jabril saw Zahra crossing the square, heading for Sofia's surgery, which reminded him that they had planned to take inventory in their surgeries after lunch. Massoud or inventory? He couldn't decide which one he wanted to do less. Finally, he decided he had to tell Massoud. Inventory would have to wait.

'Don't let work interrupt your fine lunch,' Zahra snapped without looking his way.

He had hoped the idea of this new plan where no one got hurt would have appeased her, but Zahra had not wanted to hear about it. That evening he hoped he would have good news for her, but first he had to tell her and Sofia he was not going to be able to help take the inventory. Jabril sighed loudly for Mustafa's benefit. 'Some days are better than others, my friend. This day is not one of my best.'

Jabril saw the man walking toward him as he rose from his chair and in that moment he knew. The first bullet ripped through his shoulder like a ball of fire, shattering bone, severing blood vessels and ripping through muscle as it spun him sideward. Knees buckling under him, Jabril instinctively grabbed the side of the table to break his fall. When the second bullet smashed into his abdomen, the shock to his body ended all conscious thought.

41

SOFIA HAD BEEN standing by the window looking down over the square while Zahra was in the bathroom. Later she would often think back to the fact that she had noticed the stranger in the square immediately and had been watching him, but she could not say why. Perhaps it was the way he was walking. Most people generally strolled into the square, but this man was in a hurry, heading with purpose toward the *chaikhana* where Jabril and Mustafa were sitting. Maybe that was it, or maybe what was about to happen had registered in her subconscious before it had time to register as a thought? She watched him pull out the gun. Her scream reached Jabril long after the bullets. That's part of the horror of the memory: knowing and not being able to stop it. Like when you know a car accident is about to happen and there's nothing you can do, or you see a child's foot slip and know they are going to fall, or you see words coming out of a mouth moving through the air toward you, words that you somehow know will shatter you, but you can't stop them from arriving. Those moments are strangely drawn out, as if you're being given a fraction more time to prepare yourself.

As Jabril collapsed, taking the table with him, Sofia turned and ran. Taking the stairs two at a time, swinging off the rail, she ran out into the square to see Rashid standing over the man's body, his AK-47 pointed at his head. By the way the body was sprawled out on the cobblestones she guessed he was already dead. She watched Rashid lift his gun and fire into the corpse. She saw the recoil of the gun and the corpse jump but there was no sound in her ears. The world was filled with the white noise of shock.

In front of the *chaikhana* Jabril's body was lying motionless in a pool of blood. The upturned table had rolled on top of him and Babur and another man were lifting it off before kneeling down beside Jabril. Mustafa, confused and frightened with his unseeing eyes, was frozen, standing behind his upturned chair as Babur's cook reached him to take his arm and lead him away.

'Get out of the way,' Sofia yelled at Babur, unaware she was speaking English, bringing noise back into the world. She pushed through the men. 'Move!' Blood was seeping out of Jabril's lower abdomen and his shoulder, dark crimson stains spreading out at an alarming rate across his white shirt and the cobblestones beneath him, but he was still breathing.

'Stay with me,' Sofia said, ripping open his shirt to send small white buttons skipping across the cobblestones. 'Call an ambulance!' she yelled in English. When no one responded she realised her mistake. She looked directly at Babur and spoke again in Dari.

'It's coming,' Babur said. Jabril was going into shock. She would have to deal with that later. She did a quick scan. The shoulder was shattered, but it was his stomach that really worried her. 'I need to put pressure here. Get me something,' she said to no one in particular, holding out her hand. A man handed her his soft felt hat. For a second she looked at it before applying it to the hole in Jabril's abdomen. 'Here,' she said, moving over to make room for the man to kneel beside her. 'Apply pressure here, like this. That's right.' With the fellow holding his hat in Jabril's stomach, Sofia turned her attention to the shoulder before looking up at Babur. 'I need something to tie this off. A belt, something ... anything.' She held out her hand and Babur undid his apron and handed it to Sofia. She used it to make a tourniquet. With that secure she took over from the man plugging up the hole in Jabril's gut. 'The ambulance. Where's the ambulance?' she said more calmly.

'It's coming.'

Leaning down, she whispered, 'I'm here, my friend. You're going to be just fine. I'm going to take good care of you. Do you hear me? You're going to be just fine. I love you, Jabril.'

She heard Zahra scream from behind and for those few seconds she didn't want Zahra there. She didn't need a hysterical wife. She needed to concentrate on keeping Jabril alive. She felt herself being pushed to one side as Zahra collapsed to her knees to take her husband's head into her arms. Leaning back in, Sofia applied pressure to the stomach again, checking with her eyes that the tourniquet was still holding. Zahra began crooning to Jabril, rocking him back and forth until she looked up at Sofia with the question in her eyes.

'I don't know,' she said, shaking her head. 'I just don't know.'

Sofia heard the ambulance approaching the square but knew more time would be wasted when the driver discovered the vehicle couldn't fit down the alleyway. When the medics finally came running she told them what she knew of his wounds and stepped away.

As she stood watching them work, strong arms were being

wrapped around her, pulling her away from the crowd that had gathered around Jabril. 'Come, come inside,' Behnaz said.

'No,' Sofia pulled against the grip. She needed to know he was in good hands. As she watched the medics working on him she desperately searched for something constructive to do but her mind was no longer functioning. This was not the time to lose it. Looking around the square she saw Ahmad, Hadi, Iqbal and Iman standing together out the front of Ahmad's shop. She focused on them, willing them to bring her back to the moment and to Jabril.

'You must come inside, quickly,' Behnaz was saying to her as the medics picked Jabril up and began to carry him out of the square on a stretcher. When Sofia didn't react Behnaz took Sofia's face in both her hands, forcing her to look at her. 'Quickly. It's not safe for you out here.'

Omar, who had been having his lunchtime nap when the shots woke him, began helping Behnaz move Sofia away. 'Go inside now,' he said when they reached the turquoise gate. 'I'll guard this door with my life. No one will hurt Dr Sofia.'

Inside the house Behnaz sat Sofia down on the brown floral lounge, still covered in the hard plastic it had arrived in three years earlier. Crouching down in front of Sofia, Behnaz began pulling her hair away from her face, threading it back behind her ears as she had seen Sofia do a thousand times before. As Behnaz began wiping away Sofia's tears with the end of her black headscarf, Sofia stared at her hands cupped in her lap until she realised they were covered in Jabril's blood.

'I need to go to the hospital,' she said, wiping her nose on her sleeve as she tried to stand. Behnaz pushed her back down again.

'The ambulance has gone. There's nothing you can do there,' Chief Wasim said as he walked into the room. 'There are things I need to ask you now, Dr Sofia.'

42

EASING HIS WEARY bulk onto the vinyl pouf in front of Dr Sofia, Wasim took his time studying her. He needed to know her state of mind and whether she could be trusted to act rationally. He also needed the time to gather himself. What happened next was critical for everyone. There was no confusion in Wasim's mind about what he had to do.

'Did you see anything?' Sofia looked up at him frowning, as if she couldn't understand the question. 'Did you see anything of the shooting?'

'Yes.'

Wasim waited for her to continue until he realised she wasn't going to. 'Tell me what you saw.'

She rubbed her forehead as if trying to recall. 'I saw a stranger walking into the square, heading for Babur's *chaikhana* … for Jabril.' She shook her head. 'I saw him pull out his gun and shoot. I remember seeing Rashid shooting a corpse.' She shook her head again before looking up at Wasim. 'That's it.'

Thankfully Rashid had solved the problem of the shooter for him. Dead men didn't talk, just like those men who had taken the boys. 'Okay, we'll deal with that later. Have you seen this man or any strangers in the square lately?' Again, Sofia looked at him as if she couldn't understand what he was saying. 'Anyone watching you?'

'No.'

Wasim leaned forward and patted her hand. 'That's good. Don't worry, we'll find who did this.'

Sofia had been agitated, wringing her bloodied hands, her eyes darting around the room, but now her eyes were fixed on him. 'You know who did this.'

'We must not jump ahead of ourselves,' Wasim offered calmly. 'We need to wait until we've finished our investigations before we can decide.'

'Minister Massoud shot Dr Jabril because of the article. Who else could it be?'

'That's not Minister Massoud's body out in the square. He didn't shoot Dr Jabril.' She was staring at him again as if his words were confusing her. She was in shock. This was understandable. 'Behnaz, can you get Dr Sofia a blanket please?'

Sofia frowned again. 'Of course it isn't Massoud's body in the square. It's someone he hired to do the job.'

'We should not jump to conclusions. I understand Dr Jabril has been getting *shabnamah* from the Taliban long before the article.'

He had never thought anyone would ever think the notes he had written to warn Jabril would be considered *shabnamah*. From the little he had been able to gather from Omar before he came into the house, the idea that the notes on his own gate had been *shabnamah* had arisen from Omar's drug-addled imagination, but he could now see how he might use this idea of *shabnamah* to his advantage, although he needed to be careful because neither Zahra nor Jabril had told him about their notes. Officially, he didn't know they existed. Hopefully, no one else had seen them either, but if they had it was still in his interests to encourage this idea that they too were Taliban night letters.

'So,' Wasim said, clearing his throat, 'it seems to me that it is more likely this was the work of the Taliban, not Minister Massoud.' Wasim held up his hand to stop Sofia speaking. 'Until we know the reasons why, we cannot know the who.'

Sofia was shaking her head violently. 'No, this is Massoud. He just wants you to think it's the Taliban.'

'Dr Sofia, please, I need you to think about this. What you are saying doesn't make sense. How could Minister Massoud have known about the article?'

'Why would the Taliban want to shoot Jabril?' she fired back at him.

'It could have been because he hired you to work with the women here. It could have been anything.'

He watched the blood draining from her face. 'You think they wanted to kill him because of me?'

'That's not what I said. I don't know their reasons. Until I investigate, none of us knows what Dr Jabril was doing that may have enraged the Taliban. What I do know is that the minister could not have known about the article.'

He watched Dr Sofia push her fingers deep into her temples. 'You of all people, chief, know what it's like around here. He's a powerful man and people like him have spies everywhere. You even said you might have spies in your office.'

'No, I believe Dr Jabril said I might have spies in my office. I personally don't know of any spies.'

He watched a dark cloud passing over her face until she frowned. 'How do *you* know about the article, Chief Wasim? No one knew about the article but Zahra, me, Dr Daniel and the editor.'

Luckily he had his answer ready for this. 'Dr Jabril told me last night when I went to see him about the boys being rescued.' Thankfully, she accepted this.

'You know Massoud threatened Dr Jabril?'

Wasim sat up on the pouf. This was not good news. A threat from Massoud would complicate things. 'What do you mean?'

'He said something to Dr Daniel about it being a shame if Dr Jabril couldn't continue his good work.'

'And this Dr Daniel is the same person who gave you the information about the boys?'

'It is.'

'When did this alleged threat happen?'

'It's not "alleged". It was a few days ago, I think. Maybe four. I don't know. Two? I can't remember. Ask Dr Daniel. He'll tell you.'

'Are there any witnesses to this conversation?'

'I don't think so.'

'It doesn't sound like a threat to me. It could have been an observation by Minister Massoud of Dr Jabril's good works.' Sofia looked incredulous. 'I'm just saying this is what his lawyer will say, although the minister will probably deny the conversation completely.'

'Oh,' she cried, burying her face in her hands as Behnaz reached out to put her arm around Dr Sofia's shoulders, shooting Wasim flames of anger. His wife wanted him to leave Dr Sofia alone but he could not do that.

'I'm sorry, Dr Sofia, but I have a few more questions I need to ask you while everything is still fresh in your mind.'

'Talk to Dr Daniel,' Sofia said, looking up at him through red-rimmed eyes. 'He'll tell you. It was when he saw Minister Massoud's boy dancing.'

Wasim held up his hand again. 'Please, I must warn you in the strongest possible terms not to say things like that about the minister.' Wasim took his glasses off to polish, but when he reached for the hem of his *perahan* he discovered he was wearing his police uniform. He put the smudged glasses back on his nose. It had been a long week and there were longer and more dangerous days to come. Wasim considered his options again and came to the same conclusion: there was only one thing he had to do and that was protect Minister Massoud.

'There's a slight problem with your logic. Minister Massoud could not have threatened Dr Jabril because of the article before it was even thought of.'

Sofia looked confused. 'I don't know, maybe it was because of this campaign or because of the boys.'

'Then why didn't he threaten you when he was talking with Dr Daniel? You see, we got *shabnamah* too.'

As soon as he spoke he realised his mistake. Behnaz had never told him about their notes.

'Ahhhh!' Behnaz cried, slapping herself on the cheeks in frustration. 'Why did you tell her? Now she'll leave.'

Ah, thought Wasim, so that was why she'd hidden the notes. He thought once his wife saw them she'd warn Dr Sofia, who'd tell Jabril about the letters, who would then finally get the message that this was serious. Instead, she'd hidden them so Dr Sofia wouldn't leave. What a fool he'd been.

Wasim knew now Behnaz would only see that he had betrayed her by telling Dr Sofia. No one would ever understand that he had been trying to save Jabril. He also knew that Behnaz would soon begin to wonder how he knew about the notes when she hadn't told him. Luckily for him, Omar, who was probably still guarding their gate even though he'd stationed one of his men there, had told him about the *shabnamah* before he'd come in.

'We've been getting night letters too?' Sofia asked. 'What did they say?'

'We only had one,' offered Behnaz. 'Only one and it wasn't a *shabnamah*. It could have been a mistake. Maybe it was on the wrong gate.'

Wasim, who knew from Omar his wife was in possession of both his notes now, was surprised to hear how easily she lied. He'd never seen this before.

'What did it say?' demanded Sofia.

'That we should tell our friend to stop,' offered Wasim, before seeing the look on Behnaz's face and realising his mistake.

'How do you know what they said?' Behnaz asked, her eyes narrowing as she looked at her husband. 'I never told you about the notes.' She was no fool but she'd just given her lie away by using the plural.

'Omar told me.' Thankfully, his explanation seemed to satisfy her and the ferocious look she had given him relaxed. In Wasim's experience, if you needed to lie you needed to stick as close as possible to the truth: do not elaborate, do not offer more than what is being asked for and say as little as possible. He'd dealt with enough criminals and their lawyers to know this.

'What friend?' Sofia asked angrily. 'Me or Dr Jabril? And stop what? Should I stop working in the square? Should I stop talking about *bacha bazi*? Should I stop brushing my teeth in the morning? What?'

'Dr Sofia,' Wasim said, holding up his hand in the hope of calming her hysteria.

'Who were they talking about, Chief Wasim? And what were they talking about? Should Hadi stop cheating his customers, should Ahmad start going to …' Dr Sofia's words trailed off as realisation dawned. 'Everyone in the square knew about these night letters, didn't they? That's why Ahmad's been going to mosque in the morning and Tawfiq's worried. That's why everyone's been acting strange. That's why my security was upped. Everyone knew but me.'

'Dr Jabril didn't know about our letters and no one knew about his. You were not the only person who was ignorant. Now, Dr Sofia –'

'Show it to me,' she demanded, holding out her hand.

Wasim looked to Behnaz. Reaching into the pocket of her coat she took out one of his typed notes. He suspected the other one was secreted away in the same place. Somehow he had to take possession of all the notes he'd written and destroy them, but he would worry about that later.

Sofia looked at it. 'This isn't a night letter from the Taliban. The Taliban write essays, not one-line mysteries. The Taliban always *want* you to know what you're doing to upset them. This doesn't tell you anything.'

'I think who wrote the *shabnamah* is not important. Who shot Dr Jabril is what's important.' Wasim watched Sofia's face collapse into tears again.

'I need to know what's happening to Jabril,' she said, getting up out of the seat.

'Please sit down, Dr Sofia.' He motioned with his hand for her to sit and, to his great surprise, she did. 'One of my men is at the hospital now and he'll let me know when there's any news. I promise, you will be the first person I tell.'

'His injuries were really serious, Wasim,' she said, her words coming out in tiny sobbing spaces.

'I know.' As he watched, her look of misery began to morph into something else. His heart sank. What bad news was about to fall on his head now?

'Why didn't you put someone outside Dr Jabril's house to protect him? That might have been a good idea, don't you think, Chief Wasim?'

'Dr Jabril didn't ask for someone to protect him.' At least that was the truth.

'*Namoos. Nang*,' Behnaz cried out in disgust. 'This is all Afghan men think about: their pride and their honour when their families are dying. You're all fools and now Dr Jabril's going to die and Dr Sofia's going back to Sydney.'

Sofia looked directly at Behnaz, her eyes blazing. 'Dr Jabril's *not* going to die and I'm *not* going back to Sydney. This is my home. Here,' she said pointing to the floor. 'Right here.'

Her words stunned Wasim. How could she even consider not leaving? Did she not understand the danger she was in? Hadn't Dr Jabril's shooting been enough? He had to straighten this out before she was shot also. 'I think your visa has been cancelled so you have no choice, Dr Sofia. You must go back to Australia immediately.'

Behnaz made a sound like a wounded animal. 'Dr Sofia's visa's been cancelled? Why?'

They both ignored her. Wasim was watching Sofia, fascinated by how her face was a perfect signpost to her rapidly changing emotions. She was looking at him calmly now, all anger having vanished. If he were to describe the way she looked, he thought, it would be an animal that had just seen its dinner. This concerned him more than her hysteria.

'How did you know my visa was cancelled?'

As Wasim swallowed his alarm he could feel the sweat prickling under his arms. Although he didn't look at her, he suspected Behnaz, who knew him better than most, was beginning to understand something was not quite right. He had to be particularly careful with his answer. It was Massoud who had told him about cancelling Dr Sofia's visa. The only way he could possibly get out of this bind was if Dr Jabril had known about the cancellation also. He had no choice. 'Dr Jabril told me.' He watched Dr Sofia carefully to see her shoulders collapse as she sank further into the chair. He had been right. Wasim was back in control.

'What I am going to do now is discover who shot Dr Jabril.' That was not what Wasim was intending to do. What he was intending on doing was getting back outside and taking control of the investigation before one of his men found something he was not supposed to find. Wasim stood. 'Under no circumstances can you go back out into the square today, Dr Sofia, do you understand? And you must leave the country as soon as possible. Tomorrow.'

'Tomorrow?' Sofia said, looking at him in confusion.

'Today. Tomorrow. You need to leave now, Dr Sofia, because

your life might also be in danger. I'm sorry.' And he was sorry. He did not want to see her go as much as Behnaz didn't, but her life might depend on her leaving. Who knew what Massoud would do next? If he remained angry, Dr Sofia was sure to be the next target.

As he walked out of the house, Wasim heard his wife crying again. Things were not going to be so good at home for a long time after Dr Sofia left.

Once outside the gate, the chief of police ignored Omar as he fumbled around in his pocket to retrieve his cigarettes, his second packet for the day. He took a deep, calming breath.

Ordinary people like Behnaz and Dr Sofia, or even a Western-educated man like Dr Jabril, didn't understand how this world worked but he, Chief Wasim, did, and while it was not how he would have wanted things to be, he was a realist. There had been a time, though, when as a young policeman he had seen the world more simply, with enthusiasm for his job and love for his country, but inevitably, as time passed, he began to learn secrets. At first it had felt powerful to know these things, but in time the secrets you kept made you someone else's property. Wasim took another drag on his cigarette. With all his heart he wished those secrets had not passed his way. With that useless thought he turned to Omar. 'You must not tell anyone about the *shabnamah*.' When he saw the look of fear on Omar's face his heart sank. What had that fool Omar done now? Wasim could feel his ulcer playing up.

'I think it might be a little bit late for that, Chief Wasim,' Omar offered sheepishly. By the time he had finished telling Wasim about his efforts to find the mysterious 'friend' in the square, Wasim understood that the only people who should have known about his notes on their gate, Dr Sofia and Dr Jabril, were probably the only people who didn't, while the rest of the square, and possibly half of Kabul, did. Disgusted, Wasim threw his cigarette down before walking over to the police tape. Lifting it, he walked under.

'This didn't have to happen, my friend,' he said, as he stood over Jabril's blood still drying on the cobblestones. 'It didn't have be this way. If only you'd listened.'

'The woman was easy to take care of,' Massoud had said to Wasim the previous evening after he'd reported his failure to convince Dr Jabril to withdraw the article and forget about funding a campaign. 'Without a visa she'll be gone soon enough. It's Jabril who's our real problem. The fool needs to be stopped.'

Massoud hadn't been overly worried about Jabil's idea of a campaign initially because he knew no one would want anything to do with it. It had only become an 'irritant', as Massoud called it, when Jabril wouldn't let the subject drop, but when he heard that Jabril was intending to fund the campaign himself Massoud had become concerned. And then this article business. Wasim had never seen the man so angry. He had no idea how the minister knew about the article but he suspected Massoud had 'friends' at the newspaper, like he had 'friends' everywhere, like he had 'friends' among Wasim's staff.

'Give me more time,' Wasim had pleaded with the minister. 'I'm sure I can get him to change his mind.'

Like everyone else, Minister Massoud owned him. It was the secrets. Keep one secret and then you will keep another and then another and soon it was secrets within secrets until no one could remember where they began, but everyone knew where they ended. Wasim's shoulders slumped. He'd failed his friend. If only he had been able to report back to Massoud that he had been able talk Dr Jabril out of publishing the article and forgetting about the campaign, none of this would have happened. And now he had no idea whether Massoud would turn on Sofia. The man was out of control.

Straightening up, he looked around the square. Nearly all the shops were closed already. He would have liked to go home too but he had work to do. He needed to respectfully suggest to the minister that one shooting was enough. He also had to make sure Dr Jabril's friend withdrew the article, although he didn't think that would be a problem after what had just happened. He also needed to speak with this Dr Daniel and convince him that Minister Massoud had not threatened Dr Jabril. And finally, he had to take possession of the three notes he'd written Jabril and the two in Behnaz's possession, because if Massoud discovered he'd written them to warn his friends then his life was as good as over. Wasim sighed. Getting the notes wouldn't be so hard. He'd just tell Behnaz and Zahra they were needed for evidence. If he could then perform a miracle and make sure the investigation went in the opposite direction to Minister Massoud and make sure Sofia was safe they might all survive this mess. All except Dr Jabril, he reminded himself, feeling the weight of guilt heavy on his heart.

43

SOFIA'S HEAD ACHED and her heart felt like it had been smashed into a thousand tiny pieces. Zahra had rung the night before to say Jabril was out of surgery and in a critical but stable condition. The bullet in his shoulder had shattered the joint and he would need further surgery. The one in the stomach had done the real damage and it was now a matter of wait and see.

In the morning Sofia rang Zahra, who was still at the hospital, to learn his condition had not changed. Zahra was being swamped with calls and was about to turn her phone off. She would ring Sofia if there was any change. Sofia then spoke to Chief Wasim. The shooter was not on any police database so they couldn't identify him unless someone reported him missing. Chief Wasim said he suspected the man might be from Iran or Pakistan, and in that case they'd never identify him. When Sofia offered to have Dr Daniel ask his friend if he knew anything about the last two missing boys Chief Wasim told her no, stressing again that for her own safety she needed to leave Afghanistan within the next couple of days and should not, under any circumstances, leave the square except to go to the airport. She also needed to keep Rashid by her side at all times.

Sofia wandered around the apartment, taking her time getting ready for work, but before she left she called Taban to ask about Farahnaz's little brother and offering to ask Dr Daniel to contact his friend about the other missing boys. Taban's response had surprised her.

'There are powerful people behind this, Sofia. Leave it alone.'

'You mean you don't want to try to find them?'

'I mean I need to rethink strategy.'

Out in the courtyard, Behnaz told Sofia that Dr Daniel had arrived the night before wanting to see her but she had told him Dr Sofia needed to rest.

A sombre pall hung over the square that morning. Two policemen were stationed outside Behnaz's gate along with Rashid, while another two were stationed across the square. Police tape still cordoned off Babur's *chaikhana*, which for the first time anyone could remember hadn't opened. She noticed someone had cleaned away Jabril's blood from the cobblestones, but the chalk outline of the body of the shooter and his blood were still there. No one called out greetings or stopped to have a chat as Sofia crossed the square with Rashid and the policemen.

'They're going to shoot you too, aren't they?' said Iman, bursting into tears when Sofia walked into reception. Walking around the desk to kneel down beside her, Sofia took the young woman's hands in hers. 'No one's going to shoot me. Do you hear?' She spoke with a calmness she did not feel. Iman nodded. Sofia then talked to her about Jabril's condition and the hope that he would regain consciousness soon.

It had been a busy morning, with a number of the women spending an especially long time wanting to talk about Jabril's shooting, something she didn't want to talk about. When her last patient left before lunch Sofia emerged into reception to find Clementine waiting for her.

'Can I have a word?' Clementine asked, rising from the chair she was sitting on.

'Sure,' was all Sofia said, but as she turned to go back into her surgery she looked over at Iman, who simply raised her eyebrows as if to say, 'Don't ask me.'

'Is this about the midwives?' Sofia asked, taking her seat behind the desk.

'No, it's about Daniel.'

'Is something wrong with Daniel?'

'He hasn't told you, has he?' Clementine put her tote back on the ground beside the chair before crossing her long legs. She was in control, the gestures said. She was the one with all the information.

'I've no idea what you're talking about, Clementine.'

'I know he cares about you so you should talk with him.'

'As I said, I've no idea what you're talking about, but if Daniel hasn't told me something, I can only assume he doesn't want me to know.' She didn't have time for whatever it was Clementine was talking about. She wished the woman would go.

'That's probably true, but Daniel doesn't always know what's best for him.'

Sofia bristled. What sort of friend told a stranger that a grown man didn't always know what was best for him? She didn't like Clementine, no point in pretending otherwise. She wondered whether she should put an end to the discussion there and then.

'Daniel was lost in so many ways for such a long time, but the other morning at breakfast, when he was talking about you, he was happier than I'd seen him in years, and then I watched

you two together in Kandahar. There's something there that
I've not seen in him for a very long time. He won't be willing
to tell you. He won't ever bring it up, but if you care about him
you need to know.'

'You're here asking me to ask Daniel about something even
you say he doesn't want to talk about because he was happy
to see me the other morning and you think there's something
between us?' She was pretty sure what Clementine was about
to tell her was gossip. She had no intention of making it easy
for her.

'Can you at least think about it?'

Sofia lost her patience. 'I have no idea what you're talking
about. Why don't you just stop talking in riddles? Do you even
know what happened here in the square yesterday, Clementine?'

'No.' She looked genuinely surprised.

'One of my best friends was shot here and he's on life
support. So your riddles I do not need.'

'I'm so sorry. I did hear of a shooting, but I had no idea
it was here or he was your friend. Look,' she said, sounding
uncomfortable now and apologetic, 'my timing isn't very good,
to say the least, but I'm here now and … Well, if I don't say it
now I might never say it. It's for Daniel, you see.'

Sofia sat back in her chair, examining Clementine. 'Can you
not see how confusing this is?' Sofia said. 'What makes you
think he even wants to talk with me? In fact, didn't you just say
he wouldn't want to talk to me?'

Clementine ignored her questions. 'I've loved Daniel for as
long as I can remember and I believe I know him probably
better than anyone. Oh, don't look at me like that,' she said to
Sofia. 'I'm sure you've guessed.'

'I'm just a little surprised you'd say it to me.'

'Why wouldn't I? I've nothing to hide and I've got nothing to lose. He'll never love me because of what happened, but he needs to open up to someone about it. I know he's never talked to anyone about it, but I think that if he'll talk to anyone, it'll be you.'

'You're giving me far more importance in Daniel's life than I have and, as I said, I don't need riddles.'

She watched Clementine searching for the right words. 'All I can say is that what I did all but destroyed him – that day destroyed so many lives.' She looked up at Sofia again, more sure of her words. 'And so, you see, I don't only love him but I owe him, because of his wife.'

'His wife?' Sofia repeated, feeling like stone.

'Now you have to ask him, don't you?' Clementine said as she stood and, without another word, left.

Sofia was still staring at the door when Iman poked her head around the corner. 'What was ...' Seeing the look on Sofia's face, Iman stopped. 'Has something else happened?'

'No. Can you please close the door, Iman? I need a few minutes. When the door clicked shut, Sofia lay her head down on her arms on her desk. *I don't need this shit. I don't need this shit.* The words kept going around in her head like some crazy tape stuck in a loop. *I don't need this shit.*

When there was a soft knock on the door Sofia looked up to see Iman poke her head around the corner again. 'Do you want lunch?' she asked. Sofia shook her head.

She worked through the afternoon, trying not to think about Jabril, or Clementine or Daniel or her visa, until she was packing up for the day and her phone rang. It was Daniel.

Sofia sat looking at the incoming call and let it go through to voice mail. When Zahra rang a few minutes later she picked it up immediately. There was no change in Jabril's condition, she said, but she was about to head home for a shower and a change of clothes and wanted to know whether Sofia would drop around to the house.

'Did you know Daniel has come by the hospital twice today?' Zahra said, as the two women sat together on the lounge nursing their tea. 'He's an expert in gunshot trauma.'

'I had no idea. Stands to reason, I suppose.'

'He's offered his services, and anything the surgeon might need that MSF can supply. He also took the time to explain what was happening to Jabril in language I can understand. I'm sure the surgeon had already explained it all but I wasn't able to take it all in. I like him, Sofia,' she said, turning to look at her friend.

Sofia didn't answer immediately, wondering if Zahra really needed to know her problems at such a time, but as is the way of friends, she needed to open her heart to someone she could trust.

'I had a strange conversation this afternoon with a friend of Daniel's. She thinks something's going on between me and Daniel and wants me to talk to him about something that, in her words, almost destroyed him.'

Zahra turned to look at Sofia. 'Did she say what?'

'I think it's got something to do with his wife.' Sofia waited for Zahra's reaction.

'Daniel's married? He didn't tell you?'

'Nope.'

Zahra reached across to squeeze Sofia's hand. 'I'm so sorry, Sofia. That must hurt.'

'A little ... maybe more than a little.' She'd never considered him married. Not in the mountains and not now in Kabul. She felt like such a fool.

'Are you going to ask him about it?'

'No, I really can't deal with this at the moment.' Despite what she said, Sofia was not so sure she could stay silent.

'I think you should. You won't be satisfied until you know what's going on.'

'Maybe.'

'Do you know,' Zahra said, leaning back into the cushions, 'I thought of pouring myself a glass of scotch when I got home this afternoon. Isn't that strange? I hate the stuff. It must have been Jabril in my head telling me to have a glass for him. It's just the sort of thing he'd do after a day like today.' Sofia watched the tears gathering in her friend's eyes. 'We know each other so well. Probably better than we know ourselves. How can that be? How can you be so familiar to someone and yet a mystery to yourself? He's always been my compass, my true north, and that's what got him shot. What sort of world are we living in, Sofia, when they want to kill someone because they're good?'

Sofia had no answer to that question and was pretty sure she never would.

'You know, Jabril truly wasn't worried about the notes from Massoud. Of course, he didn't realise they were from him at first. He thought that having Rashid and Tawfiq stick closer to you would be enough. When you think about the notes, they were so childish, so amateurish. *If you don't stop, someone will get hurt.* Who writes stuff like that?'

'Just because Massoud's evil doesn't mean he's intelligent.'

'Chief Wasim will never catch him, you know. Men like

Massoud are too powerful and their reach too deep and people like Chief Wasim are completely powerless, not to mention hopeless.'

'Let's give him the benefit of the doubt and some time.'

'But we don't have time, do we? You're going home, aren't you?'

'Not home.'

44

LATER THAT NIGHT, Sofia sat by the window looking out over Shaahir Square, making her memories for the time when she would no longer be there. As she watched, a taxi drove into the square, pulling up outside the gate. Although she couldn't see who got out, she knew who it would be. A few minutes later she heard Behnaz shuffling up the stairs and a knock.

Opening the door, she held out her arms to Behnaz. 'Can I hug you, please?'

Her landlady gave a short, sharp nod before wrapping her arms tight around Sofia's middle.

'Shhh, Mrs B,' Sofia said, patting her on the back as she rested her chin on the top of Behnaz's head. 'I'll be back before you know it and everything will be just like it was before.'

Pulling herself free, Behnaz wiped her tears on her scarf. 'That doctor from the UN is here to see you.'

It was the first time a man had visited Sofia in the apartment. 'I'd like him to come up. Is that okay?' she asked, nodding as if encouraging Behnaz to agree.

'I'll tell him.'

'Well,' said Daniel, when he came to the door and saw Sofia's swollen eyes and tear-stained face.

'Mrs B got a bit emotional,' she offered.

'Doesn't look like she was the only one.'

'It's been an emotional time. Come and sit with me by the window,' Sofia said, leading him out to the covered balcony and the two cane chairs, only to realise for the first time how small the balcony and the chairs were. As he took the seat opposite her, Sofia watched him trying to adjust the cushion at the back to find more room on the chair. 'Here,' she said, holding out her hand, 'give that to me.' Pulling the cushion out from behind him, Sofia put it on the floor beside her chair.

'So this is where you live,' he said, looking around.

Following his gaze, she tried to see the familiar space as a stranger would. It probably looked small and shabby. 'Yep, this is my home ... was my home.'

'And that's the window escape route,' he said, nodding toward the kitchen. 'And that must be the infamous cupboard.'

'Yep.'

'On the strength of what I'm seeing, it's probably a good thing you're leaving.' He relaxed back in the chair as best he could, watching her.

'You've heard?' she said.

'You just said "was my home". Past tense. Your landlord also told me, along with a few interesting theories about who might want to shoot Jabril.'

'Any of those to do with Massoud?'

'Not a one.'

'I suppose he can't do much, can he, considering Massoud's

his boss? Did he tell you that both Jabril and Behnaz were getting threatening notes?'

'Surprisingly,' he said, not looking surprised at all, 'he didn't mention them.'

'We're not sure if the messages were meant for Jabril or both of us, but the chief's pretty adamant I have to leave ASAP in case I'm the next target. Maybe it would also be better to try to sort out the visa thing back in Sydney, although if it's Massoud then we all know I'm not ever coming back.'

'Unless something happens to Massoud.'

'Now that's a happy thought,' she said, trying to smile.

Daniel moved around in the chair, trying to make himself comfortable before crossing his legs. 'I'm pushing for this study, which is looking more viable every day. If they can finger Massoud he'll probably, at least, be forced to leave the government, and you might get your visa back.'

'They're big ifs. God, Daniel,' she said dragging her hands down her face, 'I've no idea what I'm going to do back in Sydney.'

'You're going to make a new life for yourself,' he offered, sitting forward in the chair.

'It'd be really good if someone could tell me what this new life looked like because I've absolutely no idea.' She hated how sorry for herself she sounded but there was no getting around it, she was.

'I know it's hard to start again when you're feeling like you've lost everything, but you will. You must. Life moves on.'

'Sounds like you're speaking from experience.' Sofia watched him shrug. He was not going to elaborate. She wondered if she would ever really know Daniel Abiteboul. 'Clementine came to see me this afternoon and said I needed to ask you about something. She was pretty cryptic, but apparently it has something to do with your wife.' Sofia had been watching Daniel closely and saw his body stiffen, his jaw tense. So it was true, she thought. He has a wife. She didn't need to know any more. 'I've got no idea what that has to do with me. It's none of my business. I'm sorry I said anything.'

'She told you about Amahoro?'

'No, she just mentioned you had a wife and how she was sorry, and how she owes you, and thinks it might help to talk with me, which is ridiculous. God knows how talking with me is supposed to help you with your wife.'

Daniel shook his head. 'My wife's dead, Sofia. She died a long time ago, but both Clem and I carry guilt over her death. I lost Amahoro –'

Sofia held up her hand. 'You don't have to tell me. I seriously don't need to know.'

'But you do. I wanted to tell you way back in the village. Amahoro, my wife, was pregnant with our first child when she was killed in a car accident, and Clem, who grew up with Amahoro, was driving. It should have been me but I'd said I had too much work, so Clem took Amahoro for her check-up.'

She could see the pain that talking about his wife's death elicited. She wanted so badly to put her arms around him but had no idea whether it would be welcome. 'Oh, Daniel, I'm so, so sorry.'

'It's the connection Clem and I'll always have, our shared guilt, I suppose, over Amahoro's death. I wished I'd been driving the car and she wished she hadn't. Neither of us blamed the other. We blamed ourselves. After it happened I thought I'd never be happy again. I didn't just lose my wife and our child, I lost the life we had together and the one we dreamed of creating. Like you, I couldn't see a future back then, but I promise you there is one. This life I have now isn't the one I imagined when I was thirty, but it's a good life and, despite everything, I fell in love again. You'll create another one too, Sofia. It just won't be the one you've been imagining for the last five years.'

'It all makes my being upset about going back to Australia seem pathetic.'

'Absolutely not. No one should compare their pain to another's. Pain is pain. Grief is grief. Yes, mine was bad, but even back then I could think of worse. What about the parent whose child just disappears off the face of the earth one day? They must live their whole life wondering if that child will ever return to them. At least I could bury my wife and child – I knew what happened to them and I had the opportunity to move on. I could grieve, but those parents will spend their life waiting. That's what you call hell and there's no moving on for them. To me, that was much worse, but like I said, grief is grief. You shouldn't compare.'

'Not many people would have been able to stay friends with Clementine after that.'

He shook his head. 'As I said, I never blamed Clem. I blamed myself. I should've been driving that car, and if I had been, everything would have been different. We wouldn't have been in the exact place and time when the driver of the other car fell asleep at the wheel and came across to the wrong side of the road. Clem lost so much too, you know. She lost her best friend, and for the rest of her life she'll probably blame herself.' Daniel looked at his watch and stood. 'I'm sorry, Sofia, but I've gotta go.'

'Will I see you again?' she asked, standing too.

'Absolutely. I'm not letting you go without a proper goodbye this time.'

* * *

As THE FIRST light of morning crept through her window, Sofia got out of bed, made a cup of tea and took it out to the balcony. Would Behnaz's next tenant sit in this same chair and watch over the square? Would they build a life here or would they just be passing through, a short stop on a longer journey? Below her, the men had left the mosque and Hadi and Ahmad had rolled up their shutters and carried goods out for display. It was time for her to get ready for work.

'Walk with me, my friend,' she said to Rashid when she found him and a policeman outside the gate. She noticed that the police and the tape were now gone from Babur's *chaikhana* but Babur wasn't there opening up. For the second day no one called to her or stopped to talk as she crossed the square, and as they approached Ahmad and Hadi the two men fell silent.

'*As-salaam alaikum*,' Sofia called.

'*Wa alaikum as-salaam*, Dr Sofia,' they replied in unison.

With the policeman taking up his position at the bottom of the stairs, Rashid accompanied Sofia to reception where they found Iman polishing an already spotless desktop, her eyes red and the bin beside her desk full of tissues. Rashid returned downstairs.

'Hug me, please,' Sofia said, holding out her arms. As Iman came around her desk to embrace her, Sofia noticed that the door between her waiting area and Jabril's surgery had been opened. 'What's this?' she asked, letting Iman go.

'I don't know,' she said, swiping away the tears filling her eyes again. 'I was just looking.'

Sofia put her hands on Iman's shoulders. 'It's going to be okay,' she said, looking into her eyes. 'Do you hear me? It's going to be okay.' When Iman nodded she let her shoulders go.

'Omar told Hadi that someone was trying to kill you, but Behnaz said he's lying. They're not trying to kill you, are they, Dr Sofia?'

Sofia sat on the corner of Iman's desk. 'I don't think so, but we don't know exactly what this is until the chief finishes his investigation.'

'Everyone's saying Chief Wasim will never find the killer because it's someone powerful.'

Sofia didn't comment as she pulled the patient list toward her to discover it was blank.

'Everyone cancelled,' Iman offered.

Sofia gave the list back to Iman. 'You know I'm going to have to leave, don't you?'

'Leave where?'

'Here.'

'You don't have to go.'

'I think I do,' Sofia said, hopping off the desk. 'Look, it's probably only going to be for a short time, until Chief Wasim finishes his investigation. Let's just think of it as if I'm going on holidays back to Sydney, like I always do.'

'Okay.' Iman opened her mouth to say more but decided against it.

Giving Iman the rest of the day off, Sofia sat down at her desk contemplating what she was about to do. Within ten minutes she had checked that Dr Suraya Samar, the female doctor who took Sofia's place whenever she was on holidays, could locum for the next three months. She then rang her travel agent in Kabul, asking her to book a ticket back to Australia. There was a seat available on a flight that evening, she was told, otherwise she would have to wait another three days.

'That soon?' Sofia said. She heard the woman tapping away on the keyboard again.

'Or standby next Friday.'

Sofia hesitated only a few seconds.

When she'd finished at lunchtime she was sitting at her desk, wondering where to start packing up the surgery and how to tell Iman, when Zahra rang to report there was still no change in Jabril's condition. When Sofia told her the news, Zahra was at the surgery within the hour. Carrying two chairs to the window they sat looking out over the square, although Sofia was careful to take the chair facing the *chaikhana*.

Neither Omar nor Behnaz could be seen in the square, and while Hadi and Ahmad were hidden by the awning, there were people shopping and moving around as if nothing had changed. Like any normal day, Sofia thought. She and Jabril had been part of their world but they weren't the centre of it, and life had to go on. Sofia looked at Zahra and gave her a smile. 'How are you feeling today?'

'Okay. I think he'll pull through. The doctors aren't saying that yet, but it's what I believe.' She looked at Sofia, as if daring her to deny this. 'Daniel came by again this morning,' Zahra offered.

'What did *he* say about Jabril?'

'That he has every faith in the surgeon and the treatment Jabril's getting. That doesn't sound too good, does it?'

381

'It doesn't sound bad either. He must be in the best hands.'

'But he didn't say Jabril's going to recover.'

Sofia leaned over and took Zahra's hand. 'You know he can't say that, even if he thinks it.'

'I know. Did you get to talk to him about his wife?'

Sofia let go of Zahra's hand and sat back. 'She's dead.'

'Then this friend of his was just trying to cause trouble.'

Sofia considered this and shook her head. 'I don't think so. I think she really loves him.'

'Sometimes you're too generous,' Zahra said, throwing her hair behind her shoulder before leaning in to squeeze Sofia's arm. 'I'm sorry you won't be able to see Jabril before you go, but you will come back to us, won't you?'

'I'll try.'

'As you can guess, they're not publishing the article about Massoud.'

Sofia nodded. 'I guessed as much.'

'No one will risk their life for these boys now.'

Although Sofia agreed with Zahra, she didn't say so. She did, however, need to know her friend was not completely in denial. 'I've got Dr Samar for three months to cover for me but after that … It's early days, but have you thought about what you might do until Jabril gets better?'

'Oh,' Zahra waved Sofia's concerns away, 'I'll have no trouble getting doctors who want to work in an established private practice. Can you believe it? I've already had calls.' Zahra looked over to her friend. 'I'll hire someone for a while and see where we go from there. You will come back, won't you?'

'I'll do my best.'

'He was always such an irritating man.' Zahra wrapped her

arms around her body and began to rock, no longer able to hold back her tears. 'Seriously, he was irritating, wasn't he? Tell me he was irritating.'

Sofia smiled. 'I can see that he would have been for you.'

'Oh,' Zahra said, 'I can't stop thinking about all the times I was too bossy.' She looked at Sofia, her eyes pleading. 'Do you think he'll ever forgive me?'

'Zahra,' she said, unravelling her friend's arms to take her hands, 'he would forgive you anything. You were his world.'

Too late, Sofia realised she'd used the past tense.

45

AFTER ZAHRA LEFT Sofia began tidying her files for Dr Samar's arrival, but as she did, five years of memories came flooding back until she could bear it no longer. Returning the files to their proper place, she locked the cabinets for the last time and sat back in front of her laptop, opening up the one surgery file that only she knew existed. She hesitated. What if she came back? But what if something happened to her? If someone else found it, it would be a catastrophe. She thought of emailing it to herself so she would have a record but decided against it. The information in that file did not belong to her. Taking a deep breath, Sofia pressed the delete button and the secret file recording all the intimate minutiae of her patients' lives disappeared. She then cleared the trash file and it was gone forever. Closing her laptop, Sofia carried the two chairs she and Zahra had sat on back to the desk, took one last look around the room and walked out, locking the door behind her.

At the bottom of the stairs, Rashid and the policeman were waiting for her while Iman was sitting on the ground beside Iqbal.

'Can I join you?' Sofia asked.

'Of course,' said Iqbal, moving over, 'you're always welcome in my kingdom. Iman tells me you're leaving soon.'

'Tonight.'

Iman jumped to her feet. 'I knew you'd do this. I knew it! Who'll look after the women when you go?'

'Dr Samar, and then, if she needs to, Zahra will find someone to take my place, but hopefully I'll be back before then.'

'We don't want someone to take your place. We want you,' Iman said, staring down at Sofia, who was still sitting on the ground next to Iqbal.

'I'm sure it won't be long.' Sofia reached up to take Iman's hand but she pulled it out of reach.

'What about the visa?'

'I'll sort that out from Australia.'

'No, you'll go back to Australia and you'll never return.'

'Why would I do that?' Sofia said in a calm voice, hoping it would help calm Iman.

'Because that's what I'd do.'

'I have to think I'm coming back or it's way too hard to leave. Please,' Sofia said, rising to her feet, 'it's not easy for me to say goodbye to you, Iman. Can we not do it like this?'

'I don't want to make it easy for you,' she cried.

'Iman, if I don't come back …' she started, stepping toward the young woman, who just as quickly stepped away. Sofia put out her hand, again trying to calm her. 'I was just saying that if I don't come back then perhaps you can see this as an opportunity to go to university. Why don't we try to turn this into a positive?'

'I don't want to turn this into a positive,' Iman said, her

beautiful face flushed with anger as she turned and walked away. 'I knew you'd leave us,' she called over her shoulder.

Iqbal, Rashid and Sofia watched her go. 'I didn't want our parting to be like that,' Sofia said, trying unsuccessfully to hold back the tears.

'She's young and she loves you, and I don't think she's lost anyone she loves before,' Iqbal said. 'This generation is soft. They haven't been through what many of us have. They don't know how to deal with loss.'

Sofia turned and squatted down to Iqbal's level again. 'I'll miss you, Iqbal.'

'And I you, and if Allah wishes it we will meet again in this life or the next.'

'*Insha'Allah.*'

Wiping her tears, Sofia stood again before turning to look around the square. Babur was still nowhere to be seen, while Hadi had already packed up and gone home. Ahmad was sorting through a box of shoes so she made her way over to him, Rashid and the policeman in tow.

'I'm sorry, I have to go back to Sydney for a while, Ahmad.'

'I know.' He abandoned the shoes and got up off his knees.

'I'd like you to promise me one thing before I go.'

'Of course, anything.'

'Can you take Badria to the hospital for an ultrasound?'

'Is there something wrong with the baby?' he asked, concern written all over his face.

'No, absolutely not, but I need you to do this for me. Promise?'

'I will, but you'll be back to deliver Badria's baby, won't you?'

Babies, thought Sofia. It was a little too early to tell yet but she suspected Badria was having twins. 'I'll try but I can't promise.'

When Sofia heard her name being called she turned to see Tawfiq hurrying into the square. Turning back to Ahmad, she said, 'I'm sorry to be leaving you. We can only hope that Allah, in His wisdom, allows us to meet again, my friend.'

Ahmad put his hand on his heart. 'Let us hope He is kinder to you than He has been to me and my stool.'

They both laughed. 'Take care, Ahmad, and give Badria and your children a big hug from me,' said Sofia, feeling the inadequacy of her goodbye.

She walked over to where Tawfiq was waiting for her under the pistachio tree. 'Tawfiq, my very special friend, my brother, how do I say goodbye to you?'

'It is true? You're going back to Australia?'

'Yes, tonight,' she said, putting her hand on his shoulder, which she knew she shouldn't have done, especially in public, 'but I'll try my very best to come back soon, and hopefully Dr Jabril will be back in his surgery and life will be just as it always was.'

'You don't have to go. Rashid and I will protect you,' he said, looking at Rashid, who was standing behind her, for confirmation. 'See,' he said, when Rashid nodded.

'Thank you, but I think it's best that I go for a little while.'

'No,' Tawfiq said, shaking his head violently. 'No, this is your home. You mustn't go.'

'I'm sorry but I must – you see, my visa's been cancelled.' As she watched the reality sink in for Tawfiq that it wasn't about protecting her anymore and there was nothing they could do to keep her there, she felt the grief rising up in her throat, so sharp and sudden that Sofia found it hard to speak. The two unlikely friends, whose lives had threaded through and around each other in so many unexpected ways, stood together in Shaahir Square under the pistachio tree, with no idea how to say what was truly in their hearts.

'I'll try to get back, Tawfiq. I'll try really hard, I promise.' Without realising what she was about to do, Sofia grabbed Tawfiq's hands and held them up to her face, leaning her cheek on them. A stranger in the square might have thought it a wanton display of affection, but those who knew Sofia and Tawfiq understood and turned away.

'Where your heart goes, there your feet will go, they say in my country,' Tawfiq said, emotion catching in his voice.

'If it is true then surely I will return.'

Looking around the square, which was unusually deserted for this time of day, Sofia could not see anyone else she needed to say goodbye to. Mustafa had taken to his bed after the shooting, Babur had not returned to the *chaikhana* and Omar was probably asleep inside his shop. Walking over to Behnaz's gate, she turned to Rashid and handed him the surgery keys, asking if he could give them to Zahra. She wanted to hug him goodbye but that would have been going too far. Instead she put her hand on her heart and thanked him for being such a good friend and keeping her safe these past few years before telling him how much she was going to miss him. Again, her words fell far short of what she really wanted to say, which is always the way when parting with friends, she thought.

Rashid bowed low to Sofia with his hand over his heart. 'Dr Sofia,' was all he could say as she disappeared behind the gate. Sofia knocked on Behnaz's door. When she didn't answer she called, 'I have something to tell you.' Behnaz slowly opened the door.

'I'm catching a flight this evening back to Sydney but –'

As Behnaz's face collapsed she turned and rushed back inside the apartment, leaving Sofia standing at the door, not knowing what to do. She could hear Behnaz sobbing in her bedroom and desperately wanted to comfort her but found herself unable to enter Behnaz and Wasim's private space without an invitation. Not knowing what else to do, she softly closed the door and made her way upstairs.

Back in her apartment, Sofia rang Taban to tell her she was leaving and then looked around to take stock. Nothing much had changed in the last five years. She had bought a bamboo shade for the naked bulb in the bedroom and in the first week she had moved the two cane chairs from the lounge out onto the enclosed balcony where they had stayed. A small hand-me-down two-seater lounge from Zahra – with Behnaz's approval – had replaced the chairs in the sitting room.

Five years and that's all I've changed, she thought. I haven't left much of a mark.

The laminated kitchen cupboards had been badly painted green by Behnaz's nephew two years earlier, and while more green tiles had found their way into the bathroom to replace the disintegrating white ones, the last two were pink. When Sofia commented on this Behnaz had explained that the green tiles she preferred were discontinued and the only ones she could get for the price she was willing to pay were pink. She thought the pink tiles looked very nice.

'Very retro,' Sofia had offered.

Taking her suitcase off the top of the wardrobe, Sofia laid it on the bed. There really wasn't much she needed to take back to Sydney, unlike the overstuffed suitcase she had arrived with. She

sorted the clothes into two piles: one for Taban to distribute in
Jamal Mina and a much smaller pile to take home. When she'd
finished she closed the suitcase, stuffed the clothes for Taban
in an overly large Chinese carry bag she'd bought from Ahmad
some years before and sat on the bed. She thought again of
the first time she had seen Jabril waiting at the airport in his
shiny gabardine pants, holding a sign with his name on it and
wearing the biggest smile she had ever seen. It seemed like
yesterday; it seemed like a lifetime ago.

46

Wasim had received such an earful from his wife about catching the culprit before Dr Sofia went back to Sydney that his ulcer was giving him hell and he was suffering from a constant headache. There was no way he could make Behnaz understand that he couldn't catch the culprit when the culprit was Minister Massoud. By lunchtime, though, Wasim had formed a plan, and if he was very careful, and if he did everything right, it just might solve all their problems.

Climbing the stairs to Dr Sofia's apartment, Wasim realised that he had never visited her before, although he had been in the apartment a few days earlier looking for her passport. When she saw it on her bedside table he had hoped she might understand that someone who cared about her was sending her a message to leave, but that plan, like the other plans he had hatched to keep his friends safe, had not worked. He hoped this last one would.

Dr Sofia invited him in but he was reluctant to enter, preferring to remain standing by the open door. He was a bit embarrassed about being alone with Dr Sofia in her apartment, but more importantly, he was nervous about the conversation he was about to have, and the message he was about to deliver. Staying by the door would give him an easier exit.

'I'm sorry you have to leave so soon, Dr Sofia, but for the moment I believe in my heart that it's for the best. Definitely, when I find who killed Dr Jabril –'

'Who *tried* to kill Dr Jabril!' she snapped.

Wasim looked suitably chastened. It had been a stupid error. 'Of course. You're right. When I find who *tried* to kill Dr Jabril and understand their correct motives, I'll let you know and you can return. We would all like that, especially Behnaz.'

'Thank you, Chief Wasim. Would you like to come in and sit down?' she asked again as they stood awkwardly by the door.

'It's not necessary. What I have to say won't take long. It's about my wife.' Clearing his throat, Wasim moved his weight from one foot to the other before he cleared his throat again. 'This is a highly … irregular conversation, Dr Sofia, and I hope you can forgive me for what I'm about to say.'

'I'm sure I can.'

'We shall see.' Wasim fidgeted some more before forcing himself to look directly at Sofia. 'Behnaz has never been able to give me a child, and even though she's my cousin, my family said I should take another wife, but I never did.' Wasim could feel his insides twisting. He would have given a lot not to be having this conversation. It was not an easy topic, but it was something he had to do for the woman he loved.

'I've known Behnaz since we were children. I've never wanted any other wife, but she wanted children very much, and she begged me to marry again so there might be children in our home. I disappointed my wife because I wouldn't take another wife.' Wasim was looking past Sofia, shaking his head.

'Who can believe that?' When he looked back he gave Sofia a nervous smile. 'I assure you, Dr Sofia, one wife is enough trouble for any man.'

Wasim became serious again, focusing his attention on a spot on the floor as he sighed. 'Over time she became more and more unhappy. She couldn't understand why we hadn't been blessed and neither could I. Then you arrived, Dr Sofia, and you became the daughter she never had, and for the first time in many years she was happy. Forgive me for saying this but when she learned your mother was dead she truly believed you had been sent to her for a reason, but now you are leaving and she feels like she is losing her child and it's all my fault.'

'No, Chief Wasim, it's not your fault.'

'That's what I told her, but it's no good. She won't listen.'

'Do you want me to talk to her?'

Wasim shook his head. 'No. She must not know I'm telling you these things.'

'Then can you please tell Behnaz that she's been like a mother to me and that I'm sure my mother would have approved.'

'Thank you, I'm sure it'll help.'

Wasim looked down at the floor again. Earlier in the day his plan had seemed like a good one, but now he was not so sure. He sighed again. Being the chief of police took the balancing skills of an acrobat on a high wire over the tallest peak of the Hindu Kush. His talk with Dr Daniel had not gone as well as he had hoped but as he had expected. He had hoped this conversation might go a little better.

'I have been thinking. Perhaps I might be able to have a word with ... some people and it might be possible for you to

393

stay if you agree not to speak about *bacha bazi* again ... or about men with boys.' Wasim looked directly at Sofia. 'I hope you understand what I mean.' He watched the colour drain from her face and knew he was in trouble.

'You mean you'll have a word with Massoud?'

'That's not what I said.'

'But it is what you meant, isn't it? You will have a word with the good Minister Massoud, and if I agree to never speak about the fact that he and all those bottom-feeders like him get their sexual gratification from raping little boys then I might be able to stay here. That's what you're saying, isn't it?'

'Possibly that might have been what I was thinking.' He wished she would stop.

'You'll speak to the man who shot our dear friend who is now fighting for his life in hospital, and if I don't cause him any trouble he won't try to kill me too. And this is the really good part.' She gave Wasim a sweet smile. 'If I say nothing I can stay! Tell me if I've got any of that wrong.'

Wasim took his handkerchief out of his pocket and wiped his brow. He had never in all the years he'd known Dr Sofia suspected this woman of steel existed. He was good at assessing people. How had he missed that? And then he knew. Nothing had ever stood in her way before. No one had threatened her. He had to admire her for that.

'Please, Dr Sofia, word has come to me that whoever did this is not angry with you anymore so I think this is an option that will allow you to stay. Behnaz, she doesn't want you to go and I don't want you to go. No one wants you to go, but we do want you to be safe. I thought you might be happy with this.' He knew immediately his last words were a mistake.

'That the man who tried to kill Dr Jabril will let me stay if I don't speak out about him interfering with little boys?'

Time to back-pedal. 'We don't know this. We do not know Minister Massoud was behind it. Personally, I think it was the Taliban, and this idea of mine might all be for nothing.' He could no longer read the look on Sofia's face, which worried him more than her anger, or her hysteria, or even those moments of quiet calm from two days before.

Women would always be a mystery to Wasim. Dr Jabril used to say that women should rule the world, but Wasim knew that was not a very good idea. Women were too unpredictable, while men ... well, he could understand men. They behaved as expected. Case in point: Massoud had no interest in the boys who had been taken and yet he had ordered Wasim to delay the first raid until they could be moved. Why? Because the owner of the boys would then owe Massoud. That was the way business was done by the rich and powerful – trade-offs, favours and debts. Once you understood that, you understood everything. All very predictable. Then when Wasim rang Massoud to tell him that he'd just heard where the boys were from the head of the UN and pleaded to be allowed to rescue the boys, the minister had conceded on the condition that Wasim made sure Dr Jabril stopped the publication of the article, forgot his campaign and never said anything to anyone about Massoud's boy. While this might have seemed strange to some, this was also entirely understandable and predictable. The man who owned the boys was of lesser value to Massoud than the silencing of Jabril, so the warlord traded the lesser for the more advantageous outcome. That Massoud had not given Wasim enough time to convince Dr Jabril had been less predictable, but he guessed Massoud knew the article was about to be published and felt he had no option but to get rid of Jabril.

Deaths, threats, silences, secrets and pay-offs was how people like Massoud operated, while Wasim liked to think that his primary job was to maintain order. Unfortunately, that often meant maintaining a crooked and corrupt status quo. The job was no longer giving him the satisfaction it once had.

'I'll think about your offer,' he heard Dr Sofia say.

As he went back down the stairs, Wasim hoped that Dr Sofia would see the wisdom of the offer and not cause any more trouble. A man, he knew, would understand the sense of this; a man would consider what was best for him. No hysterics would be involved. In fact, Wasim thought he could almost see a man's thought process, but a woman's ... That was an unsolvable puzzle.

Wasim had a complicated investigation to finish in a satis-factory and timely manner and a very tricky negotiation to begin with Minister Massoud, who was not the most trust-worthy of partners. He prayed to Allah that what he was about to do would not be adding tinder to the fire. Wasim sighed again. No one knew the risks he had taken to save his friends, and hopefully no one ever would. Massoud had been furious with him when he had failed to convince Dr Jabril to withdraw the article and abandon the campaign because he said he quite liked Dr Jabril and hadn't really wanted to kill him. Massoud's anger had only intensified with the botched assassination attempt, and now Wasim was about to walk into the lion's den and offer his proposal to keep Dr Sofia in Shaahir Square. It could be the tipping point with Massoud, but if the warlord ever discovered that Wasim had been writing the notes to warn Dr Jabril then he was, for sure, a dead man walking.

In hindsight, there was no doubt that the notes had not been the most promising plan, but who would have thought things would escalate so fast? He couldn't very well tell Dr Jabril about Massoud, could he? He had spoken to Dr Jabril when he first talked about his campaign, warning him of the dangers of messing with these powerful men. On a number of occasions after that he had directly asked Jabril to stop. The idea that there were *shabnamah* in the square had all been Omar's fault. If only he hadn't taken that first note off their gate. If only he didn't drink that pain draught of his as if it were tea. What more could he, Wasim, have done? His heart sank. Obviously a lot more, because whatever he did hadn't been enough and might still not be enough.

When he reached the bottom of the stairs Wasim sighed again. Despite what Dr Sofia might think, he didn't agree with what men like Minister Massoud did. In fact, unlike others, Wasim never shunned these boys when they were abandoned.

Standing outside the door to his apartment, Wasim lit a cigarette. He had two choices. He could stay and try to calm the inconsolable Behnaz, who had locked herself in their bedroom, or he could go back to the station and continue dealing with these complicated matters. Wasim headed back to the station.

47

As Sofia stood with her back against the door, knowing that despite what she had said to Chief Wasim she could not consider his offer, the phone rang.

'It is the responsibility of Afghans to fix our land,' Fatima said, without a greeting. 'I don't want to see another one of my friends die. You have to leave, Sofia *jan*.'

So, thought Sofia, as she walked back into the bedroom to collect the bags, the woman who defied the Taliban and the warlords, the woman who was not frightened of anything for herself, was frightened for her. Deep in her heart she knew she would probably never see this extraordinary woman again. 'I am leaving.'

There was a long silence. 'Good. I approve.'

'But I hope I'll be able to return one day.'

'No. As much as my heart would sing to see you again, Sofia *jan*, the only thing I want is for you to promise me you'll stay safe. Things are only going to get more dangerous for women here now the West are going.'

'And you, my friend? What about you?'

'Don't worry about me. I survived the Taliban before and I'll survive them again.'

With the two women quickly running out of things to say, for they had already said their goodbyes, Sofia carried her suitcase and the large bag for the women of Jamal Mina to the door and then went to sit by the window one last time to make the call she had been putting off all day.

'Hi, Dad.' As soon as the words were out she started crying.

'Sofia, darling, what's wrong?'

'I'm fine, Dad,' she said, trying to control her tears. 'I'm just ringing to say I'm coming home.'

'Sure, sure, honey. So how long are you staying?'

'It's not a holiday, Dad. I'm coming home for good, or at least I'm leaving Afghanistan. I suppose they're not the same thing, are they?'

'No, honey, they're not the same thing, but I'm glad. I'm really glad you're getting out of that place.'

She could hear the relief in his voice. There was no point trying to tell him anymore that she was safe.

'Are you alright? Did something happen? You don't sound so good.'

'I'll tell you when I get home.'

'You can't leave me like that. What happened to you?'

'Nothing happened to me. I'll be home on Saturday. Okay?'

'Are you telling me the truth?'

'The absolute truth. I promise you I'm okay.'

'Saturday. That's quick.' The worry was back in his voice.

So many years and so much heartache she had given him. Why must the ones we love pay for the decisions we make?

'Ah, you'll see Jack,' he said, his voice lightening. 'He's such a serious little fellow. Reminds me of you when you were young.'

'I wasn't serious, was I?'

'You were.'

'Wasn't I ever funny?'

'Well, there was one time when you were a little tot and you fell over and scraped your knees and then stood up wiping the dirt off with an "oops", like it was a big joke. Your mother and I laughed at that.'

'That's it? That's the sum total of my funny?' They considered the question. 'I suppose I'm not that funny, am I?'

'You're perfect. You're my perfect princess. You are so perfect I can't even begin to tell you how proud I am of you and who you've become. You remind me so much of your mother.'

'You've said that before.'

'She was a beautiful, serious, extraordinary woman and I wish she could be here to see you now. She would've been proud. And little Jack. If only she could have met him.'

'Dad, you're making me cry.'

'No, no,' he said. 'Nothing to cry about now my girl's coming home.'

'Come on, Dad, now you're really making me cry.'

Sofia realised that she'd be landing back in Sydney smack bang in the middle of Michelle's return with a fiancé and child. Did her father even have a bedroom for her? 'Is the baby sleeping with Michelle in her old room?'

'No, he's in your room. She doesn't like him in her room because she says his snuffling at night keeps them awake.'

That's motherly love for you, Sofia thought. She'd have to get a hotel and find some share accommodation quickly, which could be a problem considering she didn't have much money or a job. Afghan currency didn't translate particularly well into Australian dollars and, as Jabril had said that first day, she'd never get rich working in Shaahir Square. 'I'll find a hotel room until I can get a flat.'

'No, no, there's no need, really. Michelle and Shane are driving up to Queensland tomorrow morning. Looks like there might be a job there for him.'

So that's his name, Sofia thought. 'And Jack? Are they taking Jack?'

'They're leaving him with me until they get settled.'

Oh my god, Sofia thought in horror. Oh my god. They're going to leave their baby with Dad. That had obviously been the plan all along. Michelle hadn't changed one little bit and she'd hooked up with someone just as bad as her. Bastards. 'I can help you look after him when I get home then.' She had no idea how that was going to happen, considering she had to get a job as soon as possible and her dad had to work. How was he going to look after a baby anyway? She decided that would have to be a discussion when she got back home. Perhaps they could coordinate shifts if they took her back in the emergency department of the hospital?

After hanging up from her father, Sofia sat staring out into the square. Five years and no one had even begun restoring the timber houses with their fine fretwork. They had been put up for sale two years before, but no one had even come to look. The square was not a good commercial proposition.

She walked back into her bedroom and lay down. Sydney was not her home. She thought about Chief Wasim's offer again and dismissed it. Sounded like her father needed her now. It was about time she did something for him.

Opening her phone, she scrolled through the photos until she found the one she had been looking for.

She could remember the boy who had taken the photo. He couldn't have been more than fifteen. Neatly dressed and washed with his hair combed to one side, a thin chest and soft down on his upper lip. Had he been on his way to meet a girl or play with his friends when she had stopped him? Did he still remember the three people in Bagh-e Babur he took a photo of on a beautiful spring day? A serious boy, he'd been eager to make sure it was a good photo, and it had been, for he had captured their love. Why had that boy and that day remained so vivid in her memory when nearly everything else in life faded away to nothing? Was it only because of the photo? She thought not.

It had been one of those glorious early spring days heralding the end of the long Kabul winter. They had taken a picnic lunch to the gardens built by Babur's famous namesake, and had been sitting on the grass on blankets under a tree, reading and talking of small, inconsequential things, when Zahra put her book down to ask where each of them wanted to go before they died.

'Bali,' Jabril piped up without hesitation. He wanted to go to a place where the water was deep blue and crystal clear, where the sand was warm and squeaky clean under his feet, and where palm trees swayed over his head. He would walk under waterfalls, get lost in jungles and every evening sit with a drink gazing out over green paddy terraces as the sun set behind the jungle. When Jabril had finished he was quiet for a moment. They both waited. 'Yes, that's what I want,' he said, as if he had examined his choice again and still found it pleasing.

'Nice,' Sofia had said, imagining Jabril's perfection, unspoilt by the possibility of black sand, hordes of rowdy Australian tourists and the overdevelopment that was destroying the paradise Bali had once been. She said none of this. It had not been a day to destroy dreams.

Sofia had chosen Ireland in her old age. 'I want to sit contentedly in an Irish pub, drinking Guinness and eating mussels in white wine and cream sauce, surrounded by the sing-song lilt of Irish voices, and maybe a bit of live music in the evening. Definitely. Music would be good.' She thought it had been an inspired choice, considering she'd really never thought about where she wanted to go before she died. Zahra did that sort of thing sometimes: hitting you with a searching question she'd obviously been mulling over for a while when all you'd been thinking about was what was for dinner, or what you had to get at the shops.

'You don't like beer,' Jabril countered, 'so I'm not sure why you'd want to drink it.'

'Precisely,' added Zahra. 'Exactly what I was thinking. Besides, your choice is too ordinary.'

Sofia had laughed. 'You didn't say it had to be exotic, and I think you have to drink Guinness when you're in Ireland whether you like it or not.' How could she make it more appealing? 'Okay,' she started again, 'I want to be living in an old white house somewhere on the Wild Atlantic Way that has ancient stone walls, and sheep on sodden clods of earth, and impossibly green grass that cushions bare feet, and open ridges of peat flowing down to the cliff's edge. Oh, and I want an old wrinkled face, and I will be smiling all the time because I have lived a life well and full of grace.'

Zahra sat looking at Sofia, as if trying to imagine her in this picture. 'I could do that too,' she said, nodding. 'Sounds good.'

'Then come and join me,' Sofia offered with a smile.

'No, I want Antarctica and slow travel.' A working boat, where at night she would sit outside all rugged up, drinking hot tea and gazing up at a zillion stars. In the day she would venture out onto the ice floes in a rubber boat with a biologist. 'Or maybe a marine geologist.' Zahra wanted chattering colonies of nesting seabirds, sleek brown seals, ice walls breaking off glaciers. She wanted days that never ended. She wanted deep blue, cold and clear white as far as the eye could see.

'And does this biologist or marine geologist have to be young?' Jabril had asked as he moved to rest his back against the tree.

Zahra considered her answer as she began packing up the food containers. 'I think that would be an essential part of the job description, don't you, Sofia?'

'Definitely.'

'No room for me then on your little boat with your young men,' he said, handing her his plate.

Zahra stopped and looked at her husband. 'I didn't see you inviting me to Bali, my love.'

'Ah,' he smiled, reaching out to touch her hand. 'You must have missed the beach towel lying next to mine on the sand.'

Sofia had seen the smiles that passed between them and she had wanted that with all her heart. She wanted a relationship like they had.

Rolling over in her bed, she stared out the window. What would it be like to never see the sun light up the peaks of the Hindu Kush on a cold winter's morning again, or to hear the morning call to prayer from Mustafa's mosque? How would it feel to know that every morning Ahmad was going through the ritual of laying out his shop without her there to witness it?

To never smell the sizzling goat from Babur's *chaikhana* as she crossed the square to work, or to travel with Tawfiq through the streets of that dusty, smelly, dirty, crazy place? The enormity of loss rose from deep within her, a dark, heavy mass leaning heavily on her heart. Sofia choked back a sob.

She knew she had been lying when she had told her friends she would return. She was never going to return while Massoud was alive, and there was no good reason to believe he would not live a very long and eventful life. Sofia thought of her new life back in Sydney. Perhaps she *would* eventually live her father's version of 'normal'. Turning over onto her back, she rested her arm across her forehead and stared up at the light bulb inside its dusty cane shade.

In the past week she had been skirting around a truth, as if it had been a puzzle she could solve, or something she could control, but it wasn't and it never had been. The man she loved was here, in Afghanistan. It was impossible that she loved a man she'd only spent ten days with in a village and a few days with in Kabul but love him she did. Sofia grabbed her phone again and looked at the time. Four and a half hours until she had to head to the airport for her flight. She sat up on the bed. She had one more thing to do.

After ringing Tawfiq, Sofia took one last look around the apartment, hitched her bag over her shoulder, picked up her suitcase and the bag for Taban and made her way downstairs. Knocking on Behnaz's door she waited. No answer. Putting her ear to the door, she listened. Silence. Sofia stood back, wondering what she should do. She couldn't phone Behnaz because she didn't own a mobile phone. The *Amreekawees* kept tabs on everyone in Afghanistan through the phones, she used to say, in case they needed to kill you with a drone strike.

How could she possibly leave without trying to say goodbye to Behnaz? She loved Behnaz and Behnaz loved her. Sofia checked the time on her phone again. It was either him or Behnaz. Leaving the keys by the door, Sofia picked up the two bags and walked out, like a thief in the night.

Outside the gate Tawfiq was waiting for her. The policeman was still there but Rashid had gone home.

'Can you please give this to Taban?' she asked, offering him the large bag full of clothes. As Tawfiq lifted her suitcase into the car, she heard her name being called and turned to see Omar crossing the square, barely visible in the last of the evening light. The only other person in the square was the man who sold corn from his portable kitchen in the old city, pushing his kitchen before him on his way home.

'You're leaving,' Omar said as he came to stand before her.

'I am,' she said, examining her friend in the fading light.

'Will you come back?'

'I'd like to.'

Tawfiq and the policeman climbed into the car, closing the doors quietly behind them.

'I didn't know it was Dr Jabril,' Omar said with such sadness that Sofia found herself fighting back tears yet again.

'None of us did.'

'I couldn't save him.'

'No, Omar, none of us could. It wasn't your fault.'

Everything about Omar had shrunk. She was sure he had not always been so short. His old wool *pakol* cap no longer fitted his head, while his *perahan tunban* fell loosely over his thin frame. His once mischievous green eyes had grown cloudy and surely the lines on his face had deepened? Sofia put her hand on his shoulder to discover only bone. Letting go of his shoulder, she took his hands in hers to find them frail and bird-like. Searching his face in the dying light, she saw what she should have seen a long time ago. Her heart sank. How neglectful she had been of this dear man.

'I have to go now, Omar, and I don't honestly think I'll be coming back, but before I go, is there anything I can do to help you? Anything I can get for you? You could go to the hospital, you know? I've got friends there who could help you.'

He shook his head. 'Remember me. That's all I ask.'

'Always, Omar, always.' Sofia let the tears fall. If they couldn't fall now, when could they? 'I pray that we meet again soon, my friend.'

'I think maybe it will be in Jannah.'

'Then Jannah it will be,' she said, offering her love for him in a smile.

As they drove out of Shaahir Square, Sofia turned for the last time to see Omar waiting alone in the dark beside Behnaz's turquoise gate.

48

'I TOLD YOU I wouldn't let you leave without seeing you again,' Daniel said when he opened the door.

'Only because Mohammad had to come to the mountain,' she replied, walking past him into the room. 'Seriously?' she said, frowning and shaking her head. It wasn't a room, it was a suite, decorated in dark brown timber with splashes of red and yellow in the rugs and artisan work on the walls. There was an enormous full-sized lounge, two armchairs, a king bed, a large elegant desk and two TVs. 'If this is how the UN house their staff, I want a job with them. I'm also going to stop my contributions to UNHCR forthwith.'

Daniel laughed. 'They're not paying for all this, believe me.'

Sofia raised an eyebrow. 'So you're rich as well.'

'As well as what?'

'Never mind,' she said, sitting in one of the armchairs.

'Can I get you something to drink?' he asked, opening the bar fridge. 'We have a range of teas and fizzy drinks for your pleasure. There might even be a coffee sachet if I look really hard.'

'A soda water?'

After choosing two sodas, he sat in the armchair opposite her.

'The hotel wasn't full so I was upgraded to this executive suite, but it's all smoke and mirrors and it's going to disappear tomorrow when I'm being kicked back to the cubbyhole in the new wing, after which I'll probably be moved into some tiny shared accommodation.'

'I'm flying out tonight.'

Daniel leaned back in his chair, watching her. 'I guessed as much. When?'

Leaning across the coffee table between them, she took his wrist, turning it so she could see his watch face. 'Four and a bit hours.'

'I see. Anywhere else you need to be before then?'

'Not that I can think of. Tell me how Jabril really is.'

'He's picked up a staph infection in the last couple of hours.' Sofia groaned and shook her head. 'His body's fighting hard and he's in the very best hands. They're pretty good with gunshot wounds and they've got everything they need, so all any of us can do now is wait.'

'He can't die, Daniel,' she said, shaking her head as she bit her bottom lip. 'He can't die. I haven't said goodbye to him and I might never see him again.' She ran her hand though her hair. 'I owe him so much. It's because of him I have this life here ... had this life here.'

'I know.'

She sat back in her chair. 'Chief Wasim says I might be able to stay if I promise not to say anything about Massoud and *bacha bazi* ever again.'

'So I heard.'

'You did?'

'Wasim told me when he rang this morning to try to convince me again that I must have been mistaken about Massoud's threat. Look, Sofia,' he said, sitting forward, 'you're probably not going to like what I'm about to say, but it seems to me that whoever ordered Jabril's killing is so powerful they'll never be caught. So perhaps another way for you to look at Chief Wasim's offer is that you're being given the chance to stay and continue your work if you keep out of Afghan affairs.'

'What would you do?'

'Oh, no,' he said, sitting back again and shaking his head as he held up his hands as if to ward off the question. 'Wrong question, wrong person. I won't be responsible for anyone else's decisions. Besides, it's irrelevant what I'd do.'

'But I'm asking you anyway.'

'Sofia, I'm not going to decide for you, but I can offer some advice. I don't think you should be so hard on Chief Wasim. He can't afford to cross someone like Massoud. I also imagine he's under a lot of pressure to make this all go away, but at the same time he wants you to stay, and he wants you to be safe. If I was the chief and those were my goals then a deal with Massoud is probably the only way that's going to happen. Presenting that sort of proposition to Massoud or you couldn't have been easy for Wasim, to say the least.'

'I know he's trying to help,' she said, smiling, 'although it might also be an effort to please his wife.'

'So,' he said, nodding as if considering the possibilities, 'the chief of police has the choice of confronting the powerful and murderous warlord or his wife and he chooses the warlord. From what I've seen, that's probably a wise decision.'

Sofia smiled before kicking her shoes off and curling her feet up under her on the chair. 'Do you ever think about the village?'

'Yeah, a lot lately.' Daniel took a swig of his drink from the bottle.

'I've been thinking about it a lot too. When you left that last time you didn't say goodbye.'

'That's because I didn't know it was goodbye.'

'But you didn't come back.'

'I did.' His words, simply stated, dared her to doubt him.

'But I waited. You couldn't have come back.'

'You didn't wait long enough.'

Sofia stared at Daniel as she began to understand. Had he come back for her? He had come back for her. And if he'd come back then everything she had imagined about him for the past five years had been based on a misunderstanding.

Daniel sat forward on the lounge again, facing her with his elbows resting on his knees and his hands clasped in front of him. 'After I left you that last morning, a messenger from the village down the valley arrived to say that someone I'd been treating was dying. I thought I'd only be gone for maybe half a day, but by the time I got there he was dead and others had come down with the sickness. I can't tell you how many times I wished I'd left you a message to tell you what was happening. I also thought about sending someone back to tell you but I worried that you'd insist on coming to help, or that the messenger would pass the sickness on to you and the village. For all I knew, I was contagious. There wasn't an hour that I didn't think about getting back to you but I couldn't. By the time the threat had passed the weather had closed in and I should've headed back down the mountain, but instead I came back only to find you'd already gone. Back in Kabul I learned that you'd returned my dictionary and hadn't wanted to leave a message. What was I supposed to think?' Daniel leaned forward and took her hands across the coffee table. 'Back then I didn't know what the ending was supposed to be between us. Fuck,' he said, letting her hands go to run both of his through his hair, 'I didn't even know what was between us, but I never wanted it to end the way it did.'

'All these years I thought you'd gone without a word.'

'It was in a strange time back then for me. I've already told you about Amahoro and how I felt responsible for her death, but that's only half the story,' he said, sitting back on the lounge. 'Three months before I met you in the village, another woman I cared a great deal for died – killed by the Taliban. And I was the reason she died. No,' he said, holding up his hand to stop her speaking, 'it's true. Alice hadn't wanted to return to Afghanistan but I talked her into it. You see,' he said, stressing his next words, 'she came back for me, and that was what got her killed.'

'I'm so sorry, Daniel. I can only imagine how you must have been hurting then.'

'You asked me once about the tattoos. The Arabic one says, *Without pain you can't know joy.* That was something my Moroccan cook used to say to me when I was a little boy. I got that tattoo when Amahoro died.' She could see him retreating back into the memories. 'There are times when I think most of us would forgo the love to avoid that much pain afterward. I never wanted to know that kind of pain again.' He gave her an apologetic smile. 'I'm not a great believer in the adage that it is better to have loved and lost than never to have loved at all.

The numbers tattooed into my skin are the dates of Amahoro and Alice's deaths.' He smiled apologetically again. 'All that's to explain why I'm not willing to tell you if you should go or stay. I can't be responsible for those sorts of decisions. In any event, that was the space my head was in when you turned up in the village.

'I hadn't expected to be attracted to anyone. I thought I owed Alice my loyalty for longer than three months, and I still think that. Meeting you, and feeling the way I did about you, rocked me to the core. Every day I promised myself that I wouldn't go back to your hut but every night I did. And then every morning when I left I beat myself up over it.'

'I wish you hadn't felt like that about us.'

'Well, I did, and for a long time I've wanted to explain all this to you, so when I discovered you were in Kabul I knew I had to do it.'

'But you didn't.'

'No, I didn't.' He looked amused. He also looked relaxed again, like he had the evening of the fundraiser. 'That's my weakness around you again, Sofia Raso.'

Uncurling her legs, Sofia slipped her feet back into her shoes and sat forward in her chair, her knees touching the coffee table. She had no idea whether what she was about to say would be a mistake, but she was leaving Kabul, and she was leaving him, and she had to say something to let him know how she felt. As her father would say, she needed to lay her cards on the table.

'It feels like … and it might not feel this way to you … and maybe I'm being overly dramatic and making a fool of myself …' She laughed, aware that she was making a muddle of it. 'I think of all the possibilities and how much we've lost by not

413

giving us a go.' They hadn't been the words she really wanted to say but they were the best she could do.

He shook his head. 'Maybe it just wasn't our time back then, Sofia.'

Her shoulders slumped. That had not been what she had been hoping to hear. 'Maybe.'

'I have something I want to give you,' he said. Rising from the chair, he walked over to the desk where he shuffled through some papers until he found what he was looking for. Sitting back down again, he handed her an old envelope.

'After returning to Kabul to discover you'd been to the office but hadn't wanted to leave a message, I began looking for you. I asked around everywhere but no one seemed to have heard of you, so in the early hours of the morning before I left Afghanistan – for what I thought would be the last time – I wrote this letter to you. In it I tried to explain what had been happening for me when we'd been together and how important it had been to meet you and how I'd hate it if we never met again. I thought about leaving the letter in the Kabul office in case you ever returned but decided you probably never would, so I've carried it around with me ever since in case one day I ran into you again. You should also know that I've never opened it.' He smiled at her. 'I've always thought of it as my night letter, written in those early hours of the morning when everything is so raw and there's no place to hide. I think it's a love letter to you, Sofia Raso, but you're the only one who can be the judge of that.'

When he saw the tears in her eyes, he leaned over and wiped them away with his thumbs. 'It's not that bad,' he said, making light of the letter, but when she went to open it he reached out and covered her hand with his. 'Not now. Later, when you're on the plane.'

'What do you want from me, Daniel?' she asked. Despite all he said she still felt unsure of herself. He may have written a love letter to her five years before, but what did he feel now? 'I don't know what you want from me, or even if you want anything. I feel like I could be making a complete fool of myself here.'

Pushing the coffee table between them aside, he leaned in and grabbed hold of both sides of her chair to pull her in closer to him.

'And that's the difference between you and me. I'm a negotiator and I close deals so I've learned to hide my emotions, but you're different. I've always known what you want. You give yourself away. Did you know that? You lay yourself bare for the world to see. There's no subterfuge, no silly games. There's no hiding. What you're feeling is written all over your face and I can tell you now that I feel exactly the way you do.'

'Oh, we'd probably be a disaster,' she said, crying and laughing at the same time.

'Maybe.' He pulled her chair in closer until she was sitting between his legs.

'It probably wouldn't work.'

'Why not?' he asked.

'You live nowhere in particular and I'll be living back in Sydney.'

'And there's no way two intelligent, resourceful people who want the same thing could possibly find a way to make that work?' he asked, making a point of looking at his watch before leaning in closer and putting his hands on her knees. 'Do you think three hours and forty minutes, give or take, might be enough time for us to start again?'

415

49

BEHNAZ HAS FINISHED sweeping the dust out of the courtyard and is leaning on her broom, looking up at the balcony. It has been seven months since Dr Sofia left. Her nephew lives in the apartment now with the clear understanding that he must leave if Dr Sofia returns. He's a good boy who has grown in her regard, especially after he retiled the bathroom pink at his own expense. Recently, he has been making noises about fixing the balcony, which he hasn't been willing to use because he says it isn't safe. The idea holds no traction with Behnaz. Dr Sofia sat there every morning and every afternoon for five years without complaining. If it was good enough for Dr Sofia it should be good enough for him. Still, if he wants to pay for it himself she would be a fool to say no.

It's a strange thing but lately she has found herself thinking more about the past. 'It's the way of the old,' she told Wasim that very morning, as she sat watching her husband eat his breakfast, thinking how quickly the years have passed and how dull and grey their lives have become. It's not the life she had imagined all those years back in Jalalabad when she was told she would be marrying her cousin, the policeman from Kabul.

Behnaz knows Wasim doesn't much like thinking about 'the way of the old'. He says he has enough problems dealing with 'the way of the present', but what did he expect making his bed with criminals like Massoud? She will offer him no sympathy. Massoud is the reason Dr Jabril was shot and Dr Sofia is gone.

Behnaz curses Massoud when she wakes each morning and when she goes to bed at night. He took away her beloved Sofia and now the criminal is talking about running for president.

Opening the gate, Behnaz steps out into the square and looks, as she always does these mornings, to see if Omar is up. He isn't. She leans again on her broom, letting her mind travel back to the first time she saw the handsome young apothecary with the green eyes. That night, as she lay with her new husband, she thought only of the apothecary. With the memory the old familiar sadness wells up in her heart until it feels as if it might burst. She gives the cobblestones a sweep, as if sweeping away the memory is sweeping away the pain. Behnaz looks up at Omar's bedroom window again. The memories will not be chased away today. She is not sure whether she even cares.

It was Omar who had shown Behnaz what it truly meant to be a woman, and once that thing is known it can never be unknown.

Nor can it ever be undone.

The old woman she is today says she hates him, but she knows that the young woman she once was still loves him.

'There is a path that leads from heart to heart,' he had once said to her, as they lay in his bed. 'That path will always lead me back to you, my sweet Behnaz.' The young woman believed him all those years ago. The young woman still believes him.

Behnaz knows Omar will soon be gone. When she was

young she cried countless tears because their time together had been so pitifully short, but now that she is old she knows it was a blessing. The love she had for Omar had burnt so fiercely under her skin that it would surely have eventually destroyed all their lives. To this day she doesn't know whether Wasim knows about Omar. It's a question she will never ask.

Like all the women of Afghanistan, Behnaz was forced back behind the walls of her home during the civil war and the rise of the Taliban. Their miniskirts, shorts and make-up, their knowing smiles and raucous laughter all disappeared; their voices no longer heard; their beauty no longer seen; their lives no longer worthy. It had been a time of great fear for women, but it had also been a time of great loss, especially for Behnaz. It was during those years, when she hid behind the walls of her home, that Behnaz discovered she would never bear a living child. And as she grieved her losses, she watched the young Omar take a wife, and then a second and a third, and all these dour wives knew how to produce children for Behnaz's lover. Daughter after daughter after daughter had slipped seamlessly into the world, as if the magic of breath, and the gift of life, was their right, but not that of her own dead babies. And with each new girl child Behnaz found herself thinking, 'This one should have been mine. This one should have been mine.'

Under the cover of the burqa, and through all the miscarriages and losses, Behnaz's laughter had dried up and her heart had hardened, as if the young Behnaz had been picked up and thrown away to be replaced by an older, bitter version. Having sunk so deep into the loss of her youth and her womanhood, Behnaz emerged from her home when the Americans came, unrecognisable to all those who had known her, but especially to her lover. Those were the dark years; Omar the wound that would never heal.

In these last days before Omar goes, she is allowing herself to remember, but she knows it will soon be time to pack all the memories away again.

Behnaz begins to sweep in earnest now, sweeping away the dust and the memories until she stops and looks up. But what if she doesn't want the memories to disappear? What if they are all she has? Are they not the precious gifts the young woman she once was has given to the old woman she is today? Without those gifts, what joy would there have been in her life? Behnaz looks up at Omar's window again, wondering whether he ever thinks of those days as she does, or whether the memory of her has been erased by the young wives and the beautiful babies that followed.

Very soon Behnaz knows she will have to ask Wasim to climb the stairs to Omar's bedroom and carry his body out. She has no doubt she will know when the time has come. *There is a path that leads from heart to heart.*

'*As-salaam alaikum,*' Ahmad calls to her, releasing Behnaz from her thoughts.

'*Wa alaikum as-salaam,*' she responds as she rests her broom against the wall near the gate and wanders out into the square to pick up the papers that have gathered around the fig and pistachio trees. She will not be able to do this much longer. The pain in her joints is getting worse.

Behnaz has noticed that Ahmad is not going to morning prayers again. She also thinks he is not taking such good care of his shop either. He seems to prefer to spend his time sitting on his green stool smoking cigarettes to chasing customers. She watches Ahmad come back out of his shop with a box he adds to the already growing display before stopping to glance up at Dr Sofia's balcony. She knows what he is looking for.

Ahmad's wife, Badria, recently produced twins. As if she is a baby-making machine, thinks Behnaz, stuffing the papers into the pocket of her coat as she walks back to retrieve her broom. It annoys her when Ahmad complains about how much six children cost, for it is another reminder of her great loss, mirrored back to her in other people's joys. Sometimes she imagines that if she cleans hard enough she might clean away the pain of her barren womb.

A couple of months ago Dr Jabril emerged from his hospital bed, a pale imitation of his former self. Thin and gaunt, with a useless arm hanging by his side, he came back to the surgery only to forget the names of his old friends. With the birth of Dr Jabril and Zahra's first grandchild in *Amreekaw*, Zahra has taken Jabril away to see him. The gossips of the square have counted the months since the wedding and purse their lips in disapproval, but Behnaz refuses to join them. A baby is a baby. Who cares when it was made?

While the new male doctor seems acceptable to the men of the square, the female doctor, who took over from Dr Suraya and only bothers coming three days a week, has not been so well received. 'She only thinks about the ache in your body. She doesn't care about the ache in your heart,' Behnaz likes to say to her friends, her words reminding the women of the square of the babies she lost. 'That is the real pain that steals your heart.' The women agree, for most know of Behnaz's miscarriages and have felt the pain of their own.

Rashid, who disliked this new female doctor more than even

the women did, has gone to Iran to be with his family, although he told Tawfiq, who is living back in Mazar-i Sharif with his wife, that he will return when Dr Sofia returns. Tawfiq says he will too.

Iqbal recently moved his cobbler business from next to Dr Sofia's surgery steps to the pavement between the mosque and Babur's *chaikhana*. While he is not one of the new doctor's greatest fans, the move has more to do with the fact that she is not one of his. With the loss of Rashid and Dr Sofia, Iqbal says he is happier sitting between his two friends, Imam Mustafa and Babur. 'It is where I can do more good,' he told Behnaz the other day.

Babur, who has moved into the back rooms of his *chaikhana*, still sets up the table and chairs out the front for Dr Jabril and Imam Mustafa, although since Dr Jabril has gone and Mustafa no longer comes, they are only ever used by strangers who wander into the square. It upsets Behnaz to see the chairs and the strangers sitting in them because they are a daily reminder of the loss they all have suffered. She would like to ask Babur to stop putting them out but she knows that he's been badly affected by the loss of his friend and she will not cause him any more pain.

Behnaz must still wake her snoring husband with a jab in the ribs to get him out of bed in time for mosque, but these days he's not gone for so long. When she questioned Wasim about it this morning he told her Mustafa's sermons were becoming shorter every week, 'as if he's running out of things to say.'

'Perhaps he's running out of life, like the rest of us,' Behnaz offered, knowing this wouldn't please Wasim. For a man who deals with death every day she is always surprised by her husband's fear of his own. It's not a fear she shares. What more can Allah take from her?

Because Mustafa has not been himself since the shooting, Babur has taken to carrying the imam's favourite lunch of goat skewers and *palau* to him in the mosque, where she is told they sit talking for hours. She wonders whether they ever speak of Dr Jabril or Dr Sofia. She has noticed that their names are seldom mentioned in the square, not because they have been forgotten but because the memory of that day, and all that was lost, is too painful for some.

Behnaz spots Iman, who took Dr Sofia's departure especially hard, making her way across the square to her. Last month, Iman and a lot of other women rode their bikes in the street in Kabul, causing a serious traffic jam. Behnaz shakes her head with the memory. Sooner or later someone who isn't so forgiving of the girl's crazy schemes, like the Taliban, who are gaining more power each day now, is going to take offence. Only last week Iman, who doesn't like working for this new doctor, told Behnaz she was thinking of applying for a scholarship to a foreign university. This didn't sit well with Behnaz. 'You should stay at home and have babies,' she told her. When Iman said she didn't want babies Behnaz had felt mortally wounded and had avoided Iman, but now the girl is standing in front of her.

'I've been thinking about what you said, Behnaz,' Iman says as she flicks her hair over her shoulder. 'Of course I'll have babies someday, but first I need to get a good education so I can help my country, and then I can find a handsome man who I love and then,' she says beaming, 'when I have my babies, perhaps you can take care of them so I can work?'

Behnaz takes a few seconds to absorb the magnitude

of Iman's offer. No one understands what it is like to be old without children. There's no one to look up at you, no grandchildren to pull at your skirt and ask you to kiss the scrape on their knee. The offer is more than she could ever have imagined.

'Humph,' Behnaz says, wanting but not wanting to embrace this new idea, in case it is snatched away from her. 'What about your own mother?'

'Oh, you know my mother. She has her work.'

'We will see, but you mustn't leave the babies too late or your body will get old and dry up,' Behnaz says. She feels the unfamiliar sting of tears in her eyes and shooes Iman away.

For years she had secretly hoped that Dr Sofia would have babies and she would look after them, but now she knows this will never happen. Yesterday she overheard Mustafa, who couldn't see her, telling Babur, who could see her, that Dr Sofia is going to work with Dr Daniel in Syria. She wonders how long this secret has been known to everyone but her. Do they all think she is a speck of dust so light that she can be blown away with a puff of wind? Has she not weathered more storms than most? Behnaz is a rock. She is a sentinel of resistance. A mountain. She sweeps outside the gate, drinking in this thought.

Behnaz wonders whether she will ever see Dr Daniel again. Since Sofia left he has returned twice to the square, and each time he has brought messages and small gifts from her for Behnaz, who now possesses a furry kangaroo with a baby in its front pocket that you can take out, and a fluffy koala with a hard black plastic nose. She also has a beautiful box of soaps made from Australian eucalypts that she keeps in its cellophane wrapper, and a cup that says *I love Sydney*, where the 'love' is a red heart. She has seen these cups in Ahmad's shop only they say *I love Kabul*. Who loves Kabul? She doesn't see any tourists coming into the square asking for one of Ahmad's 'I love Kabul' cups. Her favourite present of all is the miniature Sydney Opera House in its plastic dome that snows when you shake it. Behnaz knows it doesn't snow in Sydney but she loves it anyway. This most precious of all gifts is sitting on her bedside table, along with the fake yellow canary Sofia sent to keep the canary in the courtyard company. Unfortunately, the bird is dead. Such a waste of good afghani it turned out to be.

Everyone in the square now knows that Omar stole her letter, which they all still think was a *shabnamah*, but Behnaz knows who really wrote them. And everyone knows Babur bought alcohol and Hadi was free with his scales, although everyone knew that already. She recently overheard Hadi grumbling that his new-found generosity could not last, but she thinks it has already not lasted.

The day before Dr Jabril was shot, she overheard a conversation between Wasim and Tawfiq, who was enquiring on behalf of a 'friend' if someone could be arrested for looking at photos of naked women on the internet. Wasim had reassured him that his friend would not be arrested for such a thing. After returning to his family in Mazar-i Sharif, Tawfiq rang Wasim to say that his friend had successfully kicked his night-time addiction. Behnaz suspected it had more to do with the fact that he was back with his wife.

Behnaz stops sweeping and leans on her broom again. After all these years of living in fear that the square might discover her secret, the idea of Omar taking it with him to the grave brings her only sadness. Surely a secret has to be a shared thing? It really isn't much of a secret if you're the only one left who knows it. Behnaz wonders what will happen if, as she grows older, her mind misplaces their secret? Will that mean it never happened, or has it been folding into the fabric of time for someone to uncover long after they are both gone? Behnaz feels the prick of tears in the back of her eyes and swipes them away. I am getting old and sentimental, she thinks.

As she disappears behind her turquoise gate, Behnaz looks over to Omar's bedroom window once more and then up to the crooked balcony still sitting above her front door. All these paths, she thinks … all these paths that lead from heart to heart are tangled up here in Shaahir Square.

In her young woman's heart, which she knows is the same as her old woman's heart, these are the things that matter. These are the things that hold life together.

ACKNOWLEDGEMENTS

ACKNOWLEDGEMENTS ARE AN important part of a book for an author. Writing them usually marks the end of the writing process and is the time you finally get to say thank you to all the important people in the writing process who would otherwise remain nameless. Like any good speech, you usually build to a crescendo. With *The Night Letters*, I want to change that process.

Jane Curry, the owner and managing director of Ventura Press, wrote: 'It is very rare for an editor to receive credit for their work on a book or get a mention in the sales points. Any appreciation shown is usually from the author, tucked away in the acknowledgements. And yet at the very core of our industry is the quality of the writing.' While my thanks to my editors are still 'tucked away' in the acknowledgements, I want to make them first in that process, for they are an essential part of that 'core'. What makes a book rise above the ordinary is the work of the editors. I am aware that too many superlatives eventually mean nothing, so I'm going to try to keep this simple.

Thank you, Zoe Hale, for your tough questions, persistence, honesty and kindness. You're not too tough. Simone Ford, I want to thank you for just about everything, or more precisely, a copyedit and an editor–writer relationship that, for me, was perfection (except for the 'Track Changes' thing that we won't mention again … sorry). I hope these few words sufficiently convey my deep gratitude and admiration to you both. Will you work with me on the next one?

Jane Curry, you are a gem. Thank you for seeing the value in my manuscript and for your joy and enthusiasm. It is infectious. Thank you for the title also, and ditto to all of the above.

I also want to thank Emily O'Neill for the evocative cover design and Holly Jeffery for her marketing expertise. Special appreciation to Jeannette Encinias for allowing me to use 'Beneath the Sweater and the Skin', the poem she wrote for her mother.

A few years ago I had the privilege of mentoring women writers living in Afghanistan through the Afghan Women's Writing Project until that project folded due to lack of funding. I remain humbled by the strength and beauty of the Afghan women writers I worked with. They want war to end, a better life, and equality and freedom for all Afghan women. Their fight for these basic human rights has been long and hard but they remain undeterred. Like so many others, I fear for them with the resurgence of the Taliban. My heart is with them always.

Afghanistan is one of the poorest countries on Earth. It is estimated that forty-two per cent of people live below the poverty line (in the rural areas it is higher), while twenty per cent live just above that line and could fall below it at any time. By all accounts over ninety per cent of Afghan women have been sexually abused. And yet, for the vast majority of women their main concern is not their rights but surviving the daily struggle to keep themselves and their children fed, sheltered, safe and alive.

Richard Flanagan once said that as fiction writers we write what we don't know, otherwise we are simply writing autobiography. While this is true, have you ever wondered why anyone would want to write about what they don't know? Elizabeth Strout (*Olive Kitteridge*) believes it is because writers need to know what it feels like to be another person: 'to help ourselves bear the burden of the mystery of who we are (and) the mystery of who others are.' We also write to bring you on this journey with us so that you too might imagine what it is like to be another and to share the 'burden' of this 'mystery'. As both writers and readers, we are, together, intrinsically and intuitively entangled in this mystery of fiction and life.

The Night Letters is a work of fiction, apart from Commander Kaftar. Afghanistan's only female warlord is such an extraordinary character that I could not resist introducing her to you through a cameo role. Because I wanted my representation of Kaftar to be authentic, I relied heavily on Jennifer Percy's riveting account of meeting the commander, 'My Terrifying Night with Afghanistan's Only Female Warlord'. If you read it you will recognise much of Sofia's interaction with the warlord. For the same reason I have also taken, verbatim, the radio communication between Taliban leader Mullah Baqi and Commander Kaftar, as reported by Tom A. Peter in 'A Woman's War: The rise and fall of Afghanistan's female warlord'. It was just too good to pass up.

A number of years ago I learned of a female entrepreneur running a taxi service out of Kandahar. She became my original inspiration for Fatima, although the taxi service is the only thing the real woman (who otherwise remains a mystery to me) and my invented character of Fatima have in common.

In light of Sofia's work with midwives, it would be remiss not to mention the work of the Afghan Midwives Association (AMA), the primary purpose of which is to strengthen and support midwives in Afghanistan through education and training. Among their many innovations is a field-based program that aims to increase 'the visibility, status and respect of midwives within their [remote] communities'. You can read more about the AMA on their website. My apologies to the female doctors of Afghanistan for inserting a Western doctor within your midst. It was the only way I could tell this story.

If you have not heard of *bacha bazi* and want to know more, I suggest you begin by watching the 2010 documentary by Afghan journalist Najibullah Quraishi, *The Dancing Boys of Afghanistan*. The practice is well recognised in Afghanistan, although not accepted. There are also many personal and public reports of Western aid workers and soldiers confronted with the practice being told by their superiors to ignore it. Successive Afghan governments have made little effort to confront it. Paedophilia is the abhorrent underbelly of society in Afghanistan as much as it is in the West. Nowhere is immune.

My research for *The Night Letters* was exhaustive but I am not an Afghan. Broad brushstrokes were easier to discern; imagination is important, but the nuances of a culture – the things that bring it to life – are harder to grasp. When the manuscript was completed I asked two Afghan women to read it with an eye to authenticity and accuracy. Their input was enlightening and invaluable. My deepest appreciation goes to

Humaira Ghilzai, a professional cultural advisor for all things Afghan, and to Aalam Gul Farhad, an Afghan woman with a Master of Women's Studies. Thank you both again and again. I also would like to mention Drukhshan Farhad, who I had the pleasure of mentoring for a short time. A talented and intelligent woman, it was Drukhshan who suggested her sister, Aalam, read the manuscript.

I want to thank all those friends (listed in order of reading) who were generous enough to review various drafts of the manuscript (I still cringe at some of the things you had to read): Alan Leith, Jane Morgan, Rosie Scott (my dear Rosie, I hope you would have approved of the finished product), Sophie Haythornthwaite, Sally Fitzpatrick, Michael Robotham and Sally Tabner from Bookoccino. Have I forgotten anyone? Thank you, Matthew Haymes, for Bali and the peace and quiet I needed to finish the first draft all those years ago.

While all of you gave me precious gifts and insights, I especially need to thank Michael Robotham, who told me I was trying to write two books in one and that I needed to decide which story I actually wanted to tell. As a writer you can get so stuck on what *you* want the story to be that you cannot see what *it* wants to be. Throwing away a third of the manuscript, I started again. Only then did all the pieces begin to fall into place and the people of Shaahir Square really come to life.

Thank you to all my dear friends. You sustain me. You know who you are.

And finally, to the man I have loved for over forty years. *There is a path that leads from heart to heart.*

431

DENISE LEITH IS a Sydney author, and former lecturer of International Relations, and Middle East politics at Macquarie University. Her debut novel, *What Remains* (Allen & Unwin, 2012) was shortlisted for the Asher Award and the Fellowship of Australian Writers National Literary Awards - Christina Stead Award. She has also published two non-fiction works, *The Politics of Power* (University of Hawaii Press, 2002), and *Bearing Witness: the Lives of War Correspondents and Photojournalists* (Random House Australia, 2004). Denise's work has involved extensive travel, including time in an AIDS hospital in South Africa, in a refugee camp in the Middle East and in an isolated village in the mountains of West Papua. Denise has spent a number of years mentoring Afghan women in fiction and non-fiction. She currently resides on the Northern Beaches of Sydney.